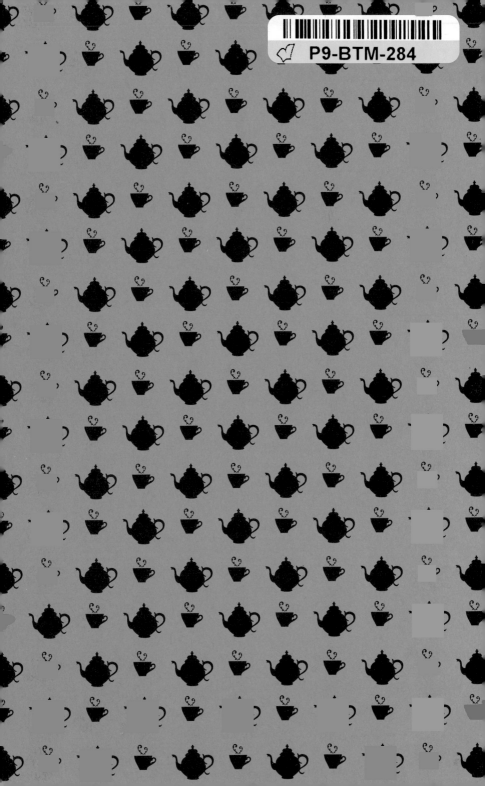

A MAD
ZOMBIE PARTY

A MAD
Z⊗MBIE PARTY

GENA SHOWALTER

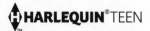

ISBN-13: 978-0-373-21182-1

A Mad Zombie Party

www.HarlequinTEEN.com

Printed in U.S.A.

To Natashya Wilson—of course!—an extraordinary woman and editor who believed in this series from the very beginning. You rock my socks.

To Blue Romero, because you are awesome on every level.

To anyone who's ever made a mistake you're certain you'll never recover from—no storm can last forever! The light *will* chase away the darkness.

To all the readers who said, "We want one more!" and "What about Frosty?"
THANK YOU!

To God, who is Love, and gives love.
Your mercies are everlasting, and I'm living proof.

COME, HEARKEN THEN,
ERE VOICE OF DREAD,
WITH BITTER TIDINGS LADEN,
SHALL SUMMON TO UNWELCOME BED
A MELANCHOLY MAIDEN!
WE ARE BUT OLDER CHILDREN, DEAR,
WHO FRET TO FIND OUR BEDTIME NEAR.

WITHOUT THE FROST,
THE BLINDING SNOW,
THE STORM-WIND'S MOODY MADNESS—
WITHIN, THE FIRELIGHT'S RUDDY GLOW,
AND CHILDHOOD'S NEST OF GLADNESS.
THE MAGIC WORDS SHALL HOLD THEE FAST:
THOU SHALT NOT HEED THE RAVING BLAST.

—FROM THROUGH THE LOOKING-GLASS AND
WHAT ALICE FOUND THERE, LEWIS CARROLL

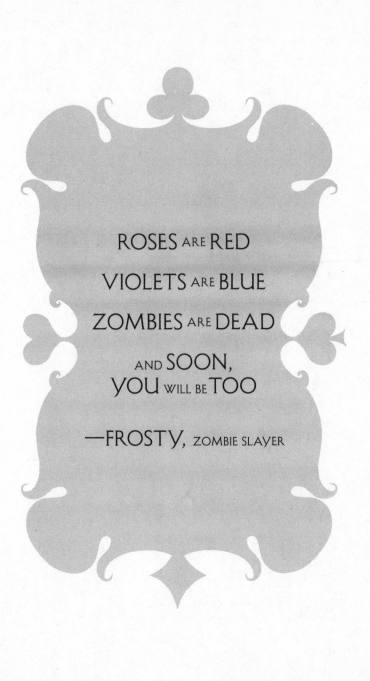

ROSES ARE RED

VIOLETS ARE BLUE

ZOMBIES ARE DEAD

AND SOON,
YOU WILL BE TOO

—FROSTY, ZOMBIE SLAYER

A NOTE FROM ALI

Check it. I'm only eighteen years old but I've already got the *coolest* résumé in the history of ever.

Mission statement: to save the entire world from the destructive forces of evil.

Abilities: seeing into the spirit realm, pushing *my* spirit out of my body, covering a person's memories with a single swipe of my hand, predicting the future and moving at speeds the average human can't even hope to track. Oh, and creating bursts of energy that toss zombies into the air.

Yes. Zombies exist. Get over it.

I'm a zombie slayer. While there are other slayers in the world, there are no others quite like me. (What? It's not bragging if it's true.) Two things we can all do? Set ourselves on fire with only a thought—*without* actually burning ourselves—and turn our enemy into a pile of ash with a single touch.

Don't be jealous! Be *re-e-eally* jealous.

Just FYI, real zombies are unlike anything seen in movies or read about in books. They are spirits that have to be fought by other spirits. Like to like. They don't hunger for blood and brains but for the very thing they've lost: the essence of life. My life... and yours.

They are pitiless darkness and we are shining lights.

But okay, okay, back to me. I won't mention my other award-winning qualities...like my killer instincts. My rapier wit. Oh, oh, or the fact that I bagged and tagged Cole Holland, the baddest bad boy every girl in Bama—and probably the world—hoped to tame. Nope, not gonna mention. I'm humble like that.

But, despite all my amazing amazingness, there's one thing I haven't been able to do, and the failure is tearing me up inside.

I haven't helped my friend Frosty.

I've tried. Oh, I've tried. Four months ago, Kat Parker—my best friend and Frosty's girlfriend—did the unthinkable and...and... passed away. Exited earth. Kicked the bucket.

Good glory, there's no easy way to say it, is there?

Anima Industries, the company determined to control zombies, bombed our house and gunned her down. (May they forever rot like their creations.)

Frosty witnessed every agonizing second of Kat's death, unable to save her, and it changed him. The fun, sarcastic and wickedly irreverent boy I once admired is gone. Now he's moody, and every mood is darker than the last. One moment he wants me to use my ability to cover his memories, the next he curses me for even daring to consider saying yes. He takes off for days, even weeks, at a time without contacting us to let us know he's okay. He drinks at all hours of the day and night, and he's sleeping around, discarding girls as if they're sexual tissues. One and done. Bang and bail. Hit it and quit it.

I know he hates what he's become. But how can I help him, truly help him, when I'm having so much trouble helping myself?

There's an ache deep in my chest now, humming in tune to the movies playing in the back of my mind. Movies on a constant loop—memories of times I shared with my bestie, the coolest chick I've ever known.

The first time we met. "I'm Kathryn, but everyone calls me Kat. And do not make any cat jokes or I'll have to hurt you. With my claws. Truth is, I stopped speaking meow a long time ago."

My first day at my new school. "Well, well, look what the Kat dragged in. Get it? Of course you do. I only make awesome jokes. But enough of my brilliant banter. I'm so glad you're here!"

When she first confessed to being sick. "My kidneys don't exactly work right. I need dialysis, like, a lot."

Our first squabble. "I told you about my illness, but you won't tell me what's going on with you? And I know something's going on. You're spending more and more time with Cole, you're bruised all the time and I would think he was beating you if I hadn't seen the bruises on everyone else you're hanging out with. I know you're involved in whatever Frosty's involved in, and I know you're keeping secrets from me."

We'd made up quickly. We'd always made up quickly. We were sisters of heart rather than blood. But as much as I love those flashbacks of our lives together, I wish they'd stop. My heartache is almost unbearable. And if I feel this way, even though Cole soothes me—even though I occasionally interact with Kat's spirit—Frosty has to be falling down a pit of never-ending despair. His only source of comfort has been taken away.

Crap! I need a sec to wipe my eyes. Got dirt in them...or something.

An indisputable fact: Frosty loves Kat the way I love Cole. All-encompassing, all-consuming, nothing held back—forever. I've heard him say he has nothing to live for, that death would bring him peace.

He's never been more wrong. He also can't go on like this. I've seen a glimpse of the future, and it isn't pretty.

The worst is yet to come.

We thought we'd won the war against Anima. We thought wrong. And how freaking sad is that? During our last battle, we lost six of our closest friends, and only consoled ourselves with Anima's defeat, certain they'd never again hurt another living soul. We should have known the company would rise from the grave just like the zombies they helped create.

Together we slayers must stand. Or one by one we will fall.

We have to— Argh! Kat! Did I forget to mention she's a witness now? When she died, her spirit went up. She lives in a spirit realm with my biological mom, Helen, and my little sister, Emma. They watch over us, cheering us on and even helping when they can. Sometimes they're even allowed to visit with me.

I can see and hear them while other slayers cannot. Yes, I did the sweet thing and shared the ability with every member of my crew—another ability to add to my résumé—but soon after, everyone lost it. Just *boom*, it was gone.

Emma once told me, her voice ominous, "There can be only one," before she burst out laughing. She then added, "You slayers...you operate in the spirit realm, where faith is your only source of strength. Some of your abilities require more faith than others and right now, only yours is strong enough to see us. Yes, we can help the others out and reveal ourselves through faith of our own, but we need permission from the Supreme Judge for that."

An-n-nd Kat is now snapping her fingers in front of my face. She won't stop talking, even though I've told her a thousand times she's probably the worst witness ever, always focused on her— Ow! She's found a way to pinch my spirit inside my body.

She wants me to add that we slayers will do whatever it takes to save Frosty. And by "whatever," I mean "*whatever.*" We have to find a way to reach him before it's too late. And we will.

Did you hear that, Kat? We will.

We'll strive for the best...but plan for the worst.

Ow! And save Frosty. Yes, yes. I get it. They get it.

Let your light shine,

Ali Bell
Ow! And Kat Parker

1

Frosty

DEATH KNOCKED, BUT I WASN'T HOME

I crawl out of bed like I'm one of the walking dead and rub my gritty eyes. My temples throb, and my mouth tastes like something furry crawled inside, nested, had babies and died. I'm on my way to the bathroom to brush my teeth with a gallon of bleach when I realize my surroundings are unfamiliar. Ignoring a flood of dizziness, I scan a bedroom that has pictures of flowers hanging on pink walls, sparkly shirts and skirts spilling from an oversized closet and a vanity scattered with a thousand different kinds of makeup.

Not exactly my style.

A sleepy sigh draws my attention to the bed, and memories rush in fast. I spent the night with a girl—the newest in a long line of randoms I've selected for one reason and one reason only. A resemblance to Kat. This particular hookup has dark hair and sun-kissed skin...or so I thought. Now, in the bright light of the morning, I see the strands aren't quite dark enough and her skin is more sun-screwed.

My stomach clenches, and my hands curl into fists as hard as hammerheads. Usually I leave two seconds after the deed is done. Just enough time to zip my pants. What can I say? I'm a class A dick. But at least I'm at the top of my field. Counts for something, right?

I hate the things I'm doing, but I won't stop doing them. I'm not sure I can. After a few shots of whiskey, I'm able to pretend the girl I'm with *is* my sweet little Kitty Kat, and I'm touching her again and she's loving it, begging me for more, and everything will be okay, because we'll be together forever. I imagine she'll cuddle close afterward and say things like, "You're the luckiest guy in the world and you don't deserve me, but don't worry, no one does," and I'll laugh, because she's ridiculous and adorable and everything right in my world. In the morning, she'll demand I apologize for doing bad things in her dreams.

She'll make my life worth living.

Then morning will actually arrive, and I'll realize she won't be doing any of those things because she's dead, and I'm the puss who couldn't save her. A fact that still haunts me. But I deserve to be haunted. I deserve to be punished.

Kat deserved my loyalty until the very end—*my* end. And this crap? I'm cheating on her memory with girls I don't know, don't even like, and will always resent. They're not my Kat, they'll never be my Kat and they have no right to put their hands on her property.

Hell. Even still, they deserve better.

What I'm doing...it's wrong. It's seriously messed up. I'm

not this guy. Only assholes use and lose, and once upon a time I would have been the guy who beat a prick like me into blood, pulp and powder.

Ask me if I care.

Before my newest mistake wakes up, I gather my discarded clothing and dress in a hurry. My shirt is wrinkled, ripped and stained with lipstick and whiskey. I don't bother fastening my pants. The combat boots I leave untied. I look like exactly what I am: a hungover piece of scum who could pass for a zombie. I make my way out the front door and realize I'm on the second floor of an apartment building. I scan the surrounding parking lot but find no sign of my truck.

How the hell did I get here?

I remember going to a nightclub, throwing back one shot after another, dancing with the brunette, throwing back a few more shots and…yeah, okay, piling inside her little sedan. I'd been too wasted to drive. Now I'll have to walk back to the club, because there's no way in hell I'm waking Hookup to ask for a ride. I'd have to answer questions about my nonexistent intentions.

As I stride down the sidewalk, the air is warmer than usual, the last vestiges of winter having surrendered to spring. The sun is in the process of rising, igniting the sky with different shades of gold and pink, and it's one of the most beautiful sights I've ever seen.

I give it the finger.

The world should be crying for the treasure it's lost. Hell, it should be snot-sobbing.

At least I don't have to worry about being ambushed by zombies right now. The scourge of the earth usually only slink out at night, the bright rays of the sun too harsh for their sensitive husks.

I come across a gas station and buy a toothbrush, tube of toothpaste and a bottle of water. In the bathroom, I take care of the furry thing and her babies still nesting in my mouth and begin to feel human again.

When I'm back outside, I pick up the pace. The sooner I get to my car, the sooner I can—

"What you doing here, pretty boy?" some guy calls. His friends laugh as if he's said something special. "You want to see what real men are like?"

—get home.

I'm in a part of Birmingham, Alabama, most kids avoid if at all possible, scared by the graffiti on crumbling building walls, the parked cars missing hubcaps and wheels, and the plethora of crimes being perpetrated in every alley—drugs, prostitution, maybe a mugging or two. I keep my head down and my hands at my sides, not because I'm afraid but because in my current mood, I will fight, and I will fight to kill.

As a zombie slayer, I have the skills necessary to make "real men" curl into a ball and beg for their momma. Taking on a group of punk kids or even gang members would be like shooting fish in a barrel—with a rocket grenade launcher.

Yeah. I have one of those. Two, actually, but I've always preferred my daggers. Eliminating someone up close and personal comes with a better rewards package.

My cell phone vibrates. I pull the device from my pocket to discover the screen is blown up with texts from Cole, Bronx and even Ali Bell, Cole's girlfriend and once, Kat's best friend. They want to know where I am and what I'm doing, if I'm visiting anytime soon. When will they realize it's too difficult to be around them? Their lives are picture-perfect in a way mine isn't—and can never be. They have the happily-ever-after I've dreamed about since eighth grade, when Kat Parker walked into Asher Jr. High our first day back from summer break. In seconds, I gave that girl my heart.

Like Cole and Ali, we couldn't keep our hands off each other. Like Bronx and his girlfriend Reeve, we worshipped the ground the other walked on. Now I have nothing but memories.

No, that's not true. I also have pain and misery.

A big brute of a guy suddenly gets in my grille. I say "brute" only because the shadow he's throwing is my size. I'm a big guy, loaded with heavy muscle and topping out well over six feet.

Clearly he thinks he's tough. He probably expects me to crap my pants and beg for mercy. Good luck with that. If he isn't careful, he won't be walking away from this encounter— he'll be crawling. But as I rake my gaze from his boots to his face, I lose the 'tude.

Here is Cole Holland in the flesh. My friend and fearless leader. I've known and loved him like a brother since our elementary school days. Over the years we've fought beside each other, bled with each other and saved each other. I'd die for him, and he'd die for me.

Too bad for him I'm not in the mood for another pep talk.

"Don't," I say. "Just don't."

"Don't speak to my best friend? How about you don't say dumb shit?"

Yeah. How about. "How'd you find me?"

"My super amazing detective skills. How else?"

"If I had to guess I'd say the GPS in my phone." Technology is such an asshole.

Cole's eyes are violet and freaky cool, especially as they glitter in the light of the sun—but they're also a little too shrewd as they stare at the collar of my shirt.

"Lipstick?" He arches a brow.

"I'm on the hunt for my perfect shade," I respond, deadpan.

"Ditch the magenta. Your olive skin tone *screams* for rose." His deadpan is better than mine.

The old me would have been all over that. The new me just wants to be left alone. "Thanks for the tip. I'll keep it in mind." I try to move around him.

He just moves with me. "Come on." He pats me on the shoulder, and if I'd been a weaker guy, I would have been drilled into the concrete. "Let's go get something to eat. Looks like you could use a solid meal rather than a liquid one."

As much as I don't want to go, I don't want to argue with him. Takes too much energy. His Jeep is idling at the curb, and I slide into the passenger seat without protest. A ten-minute drive follows, and thankfully he doesn't fight the silence. What's there to say, really? The situation is what it is, and there's no changing it.

We end up at Hash Town, and as I walk through the doors, I suddenly wish I'd argued. Ali, Bronx and Reeve are at a table in back, waiting for us. Reeve and I have never been close; she was Kat's friend, and like Kat, slaying has never been in her wheelhouse. She can't see or hear zombies, but she's watched us fight so many times, she's accepted what other civilians never have: the monsters are real, and they live among us.

Reeve lost her dad—her only living family and our wealthiest benefactor—the day I lost Kat. For the first time, I'm struck by a sense of kinship with her. Maybe this forced interaction won't be so bad.

As she smiles at me in welcome, however, I revert to my original unease. She has dark hair and even darker eyes, and for many years she and Kat pretended to be sisters from different misters. Right now it kinda hurts to look at her.

Who am I kidding? Everything hurts.

"Is this an intervention?" I take one of two empty seats and signal the waitress for coffee. I'm going to need it.

"No, but it probably should be," Ali says. "You look like dog crap that's baked in the sun a little too long." Her mouth has always lacked any type of filter, a problem exacerbated by her refusal to lie about anything. Two qualities guaranteed to turn every conversation into a battlefield. But that's okay. Give me blunt truth over charming flattery any day.

Cole sits next to her and kisses her on the cheek. She leans in to him, the action natural to her, wholly instinctive.

Kat and I used to do the same.

A sharp lance of pain rips through my chest, and I have to school my expression to hide my grimace.

"The good news is my dog crap is another man's best," I say.

"Oh, my friend," Ali replies with a shake of her head, "you clearly haven't seen yourself in the mirror."

I shrug. "You look good, at least."

"Obviously." She buffs her nails.

It's such a Kat thing to say, to hear. We both freeze.

This time, I can't school my expression. What's worse, I need a moment to steady my breathing. New conversations eventually kick off, friendly insults bouncing back and forth among the group.

Ali leans toward me and whispers, "I miss her, too."

I hike my shoulders in another shrug. It's all I can really manage at the moment.

In appearance, Ali is Kat's polar opposite. While Ali is tall and slender with a fall of pale hair and eyes of the clearest, purest blue, Kat is—was, damn it—short and curvy with dark hair and mesmerizing hazel eyes that were a perfect blend of green and gold.

In storybook terms, Ali is the innocent snow princess and Kat is the seductive evil queen.

There'd been no one prettier than my Kat. Or smarter. Or wittier. Or more adorable. And if I continue along this path, I'm going to tear the building apart brick by brick.

The waitress finally arrives with the coffeepot and fills my cup. "Your order will be out in a few minutes, hon."

I get a friendly pat on my shoulder before she ambles away.

"We took the liberty of ordering for you," Reeve tells me. "Two fried eggs, four pieces of bacon, two sausage patties, a double helping of cheesy hash browns and a stack of pecan pancakes." She nibbles on her bottom lip. "If you'd like something else…"

"I'm sure I can make do with so little." I'm not hungry, anyway. "How's Z-hunting going?"

"Better than ever." Ali takes a sip of her orange juice. "Tell him your news," she says to Reeve.

Reeve blushes. "I used my dad's notes and Ali's blood to create a new serum."

Ali practically bounces in her seat. "It's awesome because—drumroll please—she was able to extract and use the essence of my fire. We inject zombies with it, and it's as if they've bitten me. In minutes, their darkness is washed away because I am *so awesome*— What?" she says when Cole nudges her. "You know it's true. Anyway. When completely cleansed, the Zs become witnesses and float away into the hereafter."

"It's a miracle to watch," Cole says.

All slayers produce spiritual fire—inner light—the only weapon truly capable of killing zombies. But after the leader of Anima experimented on Ali, shooting her full of untested drugs, she developed the ability to *save* Zs, too. An ability she then shared with other slayers by using her fire on *them*.

Multiple times she's offered to share it with me, too, but I've always turned her down. I'm not interested in saving my enemy. Zombies bit Kat, which means I would have lost her to toxin even if I hadn't lost her to a bomb and a hail of bullets. But the thing that really kills me? The toxin ensured she suffered a far more agonizing death, no matter the cause, every bit of her pain magnified. Therefore, zombies have to die.

The downside? I don't just suffer when I'm bitten, I *suffer*, unbearable agony consuming me, the urge to destroy everything in my path utterly overwhelming me. I also can't be healed without another slayer's fire or an injection of a chemical antidote—and I have to receive either one within a ten-minute window of the bite or I'm toast.

"Do I sense a *but*?" I ask.

Excitement dwindling, Ali traces her finger over the rim

of her glass. "Supplies are limited, so we more often than not have to let the creatures bite us. The more bites we receive, the longer we take to recover."

"Makes sense. The more bites, the more toxin your spirit has to cleanse."

"More coffee?" the waitress asks.

Ali and Reeve jolt at the sound of her voice. I just nod. My guard has remained on high since I walked through the diner doors. I've known the waitress's location every second. The girls, both new to this life, are still learning.

As the coffee is poured, the waitress says, "Your order's up, gang. I'll bring it over." She walks away without giving us a "you are so weird" look. We're kids (technically) and we've discovered everyone assumes we're talking about video games.

"We need to come up with a new way to help Zs and ourselves," Bronx says. "After a battle, I'm drained for a week."

"He basically falls into a coma." Reeve rests her cheek on his shoulder, and his hand automatically sinks into her hair. "Not even true love's kiss awakens him," she adds drily.

Cole cracks a smile. "You must not be doing it right. Stop kissing his lips and start—"

Ali slaps a hand over his mouth. "Don't you dare."

He removes her hand and nips at her palm. "Punching them," he says, finishing his sentence.

Everyone laughs. Everyone but me. I shift uncomfortably and look at the door. Too rude to leave?

The food arrives a few seconds later, the waitress placing steaming plates in front of each of us. My friends dig in as if they've been starved for months. While I was drinking and cheating on Kat's memory last night, they clearly hunted zombies and did a little bite-fighting. The sleeve of Ali's shirt has risen, revealing a wealth of bruises on her arm, just above a tattoo of a white rabbit.

There are bruises on Cole and Bronx, too, and the realization hits me hard. They went into battle without me. They could have been hurt, or worse. The Z-saving thing is new, as untested as the drugs Ali was given, and we don't know all the ins and outs. Something could have gone horribly wrong, and I wasn't there to help.

I swallow a curse. I need to get my act together. Like, yesterday. But just as soon as the burst of protective energy hits me, it leaves. My friends will be fine without me. Probably even better off.

The handle of my fork bends.

"So, I have another bit of news," Reeve says, breaking through the sudden silence. "I bought a house."

Bronx swallows a bite of red velvet pancakes. He's always had a sweet tooth, and it's always amused me. With his wild, spiked green hair and multiple facial piercings, he looks as if he'd prefer rusty nails and shards of glass. "It has everything we need. Big-assed bedrooms, each with its own private bathroom. Enough for everyone on our crew and everyone we're recruiting. There's a gym. A sauna. An indoor pool. Even a basketball court. Plus, when I'm finished, security will be top-of-the-line."

My first thought: Kat would have loved living with the group. Hell, she would have loved my small, barely furnished apartment, paid for by the trust Reeve's dad left me. He left one for all of us, actually. We're all richer than we could have ever dreamed, and yet, the money is as much a curse as a blessing to me. What I can't share with Kat, well, it isn't worth having. Including my poor excuse for a life.

I grind my molars so forcefully I expect to swallow broken bits of enamel. As her image sparks to life in the back of my mind, I close my eyes. A memory begins to play with Technicolor clarity. She's sitting on my lap, and I'm toying with the ends of her silky hair.

"If I only have ten more days to live," she says, "what would you want to do with me?"

I guess her intention right away, know she's trying to prepare me. She's suffered from kidney disease her entire life, and she suspects the end will come sooner rather than later. "Hold on and never let go."

"Boring."

"Chain you to my bed."

The corners of her mouth twitch. "A possibility."

Getting serious, I say, "Die with you." And I mean the words with every fiber of my being.

She climbs to her knees and cups my face to hold my gaze. As if I would ever look away from her. When she's near, she's all I see. "You're going to live, Frost. You'll go to college and make friends and play sports and yes, date other girls."

"I don't do any of that shi—stuff now." I don't like to curse in front of her. I want to be a positive influence, never a bad one.

"You're going to meet someone else, someone special, and she's—"

"There *is* no one else." I've been lost for this girl since minute one.

Her head tilts to the side, strands of her hair lifting with

A MAD ZOMBIE PARTY

a gentle breeze. "Granted, with her you won't have as much fun and your kids won't be nearly as attractive, but I'm sure she'll make you happy...occasionally."

Not gonna happen. Ever. "You're it for me, kitten. That will never change."

In the present, someone taps my shoulder. I meet Cole's violet gaze, the concern radiating from his rugged features almost my undoing. He loves me. I know he loves me, and he only wants the best for me. But I can't have the best, and I'm not going to pretend I have something else to live for. Well, something other than revenge.

"Come with us to see the house," he says. "Pick a room."

A room I won't be sharing with Kat. "I already have a place." I breathe in...out...but I don't calm down. I stand, my chair skidding behind me. "I have to go."

A muscle jumps beneath his eye. "Where?"

Somewhere else. *Anywhere* else. "I just... I'll see you guys around." I stride out of the diner without ever looking back.

2

Milla

EYE SINK IT, YOU DRINK IT

I crouch on top of a tombstone gargoyle-style, waiting for the spirits of the recently dead to rise. I don't have to worry they'll be witnesses, the good guys. Witnesses leave the body at the moment of death and ascend. Zombies tend to linger for several hours, or even a day or two, and on rare occasions an entire week. Don't ask me why there's a difference. Zombie physiology isn't my forte. All I know is that the creatures need time to gather enough strength to crawl out.

They are always starved for what they've lost, for the most precious thing on this earth. Life.

I've been listening to police scanners, sneaking into hospitals to examine death records and patrolling cemeteries for people who have died of Antiputrefactive Syndrome. The past few days, there have been six, and all six will result in brand-spanking-new zombies.

AS is what doctors call death by zombie bite. Not that

anyone in the medical field actually knows an injection of straight-up evil is the reason portions of a victim's skin turn black and ooze pus as their organs rot...until an excruciating death finally ends the torment. Well, until the *real* torture begins. Eternity as one of the undead.

No one would believe me if I explained the truth. Hell, I might even end up in a padded room, medicated to the max. It's happened to a couple of my friends.

Former friends.

Anyway.

Fingers crossed I get to kill all six zombies tonight.

Killing is my business, and like anyone else, I'm happiest when business is good.

And I *need* a little good in life. I'm the most hated slayer in the state. With excellent reason. But even though my friends hate me, I haven't stopped loving them, which is why I'm here. The more Zs I kill, the less they have to fight. I want to make their lives better, easier—to make River's life easier.

For years, my brother protected me and my—

Can't go there right now. Depression will set in, and I'll *want* zombies to feed on me.

So. Rephrase. For years, my brother protected me from our abusive father, hiding me even though he would be punished for it, forced to take my beating as well as his own. I owe him. More than that, I adore him. There's *nothing* I won't do for him.

Steal, kill and destroy? Check, check and mate.

"Come on, come on, meat bags," I mutter. "Consider this your official invitation to my boot party." For my own en-

tertainment and okay, okay, to let off a little steam, I plan to
kick the rot right out of their brains.

I have everything I need. Earlier I pushed my spirit out of
my body, leaving the latter perched at the edge of Shady Elms
cemetery, concealed by thick foliage, waning moonlight and
eerie shadows. (What the body wears the spirit wears, which
means I'm still armed for war.)

I have to be careful, though; I can't allow even the smallest scratch. Any injury a spirit sustains manifests on the body,
the two connected through invisible tethers no matter the
distance between them. That's usually not a big deal, but I'm
on my own and I'll have to patch myself up. Basically, I'm
the world's worst patient.

Around me, locusts buzz and crickets sing, but the in-
sects aren't my only companions. A few headstones away, a
group of underage kids are drinking beer and playing truth
or dare. Definitely in the wrong place. Could be the wrong
time. Zombies prefer to chow on slayers—we're their catnip,
I guess—but any human will do.

Play with fire, get burned. A truth as old as time.

The little hairs on the back of my neck stand at full attention, and I go still. Sometimes my spirit senses something that
hasn't yet clicked in my mind.

Zombies on the rise?

I search, but find no sign there's an undead nearby. Another civilian intruder? Again, there's no sign. Not that it
would matter. I can dance, sing and shout, but to civilians,
I'm nothing more than a ghost.

Another slayer, perhaps, come to help me?

Yeah, in my dreams. As an exile of River's crew, I'm

as good as dead to all our kind. And I get it. I do. In my single-minded bid to save my brother, I made terrible life-and-death mistakes.

Commit the crime, serve your time.

My nails dig into the headstone beneath me, the entire thing doused with Blood Lines, the chemical needed to make the living world tangible to the spirit world. My brother keeps stashes of Blood Lines all over the state as a just-in-case. Used to be, I would have called him to ask for what I need, and he would have ensured I had more than enough. Now I have to raid his stashes.

Part of me wants to curl up and sob for all I've lost. Friends, a home. Acceptance, safety and security. A family. The other part of me, the stronger part, tells me to suck it up and deal. What's done is done.

Besides, I have a purpose, and that's more than most.

Laughter erupts from the kids. I call them *kids* and yet they're only a year or two younger than me. While they've probably spent the bulk of their lives having fun, I've spent the bulk of mine fighting to save the world. I'm nineteen, but my experiences have aged me.

"You gonna back out now?" one of the boys asks the only dark-haired girl. "You chicken?"

"I know what you're doing, Mr. Manipulator," she says with a smirk. "You can't goad me into doing something I don't want to do."

"Stop talking and show him your tits." Another boy throws a handful of leaves at her. "A dare is a dare."

The others chortle.

"Thankfully, I want to do it." She stands in the middle of

the group and, while Chicken Boy uses the flashlight app on his phone to illuminate her, she lifts her top to expose her boobs.

The other boys high-five and whistle. The other girls cat-call and fist-pump the sky.

I want to shout, *Stop living in the dark and open your eyes to the light. A whole other world exists around you.*

A shadow rises from the freshly packed grave site in front of me. I reach over my shoulders to palm the handles of my short swords, the kids forgotten. Metal slides against leather, whistling a beautiful tune, and I start drooling at the thought of a new kill.

Pavlov nailed it.

Another finger pokes through the dirt...soon an entire hand. There's a dull gray tint to the skin, and my heart leaps with excitement.

The creature sits up and shakes her head, clumps of dirt falling from her tangled salt-and-pepper hair. I smile with anticipation, until I note the open wounds on her forehead and cheeks, each revealing the rotted muscle and splintered bone underneath. First-time risers usually appear human, their only visual tells red eyes and graying skin. Why the change?

She locks on me, her lips curling up, showcasing yellowed teeth and thick black saliva.

Kill now, ask questions later.

She swipes a hand at me and snaps her teeth.

"Sorry, honey, but I'm not on the menu." I leap off the tombstone and end up where I want to be—in the circle of her arms. Mindless with hunger, she latches on to my waist to yank me closer, but I'm already swinging my swords. The blades crisscross at her neck before I'm in any danger, and her head falls backward, black goo spraying from her severed artery.

The civilians continue playing their silly game.

Despite the decapitation, both the zombie head and body remain animated, arms clawing at me, teeth snapping at me. Time to finish her off for good. I've been fighting the undead for so long, summoning my fire—my *dýnamis*—is as easy as breathing. By the time I sheath one of my swords and flatten my hand over her chest, flames are crackling all the way to my wrist. One minute passes, two... *Dýnamis* sinks past her skin, into her veins, traveling through her entire body. Then, suddenly, she explodes, dark ash floating through the air.

I move on to her head, making sure her teeth are firmly planted in the ground before I perform the same "fire up and wait" routine. When a second round of ash floats away on a cool spring breeze, I sheath my other sword and slap my hands together in a job well done.

I have to walk through the circle of civilians to get to the next name on my list of AS victims. Each boy has paired off with a girl, the couples making out on top of blankets, uncaring about the potential audience. Longing mixes with envy, cutting at me. I haven't had a "boyfriend" in forever. River is so protective—*was* so protective, I correct with a twist in my gut. Anyone interested in me quickly decided I wasn't worth the hassle...but usually only after I'd given up the goods. At least, I like to tell myself River is the reason I've been rejected so many times, and not my mountain of personality flaws.

Now River wouldn't care if I decided to screw anything breathing. Or hey, anything not breathing.

I never should have betrayed his trust in me, never should have tried to save his life by signing the death warrant of Ali Bell, the girlfriend of a rival crew's leader. But trading one life for another had seemed acceptable at the time. If only that's how things had gone down. Ali survived, but two innocents had not. Kat Parker and Dr. Richard Ankh. I'm not sure I'll ever be able to forgive myself for the part I played in their deaths.

Scratch that. I will *never* forgive myself.

A grunt sounds at my left, and I whip around to discover two other zombies have risen. Two zombies not from graves/ names on my list. Well, hell. As I once again unsheathe my short swords, my heart slamming against my ribs, I study my newest opponents. Two males. One is morbidly obese, while the other is short and squat. Both have a grayish tint, like the female, the same advanced stage of rot.

They race toward me without stumbling, their bones not yet brittle enough to break.

I dart to the right, their gazes alert enough to follow me. Good. I keep going, drawing the two farther away from the civilians...but I don't realize until too late that there's a small headstone in my path. I trip, land on my ass and lose my breath. I'm laid flat for only a second, maybe two, but it's enough. The pair dive for me. I somersault backward, coming up with my swords extended, ripping through each creature's torso. Multiple organs plop to the ground, but neither Z seems to notice or care that they've been disemboweled. They just keep advancing.

I kick one in the groin, sending him stumbling to the side, at the same time removing the head of the other with a single swipe of my sword. The headless wonder, now behind me, manages to clench his fingers in my hair and yank me closer. Idiot! All he can do is paw at me. I elbow his chest and kick back. As he, too, stumbles to the side, I hack at his left arm, spin and hack at his right. Both limbs hit the ground with a thud.

Pressure on my boot draws my gaze. The severed head is attempting to chew through my leather soles. I jerk my leg away and slam my sword into his ear canal, and if we were in an episode of *The Walking Dead*, my favorite show despite the inaccuracies, he would be dead. Again. But we aren't, and he isn't; he just keeps chomping at me. Now, at least, he's trapped in place. He can do no real damage while I fight the other—

A stone wall knocks me to the ground. The other zombie, back for more. I lose my grip on my swords, air exploding from my lungs and stars winking in front of my eyes. But I manage to hold him off, the heel of my palm planted firmly on his forehead. His legs move between mine, both of his hands wrapping around my neck, which he clearly hopes to use as a snack pack.

If he were human, all I'd have to do is clasp my hands together at my midsection and shoot them up, between his arms, at the same time placing my feet behind his ankles and applying enough pressure to spread his legs. He would struggle for purchase and lose his grip on me. I would then place one of my hands behind his head and smash the other underneath his chin to close his mouth, pushing with one and pulling with the other to create a counterforce, turning his body and allowing me to roll on top of him. I would balance my weight on one knee, slam the heel of a hand into his nose, breaking the cartilage and, while he writhed in pain, I would stand and stomp on his stupid face. Game over. But he isn't human, so I can do none of those things; his teeth would be too close to my vulnerable skin, and he would feel no pain.

All I can do is wiggle my free hand between our bodies. There's a dagger sheathed at my waist...there! Once the weapon is free, I wrench it up and jab it into his neck, again and again. Black goo sprays my flesh, burning me, blistering. Steam curls through the air. When his spine is the only thing holding his head in place, I drop the blade and rearrange my hands, placing one behind his head while smashing the other under his chin, careful to avoid his teeth—looks like I can use one of my moves, after all. With a push and a pull, the counterforce snaps his stupid head from his stupid body.

Panting, I toss the brand-new boxing bag several yards away and fight my way from beneath his heavy weight. Dizziness sweeps over me, but this is not the time for a break. I summon *dýnamis* and place my palm over the zombie's back. In my weakened state, my fire is not as potent and the zombie's metamorphosis from rot to ash takes longer than usual, but it *does* happen.

I push up onto shaky legs and stumble forward, relieved, searching for the head I threw. Gotta rinse and repeat. Only, I come face-to-face with more than a dozen pairs of red, glowing eyes—and every single set is locked on me.

3

Frosty

A VERY MERRY UNSLAYER DAY TO YOU

Surprise surprise, I'm back at Hearts, looking for my next hit and run.

Out of habit, I scan my surroundings. Four months ago, just days before Kat—

Yeah. Anyway. A section of the club was destroyed by Anima. Their agents bombed a wall, swooped in and attacked. We fought back hard and dirty, but damage was done. Thankfully, it took us only a month to rebuild. Out with the old, in with the new. There are now black light halogens in the ceiling, making glow-in-the-dark paint come to life around the stage, where a live band plays. The walls are covered with murals of a magical woodland, a floating Cheshire cat with a toothy grin, and a rabbit with a pocket watch. Ali's suggestion. A tribute to Kat as well as Ali's younger sister, Emma.

Once, Reeve's dad owned the club. When he died, he left most of his possessions and wealth to his daughter—his only living relative—and a million dollars each to the rest of us. The club, though, he gave to Tyler Holland, Cole's dad. I'm on the VIP list, even though I'm only eighteen years old. My ID says I'm twenty-four.

My phone vibrates, and I check the screen to find a text from Cole.

The club again? Really? Why don't U be a good boy & use UR spank bank? Yeah. I went there. Stop screwing around & come home. UR real home.

One of the employees must have called him. Friends who care are great—until they suck.

There are other texts, too.

Ali: Thought of a title 4 a zombie dating book. Ready... DYING TO MEET YOU. Thoughts???

My boy Gavin, a slayer as irreverent as I used to be: I hear UR plowing UR way through brunettes. Dude! That's my game. Play w/blondes—they R better 4 UR health. (meaning I will kill U if U don't make the switch)

Bronx: A new recruit just asked—what's the #1 thing an average person does when fighting a zombie? I told him—taste delicious. He almost soiled his pants. U should be here.

Ali again: Question. If the zombie apocalypse happens in Vegas, will it stay in Vegas???

Ali yet again: If Chuck Norris gets bitten by a zombie, will he turn in2 a zombie—or will the zombie turns in2 Chuck Norris??

There's even a text from Derek, who moved to Oklahoma to train and lead another crew.

Consider this an eternal invite 2 come C me. Miss U, man

They want to help me because they love me. When will they accept it's already too late? I'm far too damaged to be repaired.

I ignore the texts and glance at the time. It's a few minutes past midnight, and I've already had one shot of whiskey too many. If *one* is the new word for *four*. Whatever. I don't want to be here anymore. I want to be in bed, pretending.

Who's the unlucky girl tonight? I spot a possibility on the dance floor. She's twentysomething with long dark hair. Are her eyes green? Doesn't matter, I suppose. When I close my eyes, they'll be any color I want them to be.

I finish off my newest shot and stand, already drowning in a tidal wave of guilt and shame. I shouldn't be doing this. I'll regret it tomorrow. But I'm in desperate need of blackout bliss, and this is the only way to get it.

I move toward the random only to stop halfway, my heart shuddering inside my chest. I think I see... Kat? *My* Kat? Her gaze meets mine, and she offers me a tremulous smile. I know that smile. I know *all* her smiles. The good, the bad and the oh, so sad.

I'm paralyzed as I drink in every detail. The sable shine of her hair. The beauty of her hazel eyes. The delicacy of her features. The wonder of her curves. The pale skin I've caressed and kissed so many times, the texture and heat are imprinted on my soul.

It's really her.

I'm drunker than I realized and confusing a memory with reality, or maybe I'm straight-up hallucinating. I don't care which. I'll take her however I can get her. I'm across the room in seconds. Just before I reach her, she turns and glides away. I give chase. There's no way I'll allow her to escape me, whatever she is. I'll die first.

She pauses at the back exit and glances my way, even waves me over. I'll go anywhere she leads, but—she's gone a second later, vanished in a puff of light.

In a panic, I shoulder my way outside. A cool night breeze greets me, tinged with unsavory odors: old food, urine and vomit. A streetlamp illuminates the alley, revealing a row of Dumpsters and a mouse scurrying between them. Bits of shredded paper float through the air like snow.

Kat died soon after a snowstorm.

Can't lose her again. "Kat," I shout, desperate now. A few feet away, a black bird takes flight. "Kat!"

"Dude. I prefer your indoor voice. Let's tone it down a notch—or twelve."

Her voice is soft and comes from directly behind me. I swing around, every muscle in my body knotting with anticipation...but there she is. The love of my life.

Suddenly I feel as though an elephant is sitting on top of my chest. I'm struggling to breathe. I'm trembling. I want her to be real. I want her to tell me she faked her death, just to see how many people would show up at her funeral—*I put the "fun" in funeral, Frosty.* But she remains quiet, and I reach out.

She's stoic as she awaits contact. Then—

My fingers ghost through the tendrils of her hair, and I unleash a stream of profanity.

"Wow," she says with a grin. "I'm not sure some of those things are anatomically possible."

Her burst of humor calms me.

She's wearing what she died in, a white shirt and a pair of my boxers, looking adorable and beautiful at once. She's no longer littered with wounds caused by falling debris as the Ankhs' house crumbled on top of her, or the gunshots she took to the chest; she's injury-free and radiant with health.

She's everything my life has been missing.

"You're here," I say, awed to the core. "You're really here."

"Yep. But you, Frosty, are an idiot."

I smile. My first since her death. "Even your hallucination is mouthy. I like it."

"I'm not a hallucination, dummy. I'm a witness, and—get ready to be humbled by my greatness—I've come to help you." She fist-pumps the sky. "Super Kat to the rescue!"

Now I frown. My millionth since her death. I've never seen a witness, but Ali and Cole have, so I know it's possible. But my Kat has been gone for four months, and she never would have stayed away from me so long if she could get to me. Not on purpose, at least. So...maybe she is a witness, but maybe she isn't. Even my fractured mind would demand a logical explanation for the presence of a hallucination.

I still don't care. She's here, she's with me and that's all that matters.

"You want to help me," I say, the words nothing but gravel. "You stay with me. Don't leave my side."

"Tsk-tsk. Thinking only about yourself." She walks around

me, just as she used to do, pretending to be a predator who has selected the evening's prey. An action she learned from me. "I know you've had trouble parting with me. Who wouldn't? I'm amazing! But du-u-ude. I didn't expect a total meltdown. You used to dine on prime filet and now you're nomming on old cuts of mystery meat."

A very Kat way of mentioning my parade of girls. I bow my head, shamed by my behavior. A thousand apologies will not be enough. "I'm sorry, kitten. I'm so sorry. You were gone… I think I tried to punish us both. But I hate what I've—"

She holds up her hand to silence me. "Enough. I don't want to hear your excuses. You're ruining your life, and that is not acceptable to me."

"Are you kidding? Ruining my life? Kitten, without you I have no life." The words explode from me with more force than I intend. "I would rather cut off my left nut than yell at you. I'm sorry," I repeat. "I shouldn't have raised my voice."

"Well, you are *not* forgiven!" She anchors her hands on her hips. "Since I've been living up there—" she hikes her thumb toward the sky "—I've had the opportunity to watch you behind the scenes. And guess what? You've turned Beefcake TV into Bama's Crappiest Videos. Starting today, you're going out there and doing good deeds."

For her? Anything. "What do you consider a good deed?"

"To begin, you're going to help your friends by participating in the zombie-human war. And you're going to do it with a smile!" She stomps her foot. "Do you hear me?"

"Yes. Help friends. Fight. Smile. If I do these things, you'll stay with me?"

She closes her eyes for a moment, sighs. "And I told the council I had this in the bag. Bad Kat. Bad!"

"Council?" If she's a figment of my shattered imagination, shouldn't I have some sort of control over her? Shouldn't her logic match my own, considering it's, well, mine? Clearly, I have no control over this girl, and I definitely have no idea what she's talking about.

It suddenly hits me with the force of a baseball bat. She *is* a witness, real though not corporeal, and she *is* here.

Joy floods me. "Never mind." I stalk forward.

She backs into the brick wall. A wall I help douse in Blood Lines once every week, making it solid to spirits. That way, zombies can't ghost inside the building.

When she's almost within reach, I push my spirit out of my body, an action that requires faith—the spiritual power source for all slayers, just like food is a power source for our outer shell—believing I can do it before I actually do it.

Now, without my flesh to act as insulation, the air seems a thousand degrees colder. I endure because spirits can be touched only by other spirits, and I want to touch Kat with every fiber of my being. But the second I stretch out my arm, she jumps to the side to avoid contact.

"Hold on there, grabby." She gives a shake of her head, dark hair dancing over her shoulders. "I haven't always followed the rules—or ever followed the rules—but all that's behind me. You have no idea what I had to do to get here, or what will happen if I mess up, and there's no time to explain. Not during this visit. Just know that one touch of your spirit to mine will ensure I'm never allowed back."

My fists clench and unclench as I return to my body. We can't touch, fine. We won't touch.

However I can get her, I remind myself.

Her expression gentles. "I'm your past, Frosty, and for now, I'm your present. But you need to come to grips with the fact that I will never be part of your future."

"You are my past, present *and* future, kitten." I'll never come to grips with anything else.

"Frosty—"

"Kat." I flatten my hands at her temples. "Why am I just now seeing you? Why did you stay away so long?"

Her gaze remains on me, but for several heartbeats of time, I'm certain she's no longer seeing me. Her attention is far away, somewhere I've never been. Somewhere I can't go. "Like I said, there's no time to get into the nuts and bolts during this visit."

"But you will visit me again?"

She gives a sharp incline of her head. "For the next few months, you'll be the lucky recipient of one visit a day, every day."

That's not good enough. "I won't be satisfied until you're surgically attached to my side."

She rolls her eyes. "This isn't a negotiation, and you didn't let me finish. I will visit you once every day…as long as you've done something productive for our cause."

I arch a brow. "You're bribing me?"

"Oh, good. You understand." She beams at me, making my chest ache. "And no, tonight wasn't a bonus. You still have to earn the privilege."

That's my Kat, always determined to get her way. It's one

of the thousand things I love about her. She takes what she wants when she wants it, damn the consequences.

I wish I could kiss her, but if touching her means losing her, I'll keep my hands—and my mouth—to myself. "Get ready to see a whole lot more of me, kitten. I'll do *anything* to spend time with you."

"Duh. I'm so cake I'm *the* cake." Her image begins to fade, and I shake my head violently.

"Kat!"

"Listen, Frosty, I'm almost out of time and I haven't told you what you need to do. It's imperative—"

"No. You stay with me. Do you hear me? We're not done."

Her head whips to the side as if she hears a noise I do not, and her eyes widen. I follow the line of her gaze...and see a ghostly image of Ali's younger sister, Emma, whose mouth is moving. Still I hear nothing.

"Crappity crap crap. It's worse than we thought," Kat says as she faces me again. "She's alone, and they're surrounding her. She desperately needs your help, Frosty. You *have* to go to her."

"Who? Emma?"

"No, just—"

"Who?" I demand again.

"It shouldn't matter who she is," Kat says, and she's peering up at me with a wealth of concern and dread. "She's a human being and she needs help, so strap on your big-girl panties, get to Shady Elms and freaking help her! It's almost too late." A moment later, Kat is gone.

Cursing, I slam my fist into the wall. My knuckles scream in protest, but okay. All right. My girl is gone, but she won't stay gone. Not this time. She'll be back. I just have to help the mysterious "her."

Shady Elms is roughly ten minutes away. Five if I break speed records. I race to my truck, only to stop once I'm behind the wheel. I've been drinking. There's no way in hell driving will end well. Fine. I arm up with the weapons stored in the vehicle and shed my body, leaving it in the driver's seat.

As I run at a speed no human can ever achieve, pedestrians amble along the sidewalk and unwittingly move into my path. I'm forced to plow through them or spin around them. I spin, otherwise my spirit would pass through their bodies and hit *their* spirits, and that wouldn't do anyone any good. Dizziness plays chicken with my mind and nausea knocks on the door of my stomach, but I refuse to slow. The row of buildings eventually gives way to a long stretch of road, paved and smooth. I'm on constant alert for the telltale signs of the undead—grunts carried on the wind, the fetid stench of rot and the crimson glow of hunger in eyes that are windows to evil.

When the edge of the cemetery comes into view, I veer off into a patch of trees. As I pass a towering oak, a chorus of grunts assaults my ears. Then a feminine shout of frustration sounds and I pick up the pace. I leap over tombstones and shoot around a mausoleum…until finally I spot the horde. At least twenty zombies have zeroed in on a single meal while countless others writhe on the ground, cut up like pieces of old lunch meat.

The mysterious "her" is a slayer. Good. She can help me help her.

I palm my semiautomatics and push through the masses, putting a bullet in every rotting brain that moves into my way.

Not a fix-all, but at least the enemy will be slowed down, impact sending the bodies to the ground.

As the creatures catch my scent, they face me. I whirl the guns in my hands to grip the barrels. With a press of my thumb against a hidden button, serrated axes pop out at the end of each handle. I start hacking, my arms remaining in a constant sate of motion. Rotting flesh tears and limbs detach.

Because spirits are not bound to the same physical laws as bodies, I'm able to fight at a speed the hunger-fogged zombies cannot track. By the time a creature reaches for me, I've already removed its hand...followed by its head. As more and more walking corpses are cut into parts, a sea of goo and gore spreads over the ground. But at least a path opens up, granting me a good look at the slayer's backside. She's a blonde.

She's fluidly graceful, fighting with a ferocity and viciousness I admire, her short swords extensions of her arms as she slices and dices with perfect precision. Her body is lithe, displayed to perfection in pink camo, and I smile despite the situation. Kat might have worn something similar, had she been a slayer.

For once, I can think about my girl without praying I die, too.

The blonde takes down three Zs with a single swing but doesn't see the last two getting to their feet...now sneaking up behind her. I whirl my guns and squeeze off two quick shots, the boom of gunfire echoing through the night, the creatures flying backward. I race forward, there when the two hit the ground, slamming my axes into their mouths to separate their jaws. They won't be biting me or anyone else ever again.

Panting, covered in sweat and goo, I turn toward the girl. Our gazes meet—and suddenly I'm struck dumb. She must be, too. Her mouth drops open.

A shoulder-length cap of white-blond hair frames a face more delicate than a cameo, despite the silver hoops in her jet-black eyebrows. Her eyes are a dark golden brown, like honey, her bronzed skin tattooed heavily in black and white. She's beautiful in a punk-rock Barbie kind of way. I've always thought so.

When we lived in the same twenty-thousand-square-foot mansion for several months, we never had a conversation; I never had time for her, never paid her more than a passing, admiring glance, my sights always on Kat or a mission, very little else worthy of my time. But there's no doubt I'm standing before Camilla Marks. Milla to her friends.

I am not her friend.

She is River's sister, and she was once second-in-command to a group of slayers who haven't always seen eye-to-eye with Cole and me. She's the one who betrayed her own crew, and mine, destroying an entire security system so that Anima could get to Ali, all in the name of saving her brother—offering Ali's life in exchange for River's.

She's the bitch responsible for Kat's death.

I understand the need to protect your family, but I will never be okay with putting innocents at risk to do it. And okay, yeah, that's a lie. I would have done *anything*, betrayed *anyone*, to save Kat. That doesn't mean I'll ever forgive this girl.

There's no way in hell Kat would have sent me to save Camilla Marks. My kitten must not have known who needed aid. She made a mistake. One I can rectify.

"Thank you." Camilla wipes at the sweat on her brow, and I notice the word *Betrayal* scripted in bold black letters across her wrist. "You saved my life."

"Keep your thanks. I don't want it." My tone is pure grit and menace. I'm close to snapping, and there's no telling what I'll do if that happens. I've never hated anyone more than I hate her—not even myself. "And why are you wearing pink camo? You're not trying to hide in Candy Land."

She blinks at me, though she doesn't appear surprised by my malevolence. "I guess you remember me."

"I'm fighting a killing rage right now, so, yeah, I remember." I want to shout, *You're a traitor and the scum of the earth*, but I know whatever is spoken in this spirit realm comes true in the natural realm, always and forever, as long as it's believed when it's said. I believe she's a traitor and scum, but actually voicing the accusations will give power to them, perhaps making her evil side even stronger.

Sometimes it's best to keep an opinion to myself.

She flinches but says, "I'm not taking back my thanks."

The metallic twang of copper coats my tongue, and I realize I've bitten it. I spit blood at her feet. "Have you spoken to a witness? Kat Parker? You remember Kat, don't you? *My* Kat." What I really want to know: did Camilla lie to her? Convince my girl to aid the enemy? "The innocent you helped murder in cold blood."

Another flinch before she lifts her chin. "Of course I remember her, but no, I haven't spoken to her."

"You're lying," I snarl. She has to be lying.

A zombie head rolls toward me, teeth snapping, and I punt the thing in the nose, sending it soaring like a soccer ball over a hill littered with tombstones. One point, Frosty.

"I'm not." Camilla shakes her head for emphasis and rubs at her wrist. The one with the tattoo. "Trust me, I've learned my lesson about betraying other slayers."

I don't believe her, but I know I'm not doing this. I'm not having a conversation with her. I turn away and stride out of the cemetery, saying to the sky, "I've done my good deed for the day. I let Camilla Marks live. I expect to see you tomorrow, Kat. Or else."

4

Milla

WHITE KITTEN, BLACK KITTEN

I'm not a crier. When you've watched multiple friends die in the most horrendous ways, your ability to hurt is often desensitized and your emotions numbed. And when you've had to stitch your own wounds and set your own broken bones, your threshold for pain skyrockets. But tonight, as I go through the sea of zombie parts, using *dýnamis* to ash the evil—light always chases darkness away—a single tear slicks down my cheek.

That boy... Frosty. I remember every interaction I've ever had with him. How could I not? He's one of the most beautiful males on the planet. He steps into a room and all eyes gravitate to him, mine included. Girls want to bang him, and boys want to be him.

He's deliciously tall with the muscle mass of a professional football player, and the bad-boy attitude to match—snarky, maddening, yet somehow charming. He's strength personified and as lethal as the guns he carries.

So many slayers climb into a boxing ring to learn new tricks or even to play with their friends. He climbs in, and it's clear there's only one thing on his mind: delivering pain.

Why did he walk away from me, when he craves vengeance?

The way he stood before me, proud and furious, covered in battle grime, his hair pale but several shades darker than mine, the strands plastered to his cheeks, his hands twitching as he considered reaching for his weapons...yeah, he wanted to take me down. His eyes, navy blue, piercing and ice-cold—the kind of eyes you'd see on a serial killer as he explains how he's going to hack up your body and store the parts in his fridge—had stared at my heart, as if willing it to stop beating. And yet, I couldn't help remembering other times, when he looked at his girlfriend, Kat, the ice melting, his irises burning hotter than flames.

No one has ever looked at me that way. As if I'm worth something. Worth everything. As if I'm more precious than the sun, moon and stars. As if I'm a prize beyond value. I can't imagine anyone doing so now. Or ever. Not after the things I've done.

And that's okay. I sowed death, and now I'm reaping a harvest of it.

I glance at my newest tattoo. *Betrayal.* A permanent reminder of the worst thing I can do to my loved ones. The price is too high. I sigh and get back to work. By the time I finish ashing Z-parts, the civilians who never realized a war was raging around them are gone and I'm utterly exhausted.

I trudge to my body and, with a single touch, join my spirit to my body. It's as easy as slipping a hand into a glove. A few scratches are bleeding on my arms and there are bruises on my legs, but other than that I'm injury-free. All thanks to Frosty, who hates me with the passion of a thousand suns. Without him, I probably would have died tonight.

Probably, ha! There'd been too many zombies to track on my own.

I trudge forward, but stop just outside the cemetery. There are piles of ash all around me. Wonderful. Dead zombies. Except, I didn't kill any undead in this location. So...someone else did it. Frosty, on his way out? Or maybe someone who'd come with him? I spin, but find no footprints other than my own. Not many slayers think to cover their spiritual tracks. Why bother?

Whatever. I'm too tired to care. I need a shower and a few thousand hours of sleep.

I'm staying at a run-down motel a few miles down the road. It's all I can afford. When I was kicked out of the home I shared with River just outside of Birmingham, I had nothing but the clothes on my back, but I'd been socking wads of cash away for years. Just in case. A girl has to be prepared for anything. I have only fourteen hundred and thirty-seven dollars left, and I have to make it last. I can't stay up all night fighting zombies if I'm grinding away at a nine-to-five.

As I trudge up and down hills, sticking to main roads, the little hairs on the back of my neck rise again. I bend down as if I need to tie my shoe, and push my spirit out of my body to look at what's happening behind me without an onlooker knowing. But there's no sign of a tail. No moving shadows or snapping limbs. No click of a gun being cocked. No grunts or groans.

Relieved, I return to my body and motor on. Finally I reach the motel. In the parking lot, there's a guy leaning against a beat-up Nova, puffing on the end of a cancer stick. The night is nothing but a sheet of black, and there are no streetlamps nearby, so I can't make out his features, but I can tell he's roughly the same size as my brother.

My heart skips a beat. "River?"

"Excuse me?" A voice I don't recognize.

Disappointment is overwhelming. "Never mind." I reach my door and check to make sure the clear tape I placed along the frame is still intact. A split means someone entered my room while I was gone, despite the Do Not Disturb sign on the knob.

Years of being chased by Anima have made me paranoid.

But the tape hasn't been disturbed, and I'm able to enter without fear. After rigging my own special lock on the door, as well as placing bells over the top to wake me if someone manages to bypass my security measures, I shower off the gunk and sweat, clean the scratches on my arms with antiseptic and dress in a white T-shirt and a pair of shorts.

The place doesn't have a kitchenette or a microwave, so I slap peanut butter on two pieces of bread and call it good. Quick and easy with a decent amount of protein. Welcome to my breakfast, lunch and dinner. I think I'm single-handedly keeping Peter Pan in business.

I've consumed half the sandwich by the time I make it to the bed and sit. My back and feet ache like freaking crazy.

"For a villain, your evil lair sure does suck donkey balls."

The voice startles me. I'm on my feet in a blink, the precious sandwich on the floor and a 9 mm in my hand. I've

stashed weapons all over the room to ensure one is near wherever I happen to be.

A short brunette stands in front of the door. The closed
door. Overhead, the bells are silent. I frown. I…know her.
She's the girlfriend. Frosty's girlfriend, Kat Parker. But she's…
she's dead. I secretly attended her funeral—glimpsed the body
in the casket—and cursed myself for a past I will never be
able to change.

I shouldn't be seeing her here and now.

Is she my tail? The reason the hairs on my neck reacted?
No, no, she couldn't be. Otherwise I would've had a similar
reaction before she spoke. And what the hell am I doing? I
can't afford to be lost in my head right now.

"How are…what are…?" Wait. Earlier, Frosty mentioned
Kat—a witness. I've heard of witnesses appearing to loved
ones from both slayers I trust and people working for Anima,
so I know spirits of the dead *do* come back to the land of the
living to proclaim good news…or issue warnings.

"I'm not a zombie, if that's what you're thinking. I'm a witness," she confirms.

"I know you're not a zombie. If you were, I'd have already
removed your head."

"Well, well. Someone thinks highly of her skill. Too bad
for you, I'll never again be an easy target."

"I never wanted to hurt you." Keeping the gun trained on
her, I close the distance. I reach for her with my free hand…
and encounter only air. My eyes widen. She is what she says
she is. I lower my arm, my heart thudding wildly in my chest.
"You weren't supposed to be harmed."

"And that makes everything you did okay? Intentions mean nothing. Actions are everything."

She isn't wrong. "Are you here to punish me?"

As a witness, does she know what happened behind the scenes? Why I did what I did?

Does she care?

Anima had captured my brother weeks before. I broke into the facility, desperate to free him, but within minutes agents had me surrounded. Their leader, Rebecca Smith, had kept tabs on me for years. She knew my habits, knew what I'd do if River was threatened.

And she wasn't wrong.

We were in different rooms, River and I, and while I could see him, he could not see me, a blindfold over his eyes. Rebecca ordered a gun be placed at his head, and I agreed to do whatever was asked of me, on two conditions. River could never know—he would have rather died than let me aid Anima—and none of our people could be hurt.

To this day, my brother thinks he escaped that facility on his own.

And yes, I could have backed out of my promise to Anima. I could have warned Ali instead of targeting her. But Anima wasn't led by an idiot, and I'd already been informed what would happen if I failed my mission. River would be targeted in Ali's place and no expense would be spared in the quest to end his life.

"I'm supposed to forgive you, and I have," the girl finally says. "And shockingly enough, the worst of my anger has been washed away. When I died, I became part of something greater than myself, and the wrongs done to me no longer seemed—or seem—as significant. But I still don't like you. You rid the world of a national treasure."

Her overconfidence used to annoy me. Now? I kind of get it. Winning a guy like Frosty is a miracle feat. She's in a class by herself.

I return the gun to the nightstand and sit on the edge of the bed. "Not to be rude, but why are you here?" If she wants a pound of flesh, I'll give her a pound of flesh. Let's just get it over with.

"How adorable. You actually think you're in charge of this conversation." She motions to my arms with a tilt of her chin. "Question. Why are all your tattoos black and white?"

Why not tell her? "River and I learned at a very young age that there's right and there's wrong, and there is nothing in between. The tattoos serve as a reminder."

"Black and white," she says and taps her chin. "No fifty shades of gray."

I shake my head and realize I've just admitted there is no reason good enough to do what I did to her. Right: protecting the innocent. Wrong: putting them at risk. End of story. Shame floods me, sharpening already razorlike claws inside my chest.

"I want you to keep that lesson in mind as I get down to the nitty-gritty." She prances throughout the room, looking over my meager belongings with an air of distaste. "I know you fought alongside Frosty tonight."

"Yes."

"And he saved your life."

I sigh. "Yes."

"So in a way, you owe him yours. Right?"

I don't like where this is headed. "What is it you want from me? Spit it out."

The very picture of determination, she crosses her arms over her chest. "All right. You asked for it. My friend Ali— you know her, right? The girl you betrayed. Well, she had a vision, and her visions are never wrong." Kat looks away for a moment, her shoulders hunching in. A telltale sign of guilt. I know it well.

She has no reason to feel that way, but me? Yeah. *Every* reason. My shoulders sink in, too. "I've heard about the visions." Anima also tasked me with finding out more about them, but in that regard, I'd had no luck. "Go on."

Kat runs her tongue over her teeth. "In this one, you stop a woman from shooting Frosty. You save his life." Again, she looks away for several beats of silence, and I have to wonder why.

She wouldn't lie about something like this—would she?

"For that reason and that reason alone," she continues, "I'm here to ensure you never stray far from Frosty's side."

I...don't understand. "*You*, as in *me*?" I hike my thumbs at my chest for emphasis. "Guard Frosty?"

Her lip curls with a return of her distaste, but she nods. "Trust me. I'm as surprised as you are."

Well, her weird behavior finally makes sense. She's annoyed. "He can take care of himself." He's more than proved it. "Besides, he hates me. He'll never allow me to get close to him."

"We'll just have to make him. I can ensure he tolerates your presence, but I don't think I can stop him from killing you. That's your part."

Great. Wonderful. "Why don't I lasso the moon while I'm at it?"

Kat's eyes narrow on me, her hazel irises focusing with laser sharpness. "When did you become such a baby?"

Ouch. "You'll trust me not to betray him?"

"Yes, but only because of the vision. Meanwhile, I'll be watching you, and if I suspect you're doing anything wrong, my next visit won't be so pleasant."

I rub at my wrist. I didn't lie to Frosty. I've learned my lesson and won't betray him. More than that, Kat is right. I owe the boy my life. He saved me tonight. I'll gladly stand guard over him.

"I'll take care of him as if he's my brother."

This soothes her, but only slightly.

"Do you know when he's going to be attacked? Or where?" I grab a notebook and pen from the nightstand. "Any details you can give me about the vision will help."

Silence greets me.

I glance up, but she's already gone.

Sighing, I fall back on the bed. The mattress creaks, blending with the rhythmic *thump, thump, thump* of my neighbor's headboard. Frosty isn't going to like having me as a shadow. He's going to protest. Loudly. He'll insult me, and it'll hurt like crazy, and like Kat said, he might even try to kill me, but I'm tough and I'll handle it.

Who's going to attack him? A female zombie? A former employee from Anima? A new employee from Anima?

Strike those last two. One, agents are cowards. When Anima was in operation, they only approached Zs while wearing a specially designed hazmat suit, the outer layer of material made of something akin to zombie flesh, rendering the human underneath it invisible to the undead. Two, I haven't been contacted by anyone associated with the company, not since Cole and Ali burned down their facilities and wiped Rebecca's memories—a woman who would happily eat her own young if it meant surviving another day.

That memory-wiping thing... It *is* reversible. But again, if Rebecca remembered her past, or the war, she would have contacted me. Would have threatened River again.

What would I do then?

The stupid tears return to my eyes, stinging, and I roll to my side. My current situation is the sum total of the decisions I made in the past, I know that, just like I know I have to live with the consequences every day for the rest of my life.

This is no one's fault by my own, and I won't make the same mistakes. I won't.

And I'm not helpless. I can do everything in my power to create a *better* future. Starting now, with Frosty. I would forever hate anyone who hurt River, just as Frosty will forever hate the people who hurt Kat.

I can't ever make up such a loss to him, but I can damn sure try. And I will.

5

Frosty

DEAD MAN RISING

I blink open tired, gritty eyes as bright light streams through the crack in my bedroom curtains. My temples pound, a memory knocking on the door of my mind.

I reach for Kat, intending to cuddle her close, but her side of the bed is cold.

Makes sense. She's dead.

The thought hits me, a reminder of all I've lost, and agony nearly splits open my chest. But as bad as it is, it's not as bad as usual. Another memory surfaces, and I grin. Yesterday, she came to visit me; she asked me to fight zombies for another slayer, not realizing she was sending me to Camilla Marks. She promised to visit me again.

I jolt upright and scan my bedroom, hoping she's already here. Beige walls. A small bed with blue sheets and brown covers, a large dresser, the drawers hanging open. My clean clothes are piled in one corner and my dirty clothes piled in another. I've been meaning to do laundry for, oh, about four months.

There's no sign of Kat.

Still, I jump up and race into the bathroom, a small space with only a sink, toilet and shower stall. I brush my teeth and hair, but I don't bother to change my clothes. I'm shirtless, but wearing a pair of running shorts. I've worn worse.

"Kat," I call, not even trying to hide the desperation in my tone. "Kat."

She appears in a blink, as if she's been waiting for my summons, and my knees almost buckle. I step toward her out of habit, only to stop myself as yesterday's warning plays through my mind. Touch her, lose her.

No touching. Ever.

"Congrats! Today's your lucky day." She's dressed in the same T-shirt and boxers as before, but it doesn't matter. She's beautiful in a way no other girl can ever hope to be. "You call, I answer."

"I missed you," I say.

"You'd be crazy if you didn't."

I try for a scolding expression but only manage to smile at her. "When you aren't with me, where are you?" I want to know every detail about her new life.

She points to the ceiling...and then she waves her arm and whips her body into the most hideous dance of all time.

I laugh—really laugh—and say, "Stop. Before I have to bleach my eyes."

"Because your moves and grooves don't compare to mine, and watching me only reminds you of your failure?"

"Yeah, something like that."

Smiling, she wraps a lock of hair around her finger. "I had no idea how much pain my failing kidneys were causing until I was dead. Now I can walk and run and dance without a single twinge. It's… Frosty, there are no words."

"Not even *cake*?"

"Not even."

It's clear she's happy with her situation, and I love that she's happy. I do. I crave her happiness above my own. But I also…don't love it. She's happy without me. I'm miserable without her.

More tales from a grade A douche-purse.

"Are you treated well up there?" I ask.

"Dude! The best! You seriously have no idea." She saunters to the bed, which is covered in Blood Lines, and plops onto the edge. As usual, she's pure energy and excitement. A force of nature. "It's like a perfected version of here. Earth 2.0. And guess what? Contrary to popular opinion, it's not the end."

"Not the end?" My brow furrows as confusion overtakes me. "You can die again?"

"No, no, nothing like that. We're in a holding zone where we're allowed to watch over our loved ones." She taps her chin with two well-manicured fingers. "We even get to help, but only by taking opposing parties to court and winning."

"Actual court?"

"Yep. Only on a much larger scale, because it's the final authority. We have to petition for answers and ceasefires and all kinds of other things. That's where I've been all this time. In court. That's where Helen is now. In fact, she rarely leaves the courtroom."

Helen, Ali's biological mom. "Why go through so much trouble for us?" What do they actually accomplish?

Kat kicks her feet, causing the mattress to bounce. "I know you won't understand this, but sometimes to have victory down here, you first need to have victory up there. Helen, Emma and I do our best to ensure you guys have everything you need."

Realization strikes me. "You petitioned to appear to me."

"Uh, you mean I petitioned *the crap* out of the court to appear to you. Which is why I got a yes. But—boo, hiss—there are rules. More than you know."

"Such as?"

"Such as what I'm allowed to tell you…and what I'm not." She blows me a kiss. "Finally I know things you don't, and for the same reasons you couldn't tell me about the zombies once upon a time—I couldn't handle the truth—I can't tell you everything."

I don't like this. I don't like this *at all.* "What happens if you break the rules?"

"I can be forced to leave the holding zone. Some witnesses opt not to stay when they first arrive, like Miranda, Ali's adopted mom. Others, the troublemakers, can be booted out before their time." Resignation glints in eyes I want filled only with happiness. "I don't want to be booted."

Do I detect an unsaid *yet?*

"I'm helping you guys for the first time ever," she adds, "and I'm not ready to stop."

"Why would anyone opt to leave?" I cross my arms and lean against the bathroom door. "And where are the booted ones sent?"

"To the highest heaven...the True Rest. Trust me, *everyone* in the holding zone wants to enter into the True Rest. Peace beyond your understanding. Joy. And there's no such thing as heartache or pain. Only love and light exist there." She smiles wide...then frowns deeply. "But in the Rest, I will no longer have any influence over your situation, no longer be allowed to petition, so, I'll do whatever it takes to remain in the holding zone."

My mind whirls with possibilities. "Do people in the holding zone date?"

"And marry. And have babies."

Excitement blooms. If *I'm* in the holding zone, I can be with her again. We'll be a couple. With a future.

But she knows me well, knows the direction of my thoughts, and shakes her head. "Don't you dare. It's not yet your time, Frosty."

"It wasn't yours, either."

"I know. I went too early and you are now living with the consequences. And it sucks, doesn't it? So don't make your friends live with the consequences of *your* early death. They need you too badly."

"I want to be with you." Whatever the cost.

Her eyes narrow, her temper clearly pricked. "Well, I want a pony, but we don't always get what we want, do we?"

"Kat—"

"Frosty." She sighs. "I want you to date other people."

I blink. Surely I misheard her. "There's no way you just said—"

"Zip your pie hole, okay? Kitty is still talking. You knew I would die before you—"

"I didn't! I expected to die in battle long before your kidneys shut down."

"Please," she says with a roll of her eyes. "Like anyone could defeat you in a fight. But no matter how you slice it, you knew you wouldn't get a happily-ever-after with me."

"I'm not dating other girls, kitten." I'm pissed that she even suggested it.

"What about the legions you've banged since my death, huh?"

I flinch as though I've been punched by a five-hundred-pound, steroid-addicted hulk. "They were mistakes I will forever regret."

"Screw your regrets." Remaining on the mattress, she rises to her knees, her gaze heartbreakingly earnest. "You have to open your heart to love again."

"No, I—"

"You're a somewhat attractive guy," she interjects. "A good, solid five. And now that you've got money, you can probably bag a six...maybe a seven."

"Thanks," I reply drily, even as I crumble inside. She can't want me with someone else. Not really. She just can't.

Her smile is all about sadness, no hint of amusement. "All I'm saying is, there's someone out there just for you. The one who's meant to be. She won't be as good as me, of course. I'm a rare ten. Practically a unicorn. But she'll give you a reason to keep fighting in the war."

"I'll fight in the war for *you*." My tone is as rough as sandpaper. "Don't you want me anymore?"

She exhales a heavy breath. "I'm not saying that."

"Then I don't need to—"

"But," she interjects forcefully, shutting me up and erasing every bit of my relief, "I can see what you can't. The bigger picture. The endgame. The only thing that matters."

My hands fist. "*We* are what matters."

She looks away from me, as if she can no longer bear to hold my gaze. "I love you, and I'll always love you, but the moment, the very second my spirit left my body, I became part of... Well, I don't know how else to say it—I became part of one mind. A collective consciousness. I saw that you and I... we were never meant to be, Frosty. Not in a romantic sense."

Are you *kidding* me? She's just given me the afterlife version of the "It's not you, it's me" speech. Clearly, despite her "I'm not saying that," she no longer wants me the way I want her. It's a blow I wasn't prepared to take.

Acid drips through my chest, burning an already broken heart, but not by word or deed do I reveal the destruction taking place inside me.

This is another crime to place at Anima's door. A crime to place at Camilla's feet.

"Do you still want to see me?" Kat asks quietly.

"Yes." I don't have to think about my answer. I need time to change her mind and win her back, that's all.

"Good. That's good." She crawls from the bed to stand. "Now, sadly, I've got to go. The longer I'm with you, the less I know what's happening around you."

Stay, I almost roar. *Steady. Calm.* Aggression and neediness will do me no favors. "When can I see you again?"

"Tonight. You've been such a good boy, I'll gift you with another visit. But not here. Get out. Go do something. Introduce yourself to a group of cute girls. I'll find you."

★ ★ ★

I return to Hearts. Kat said she'd find me, and I want her to find me here. I want to replace the last memory she has of me in this location—going after a brunette I intended to use and lose.

Urgency is like a whip inside me, striking at me, keeping me going when all I want to do is find my girl. I've been here an hour already, but I haven't touched a single drop of whiskey, and I won't. Ginger ale is my new drink of choice.

Where is she?

A female sinks into the chair next to me. I look past her, scanning the club. The same black-light strobes flash. The same people writhe on the dance floor. The same crowd of onlookers appears a little too turned on for anyone's good. No sign of Kat, and while patience has always been one of my stronger virtues—I waited three years for Kat to say yes to a date, then another year to get her into bed—I'm hanging at the end of a very frayed rope.

"Logan?" The woman beside me nudges my shoulder. "Hi."

Logan isn't my real name. Nor is Frosty, for that matter. To be honest, I hate my real name almost as much as I love it. It's been a source of teasing most of my life, but also of envy. Tonight, however, I am who my ID says I am. Logan. The name I've been using with the girls I've bedded.

And despite a foggy memory, I know I've bedded this one. She has straight dark hair and green eyes, the reasons I would have picked her.

"How are you?" I ask, going for the polite approach. I'm

still a douche-purse, I know this, but with Kat back in my life, I'm determined to be a nice douche-purse.

"I'm good. I was hoping I'd run into you again." Smiling coyly, batting her lashes at me, she traces her fingernails along my arm. "Want to go back to my place? We never got to finish that bottle of Macallan."

"No thanks." I pull away and her cheeks heat with embarrassment. Rejection stings, no getting around that, but I won't flirt to be nice. I just won't.

Over the years, Kat and I had many conversations about the different nuances of sex. About the expectations of the guy versus the expectations of the girl. What was physical for me was probably emotional for this girl. Despite all her protests to the contrary.

Like so many others, she probably hoped I would enjoy being with her so much, I would want another night...hell, a few weeks...maybe several months with her, forgetting my "I only want one night" claim. Kat called that particular mindset "the exception fantasy."

It's a fantasy with a low rate of success.

"Are you sure?" She runs a finger between her breasts. "You'll have fun."

"Sorry, but I'm here to meet someone." The love of my life.

"That would be me. Get lost."

The newcomer leans in to my other side and waves at Macallan. I stiffen, a very dark curse exploding from me. Camilla Marks.

Her platinum hair is a wild fall of curls, the sides clipped back from her face, revealing locks of jet-black at her temples. Her ebony lashes are a mile long and spiked, a complete contrast to the glitter sparkling around her honey-colored eyes. Her cheeks are flushed to a deep rose, her lips painted bloodred.

Guys are staring at her as if she's the last piece of candy in the candy store.

I can understand why. She's wearing a black leather vest, the center veeing between small but perfect breasts, revealing more of her tattoos than it conceals. Haunting 3-D images come to startling life. My favorite is the one over her heart. The face of a little girl. Perhaps even Camilla herself, only much younger. The bone structure is similar, though the etching has jet-black ringlets.

Like the vest, her pants are black leather, and they look like they've been painted on her. Silver zippers cover both articles of clothing, and I know a blade is hidden underneath each one. Just as I know every piece of jewelry she's wearing doubles as some kind of weapon. The pendant hanging from the silver chain around her neck can be turned into a small dagger. Her bracelets have two hooks in the center. Pull them, and create a garrote.

"Who are *you*?" Macallan asks her. "Because he doesn't look happy to see you."

Camilla ignores her, turning to snipe at the guy behind her. She reveals a back completely bared, the vest held on by a prayer and a tie at her nape and waist. There are more tattoos, and the designs enthrall me. A tree of life growing from the center of a river, every branch sprouting a different type of bloom. A frying pan, of all things. A fist. A key, star and dagger. Birds are perched on several of the branches, and a flock flies above the tallest branch.

I want to trace the images with my fingers. Then she's facing me again, and I remember she's a traitor. My hatred overshadows every bit of my admiration.

"What are you doing here?" I demand.

She signals for a drink. "Ask your girlfriend."

She's spoken to Kat?

"Wait. You have a girlfriend?" Macallan asks. She's clutching her glass of froufrou whatever, clearly planning to toss the contents in my face.

Camilla acts fast, reaching over to knock the glass out of the girl's hand. "Looks like someone needs to learn her manners. I'm happy to—"

"Excuse us," I say to Macallan. I grab Camilla by the arm and yank her toward the stairs that lead to the VIP lounge.

Halfway up she wrenches from my hold. "There's no need to be so rough. I don't plan to run away. If you haven't noticed, I'm not resisting."

"Do you seriously expect me to trust you?" I say, but I don't reach for her again. The less contact we have, the better.

I march the rest of the way up. If she doesn't follow, I'll go hunting for her and she won't like what happens when I catch her.

And I will catch her.

The lounge has a bar of its own with waitstaff paid to ensure a glass never goes dry and a smile never fades. I'm recognized immediately, a waitress rushing over to greet me. I step around her and head toward the office in back. An office Ankh—Reeve's dad—once kept just for us, in case we had zombie business to discuss.

Even with the club's remodel, the pass code on the door is

the same. I put my back in front of Camilla to punch in the numbers, then motion her inside. With her head high, she sweeps past me. I'm hot on her heels, shutting the door with a hard kick of my leg. When the lock engages on its own, a wave of satisfaction hits me. Now she's stuck. She can't escape without the code. Not that the office would make a good prison. There are plush leather couches and oversized chairs. Another wet bar. A desk with multiple computers and a three-line phone system.

Camilla faces me, her dark eyes throwing venom. "Before you start hurling demands for information, yes, Kat appeared to me last night and again about an hour ago. She told me to come here and stick by your side."

"You're lying." Kat would never torture me like that.

"That's the second time you've accused me of deceit." She takes a step toward me, the menace she's throwing a match to mine. "Do it a third time, and you'll find your balls in your throat."

"I'm sure I'll love the taste of them," I retort.

"Children, please. She's not lying, Frosty." Kat appears beside Camilla, and my knees go weak with relief. She has returned, as promised. "I want Camilla at your side every minute of every day. Starting now."

What the hell? "Is this a joke? A game of 'would you rather'? Well, I'd rather play tonsil hockey with a zombie than spend another minute with your killer."

Camilla flinches, but I refuse to feel bad for speaking the truth.

"Unfortunately for you," Kat says, "this is a game of 'what

the dead girl wants, the dead girl gets.'" Her gaze pleads with me. "You're doing it, and that's final."

Damn it. She's serious about this. "Why? You know who Camilla is, right?"

"I do. Though you're wrong about one thing. She's not my killer. Not exactly." The starch drains from her. "You just have to trust me. This arrangement is necessary."

I shake my head, adamant. "No. Absolutely not."

"Frosty."

"Kitten." How can I make her understand? "I'll do anything for you. Cut out my own heart? Where's a knife? Set myself on fire? Give me a match. But I won't hang out with your murderer."

"I didn't set those bombs," Camilla rasps. "I knew nothing about them. I'm also not the one who shot her."

I spare her the briefest glance, and there's nothing nice about it. "You destroyed the security system that allowed Anima to do those things. In my eyes, you carry the most guilt."

The starch leaves her, too, and she withers. Good. Let her hurt for what she did. Let her stew in her shame. It's what she deserves.

Kat steps toward me, claiming my attention. "I'm about to drop some knowledge, big boy, so listen up. I told you I would appear on the days you performed a good deed. Well, guess what? Those good deeds begin and end with Camilla Marks. From now on, you will have breakfast with her. You will fight zombies with her. You will…" Her teeth grind together. "Sleep in the same room with her."

I give another violent shake my head. No way, no how.

"I've never asked you for anything," Kat says, and I gape at her.

"You asked me for something every day since we met. Teddy bears. Roses. Apologies. My dessert. My lunch money. My car. Hell, even my soul. Nothing was off-limits."

"I didn't ask for anything *important*," she amends, then clasps her hands together to form a steeple. "Do this for me. Please. It's the only way we'll get to see each other."

The rules, I realize. Those stupid rules.

I have more questions for her, but I blink, and she's gone. A roar of denial leaves me, echoing from the walls.

"I'll do it," I shout. I've been backed into a corner, and I know it. I feel like the mangy mutt the good people at animal control want to capture to test for rabies, but I'll still do it. "I agree to your terms. You can come back now."

But she doesn't return, and desolation begins to weigh me down.

"Why would *you* agree to this?" I demand of the traitor.

Camilla strides to the wet bar to pour herself a shot of Grey Goose. "I owe her. I owe you."

"Or you're planning to spy on me." Yeah. I bet that's it.

"Your thought process needs retooling. Who, exactly, am I supposed to report to?" She drains the glass. "Anima is nothing but rubble."

"Or so we think." I run both hands through my hair, yank at the strands. What the hell am I going to do with this girl? I don't want her in my apartment. I've had the place only a few months and it still doesn't feel like home, but it's mine and she's not welcome to *anything* that belongs to me. But I don't want her in Reeve's new place, either. I don't want her around my friends.

"Kat showed me where you live," she says. "I've already dropped my backpack there."

"The door was locked."

"Yes, and I picked it."

Rage sparks, and I punch the wall.

"Temper, temper." She doesn't look the least bit afraid of me as she strides to the exit. I'm a little surprised and a lot pissed when she plugs in the proper code and the door opens for her. "Let's go home and talk logistics."

"My home, not yours." I race to her side to keep pace, barely stopping myself from grabbing and shaking her. "The code."

She doesn't pretend to misunderstand my meaning. "I memorized the numbers when you punched them in."

"I had my back to you, blocking your view."

"Was I not supposed to peek over your shoulder? Oops. My bad."

I open my mouth to blast her.

"I didn't know what you planned to do to me and devised an evil plan of escape," she interjects. "I know, I know. How dare I take measures to protect myself. I should be ashamed."

I'll have to be more careful around her. Noted. She's the enemy, and she'll always be the enemy. Hostility and suspicion are all she'll ever get from me.

"By the way," she adds, "I'm not sorry."

"I gathered. But hang around me long enough and you will be." I'll make sure of it.

The color drains from her cheeks, but she raises her chin.

A defense mechanism. Good. Words can be weapons. Mine are arrows, and they just struck their intended target.

Downstairs, we push through the ever-growing crowd. Multiple perfumes and body sprays clash with the pungent odors of sweat and alcohol. I shift my head, getting a stronger whiff of Camilla...the roses and pecans embedded in her skin. I hiss. Talk about a prime example of false advertising. To fit her personality, she should smell like brimstone and sulfur.

We exit the building and enter the coolness of the night. I suck in the fresh air as if I've been drowning.

"If Kat wants you to stay with me, fine, you can stay with me." I'll just have to deal. "But you'll have to walk there." I climb behind the wheel of my truck.

She jumps into the bed in back, and I grit my teeth. Getting her out will be a major fight. If we weren't in public, yeah, I'd go for it. But we are, so I'll just have to deal—and make sure I hit every pothole between the club and my apartment complex. Which I do. With relish.

She doesn't speak as we take the stairs to the second floor, and neither do I. I open the door and purposely step in front of her, ensuring I enter first. One, it's rude. Two, I've watched *Dog Whisperer*, so I know the pack leader always enters first. Three, she can suck it. I don't want her here, and I'm not going to pretend like I do.

When the front door closes, she says, "We should talk about—"

But I head into my bedroom and lock her out. Footsteps register. I'm pretty sure she's pacing.

"Frosty," she says through the door.

I put my earbuds in my ears and jack up the volume of my iPod, drowning out her voice.

As morning sunlight seeps through the center crack in my curtains, I finish my exercises. One hundred push-ups. One hundred sit-ups. One hundred lunges, and a thousand other things. I go and go until I've expelled so much energy I could pass for the undead. But at least I've got myself under better control.

Camilla Marks is a means to an end. A way to see Kat. I can endure her presence in my inner sanctum without killing her. Without wanting to kill myself. Surely.

I shower, dress and at last emerge. She's sitting at the kitchen table with tubes of ink and bandages spread around her and a tattoo gun in hand. Her hair is piled into some sort of sloppy bun at the crown of her head, revealing the layer of jet-black hair usually hidden by all that snow white. Her face is free of makeup, making her look younger. So damn pretty it should be a crime.

Hate her.

She wipes blood from the image she just etched into her wrist. A compass next to the word *Betrayal.*

I won't ask. I don't care.

I make a bowl of cereal and shovel in one spoonful after another while standing at the sink. I don't say a word or glance in her direction.

"Oh, no," she says, her tone dry. "The mean boy is ignoring me. Whatever shall I do?"

"Say thank-you," I mutter.

"You can't ignore me *and* make implied threats." She wraps

a bandage around the new image, gathers up the equipment. "You have to pick one."

I drain the milk from the bowl and wash my dishes, silent.

"Sweet," she says. "You picked my favorite."

Does nothing faze her?

Usually at this time of day, I run a million errands to keep my mind off Kat. Today, I park my ass in front of the TV and turn on the sports channel, hoping to annoy Camilla. When I realize she's watching and actually engaged in the game, I flip to a "who's your baby daddy" talk show. But she watches that, too, and even yells at the screen.

"You're too good for him. Leave him!"

Next I try a soap opera, and she finally turns away, uninterested.

I smirk—until I realize I'm stuck watching a guy's evil twin seduce his wife.

After fifteen minutes of praying for the world to end, I head into my room to do a little schoolwork. I'm a senior, though I left public school in favor of a homeschool program a few weeks before Kat died. Considering how many days I'd have missed as I was hunted and attacked by Anima, I'd had no other choice. Flunking out wasn't—isn't—in my life plan. What is? Graduation in a little over a month. College. Becoming a detective. According to Kat, I'll be the youngest and hottest ever. One day I'll hunt human bad guys rather than zombies. Not because I don't like what I do now, but because I also plan to eradicate spirit-evil once and for all.

Somehow.

When I finish solving X, Y and Z, I return to the kitchen

to make a sandwich. She's still in front of the TV, watching a new game, eating a granola bar.

I walk over and snatch the bar out of her hand. "What's mine is mine."

Her cheeks flush. "We could be together for a few days or a few years. From what I gather, there's no time stamp on Ali's vision. Why don't you pretend to be a mature adult and—"

I flip her off without glancing in her direction. I throw the bar in the trash, fix my sandwich and take an exaggerated bite as she peers at me.

"Wow. *So* mature," she mutters. "Can you at least *try* to be civil?"

"You're still alive. That's all the civil you're going to get from me."

She looks away, her shoulders rolling in. "Fair enough."

The sandwich settles like lead in my stomach. I return to my room, where I stay for several hours, just lying in bed, staring up at the ceiling, hoping Kat will visit me. But she doesn't, even when I call her name.

Where the hell is she? She owes me a visit. I've done everything she—

No, I realize. I haven't. *Help friends. Fight. Smile.*

I arm up before returning to the living room. Camilla is still on the couch, but this time she's cleaning a semiautomatic.

"We're going out to hunt zombies," I announce.

Her relief is palpable as she puts the gun back together. "I want to return to Shady Elms."

The cemetery. "Why? Hordes take weeks and months to form, and we left nothing of the last one. At least, I'm assuming you weren't dumb enough to leave the parts behind."

"I ashed them, but…there was something odd about these zombies. They were more rotted than usual for first-timers."

"Here's an idea. They weren't first-timers."

"But they rose from graves. Why would zombies return to their bodies, just to rise again?"

"How would I know? I'm not a zombie." But fine, whatever. "We'll go to Shady Elms." I grab my keys and head to my truck.

The moon is full, the sky completely black. No clouds, no stars. Just a sense of gloom and doom.

Nothing new.

Wait. A rabbit cloud whisks overhead, and I stiffen. Rabbit clouds—Emma's way of warning Ali. Zombies are stirring tonight.

Adrenaline jacks me up. "There will be a battle tonight." All I have to do is find the nest.

"How do you know?"

"I just do."

Camilla jumps into the passenger seat rather than the back bed and casts me a mutinous glare, daring me to comment. I don't. What good will it do?

We maintain terse silence the entire drive. I continually scan for any sign of zombies. Nothing…nothing…for a moment the scent of roses and pecans distracts me. A scent that clings to Camilla no matter where she is or what she's doing.

When we reach the cemetery, I park between two towering oaks, surprised to find Cole's Jeep there. Camilla and I exit, and I use my phone to shine light inside the vehicle. Cole, Ali and Gavin are sitting inside, as still as death, their spirits obviously elsewhere.

"Great," Camilla says. "Now I have to fight the living *and* the undead."

I know the words aren't a threat, but I react as if they are. "Go after my friends, and I'll end you."

She sucks in a breath. "I'm not going to hurt them. I just—"

"Save it. Don't want to hear it." I stalk forward, listening for an indication a battle is waging. Searching…searching…

The sky is even more ominous out here, the sense of doom and gloom stronger.

A twig snaps about ten yards away. I palm two .44's just as Bronx steps from behind a statue of an angel, .44's of his own extended. The second our identities click, we lower our weapons.

"Frosty the Ice Man. You don't call, you don't write. You just show up to the battlefield unannounced." His gaze flicks to Camilla and narrows. "At least you've spoken with Kat."

He knows what's going on? "What are you doing here?"

"Guarding the Jeep and the bodies inside it." Bronx isn't stupid. He knows I asked why he's in the cemetery; he simply chose not to answer. "I'll guard you and yours, if you want to join the others. But don't be surprised if you have a few cuts and bruises when you return."

He's pissed at me. I get it. "If using me as a punching bag will untwist your panties, go for it."

He flips me off, but he can't hide the amused glitter in his eyes.

"Any zombies?" I ask.

"A few."

I step out of my body as easily as breathing. As I wind through the cemetery, Camilla's spirit catches up to me. We come across Cole first. He's leaning against a gnarled tree, the limbs seeming to embrace him and push him away at the same time. His arms are folded over his chest.

"What the hell is going on out here?" I ask.

Just like Bronx, he flicks a glance in Camilla's direction. I know he's debating what to say in front of someone so untrustworthy.

Camilla notices, lifts her chin and squares her shoulders.

"We were on patrol and spread out all over the place," Cole says. "Bronx found and cleansed three zombies, but more and more began to rise from the graves so he texted the rest of us and we rushed over."

"You cleansed the rest." Otherwise he wouldn't be standing here. He'd be at Ali's side. "So where are the other slayers?"

"Walking through the graveyard, watching for other zombies. Ali and I had a vision and we think at least a dozen more will rise tonight."

"They shouldn't. We obliterated a couple hordes just last night."

"If we're lucky," Camilla says, "we'll get to obliterate another one." She withdraws two daggers from the zips in her pants. "Why don't I start with the one sneaking up on Cole?"

Milla

VACANCY IN THE CORPSE ASYLUM

I reach the zombie, but he's already writhing on the ground, restrained by an arrow in each hand. Realization dawns. Cole knew all along that the creature was rising, without ever turning around. He'd been stealthily aiming his bow as he spoke to us, and I'd had no idea. Ugh. These slayers are more dangerous than I ever realized.

I crouch beside the zombie and summon my fire.

"There's no need for that," Cole says.

I ignore him, pressing my hand against the creature's sunken torso. A minute passes, my light working through the rot. Frosty stomps to the other side, bends down and punches his blazing fist straight into the chest cavity. Ash rains a few seconds later, the scent of death suddenly replaced by burning flesh.

I'm not sure which is worse.

"Thank you," I say.

"You were taking too long," he snaps.

No kind words for me, ever. Got it. "You should consider becoming a motivational speaker. In two seconds, you've inspired me to *kill...everyone.*"

"Funny."

"I'm not joking."

Cole steps between us and shoves us apart. "Enough."

How did I not realize we'd gotten in each other's face?

"Zombies can be saved," Cole says. "This one didn't have to die."

Saved? Excuse me?

Not just no, but hell, no.

Frosty shrugs, his "I don't care about anything" attitude firmly in place. "I'm sorry...that I'm not sorry. I didn't want the bastard saved."

"I'm still your leader." Cole is more intense than the night, like a predator about to pounce. "You're subject to my rules."

Tension grows between them, so thick my swords couldn't cut through it.

"Cole!" Ali calls, her agitation echoing from the trees. "It's happening...worse than we thought... So many. Too many!"

In an instant, Cole is bounding forward. Frosty follows him, and I follow Frosty, determined to keep him in my sights at all times. He won't die on my watch.

We grind to a stop as we take in the scene now before us. Zombies, so many zombies, all hovering in the air above Ali. Beside her is a guy named Gavin, and Gavin's girlfriend/non-girlfriend Jaclyn. Ali's arms are extended and trembling, the motion of her fingers controlling the motion of the zombies.

I've seen her do this a few times before, and it always amazes me.

"I'm expending too much energy...out of serum," Ali gasps out.

"Drop them." Cole moves beside her. "I'll let them bite me."

Bite him? Uh, what the what now?

"No." Ali shakes her head. "Too many for that...we can't—"

"There's only one way this plays out successfully." Frosty's tone is hard as steel. "For our entire group to walk out of this alive, some of the zombies have to die."

Tears well in Ali's ice-blue eyes, making me think she actually cares about the creatures. And maybe she does. Her dad, adopted mom and grandfather died by zombie toxin. Good people dealt a crappy hand. Maybe she sees their final hours in these monsters. Maybe she sees who these monsters *used* to be—and who they could be again.

Not that *I* believe they can be "saved."

Cole gives an almost rigid incline of his head. "You and Camilla do what you have to do," he tells Frosty. To Ali, he says, "Gavin, Jaclyn and I will save as many as we can. You're on empty, gator, so you need to work your way to the sidelines. And don't you dare cross me on this."

A minute passes, then another, and I suspect she's holding out as long as she can, trying to come up with a different plan.

Finally, a sob escapes her. "Ready?"

"Do it."

The moment she drops her arms, the horde crashes into the ground. They don't stay down for long, jumping to their feet to glom onto Cole, Gavin and Jaclyn, who have formed a shield around Ali.

I'm stunned senseless as the trio just *stands there*, willingly allowing multiple creatures to use them as pot luck dinner. At least eight sets of yellowed teeth sink into Cole's neck… shoulders…arms and legs. He's going to be ripped apart.

As commanded, Ali begins to work her way out of the fray, stumbling and crying—but she isn't trying to avoid being bitten, either.

I've seen enough, the urge to slay, to do what I was born to do, too strong to ignore. I launch forward. Or try to. Frosty grabs me by the waist to hold me in place.

"Not yet."

"We have to help them." Why can't he see that? "Let me go or I'll…I'll…"

My eyes widen as, one by one, zombies begin to vomit and fall away from slayers. The soft glow of our cars' headlights are powered by a special battery and illuminate what happens next, allowing us to witness the tinge of gray leave their skin and the red fade from their eyes. When the transformation is complete, all hint of rot gone, actual human spirits float into the air like balloons, ascending higher and higher before vanishing in the darkness.

I am baffled as the process repeats…and repeats. "How…" I begin. Only I don't know what to ask. Slayers are actually *saving* zombies—Cole used the word literally—and they are doing so *without* becoming infected by the toxin or needing an antidote.

Cole stretches his arms wider, offering both limbs as snack packs to the next line of hungry fiends clamoring forward.

"I don't think the slayers can take much more," Frosty says. "Work your way in front and force zombies to back off." He isn't done issuing the order before he's pounding forward, shooting every creature he passes in the back of the head. The undead drop like flies.

I pull myself from my awed stupor and stay close to his heels, slashing at any teeth and hands aimed in his direction. Along the way, the fine hairs on the back of my neck rise, and I stiffen. I'm being watched again, I know it, but I can't pause to look around.

We make it in front of the slayers without a scratch, but I see zombies coming in hot from behind the group and keep going, meeting the newcomers head-on. I slash, elbow and kick, always ducking to avoid fingers snagging in my hair, hopping to the side to avoid being grabbed by the ankles.

"Gavin," Cole calls. "Car!"

They're leaving? Yeah, probably for the best. By now, they have to be as weak as newborns. I only fight harder. Retreat isn't in my wheelhouse. A few minutes later, the sound of squealing tires registers, then high beams are shining up close and personal. Zombies stumble backward to avoid being burned by the light, and suddenly I'm without an opponent.

Panting, I take stock. The horde has backed away from the slayers. Ali and Jaclyn are lying on the ground and moaning in pain, more riddled with bites than the others. Guess they tasted better.

Girls are made of sugar and spice and everything nice. Boys are made of snakes and snails and rattlesnake tails.

The childhood song plays through my head as Cole, Gavin and Frosty fire up their hands. The group wasn't abandoning ship, after all. And now, I'm once again awed as the flames on Cole and Gavin extend to their shoulders...correction, all the way to their rib cages. All three boys crouch beside the girls and flatten one hand on the chest of one girl and the other hand on the chest of the other. The girls catch fire and scream, bucking and fighting to get away, but eventually they settle down, their wounds healing right before my eyes.

"Sorry about this, my man, but you need it whether you agree or not," Cole says, then flattens his palm against *Frosty's* chest.

Frosty grunts and lurches backward, quickly severing contact.

"Hey," I shout as I bound over. "You don't get to touch him without his permission."

"This isn't any of your business," Cole snaps at me. "Stay out of it."

I open my mouth to reply—

"Stay out of it," Frosty repeats. With less heat, but still. A rebuke is a rebuke.

Boys!

I look away, the hairs on the back of my neck practically dancing now, and spot a girl standing beside a tombstone. Her face is cast in shadows, but I can see her hair stretches all the way to her waist, where the light shines. The strands are so black they gleam blue. Is she a civilian?

When I take a step toward her, she scrambles backward. If she can see me, she's not a civilian. One of Cole's new recruits, here to observe the battle? To learn?

"Hey," I call, and she bolts. Nope. Not a recruit. I give

chase. Anima wouldn't be stupid enough to send someone to observe us so openly. Right?

Right, because Anima no longer exists. I wonder how many years I'll have to remind myself of that fact before it actually feels real.

Maybe the girl witnessed the fight but doesn't know she's a slayer. Maybe she's freaked out. Or, maybe she's a spy from my brother's camp, because River still cares about me and wants to know I'm okay.

A pang of homesickness nearly slices me in two.

A zombie steps into my path and I twist to the side, nailing him in the eye with a dagger as I whiz past him. Only then do I realize I've moved out of the light. My heartbeat picks up speed. Am I headed into a trap?

At my right a shadow shifts, and I stop, turn. A sharp sting explodes in my neck...my arm...my neck again. Definitely a trap!

A wave of dizziness nearly topples me as I pull three darts out of my skin. Well, well. Two of my theories are now vapor in the wind. The girl doesn't work for my brother and she knows she's a slayer. For her weapon to affect me, she had to shoot it from the spirit realm, where I'm currently located. That's not something civilians can do, even by accident.

The only other option that makes any sense is...Anima.

"Camilla!" Frosty's voice echoes through the night, anger causing the "a" to vibrate.

The dizziness fades, and I breathe a sigh of relief as I stuff the darts in my pocket.

I step toward the girl, who hasn't moved from the trees. She steps backward, into a higher beam of light, and I see that she's pretty, with wide frightened eyes and skin covered in freckles; one moment she's standing in place, frozen in terror, the next she's running away.

I kick into gear, prepared to follow her again—

"Camilla!"

But I can't leave Frosty behind. I just can't. Cursing, I backtrack. He's my first priority, not the girl.

Cole and Frosty are nose-to-nose, arguing.

"—like I told you," Cole is saying. "I had to make sure you'd heal from a zombie bite without the antidote. That was the only way."

"And I told you weeks ago I didn't want the 'save the bastards' ability. Camilla!" he shouts a second later.

I haven't been spotted, I guess. "Guys," I say. And...did Cole just admit he shared the ability by using *dýnamis* on Frosty?

Neither boy faces me. They just keep staring daggers at the other, but at least some of the tension has drained from Frosty.

Across the way, Ali is standing between Gavin and Jaclyn, pushing the two apart. "Enough!"

"I would slap you," Jaclyn growls at the smirking man-boy, "but it would be considered animal abuse."

"I'm sorry," Gavin replies, "but I can't hear you over the sound of your bitchiness."

"Children." Ali slaps Gavin's shoulder before waving a finger at Jaclyn. "This is no place to continue your weird seduction of each other."

"I'm not seducing. I'm punishing. She allowed too many zombies to bite her," Gavin says. "I can still see the toxin under her skin."

Jaclyn throws her arms into the air, clearly exasperated. "Don't fight them, you told me yesterday. Fight them, you told me today. Why don't you make up your stupid mind?"

"Guys!" I shout. "There's a girl out there. She tried to sedate me." I show them the darts. "We need to find her, like, now." Before it's too late. Hell, it's probably too late already.

A twig snaps behind me, and my first thought is that she's come back to finish what she started. I spin, a short sword palmed and raised. Not a girl, but a zombie on his hands and knees. He's closer than I would have guessed, as if he just rose from the grave at my feet. He looks to be my age, maybe younger, a boy who never really had a chance to live. I hesitate—the younger ones always trip me up—and that single second of inactivity allows him to yank my feet out from underneath me.

I fall, landing with a thud, losing my breath. Having trained for this, I roll backward, into the light still shining from the car, and spring into a crouch while reaching out to swipe my sword across his neck.

His head tilts to the side before flopping onto a fresh mound of dirt. Frosty arrives on the scene, his entire arm already engulfed in flames. I blink, and his face, neck and chest are consumed, too. I gape at him. I think he gapes at himself. It's hard to see his expression underneath all that fire.

"This is your fault," he says as he turns to point an accusing finger at Cole, who spreads his arms, all *I love you, so get used to it.*

Oh, to be loved that way.

Frosty touches the zombie, just touches him—a brush of his fingertips against the creature's head and body—and the pieces burst into black ash. The flames on Frosty's arms die. He stares at the limbs as if he's never seen them before.

"Thank you," I say, only to remember he doesn't want my thanks. But this time, he doesn't reply. I guess he's ignoring me again.

I push to shaky legs. Frosty's shirt is unmarred by the flames but ripped at the collar, gaping all the way to his navel. You'd think *I'd* never seen a tanned, toned, tattooed guy before, because I suddenly can't tear my gaze away, too star-struck by the beauty of him. An angel. A fallen angel. He's my tormentor and my salvation—and what the hell is wrong with me? Did I hit my head when I fell?

"I could have saved that zombie." Ali marches over to frown at me, as if I'm the problem. I hate how tall she is, and how tiny she makes me feel. "I could have turned him into a witness."

"Could you really?" Gavin mentioned seeing toxin underneath Jaclyn's skin, and I can see it underneath Ali's, black lines branching from her eyes and mouth. "You were almost completely tapped before you started fighting. Now you're telling me you're good as gold?"

Up goes Ali's chin—a defensive action I know well. "I'm not the problem here. You were supposed to stay by Frosty's side, not run off to—"

"I told you. I saw someone. A girl. She watched the battle and bolted when I noticed her. I chased her. She shot me up with darts. We need to catch her and question her."

"If there *is* a girl out there, and I'm not saying there is— we both know you could have brought those darts with you, intending to feed us this story—she probably doesn't know she's a slayer and that there's a war waging all around her."

I bite the inside of my cheek until I taste the copper tinge of blood. "She was in spirit form. She knows what she is." Slayers can separate spirit from body naturally, but it's something we have to learn. Anima long ago found a way to force the action through electronic pulses.

Ali gives me a once-over. "You don't look like you've been tranqed."

"That I can't explain. Unless she shot me up with something else." Like…what? The opposite of a tranq—happy juice? But I'm not exactly happy. Medication of some sort? Poison?

Oh, crap. Bile rises, burning again my sternum. The possibilities are endless, and very few are actually good for me.

"Take these," I say, shoving the darts into her hand. "Have them tested. Tell me what she's done to me."

My panic must penetrate Ali's suspicions, because she pales. "As soon as I get home, I'll give them to Reeve and Weber, our new medical advisor."

Cole massages the back of his neck. "It's late. It's dark. We're all in bad shape. We're in no condition to go after the girl. I'll follow her tracks tomorrow."

I grit my teeth, but also nod. He's right. We're all operating on fumes.

"One more thing. Don't go running around just because you see someone," Ali tells me. "Next time stick to Frosty's side as if you've been glued." Like Kat, she has trouble maintaining eye contact while discussing this particular subject. Why? "I want you with him every second of every day. Got it?"

"Am I allowed bathroom breaks?" I ask drily.

"No. Wear a diaper."

I give her the finger. I'm not wearing a diaper. Ever.

Frosty closes in, the heat he radiates enveloping me, caus-ing goose bumps to break out from head to toe. What the hell kind of reaction is this? I shift uncomfortably from one foot to the other, rubbing my arms to pretend I'm cold.

"Were you bitten?" he asks.

"Why, are you worried about me?" I hear the hope in my voice and cringe. I think a part of me longs to hear *yes*, some-one—anyone—cares that I exist.

Fury claims his expression, twisting his features. "You are a means to an end. A way to see Kat. Never doubt it."

Bile rises again, only hotter, but I manage a smile. "Don't worry. I won't." Did I really expect him to soften so quickly—or ever?

This is my penance, my only means of atonement, and I'll see it through to the end. No matter what.

"Let's go." His expression is softer, at least. But of course, he takes off without looking back to ensure I've followed.

I race after him.

"Don't forget," Ali calls. "Hash Town. Seven a.m. If you're late, I'll post naked pictures of you all over the internet. And I promise you I'm not bluffing. Kat told me where to find one of her old phones."

He waves without looking back.

"You and Ali are having breakfast together?" I ask.

"Yes. You're not invited."

Ouch. "Try to leave me behind. See what happens."

He has no reply, but then, he rarely does with me.

We reach our bodies and with a single touch, we're paired back up. As he stops to answer a question from Bronx—*what happened out there?*—I pile inside his truck and buckle my belt.

Yesterday, Frosty demanded I walk to his apartment. Tonight, I'm not taking any chances. He'll have to drag me out of the vehicle kicking and screaming—and then he'll have to crawl back inside it, because I won't leave him unscathed.

When he settles behind the wheel, he doesn't even glance in my direction. And yet, it isn't until he pulls out of the cemetery that I relax. Or try to. Every muscle I possess is knotted and trembling, the stress of not knowing what's been done to me jacking me up.

"Great fight," I say, hoping to make conversation and distract myself. "You worked magic out there."

He turns up the radio.

I jab my finger at the button, switching the music off. "We're partners, Frosty. You have to start—"

He speaks over me. "I don't have to start *anything*. And we aren't partners. You and I will never be partners."

A painful burn returns to my chest. "Look. I'm sorry for my actions in the past. I am. You'll never know how sorry. I hate what I did, I hate the outcome, but I was backed into a corner. Anima would have killed River, and he's my only family. I wish I could go back and protect Kat with my own life, but I can't. All I can do is protect yours now. But if I'm going to do so, you've got to start trusting me. At least a little. You can start by talking to me as if I'm a real person with feelings." *Because I am.*

"That will happen in never. You aren't a real person to me. You're a murderer." He sounds as cold and merciless as his navy eyes appear. "And just so you know, an apology means nothing without action to back it up."

"I do know. I just need time to prove myself."

"Time I'd rather not give you. I don't need protecting."

"Kat says otherwise. You heard her. Ali had a vision. At some point, I *will* save your life. Without me, you'll die."

He slams on the breaks as he pulls over to the side of the road. "Dying wouldn't be such a bad thing. I'd be with Kat. So why don't you do us both a favor and get out. Your services are no longer needed."

"But—"

"Now."

My lips compress into a thin line. My hand shakes as I open the door. I'm hurt by his refusal, yes, but as my feet hit the pavement, I'm also suddenly and inexplicably angry. "You would rather be shot in the chest than spend time with me?" I shout. "I'm that bad? I'm so despicable you feel it's okay to abandon me on the side of a road, alone, in the middle of the night when light is scarce?"

I palm my daggers. Before Frosty can speed away, I stomp in front of the truck and, glaring at him through the front windshield, slam the tips of both weapons into a tire.

7

Frosty

THE ROT HITS THE FAN

Maintaining a good mad is impossible right now. I'm just too freaking tired. Why did Camilla have to go and be all adorable and crap, throwing a bona fide slayer tantrum?

I stick my head out the window to yell at her, but all I end up saying is "Just...I don't know...get in or something."

A moment passes before she climbs back into the truck. She doesn't meet my gaze. I get out and change the tire, then return to the wheel, gunning the engine.

"If we're playing *would you rather*... I'd rather kiss a viper than continue our conversation," I say. "So maybe let's play the quiet game instead."

No response. She doesn't even stiffen.

This bothers me.

I'm the moron who keeps going. "Have you ever considered therapy? That temper of yours—"

"Doesn't come out to play nearly as much as yours."

Good point. "Difference is, rage is sexy on guys."

As calm as can be, she says, "The guys you're crushing on must not rage correctly. True rage? It's a total loss of control, and it's ugly. What I did to your tires? I meant to do."

There's a story there. One I'm strangely eager to hear. But I don't ask.

Use her and lose her, don't get to know her.

"Anything else you'd like to say before we get started on that quiet game?" I ask.

Silence.

Again it bothers me and I don't know why.

Then she asks, "Did Cole really share his slayer abilities with *dýnamis*?"

"*Dýnamis?*"

"Slayer fire. The stuff that makes zombies go boom."

I roll my eyes. "Yes. He shared the ability with me. Maybe shared a little extra, too." I'm not actually sure what I'll be able to do now. Not everyone gets everything. But there's no question I can now summon slayer fire—*dýnamis*—to every part of my body, rather than to just my hands. Just like that. As easily as breathing. And Cole seemed pretty confident I'll now be immune to zombie toxin, as if he controlled what he passed on. Maybe he did. It's a skill Ali learned through her mother, Helen.

When Camilla and I get to my apartment, I lock myself in the bedroom. I don't care what she does or where she sleeps. I just know I don't want to see her or think about her right now.

I fall into bed, where I sleep like the truly dead, only rising with the sun. I shower, arm up and emerge to see her awake and perched on the couch, watching TV. We don't say a word to each other.

I grab my keys and head to the truck. She follows me. Whatever. This is what Kat wants, so this is what Kat will get.

The silence continues the entire drive to Hash Town. The old-school building is made of redbrick and cracked mortar. Charming, in a way. Inside, the walls are painted pale blue and the floors are tiled in black and white.

Cole and Ali are situated at a table in back…with a brunette I don't recognize. A new recruit?

Camilla and I slide into the only two chairs available, on opposite sides of the stranger.

"Raina, this is Frosty," Ali says. She's exchanged her black leather fighting clothes for a pink dress, and she looks beautiful. Reminds me a bit of Taylor Swift, to be honest. Tall and blonde and slender, with a delicacy Cole claims brings out his inner animal. "Frosty, this is Raina. And no shop talk, okay? This is purely social."

I get the hint. The girl isn't a recruit.

The brunette offers a shy smile and wave. She's pretty in a "touch me and I'll break" sort of way, but I like her eyes. They're so dark they're almost black.

"Wow," she says to me. "I didn't know there was anyone else in the world as large as Cole."

I nod—what can I say, really?—and signal the waitress for coffee.

Ali slides a thick, rolled-up napkin in Camilla's direction. "What you asked for. You'll want a moment alone."

Raina looks at the napkin, then at Ali, then at the napkin again. "Um, what's going on?"

"I... She..." Ali looks to Cole for help, but in the end it's Camilla who comes to the rescue.

"Tampons. A lady must be discreet." Camilla winks, then stands and walks away.

"Excuse me." Curiosity propels me to my feet, and I follow her—straight into the ladies' bathroom.

"I should have known," she says on a sigh.

"You're not supposed to leave my side, remember?"

"Whatever." She unrolls the napkin. A piece of paper and a syringe fall out.

I catch them before they hit the ground and hand them over. She pales as she reads the note, then curses under her breath.

I snatch the paper from her to read it for myself.

Reeve was able to extract liquid from the darts. You were shot up w/some kind of slow-acting zombie toxin. She's never seen anything like it. While she studies the ins and outs, this concentrated antidote should help. It's a gift from Helen. Well, the recipe is. Reeve mixed everything together. In a perfect world, it will completely negate what's flowing through your veins. Also, Cole & I searched for tracks at the cemetery, but there were too many to pinpoint the girl. I'm sorry.

The news is bad, but it isn't the worst.

"This is going to hurt." I pull the top from the syringe and jab her in the arm.

She doesn't flinch, doesn't even frown. I do the latter. I've had broken bones and torn muscles, but I still howl like a baby when I'm stabbed, no matter how tiny the blade.

I cap the needle, roll it with paper towels and toss the wad into the trash. "Tell me if you start to feel sick. Even the smallest twinge." I'll put her out of her misery. Because I'm sweet like that.

"Sir, yes, sir." She gives me a jaunty salute.

We return to the table, where Ali is regaling Raina with a story about her grandmother. "—walked in when Cole and I were kissing. I just about had a heart attack. But Nana, she remains the picture of calm as she sits beside us on the couch and asks if we're the evening's entertainment or if we'd like to watch a movie with her."

"I wish my grandmother was so cool." Raina smiles and focuses on me. "Frosty. That's an interesting nickname. Who gave it to you?"

"Cole." Coffee is poured at last, and I drink it hot and black. The hotter and blacker the better. I'd drink motor oil if it wouldn't kill me. Camilla, I notice, pours four sugars and half a carton of cream into hers.

Raina continues to look at me, as if expecting more of an answer. Finally, she says, "When did he give it to you?"

"Elementary school."

Silence.

Ali kicks me under the table. I frown at her.

"There are a thousand rumors floating around about why." Ali leans her head against Cole's shoulder and pets his chest. "Most believe he got trapped outside after an ice storm and lost two of his toes to frostbite."

"That's my favorite." Kat had somehow convinced herself it

was true, and that I'd had the two toes surgically reattached, despite the impossibility of reviving dead flesh.

"Unfortunately," I add, "the real story is far less exciting."

"Well...?" Ali insists.

"I'd just moved to a new school for the third time that year, and on my first day, I knew I had to prove my prowess or I'd end up being every bully's whipping boy. Again. I was small back then. I slinked through the halls, determined to take down the reigning badass, which just happened to be Cole. I provoked him into a fight, and he punched me. I fell, but quickly got back up. This happened again and again until finally he stopped and told me I must have ice in my veins, since I was practically begging for more hits rather than curling into a ball and crying."

"First time anyone ever got up," Cole says with a fond smile. "And he did it more than once..."

"Well, you hit like a baby." I give him a smile of my own. "It was either stay down and laugh, or get up and let you try again."

Cole snorts, and Ali laughs outright.

"Did you give him a nickname in return?" Raina asks me.

"Yes. Asshole."

This time Ali snorts, and Cole laughs. Camilla nods with approval.

Raina leans closer to me, a slow grin spreading. "What nickname would you give *me*?"

Right now? Inquisitor. For some chick I just met, she sure asks a lot of questions. "I don't know you well enough."

"Well, hopefully we can change that."

I shrug noncommittally and take another drink of coffee.

Cole clears his throat and I meet his gaze. His lips are twitching at the corners as he gives a sharp shake of his head.

"What?" I demand.

"He's amused by the fact that you haven't figured out this is a setup." Camilla opens a packet of strawberry jelly and eats the inside. "A meet-and-greet. An arranged blind date."

Shut the hell up. Raina is *flirting* with me?

"Ali." I do my best to keep the anger out of my tone. "A word."

"Oh. No, thanks. I'm good." She looks everywhere but at me.

"Now." I stand and "help" her to her feet, then drag her through the maze of tables and into the bathroom hallway. I whirl on her, saying, "What the hell, Ali?"

"Hey, don't blame me." She spreads her arms wide. "I'm simply obeying Kat's orders."

Kat *told* her to set me up with another girl? Damn it. I don't… I can't… The anger burns out of control, setting fire to my shock, and all I can do is choke on the fumes. I would never—never!—push Kat at another guy. I still love her. I still want her.

But she doesn't want me.

Is she up there, watching me? Will it hurt her to see me flirt with another girl?

I guess we'll find out.

"I'm sorry," Ali says. "I know this isn't—"

"Where'd you meet Raina?" I'm not interested in her pity. "What kind of girl am I dealing with?"

"Before I moved in with Nana and started going to Asher, I attended Carver Academy with her." She nibbles on her bottom lip. "She's a senior like you, a cheerleader with a sweet heart, and she knows nothing about Zs."

Kat was a cheerleader in junior high, before kidney disease rendered her too weak. "Let's get this over with."

Ali grabs my arm as I walk away, stopping me. "One thing. Be nice to her, or I'll be wearing your testicles as earrings tomorrow."

"Set me up on another date," I tell her, "and I'll be using your lady balls as a coin purse."

Snorting, she bumps my shoulder with her own. "You'd look good carrying a purse, but if you reach for my lady balls, Cole will cut off your hand."

"I'm willing to risk it."

"And it'll be your loss."

We head back to the table.

"—last boyfriend," Raina is saying to Camilla.

Camilla opens her mouth to reply, sees me and stays quiet. The waitress arrives, and we place our orders.

Raina offers me a nervous smile. "Alice—I mean Ali—tells me you're a boxer like Cole."

The truth and yet…not. "I taught him everything he knows. He still needs some work, and he'll never be able to beat me, but I'll never give up on him."

Ali beams at me. Cole chokes on a drink of orange juice, and Camilla pours another packet of sugar into her cup.

"Would you like some coffee with your sugar?" I ask her.

"No, thanks. Did you see the sign? You have to pay for every refill," she whispers as if it's some terrible secret. "My first cup is my last."

Because she can't afford more? Something clenches in my

chest. Before I can talk myself out of it, I lean over and give her half of my coffee. She blinks at me, baffled, and it irritates me, because I'm just as baffled.

"If you die of dehydration, you can't be my bodyguard," I growl.

"Bodyguard? Surely she's not... Are you two...?" Raina waves a finger from me to Camilla, Camilla to me.

"No," we answer quickly, both horrified by the prospect.

"Not even friends," I add.

Raina frowns in confusion. "Then why—?"

"Tell me about you," I interject in a rush.

She blushes, shifts nervously in her chair and stutters the word *I* as she tries to think of something to say. Wonderful. I've made her uncomfortable. I'm off my game. Clearly. I probably couldn't charm a rabbit out of a hat.

"I'll start," Camilla says. Taking pity on the girl? "I'm nineteen, and like the boys I'm a boxer. I recently had a falling-out with my brother, my only family. I'm afraid of spiders and I adore cherry Life Savers."

I can't imagine her being afraid of anything. "Don't forget your tire-slashing fetish."

Ali narrows her eyes and points her fork at Camilla. "Did you slash his tires? Wait. Never mind. Don't answer that. I'll have to hurt you."

Cole takes her fork and sets it on her plate. "No utensil fights. I'm still healing from the last one."

"Fine." She nudges him in the stomach, saying, "Your turn. Tell us all about you."

"Are you sure you want that? We're in a public place and you tend to rip off my clothes when I—"

"Oh, my gosh. Shut up." Ali pinches his lips together.

Raina watches their interaction, transfixed.

Cole leans back, freeing his lips while draping his arm behind Ali's chair. "I'm an adrenaline junkie and Ali-gator is my favorite high. I also like cherry Life Savers."

"How am I keeping my hands to myself?" Ali says drily.

"I don't know. Did I mention you taste better than those cherry Life Savers?"

Ali fans herself.

"Well." Raina clears her throat. "I'm a big fan of the University of Alabama. Roll Tide! I'll be starting in the fall. Though I haven't decided on a major, I'm leaning toward nursing."

I keep her talking the rest of the "date," asking questions about her past, her likes and her dislikes. She tries to question me in return, but I shut her down every time. My business is my business, and I've only ever shared with the three people closest to me. Cole, Bronx and, once upon a time, Kat.

Kat, who can't wait to get rid of me.

My coffee cup shatters, my grip suddenly too tight. Hot liquid spills over my hand and the floor as sharp porcelain cuts into my skin. The pain is nothing. I barely notice, but Raina gasps and almost faints at the sight of blood.

Camilla pats the girl on the shoulder. "Uh, don't take this the wrong way but I don't think nursing is the career for you." She rushes off to gather a cool, wet cloth. "Before you ask," she says to me, "it's clean."

I snatch the rag before she can attempt to wash the wounds. If I had two broken legs and couldn't reach a bag of Oreos—probably a fate worse than death—I still wouldn't allow her to help me. I don't even want her acting as my shield, and if it wasn't for Kat, I'd just take my chances.

Live right, or die trying.

"You're an awesome slayer, but you're a horrible date," Camilla says as we climb into my truck.

Needless to say, I won't be seeing Raina again. Nice girl, but totally not my type. "I'm sure you've been on worse."

"Uh. Hmm." Camilla says no more and stares out the window.

"Don't tell me they've all been winners. I'll know you're lying."

"I'm not telling you anything. I'm enjoying a little peace and quiet. Well, *trying* to."

Something about her snotty tone... "You *have* been on a date, haven't you? Answer, and you'll get your peace and quiet."

Her nails dig into her knees, her knuckles quickly turning white. "I'm not a virgin, if that's what you're getting at."

Do I detect...remorse? "You don't have to go on a date to get screwed." I know this firsthand, considering my behavior the past four months.

"Oh, just shut up," she says.

A deflection, which is an answer all on its own. "You *haven't* been on a date." I'm completely floored. Like Raina, she's not my type, but I have eyes and even I have to admit she's an insanely beautiful specimen.

"Boys were too afraid of my brother to be seen with me in public," she says, hurt practically dripping from her tone.

"That's what I told myself, at least. They never stuck around long enough to explain their reasons."

So, the boys hung around her secretly, almost as if they were ashamed of her, and then took off after they'd gotten what they wanted.

Did my hit-and-runs hurt like this?

Damn. Guilt winds around me and squeezes the air from my lungs.

I'm curious about Camilla's experiences, but I don't like that I'm curious. I stop asking questions, and she offers no more details. The silence continues as I go about my day, running my errands.

First up—Shady Elms. I plan to do my own tracking. Unlike Cole and Ali, Camilla knows where Dart Girl started and ended. We track her to a corner street, where a car must have been waiting for her. There are no lamps nearby, no buildings, which means no security footage.

Camilla is ticked, which is why my next stop is the gun range. She can work off some steam.

Located in the middle of nowhere, the large metal building is painted camo-style to blend into the mountain behind it. As we sign in, the guy behind the counter stares at Camilla as if she's wearing a sign that says, *Eye-Rape Me. Please.* I'm surprised she pretends not to notice rather than blinding his eyes with a one-two punch.

"Hey," I snap, and he jolts. I don't have to say a word. The displeasure I'm projecting speaks for me.

He ducks his head and starts to wipe the counter clean. "Uh…right. You two are in stalls thirteen and fourteen."

We cover our ears and make our way to our assigned spots.

There are six other guys here, and each does a double take when he catches a glimpse of Camilla. Again, she pretends not to notice. Or, hell, maybe she *doesn't* notice. Kat would have—

I lock up the wayward thought, before it leads me to do something stupid.

Motions jerky, I load my .44 and aim. *Boom. Boom, boom, boom.* I keep my shots to the torso. After I unload two rounds, I compare my hits to Camilla's. Well, well. She prefers to hit the head and groin. Should have known. Fighting dirty is her MO.

I'm impressed.

"Working through a few issues?" I ask her as we leave, our headphones off and gear stored in the truck.

"A few?" She laughs without humor. "You have no idea."

No, I don't, because I don't know her.

And I don't to want to know her.

We head to the post office, where I mail paperwork for one of my classes. Then, it's to the gym for a very necessary workout. I begrudgingly obtain a guest pass for Camilla. Does she say thank-you? No. She doesn't say anything at all, just skips off to use the elliptical, run the treadmill and even lift a few of the lighter weights. I pay no attention to her. Nope. Not even a little. I punish the boxing bag for everything I've been dealing with, every punch exorcising emotion. By the time I call it quits, my knuckles are black and blue.

After Camilla and I shower in our respective locker rooms, we practically have to crawl to the truck. But we aren't done for the day.

Next stop—the grocery store.

"Pick whatever you want," I grumble, grabbing a cart. A

few moms are there with their kids, the little boys and girls staring at me with wide eyes, as if I'm a superhero—or a monster. I just wink.

As I mosey down the first aisle, Camilla remains a few paces behind me. I grab a box of cupcakes, Twinkies, cinnamon rolls and powdered donuts. Slayers work out hard, and eat harder. Except, she grabs nothing. "Don't tell me your sweet tooth has been satisfied. The way you savaged those sugar packets, I'm pretty sure you're an addict."

A pink flush colors her cheeks. "I don't have any money with me."

"So? I'm paying."

"No." She gives a violent shake of her head. "You're not paying for my food. *I* owe *you*, not the other way around."

"If you owe me, you have to do what I say. And I say pick some food. Now. Hungry girls are bitchy girls."

She glares at me. "Chauvinist boys are dogs."

"Camilla—"

"Just drop it, Frosty. Okay?"

Anger sparks. "No, I won't drop it. You'll pick some food or you'll move out. If you're weak from hunger, you can't protect yourself and you certainly can't protect me."

"This from the boy who stole my granola bar."

I'm the one who flushes now. "Pick a fucking dessert."

"Fine." She throws in a bag of cherry-frosted brownies. "Happy now?"

Not really. But before I can respond, Kat appears before me, jumping up and down with excitement, even clapping her hands. "I tried waiting for you to return to the apartment, but I can't stand it anymore. How was the date?"

Realization is a cold, hard bitchslap. She isn't jealous. She isn't even mildly upset.

"Yeah, uh, I'll be...somewhere else," Camilla says, and beats feet to get away from us.

I take out my phone and press it to my ear, pretending to talk to someone. "Didn't you watch?" Calm. Steady.

"No. Witnesses aren't allowed to watch romantic or intimate moments."

"Nothing romantic or intimate happened."

"Something must have, because the screen went blank after you teased Camilla about her sugar intake."

Screen? And why the hell isn't Kat railing at me? Or telling me she made a big mistake?

"What happened after that?" she asks, completely unaware of my increasing turmoil.

Nothing, that's what. I'd wanted to regret the impulsive gesture but hadn't quite managed it. "Let me get this straight. You expected me to take one look at Raina and turn my full attention to her. You expected me to fall out of love with you." My voice hardens, every word like a dagger. "You don't know me at all, do you?"

The color drains from her face, but she presses on. "You fell in love with me instantly, Frosty. Why can't you fall out of love just as fast? Why can't you fall for someone else the same way? Granted, I'm amazing, but—"

"No. You don't get to praise yourself while you're breaking my fucking heart." Breaking...no. It's already broken. I'm flayed. Shattered. Hell, I'm nothing but jagged pieces of pain.

Tears well in her eyes. "I'm sorry. I was just trying to make you laugh and—"

Forget the groceries. "Camilla," I shout, and it isn't long before she appears at the end of the aisle.

I don't spare Kat another glance as I leave her crying in the middle of the store. I stomp past Camilla, and as hoped, she follows.

In the truck, my darker emotions bubble over. I growl, "This is *your* fault. If she was still alive, she'd want me."

Camilla scowls at me. "I'll take the blame for a lot of things, but not that. Not another girl's feelings for you."

"If she was alive—"

"Yeah. You said that. But are you sure you're right?"

We were never supposed to end up together, Kat said the second time she appeared to me.

I punch the steering wheel so hard the horn blasts as a piece of plastic goes flying. My already bruised skin tears and my knuckles crack, but I don't care. I hit the wheel again and again and again.

"Look." Camilla's voice is unbearably gentle. "I know you're heartbroken right now—"

"What would you know about heartbreak? You've never even been on a date. None of the guys you've been with liked you enough."

She blanches, and I curse, hating myself more now than ever before. Guilt and regret pummel me, leaving bruises deep, deep inside. I don't like her, but I'm not this guy. I won't be this guy.

"I'm sorry. I had no right to go there."

"Don't worry." There's no emotion in her tone, no emotion on her features, either, but she's rubbing her thumb against the Betrayal tattoo. "I deserve nothing less."

Anyone else, I would have corrected. No one deserves to be dumped on like this. Her, I just can't.

We reach the apartment, and she trudges in behind me. I look around and try to see the place through her eyes. Gritty, dingy. As far from a palatial bachelor pad as possible. I've hung no pictures. My furniture consists of a couch, a TV and a bed.

She picks up the bag she dropped off during her B & E. "I'm taking a shower." Without waiting for permission, she shuts herself inside the bathroom and turns on the water.

I pad into a kitchen small enough to fit inside a Barbie play-house. And yes, I have, in fact, played with one. Kat used to babysit her cousins, and I used to help, allowing the little prin-cesses to "fix" my hair and paint my nails. But I can't afford to think about the past right now. I'll have another meltdown.

I grab a Gatorade from the fridge and drain half the con-tents, the liquid cool against my parched throat.

Thud.

I recognize the sound and know Camilla just dropped the soap…in the shower…where she's naked and wet.

I hiss in a breath. I did *not* just go there. But…

I did go there and now I can't get the picture of her naked and wet out of my head.

Today's blind date clearly screwed me up. Not to mention losing Kat—again. Doesn't help that I'm a young, red-blooded male with more testosterone than most, and Camilla is hotter than hell. There's simply no getting around that fact.

Damn it. She represents everything wrong with my life. Worse, she's a wild card. Is she for real? Or is she looking for the perfect opportunity to betray my group? To punish us for telling her brother she'd sided with Anima?

If I'm being honest, I don't actually think that's the case. She fought hard-core last night, slaying zombies—and tires—without a single moment of hesitation.

My lips twitch at the corners. No one has ever attacked my truck with such adorable menace.

I should not find her adorable.

By the time she emerges, I've tamed my wayward thoughts. But a cloud of steam accompanies her, smelling of roses, pecans and my soap, and…hell. My blood heats. In anger, I tell myself. Only anger. Because I don't like my things on her body. Even my scent. *Especially* my scent.

Her mass of hair is wet, the ends dripping onto her already-damp tank top, rendering the material transparent. She's wearing short shorts, her legs a mile long, with black and white roses tattooed down one side but not the other. Her feet are bare, her toenails painted princess pink, a complete surprise. I would have guessed black. On her left foot is a tattoo of—is that a dandelion? Yeah. As the seeds float away, they morph into birds. On her other foot is a tattoo of a pink ribbon crisscrossing all the way to her ankle and culminating in a bow. It's the only etching with color and I wonder why—also wonder why my blood *boils*.

Kat has no tattoos. I never thought I'd like them on a girl, but Camilla, she wears them well. Very well.

"This is five seconds past awkward," she mutters.

Caught sizing up the enemy. I should be flayed alive. "There's not much in the fridge but feel free to take what you want." I shut myself in the bathroom and stay in the shower until the hot water is gone and I'm being pelted by shards of ice, my mind finally back in the right place. Admiring Camilla isn't allowed.

My motions are jerky as I dress in a T-shirt and a pair of sweats. When I step into the hall, the scent of bacon and eggs greets me, and my mouth waters. Camilla is sitting at the kitchen table, a plate of food in front of her and a plate of food in front of the only other chair. Finally, she's eating. And despite my deplorable treatment of her, she continues to respond to me with little gestures of kindness.

I'm more baffled by her every minute of every day.

My stomach rumbles for the first time in months, and I join her at the table to dig in. After a few bites of the best (and only) bacon pancakes I've ever had, I mutter, "Thanks for dinner."

"You're welcome."

"Did you cook for your brother's crew?" Is that how she developed such obvious culinary skill?

She doesn't comment on my uncharacteristic display of curiosity and says, "No. My mom was a chef, and me and my—" A muscle clenches in her jaw. "I used to shadow her in the kitchen."

She and...who? "*Was* a chef?"

"Still could be. She took off a little over nine years ago. I haven't heard from her since."

Making Camilla far too young to be abandoned by a loved one. But then, was there ever a right age for that kind of betrayal? "I'm sorry."

My odd display of sympathy earns a small smile of gratitude. "What about your parents?" she asks, and a moment later, she sinks deep into her chair, realizing she's asked a personal question I will most likely refuse to answer. "Never mind. Forget I said anything."

I should take the out, but I say, "Both of my parents died when I was six. I've lived with an aunt and uncle until recently." They were decent people, but they had a family of their own and it hadn't included me, the troubled boy whose parents adopted him at the age of three.

"Your parents...did they love you?"

"Yes, but they didn't know how to deal with a kid who saw monsters they couldn't."

Meeting Cole was a bona fide miracle. For the first time in my life, I'd actually felt as though I wasn't alone.

"Losing both of your parents had to suck," she says, "which makes this next part terrible for me to say, but... I kind of wish my dad left with my mom. He wasn't a nice man, and the system would have been a better place for my siblings and me."

Siblings. Plural. And just how not nice are we talking? Mentally, physically or even sexually abusive? I press my lips together to keep from asking. We're getting way personal here. Too personal for two people who only agreed to fight zombies together, each for their own reasons.

I stand, my chair skidding behind me. As I wash my dishes, I say, "If we're going to live together—"

"If? We *are*."

"—we need to set some ground rules."

"Agreed." She hands me her plate and fork and arches a brow. "I cooked, you clean."

I could refuse, just to be contrary, but I take the dishes and get to scrubbing. I want her to cook again.

"Let me guess," she says. "Rule one. I do what you say when you say."

"Yeah. That sounds good. Let's go with that." I dry my hands and face her. There's only an arm's length of distance between us. It's not enough. Up close I can see the different shades of brown in her eyes, from pale amber to rich sable, and I want to kick my own ass for noticing. I take a step back.

"Rule two," I say. "You will be honest with me at all times about everything. You get caught in a lie and you're out, no questions asked."

"In that case, I'd love to share my honest opinion about *you*. You have moments of great asshattery, and one day I'll probably disembowel you just for grins and giggles."

"That's fair."

She nudges me out of the way to fill a glass with water. "I can live with those rules."

"Good, but I wasn't done. Rule three," I say. "No more personal conversations."

Her gaze darts away from me, but not before I catch a glint of hurt. "No problem," she says. "We will forever remain strangers."

I frown, not liking that I've hurt her again and not liking that I don't like it. "Rule four. If I want to be alone, you will leave me alone."

Her lips purse as if she's just sucked on a lemon. "That kind of defeats the purpose of my presence."

"And yet it's still a rule."

"One I will not obey," she says.

Girls. Can't live with them—the end. I mean, seriously.

There are two ways to argue with them, saying yes and saying no, and neither way works.

While dating Kat, I probably learned more about girls than anyone else on the planet, and yet I still know absolutely nothing about them.

I take the water glass from Camilla and set it aside. Don't want the liquid tossed at my pretty mug as I imprison her against the counter. We were too close before and we are way too close now, but I need her to hear me and understand how serious I am.

Her eyes go wide, but not with fear. I don't know what she's projecting at me, not sure I want to know. Her breaths come fast and shallow.

"Maybe you were able to steamroll your brother's crew. Maybe the guys were intimidated by you or by River, or maybe even both of you, but I'm made of tougher stuff. You step on my toes, and I'll step on yours right back. A girl who willingly gets into the ring with me never receives special treatment. I'll dish to her what I dish to guys."

Up goes her chin. Light shines over her features, paying the bronze of her skin absolute tribute. She's only a bit taller than Kat, but the added inch puts her closer to my face than I'm used to. The smell of roses and pecans is stronger now, the heat of her intense. I like it. I like it too much.

My body is obviously attracted to hers, not caring anything for my thoughts or feelings.

My body is a traitor. And so is Kat. She wanted me to date other girls. To want—crave—other girls. *Happy now, kitten?*

"Do you understand?" I demand.

"Yes. But Frosty?" Camilla pauses, frowns as if she's just hit a brick wall. "Wait. What's your first name?"

I straighten and latch onto the subject change as if it's a life raft. In a way, it is. "That's delving into personal territory, don't you think?"

"A first name is personal to you? Hardly. I know the first name of my former mailman and believe me, there's nothing personal about our relationship. He's, like, three hundred years old."

"Don't care. I'm not telling you my name."

"Why not? Is it embarrassing? I bet it's embarrassing."

"Give me an example of what you consider embarrassing."

"Dick. Or Dijon."

"I only *wish* my name was Dijon."

"Because you like to be the condiment in a flesh sandwich?" She smirks up at me. "I remember your 'friend.'" She air quotes the word. "She would have done anything you asked, even a three-way."

"I'm not interested in a three-way. Never have been." Despite my recent behavior, I actually prefer to be in love with my partner. Don't get me wrong. I adore the act of touching and kissing and being together, but I want it to mean something, because I'm vulnerable in those moments—hours—with all my defenses down, and I like to know my girl is right there with me, giving as much as she takes. "What about you?"

"I'm a little too territorial to share."

"Do you have a *special friend*?" Someone she sleeps with on a regular basis.

Her chin goes up another inch, her cheeks reddening.

"That information *is* personal, and as we agreed, the two of us won't travel that road. Now, if you'll excuse me." She saunters to the couch, claims the remote and flips on the TV, pretending I don't exist.

Damn it. Now I'm more curious about her than ever and slightly annoyed. *Is* she sleeping with someone on a regular basis? And why the hell do I care so much about the answer?

I take the bed once again, forcing Camilla to take the couch. Ungentlemanly, I know, but I have a point to prove to us both. She's nothing to me. Nothing except a means to an end, just like I told her.

As usual, I toss and turn all night. I may have gotten my appetite back, but sleep still eludes me. And that's probably a good thing. I'd only dream about Kat's death, a horror show I've seen so many times the smallest details are forever embedded in my memory.

When the sun rises, I make my way into the living room and see Camilla asleep on the couch. She's sitting up, and she's sweating, her body shaking as if she's having a seizure. I rush to her side, but by the time I reach her, she's sagging to the side, a streak of soot left in her wake.

Soot?

She tosses and turns, and it's obvious she's trapped in a nightmare. I know better than to wake her. I study the tangle of her white-black hair, the rose-tint in her skin, the fragility of her features. She's beauty and she's the beast, rolled into one. There are cuts on her bottom lip, where she chewed just a little too hard. The strap of her tank top has fallen down her shoulder, baring bronzed, mouth-watering skin. She's already kicked off the blanket, revealing the length of her legs. I frown when I notice jagged, raised flesh underneath several of her tattoos. Scars, and lots of them.

The thing is, when scars show on the outside, scars are usually hidden on the inside.

More questions plague me. More questions to stuff inside a mental box.

When she goes still and sighs, a signal she's calming, the dream waning, I leap into action. "Time to wake up." I nudge her knee with my own and her eyelids pop open.

Though she hasn't yet focused, she kicks me in the stomach before hopping to her feet. "Frosty?" Her gaze sweeps over me, from my shirtless chest to my low-slung sweats and bare feet.

"Who else?"

Her frown is deep and intense. "If that's how you wake a girl, no wonder you've had no repeat customers lately. Don't ever jolt me like that again."

My hands curl into fists. "I haven't had any repeat customers because you killed the only customer I wanted."

"How many times do I have to tell you? I didn't kill—"

I storm to the bedroom, gather clean clothes, then lock myself in the bathroom, where I take another shower to cool down. By the time I step out of the stall, there's a handwritten note perched on my pile of clothes.

Sorry I mule-kicked you.

Camilla snuck in? She would've had to pick the lock and move so quietly my trained senses wouldn't notice.

Well, well. I don't want to be impressed. No, I really don't.

I'm calm as I dress in a plain T-shirt, ripped jeans, combat boots and a few weapons hidden for good measure. I never leave home without a semi-arsenal, at the very least.

I step into the living room to find Camilla dressed in a lacy pink shirt and supershort skirt—short enough to make a guy pray for hundred-mile-per-hour winds. She won't meet my gaze, and I soon learn she won't leave my side, either.

As one week bleeds into two...three...I grow used to my shadow. We even develop a routine. After a silent breakfast, I do any schoolwork currently due, usually finishing up in one to four hours, and she plans Z-battle strategies in a notebook. We then have lunch together—again, neither of us saying a word—and work out. I try not to watch Camilla as she runs the treadmill, parts of her I shouldn't admire bouncing.

We have dinner every night—yet another silent meal. She cooks, I do dishes. Afterward we hunt zombies. So far, there have been no new sightings. Not on our end, and not on Cole's. He and I text each other every night with a progress report. Actually, he texts me all the damn time. All my friends do. What I find on my phone this morning?

Gavin: Giving up the brunettes 4 a tattooed blonde? Sucker! I like a girl who goes 4 the home run rather than the throat.

Bronx: River showed up w/a cage full of Zs so the recruits could get real-world fighting experience. Have U ever seen a kid shit his pants, bro? Once upon a time, I could have said no. Someone bleach my corneas. Please.

Ali: Zombie pickup line! U LOOK SO GOOD I WANT 2 HAVE U OVER 4 DINNER. Hahahaha get it???

I've finally started texting back.

To Gavin: U used 2 B a player—now UR not. Get over it. Also, U suck—& I mean that from the bottom of my heart.

To Bronx: Kids these days R pussies. Wouldn't know a right cross from a left cross. Teach them—& send me vid

To Ali: What about: I love a girl w/BRAAAINS

Not everything is on track, though. Camilla has had a nightmare every night, her moans drawing me out of bed. I've witnessed the ends of her fingers catching fire. A flame here, a flame there, though they never burn more than a few seconds—but even that's too long. Explains the soot, at least.

What I can't reason out? Why the flames are the color of blood.

I dose her with antidote every morning, and a few times Reeve has come over to collect blood samples for testing. But whatever the cause of the odd-colored flames, Camilla is always in top form during the day. The perfect bodyguard.

Once, we were ambling down a sidewalk and a car backfired. She jumped in front of me, thinking someone was shooting at me. And every time I enter a building, she insists on going in first, just in case someone is lying in wait.

She takes her role seriously and…hell, it's starting to bother me. Despite everything, I don't want her taking a bullet meant for me, even if she won't be harmed. Hell, she'd probably like it better if she *was* harmed. The way she rubs that Betrayal tattoo, yeah, I know guilt is her constant companion.

"Frosty? Are you even listening to me?" Kat snaps her fingers in front of my face.

"Your words are poetry," I say out of habit. "Of course I'm listening."

She visits me once a day, as promised, but only for an hour. Today, I chose to spend our time in the kitchen rather than my bedroom. Don't ask me why.

Because the counter has been doused in Blood Lines, she's able to sit in front of me, legs crossed, as I eat a perfectly mediocre sandwich. Camilla is in the living room, watching TV and enjoying a bowl of what she calls SpaghettiOs-oh-ohs. Somehow she was able to turn a canned mess into a gourmet meal with sautéed peppers and a mix of spices.

"Frosty," Kat says on a sigh.

"I'm one hundred percent invested in this conversation." I want a bite of those SpaghettiOs-oh-ohs so bad I'm willing to risk a forking to get it.

"You're killing me here," Kat mutters.

I glare at her.

She smirks.

Every day, I've tried to charm her, to make her fall in love with me again. Today, though, my heart just isn't in it. She's resisted me at every turn, kept me in the friend zone, and my shredded heart just can't take anymore.

I love you, kitten.

I love you, too. Hey, ask Ali about such and such girl. She's pretty.

I'm tired, so tired. And hell, did Camilla just take the last bite of those SpaghettiOs-oh-ohs?

"You feeling okay?" Kat waves her hand to encompass my entire body. "Or are you coming down with something?"

Used to be, she would have given me a sizzling kiss and said something like, "If you're going to die of plague, *I'm* going to die of plague." She'd had a spark, a zest for life. Now? She's all business all the time.

"I'm fine," I say and glance—again—at Camilla.

She looks away hastily. Has she been watching me? The way I've so often found myself watching her...

"Usually I have to tell a guy to look away from my boobs," Kat says, "not another girl."

I grit my teeth. "You want me to fall for another girl, remember? You insist on it. You can't get pissed when I oblige."

"Not her," she says quietly. "Anyone but her."

I don't want Camilla, not like that—damn it, I don't.

A beep sounds from my phone, saving me from a reply. Kat attempts to lift the device, but her hand ghosts through it and she growls with frustration, banging a fist against the counter, rattling my plate.

I read the text to her. "Cole says knock, knock."

"That's it?"

I nod and set the phone aside.

"Well. Aren't you going to respond to him?"

"Later." My phone beeps again. "Knock, knock," I read.

"Frosty," Kat says on another sigh.

Fine. I type, Who's there?

Cole: Me. I'm @ UR door. Open up.

Knock, knock.

The noise actually comes from my front door. My gaze lands on Camilla, and she stands, her body tense.

"I know you're in there," Cole calls through the wood. "I'm not leaving."

Kat smiles at me with a mix of affection and sadness. "He's got a proposition for you. You'll want to say no, but I expect you to suck it up and say yes." A second later, she's gone.

Milla

BURN, BABY, BURN

Thank God for distractions. I wasn't sure how much more *Slayer and Ghost: A Love Story* I could take. And okay. All right. Part of my irritation stems from my fascination. Frosty used to transform from caterpillar to butterfly every time Kat visited. His features would freaking glow. He would laugh and joke. Today, however, not even Kat is able to cheer him up. He's as sullen and snappy with her as he is with me. Why?

Has he finally given up on her?

Do I want him to?

Well, I'm not gonna think about it right now. We have a visitor. Hopefully he'll stay awhile, and I won't have to spend the evening worrying about the coming nightmare. And it will come. I have one every night now, no exceptions.

I palm a dagger, just in case Cole's here under duress, and move in front of Frosty to open the door.

Nope. No one has a gun to Cole's head. My weapon goes back into its sheath.

The beautiful Cole is not alone, however. Ali and Gavin flank him, both giants compared to me.

Cole and Ali nod at me. Gavin wiggles his brows.

"I can answer my own door, thanks." Frosty comes up beside me.

"You can, but you won't."

He glares at me before focusing on his friends. "What's up?"

"My blood pressure if you don't let me in." Ali pushes her way past us.

Cole follows suit. "Love, Justin, Jaclyn and River are on patrol with some of our new recruits."

Love. Mackenzie Love, Cole's ex. And Justin Silverstone. About a year ago, Justin betrayed Cole's team and aided Anima, believing their "we make the world a better place" propaganda. When the company abducted and tortured his sister, Jaclyn, all in an effort to force him to do more, to do *worse* to the friends he once fought alongside, he flipped sides once again. And yes, he had to go to great lengths to earn back their trust, but in the end, he succeeded.

I can't hope for the same. Once bonded, always bonded with this group, and I've never had the luxury.

"So...River's in town," I say. He's out there. He's hunting zombies, teaching newbies, living his life without me. "He's okay?"

Ali's features soften. "Yeah. He's fine."

Recruiting is something my group has always done, but this is a first for Cole. Trust issues, I guess. But now that Anima has been defeated, he must be willing to try new things, to help kids who have no idea they're slayers; they just know they're different.

"No zombies have emerged in weeks and no one has seen a rabbit cloud in the sky," Cole says.

I'd heard Ali's sister, Emma, somehow shapes a cloud to look like a rabbit whenever she sees zombies stirring in their nests. A warning. Kinda like riding into town on a pony, shouting, "The undead are coming! The undead are coming!" But I don't rely on that cloud like these guys. Emma can see a lot, I'm sure, but she can't see everything. I think Frosty agrees with me, otherwise he'd have stayed home the past few rabbit-cloudless weeks.

"We're on call, just in case," Cole adds, "so there won't be any drinking. But. Yeah. I said *but*. We're going to Hearts and hanging out like we used to. You're coming."

"A night off? No." Frosty shakes his head.

"Why? You got a hot date with a zombie?" Ali scans him from head to toe. "Seriously. I'm not just using the best pickup line ever when I say you look good enough to eat."

Cole cracks his knuckles. "I hope you're happy, Ali-gator. Now I have to kill my best friend."

"Don't be hatin'." Frosty brushes an invisible piece of lint from his shoulder. "She can't help her crush on me. No one can."

If only a snort would be appropriate. Problem is, he *does* look good enough to eat in a black T-shirt and roughed-up denims and girls *can't* help their crush on him.

"My answer is still no," Frosty adds.

"Don't listen to him. We'd love to join you for a night out." I need to escape this apartment, like, yesterday. And whether

Frosty knows it or not, he could use some time away, too. Hanging out with a dead ex-girlfriend can't be all that great for his mental heath.

He latches on to my wrist. This is the first time he's ever purposely, willingly touched me, and the contact is electric, startling me. Suddenly, my skin burns and tingles. I don't understand such a physical reaction, but maybe he feels it, too; he lets me go as if I'm leaking toxic waste.

"We're hunting, as usual," he says.

"Wrong. You heard your friends. We'll be told if any zombies are found." I push him into the hall, and the others follow him out. I shut and lock the door. "I can't take any more of your man-pouting. Kat's dead, but guess what? You're not. Why don't you at least pretend to be alive."

Ali actually gasps. As if she isn't always that blunt. Gavin gives me the stink eye, like I've just skinned his favorite cat. They can suck it. I've spent the last three weeks with Frosty, living in his lair, watching his every move. Subtlety always flies right over his head.

"I don't need to pretend," he grits. "I know I'm alive."

"Great. Now prove it."

"Oh, I'll prove it all right." He stomps down the hall.

Like him, I'm already dressed for the occasion in an ice-blue cami, skinny jeans and knee-high boots to better hide my knives. Part of my "always be prepared for anything" plan.

The group crams into Cole's Jeep. Gavin takes the back-seat with Ali and me, putting Frosty in front with Cole. That doesn't stop my charge from glaring at me over his shoulder numerous times, blaming me for his current whereabouts.

"Bad moods are contagious. Lighten up." Ali leans forward to pat the top of his head.

"Make me," he mumbles like a child. He stares out the window, at the pine trees, giant boulders and hills illuminated by streetlamps. "FYI, if a stranger says the wrong thing to me, I'll be arrested for assault. Anyone have bail money?"

"Sorry, bro, but I only have enough for myself." Gavin pats the wallet in his pocket. "Have a feeling I'm gonna need it."

While he's talking, I stealthily palm the wallet—without his knowledge—remove the cash and return the empty container to its place.

"I'll bail you out," I tell Frosty.

The car goes silent. Crickets might as well chirp. What'd I say this time?

"Thanks," he finally mutters.

"Well, I'll leave you both behind bars to rot—and learn a valuable lesson," Ali says.

Cole squeezes her thigh. "I'm sure I'll be sitting right beside them."

"Hopefully learning the same valuable lesson." Ali nudges my shoulder. "Have you been sticking to Frosty's side?"

"Yes, Mom. I have."

"What about those bathroom breaks you wanted?"

Frosty twists in the seat, his gaze sparkling. "Did she tell you to follow me into the men's crapper, as if someone will dare attack me while I'm doing my business?"

He's looking at me with humor. Not hatred. Not disgust. And he's never looked more gorgeous. What kind of miracle is this? "Yeah. But don't worry. I've settled for listening at the door."

"How kind of you."

He turns away, but it doesn't matter. For the rest of the drive, I feel like I'm floating on clouds.

We park in back of the club, and though the lot is jam-packed with cars of all shapes, sizes and colors, Cole has no problem finding a place. One of the spots in front is empty, safeguarded by a sign that reads "Reserved for Holland."

I'm trembling with excitement as I emerge. No matter what, I'm having fun tonight. The decision has been made.

The moon looks like an upside-down smile. There are no clouds but countless stars sparkling like diamonds on a bed of black velvet. The air smells of exhaust, cologne and sweat, and even though it's unpleasant, it beats the odor of rot.

As I trail behind Frosty, I guard his six, my gaze constantly scanning for trouble. To the right, a couple is making out hardcore against a Porsche. To the left, a girl is shoving her drunken friend into the backseat of a beige sedan.

Two beefy security guards block the front doors, but they allow us to enter despite boos and hisses rising from the mile-long line. We're even allowed upstairs in the VIP lounge, where the music isn't so loud and we have an unobstructed view of the dance floor.

A hostess—young and pretty with dark hair and gorgeous skin the color of burnished copper—rushes over. "Welcome back, Mr. Holland."

Cole is all business. "Is my usual table available?"

"No, sir. We didn't know you were coming and—"

"Make it available," he says.

"Yes, yes, of course." She rushes off and returns a few minutes later to lead us to an empty booth in the far right corner, hidden from the rest of the club by black-as-night drapes.

Ali slides in, Cole right behind her. Gavin goes in at the opposite side, leaving Frosty and me standing there like idiots. I'm about to take the seat next to Gavin when another girl races over to give Frosty a hug and kiss on the cheek and if that's not enough, she clings to his arm.

"Logan! It's been weeks. I've missed you so much."

Logan—oh, yeah, his he-slut hall-of-shame name.

Frosty sits beside Cole, forcing the girl to release him. He pulls at his collar, clearly uncomfortable and probably flipping through mental files and coming up blank. The poor girl doesn't get the hint and asks him a thousand questions about his life. As if she has every right to know.

Gavin tries not to laugh. Cole doesn't notice, he's too busy cuddling Ali.

Frosty's gaze meets mine and I swear he's begging for help.

I finally claim a seat—the one right next to him. There's not really room for me, but whatever. I drape my arm around his shoulders and he leans into me. "My sweet Frosty has forgotten his manners, hasn't he? I'm Milla and you're…?"

"Patricia." The girl pales. "You're his girlfriend?"

"Well, you tell me. I've been living with this delicious slice of beefcake for three magical weeks, spending every waking moment with him." I shake a hand at the ceiling. "I try my hardest to keep my hands to myself, but…my little pookie bear needs me. Isn't that right, lollipop?"

"That's right, sugar tush."

Sugar tush? Well, I've been called worse.

The girl stammers out an apology and at last leaves.

"Thanks," Frosty mutters.

I release him and say, "Bang and bail protection is just one of the many services I offer."

Our waiter arrives to take our drink orders. He's a good-looking guy with a leanly muscled frame. His hair is purple and there are three silver piercings in his brow.

If I'm not mistaken, he gives me an extrasweet smile when I request two shots of Grey Goose. Forget Cole's no drinking rule. This is my one night off; I'm blowing my budget—well, Gavin's budget—and partying like a rock star.

"You follow instructions *so* well." Ali frowns at me. "I'll have a ginger ale."

The others order the same. Their loss.

Waiter McCutie winks at me before rushing off. I'm not asked for ID *or* payment, which is a first. And I don't have to wait while he serves other, nicer—wealthier-looking—customers. He returns a few minutes later and distributes the drinks. I've never been a top priority before.

"Thank you," Frosty says, stealing one of my shots. He drains it before I can work up a good protest. "Didn't think I'd ever have another one of those, but what the hell."

"Cheers." I drain my own. The liquid burns going down, but quickly settles in my stomach like warm honey.

"Can I get you anything else?" Waiter McCutie asks.

"Another round," I say. "And keep 'em coming."

Again, he isn't gone long.

Frosty steals a second shot. This time we clink our glasses before the liquid goes down the hatch.

Ali shakes her head in protest. "You guys suck."

"If Zs are found," I say, "and you're drunk as a skunk, so what? The monsters will be happy when they die."

Her frown returns. "One, we don't kill them if we can save them, and two, I never drink."

Cole gives her shoulders a squeeze, and it's clear he knows something about her I don't.

"What about you?" I ask him.

"I'm driving," he says. "A task I take seriously."

I admire their sense of responsibility, even as I pick up two new glasses. "More for me. Bottoms up."

"Hold on a sec." Gavin swipes one from my hand and drains the contents. "You convinced me."

Ali slaps his shoulder.

"What? She gives good argument."

"You are such a traitor," she grumbles.

"A smart traitor. Do you know how long it's been since I've had a good buzz?" He eyes each of us. "Two days."

"A torturous eternity," Frosty says drily.

I toss back my shot, then another and another. By the time I've emptied the last one, the burn is completely gone, my head swimming. I hate feeling out of control almost as much as I love feeling uninhibited and carefree.

I turn to signal Waiter McCutie…and find he's already back and crouching beside me, watching me with a grin. "Hi," he says.

"Hi," I say back.

"Came to see if you needed anything else."

"More Grey Goose, please."

"My pleasure." But he doesn't take off just yet. "This your first time at Hearts?"

"Nope." Not only had I come here looking for Frosty the night after Kat first appeared to me, but I'd also come here thanks to Anima—to pretend to fight and at last hand over Ali. The night my secret came to light and my brother disowned me. "But I'm kinda glad you missed my debut."

"Why?" His grin grows wider. "Did you trip and fall?"

"Hardly." I burp discreetly into my hand. "I'm so graceful and ladylike it's scary."

McCutie laughs out loud. "Did you drink too much and projectile-vomit on your boss's Italian loafers?"

"Please. That kind of thing only happens in books and movies."

"Honey, it happened an hour ago. And last night. And the night before."

An endearment. One he probably uses on every girl he encounters, but I don't care. I've found a person who doesn't hate me, or suspect me of wrongdoing, and I gobble it up.

I crave more.

"You're cute," I tell him.

"Thank you." His grin returns as he twines his fingers with mine. "I'm Jason, by the way."

"You're about to be dead." Frosty grabs Jason by the wrist and must apply enough pressure to hurt because Jason flinches and jerks back. "She's off-limits."

My anger is so sharp it feels like glass shards are riding a tide of acid inside my veins. "What, I'm your bodyguard, so I can't have a *special friend*?"

Ali jumps in. "No. You can't."

"Do yourself a favor and keep your opinions to yourself," I tell her.

Jason gapes at me. "You're the big guy's *bodyguard*?"

"Leave," Frosty tells him. "Now."

He scurries off.

"Rude," I say.

"No more so than you." Frosty leans toward me. "You owe me, remember. More than that, you agreed to do a job, so stop screwing around and actually do it."

"I thought you didn't need a bodyguard."

"Don't tell me you're dumb enough to believe everything I say."

We glare at each other—we glare and we don't look away. We're both panting, our tempers high, our minds fogged with alcohol and adrenaline. The tension thickens between us until I almost can't breathe through it. But I know I'm breathing, because I smell the musk of soap embedded in his skin.

I lean closer, until I see the flecks of gold sprinkled through the navy in his eyes. His lashes are longer and spikier than I realized, and if I didn't know him, I'd accuse him of wearing falsies.

He's so beautiful right now it hurts to look at him.

His lips part, drawing my gaze—holding it captive. They are full and soft and I wonder how they'll taste.

Taste?

What the hell is wrong with me?

"Come on, princess." Gavin stands, takes my hand and pulls me to my feet. "It's your lucky day. *I'm* going to be your special friend." He drags me downstairs to the dance floor, and despite the frantic pulse of music, he wraps me in his arms and moves slowly, purposely.

"I'm not sleeping with you," I tell him.

"Good to know. Now listen up, buttercup."

Ugh. "Before you turn on the charm to change my mind, you should know the answer will forever be no. You're not my type."

"You don't like perfection? That's okay. I don't like girls with bad taste. Now zip your lips. I'm not here to throw a party in your pants."

Oh. I peer up at him, my brow furrowed. "How are you going to be my special friend then?"

"By giving you a bit of advice."

Advice. Gross. "I'd rather let you throw that party."

"Too bad. My boy, Frosty, he's stubborn."

I snort. "That's not exactly a news flash."

But Gavin isn't done. "You're trying to squeeze good milk out of a rotten cow. I see that. I get it. But he's never going to drop Kat. Just ain't gonna happen. And if you try to win him away from her, you're going to end up hurt."

My mouth goes dry. "I'm not interested in him that way."

"You sure about that? You looked like you wanted to eat his face. Granted, he looked like he wanted to eat your face, too, but even if you managed to get him into bed with you, you wouldn't be able to keep him there."

A lump grows in my throat. "I don't want to talk about this."

"The truth isn't always easy or pretty, but it's the truth."

I don't know how to respond. Not that it matters. Ali and Cole come up beside us to dance. Or, more accurately, to dry-hump.

I'd be embarrassed for them, but my world is currently spinning off its axis. Faster and faster… My stomach threatens to rebel. Violently. I close my eyes and swallow a moan—and the burn of bile.

"I've got her, Gav." Frosty's voice, his warm breath suddenly tickling the locks of hair pressed against my dampened skin. "Let her go."

"Are you sure? I can—"

"Let. Her. Go." He wraps me in his arms, holding me against his side and leading me away from the dance floor. I stumble, but he keeps me upright. "Come on. Let's get you home."

Cool air hits me, and I'm glad. I hadn't realized how much I'd overheated. Unfortunately, it's too little too late. I wrench from Frosty and dive to the gravel-covered ground. When I land, half my dinner comes up in a rush.

"At least you didn't vomit on my Italian loafers," he mutters.

"That would have been…awesome," I splutter.

Strong hands hold back my hair as the other half of my dinner pulls the eject lever.

"I've been keeping track of your flaws, you know," he says.

"How kind of you." *Bastard.*

"This one, the inability to hold your liquor. It's actually kind of cute."

Double-dog bastard.

"You look so tough. You *are* tough. But get a couple shots of vodka in you and it's a total TKO."

A moment passes, or maybe an eternity. I finally stop heaving. He picks me up and carries me to Cole's Jeep, muttering softly, "What am I going to do with you?"

I want to open my eyes, want to read his expression, but

I don't have the strength. "I didn't mean to ruin your night. I'm sorry."

He sighs. "I only wish that was the crux of the problem."

His soft words are the last thing I remember until I wake up however long later, haunted by another dream of burning to death by crimson fire. *Dýnamis*, only twisted and warped.

Where I am? I ease upright to look around. Queen-size bed. The sheets are Star Wars themed. There's a dresser with one drawer open, a white T-shirt hanging over the side, but there's no other furniture.

This is… I'm in Frosty's bedroom. His inner sanctum. He's always made me sleep on the couch. Where is he?

My stomach protests as I stand. At least my dizziness is gone. I search the apartment, but find no sign of my partner…roommate…whatever. He must have dropped me off and run for the hills, hoping to salvage what he could of the night. Does he care nothing for his own safety? Do I? I never should have had those shots. I lost focus in a hurry. I also lost my dignity.

Fun only lasts a little while. Consequences are a lifetime. I know this better than most, which makes me twice the idiot for tonight's behavior.

I stalk to the front window that overlooks the apartment's parking lot. The sun is a big ball of orange-gold fire as it rises in the horizon. Beautiful, but not quite high enough in the sky to chase the shadows from the lot. At least I can see that Frosty's truck is gone.

Asshole! My cell phone is still in my pocket because I'm still dressed in my club clothes. I text Frosty—where R U?—but he doesn't respond.

Desperate, I text Ali. The fox has left the henhouse. Any idea where he is?

Her reply comes only a moment later. U had vomit breath. We ALL jumped ship.

Me, my cheeks going up in flames: He's w/U?

Her: No. He's w/the boys. Apparently he needed something called "punch in the face therapy"

Me: Why? & does PITFT mean Cole & the boys R actually hitting him?

Her: Not sure. & YES!!!

Me: They R so lucky

Frustrated, I throw my phone across the room. Of course, I suffer instant regret. If I break it, I can't afford to buy another one. But as I turn to collect it, I glimpse a shadow creeping through the parking lot. Zombies? A Peeping Tom? Spy?

My heart is nothing but a war drum as I grab the .44 hidden in a hollowed-out book on the coffee table. I'm out the door and tracking the shadow a few seconds later.

This seems to be my MO lately. Going off alone, practically begging to be ambushed. But make a move, shadow. Try to take me down. I'll give worse than I get.

I circle the entire lot twice, but find no hint of foul play. No scent of rot. Still. I'm not reassured. Just before Anima captured and tortured River, I suspected I was being followed and watched, yet I could never find proof.

When I return to the apartment, a sense of foreboding accompanies me.

Frosty

FRIENDS WITH BRAINS 'N FITS

I'm ashamed of myself—because I'm not actually ashamed of myself.

Dude. I'm a mess. A tangle of confusion, disdain, self-loathing...and desire.

At the center of all this turmoil? Camilla. In the middle of an insult-fest, I got hard for her. I'd all but called her a low-down dirty quitter, but rather than slap me, she'd looked at me with those eyes. Those luminous golden eyes. Suddenly, all I could think about—all I cared about—was that she was the embodiment of sex. A punk-rock Barbie with a jones for something rough and dirty.

I'd had a few too many shots, that was all. Vodka turns the most devoted guys into he-sluts.

But does it really matter? I'm not devoted to Kat anymore. She's certainly not devoted to me.

After the boys and I drop off the girls—Ali at slayer HQ

and Camilla at my apartment—we pick up Bronx, Justin and River, who's still in town to help to train the new recruits. New recruits I've never met and haven't vetted to make sure they're legit.

Bad Frosty. Bad.

That shit changes *now*.

We return to Hearts and reclaim our booth in the VIP lounge. It's bright and early, which means it's after hours, all the patrons and employees gone...which means it's also self-serve.

"What's this I hear about Punch Frost in the Face?" River asks.

"Hit and forgive has always been a way of life for us," Cole explains. "But we turned Frosty down. We forgave him for his stupidity a long time ago, and he didn't even have to ask."

River glares at me.

"You got a problem?" I ask.

He runs his tongue over his teeth, but remains quiet.

Whatever. I turn to Gavin. "Jaclyn is a good girl. So why haven't you committed to her yet?" When he—a single guy—put his arm around Camilla, when he danced with her, I'd wanted to get in his grille and rage. A reaction I still can't explain. I'm not into her in a romantic way.

But here's the shocker. I think I'm starting to like her in *other* ways. The way she fights. Her wit. Her determination. The way she charges forward, never trying to sidestep a difficult issue or pretend it doesn't exist. The sadness she always carries and can't hide—it makes a guy want to do whatever proves necessary just to make her smile.

Hell, maybe I've even gotten a little possessive of her, seeing her as my own personal shadow.

"Dude," Gavin says. "Are we gossiping like junior high girls now?"

"Yes," Bronx says.

"Too bad. Me and Jaclyn, we aren't up for conversation." Justin punches him in the shoulder.

Gavin frowns at him. "What the hell was that for?"

"Anytime my sister's name is mentioned, I get the urge to hurt you."

Gavin rolls his eyes. "Fine. You want the deets, you get the deets. She's pretending she isn't interested in me right now."

"Maybe she *isn't* interested," Justin quips. "Ever think about that?"

"You've seen my face, right?" Gavin proudly pats his own cheeks. "Everyone's interested. Including you guys. Don't try to deny it. *Anyway.* She'll commit to me if and when I decide I'm ready to settle down."

"Dude," I say, mimicking him, "I hope some guy comes along, sweeps her off her feet, and she leaves you in the dust."

A muscle jumps beneath his eye, but his tone is casual as he says, "You actually want her to suffer? Cruel, Frosty. Cruel. By the way, I've changed my mind about punch therapy." He leans over the table to jab his fist into my mouth.

The impact hurts like hell and sends my head whipping to the side. I smile at him, knowing there's blood on my teeth.

"What about you?" I nudge Cole before wiping my mouth. "You and Ali engaged yet?"

"Not officially. I'm still trying to plan the proposal."

"Something to melt her panties off, I'm guessing."

"I suggest a banner in the sky that reads Slay the Undead with Me Forever," River says.

Cole flips him off. "Even without the ring, she's mine. I'm smart enough to take myself out of the game before the other team steals my balls and goes home."

Gavin draws back his fist. "You wanting a little sesh with the doctor, too?"

"Bring it," Cole says with relish.

"Um, sh–should I come back later?" a small female voice asks. "Miss Ankh called and asked me to take care of you guys while you're here, but I can go. Do you want me to go?"

A waitress after hours. Sweet.

"Are we restricted to drinks or can you work a little magic in the kitchen?" River asks.

"M–magic," she stammers.

"Then we want you to stay."

We place our orders and she rushes off.

Since hitting puberty, I've noticed that slayers always get one of two reactions from the opposite sex. We scare them, or we turn them on. I scared Kat for years. That's why she turned me down again and again before finally saying yes. And even after we were together, when she trusted me with her life, she still had trouble accepting who and what I was.

Girls like Ali and Camilla are rare. They see us for what we are—violent when the situation calls for it, willing to cross any line to do what needs doing—and yet they stand by our sides anyway. Hell, they help us cross those lines.

My teeth gnash when I realize I've lumped Camilla into the same category as Ali. It's Love and Jaclyn who are like Ali, not Camilla.

I like her better now, yes, but I still don't trust her.

"What's the deal with your sister?" I ask River, and hate myself for going there. Do I back away from the subject? Hell, no.

He raises his chin the way Camilla raises hers, and for the first time, I notice how closely they resemble each other. Same pale hair with dark brows. Same golden eyes. Same flawless bronzed skin decorated with a multitude of black-and-white tattoos. Only, he doesn't make the fly of my jeans strain, so I can kind of tolerate him.

"I don't have a sister, remember?"

Right. The whole "disown her for betraying the crew" thing.

"And what do you mean, what's the deal with her?" he snaps. "Why do you even care?"

"Ali had a vision." Cole leans back, drapes his arms on the edge of the booth. "Her first on her own. In it, Camilla stops some woman from shooting Frosty, saving his life."

"It's why they've been hanging out. A lot," Gavin offers helpfully.

River drums his fingers against the table and glares at me. "How will she stop the shooter? What happens to her afterward? What, exactly, does Gavin mean by *hanging out*? And how do you know the vision will come true? The ones Ali's had with other people have been proven. But one on her own? No. The fact that it came to her in a different way must mean it, too, is different. Perhaps even changeable."

I kick myself for not asking those very questions. In my defense, I'd been too wrapped up in hate for Camilla and my love for Kat to care. "Cole. Answer the man."

"You're right," Cole says. "It *is* different. For the first time, Ali saw two versions of the same vision. In the first, without Camilla, Frosty dies. In the second, with Camilla, Frosty lives. As for how it goes down, all I know is exactly what I told you. A woman aims a gun at Frosty and Camilla stops her from shooting him. How? I don't know. Ali says Camilla and the woman have zero contact." He flicks me a "sorry, man" smile. "Now, if you want the down-and-dirty about Frosty and Camilla hanging out, you have my stamp of approval to interrogate Frosty."

"Nothing's happened," I offer without being pressed. Because it's true. "And don't worry. Nothing will." Perhaps I sound a little less confident now—River returns to glaring.

The waitress arrives with our food, the scent of different spices wafting around the table. I lose interest in conversation. Everyone does. We devour our hamburgers like the savages we are.

Afterward, we talk a little longer before deciding to call it quits and head home.

"Stay in touch," Cole says as I climb behind the wheel of my truck. The shots of vodka have long since worn off; I'm good to go. "I mean it."

"I'll come see you tomorrow. Tour the new place."

"Good. You don't, and I'll hunt you down." He reaches in to grind his knuckles into my scalp then strides to his Jeep.

I'm strangely excited to see Camilla, and I make the drive faster than I should. I just want to check on her, to assure myself she's okay. Because I'm a nice guy. Probably the nicest ever.

Once there, I slow my roll and quietly step inside, not

wanting to wake her if she's sleeping. I know how little sleep she actually gets. When I close the door, hinges squeak. Damn it.

A shadow moves from the corner and the next thing I know, I'm being tackled to the floor. The lights are off, but I would recognize Camilla's scent anywhere—roses, pecans and the musk of my shampoo—as she pins me to the floor.

"It's me," I tell her, going lax.

"I know." She swings at me, nailing me in my already sore jaw. "You want punch therapy, well, get ready. There's more where that came from."

She got the drop on me. She freaking got the drop on me.

I grab hold of her waist and flip her to her back, our lower bodies unwittingly rubbing together. Gritting my teeth, I maneuver to my knees. Our gazes lock…and it isn't long before the tension I experienced at the club returns, thickening the air.

Pale hair spills around her shoulders. Her lips are parted, as if begging for a kiss. My kiss.

"Get off me," she says without any heat.

Or stay right where I am…

No. Hell, no. I jump to my feet, looking anywhere but her direction. "You're better, I see. That's good. That's real good. Now let's get some sleep."

"Sleep? It's almost noon."

"Thanks for the update." I stride into my room. For once, I don't bother with the lock.

I snooze the rest of the day. A mistake. By the time night arrives, I'm wide-awake. I stare at the ceiling until the butt crack of dawn, finally rising to shower and dress. My plan for the day? Avoid Camilla. We could use some time apart. But she's stretched out in front of the door, drenched in sweat and tossing and turning. There are scratches all over her arms.

I close the distance—or try to. The little witch set a trip wire in my path. Not seeing it until too late, I pitch forward, land with a thud and a curse.

She jolts upright with a .22 extended and cocked.

"Careful," I say. "It's just me."

"I know that...now." She's panting as she lowers the weapon. "What are you doing?"

"Leaving." I stand slowly, not wanting to spook her further. "Just let me—"

"No. *I'm* leaving. You're staying." I pick her up by the waist, not exactly hating the way she fits my grip, and carry her to the couch, where I unceremoniously dump her. "I mean it. Stay here. You're in no condition to be out and about."

I stalk outside without another word. The sun is rising, the sky gradually brightening with vivid streaks of pink and purple I can't bring myself to hate today.

Like Camilla so rudely pointed out, I'm alive. Why not act like it? Why not enjoy what time I have left?

I slide into my truck an-n-nd she jumps in from the other side. I grip the wheel as she buckles up.

"Camilla—"

"Save your breath." She digs inside the backpack she brought with her, soon withdrawing a toothbrush, small bottle of water and tube of toothpaste. When she realizes I'm staring at her, she harrumphs. "My go bag. Just so you know, I'm ready for anything, anytime."

Wonderful. "You need a break from me. *I* need a break from you."

"Too bad," she says. "Better you need a break and live than get a break and die."

I try again. "Camilla—"

"Besides," she interjects, "I have a problem, and you're the only one I can talk to, so whether or not you decide to help me, pretend to listen." She peers out the window, as if waiting for my rejection.

I put the key in the ignition, gun the engine. "If you're about to ask me for special friend advice—"

"Hardly. It's not like I've been sneaking out to hook up with a side slice."

"Good to know." I relax into my seat, only then realizing how tense I'd grown, and ease the truck forward.

"And just so you know, I've never gone to bed with someone thinking it's a onetime bang, or that the benefits package comes with zero benefits. That's just how things turned out."

"So…you want me to tell you how to score a guy long-term?"

"Yes. No. I want to discuss my nightmares."

Okay. That I can handle. "Go on."

She releases a pent-up breath. "Every night, I dream of bloodred flames. Flames I'm calling *thánatos*."

Doesn't sound so bad. I don't mention that I've actually *seen* the flames. "First *dýnamis*, a Greek word for power, and now *thánatos*, a Greek word for death. Someone in this car is a geek at heart. Hint—it's not me."

"You know the meaning of the words. You're a geek."

"I know the meaning of the words because I play video

games, which means I get a pass. I bet you actually studied Greek."

"I was a straight A student and proud of it. Or I would have been, if I'd gone to class."

"Both a nerd and a sexy rebel. The girl next door meets the biker babe."

"Did you just call me…sexy?"

I purse my lips. "Tell me more about the nightmares."

"Well, the flames…they kind of kill me."

She *dies*? "Kind of?" I snarl.

"Definitely."

Nightmares aren't visions, I remind myself, or even premonitions. "You should have told me the first time it happened."

"Why? So you could cheer about it?"

I deserve that. "When did the nightmares start?"

"The night I was darted."

"So the toxin is probably the cause. Has the antidote helped at all?"

"Not really."

At least she is fine otherwise. "Maybe we need to hit you with a stronger dose." I reach over to press the latch on my glove box. The lid pops open, revealing a stash of syringes Reeve delivered the day after my breakfast date with Raina. Just in case. "Use two. Also, we'll have Reeve do some kind of sleep study on you." So far the blood tests haven't provided any new answers.

"Okay. Thanks." Camilla stabs the needles into her thigh, one after the other, and again, she doesn't flinch or gasp. As if the pain is insignificant or she's totally numb to it. Maybe she is.

What has this girl endured over the years?

We lapse into silence as I drive to a nearby coffee shop, where I set up my laptop to do some schoolwork. While I draft my thoughts about *The Tragedy of Macbeth*—lust for power will kill you every time, yo—I ignore Camilla. Or pretend to. At one point, I order a coffee, and she requests a glass of water. When I order a sandwich, she asks the waitress about the cheapest thing on the menu—a mini sugar cookie. That isn't a nutritious breakfast. Whatever. It's also not my problem.

Camilla suddenly reaches out and grabs my arm, shaking me. "Let's go. Now."

"I'm not done."

"I don't care." She swipes up the laptop, saves my work and shuts it down. "Please, Frosty."

Please? From Camilla Marks? I reclaim my property, intending to offer a scathing remark, but panic bathes her features, stopping me. I've never seen her like this.

"What's wrong with you?"

"I want to go." She tugs on my hand, only to release me as if I somehow burned her. She steps away from me, muttering, "I'll be outside."

"Well, well." A male voice, somewhat familiar, rises above the quiet chatter throughout the shop. "The traitor has emerged from hiding at last."

Three members of River's crew approach us. I've spoken to each guy at some point, but only really know the one in the middle. Chance. Or Knuckle Scars, as Ali calls him. He's been sniffing around Mackenzie Love.

I stand and bump knuckles with him.

He looks from me to Camilla then back again. "What's up?"

"Nothing much. You?"

"Same."

Camilla adjusts her bag on her shoulder before stuffing her hands in her pockets. "Fingers crossed we never again run into each other, Frosty—that's your name, right?" She attempts to march out of the store.

The guy on Chance's right steps into her path. "Where do you think you're going? Back to Anima?"

I swallow a retort, wondering how she'll handle the situation.

"Anima has been destroyed." She raises her chin. "The same fate you'll suffer if you don't move out of my way."

He crosses his arms over his chest. "I'm quaking in my boots, princess."

Without hesitation, she pops him in the nose once, twice, and as he goes down, howling with pain, bleeding, she says, "Oops. My hand slipped."

I fight a grin. "Both times?"

"The air is slippery." She steps around Broken Nose.

The other guy helps his friend stand up. "Bitch."

Camilla's shoulders square before she exits, letting me know she heard the insult. I also know she left the way she did, pretending to have bumped into me, because she hoped to spare me grief for hanging out with her, and it's making my chest ache.

"We just left Cole's," Chance says, picking up the conversation as if there was never a confrontation with Camilla. "We were surprised you weren't there."

"I'm headed there now. See you around." I slam into the

guy who called Camilla a bitch, knocking him down, before chasing after my girl—no, no. Not my girl. My...I don't know what she is. I only know I would rather be with her than the pricks who just hurt her.

10

Milla

ANOTHER LITTLE PIECE OF MY HEART

I'm trapped in a freaking day from hell. But the part that sucks the biggest balls? This is a day from hell in a long string of days from hell. And really, one should be indistinguishable from another by now. Somehow, though, this one stands out as the worst yet.

First, I woke up to find Frosty sneaking out. As if I was a one-night stand he couldn't wait to forget. Then, of course, I ran into Chance, my brother's best friend—and a former "boyfriend" of mine—as well as Chance's two younger cousins. Oh, and my personal fave, the Z toxin in my system is causing the nightmares and who knows what other problems.

From now on, I probably need to ask myself one very important question each and every day. *Do I want to eat my friends?*

I'm not sure how much more bad news I can take.

Frosty catches up to me, grabs me by the wrist and tugs

me to his truck. I don't protest, but I do look around to make sure no one sees us.

As he speeds down the highway, he says, "I'm not embarrassed to be seen with you. You didn't have to pretend we'd only bumped into each other."

My heart melts. Until he adds, "Besides, they probably know about the vision."

Right. Because he wouldn't hang around me for any other reason.

I won't cry. It's not like this is news.

"Do you miss your crew?"

I'm not sure I like the way he hammers to the heart of the matter. "I do. As much as a limb." Seeing the trio had hurt like hell. They might have lost all respect for me, might hate me to my rotten core, but I still love them.

"Your betrayal put them at risk, saved only your brother."

At least he's not spitting the words at me. His tone is calm, factual. I rub my Betrayal tattoo—and the compass next to it. A reminder that no matter how lost I am, there's still a way home. I just have to find it.

Needing a reprieve, I stare out the window. The sky is pretty, baby blue with puffy white clouds. Towering oaks line the side of the road and dot the rolling hills. I've lived in Bama all my life, but I'm still awed by the scenery.

"Camilla?"

If I continue to maintain my silence, Frosty will let the subject drop. I know this. Personal conversations aren't our thing. But I finally say, "At the time, I had tunnel vision. Save River. My eye was on the prize, and I was blind to everything else."

"I still don't understand how you did what you did to them...to Ali."

She's easier to talk about, so I say, "Before I'd even met her, I knew I had to betray her. I decided to find fault with her, no matter what. A smile meant she was making fun of me. A frown meant she disapproved of me."

"Seems pretty twisted."

"It was." Anytime I felt myself softening toward her, I purposely snipped and snapped at her, creating strife between us. A task my inner bitch enjoyed. "Desperate girls do desperate things."

A moment of silence. "Where we're headed... River is there. He's been staying there. Can you handle seeing him?"

Good question. The brother who used to hold me when I cried, who used to tell me everything would be okay, that he would always take care of me, the brother who did his best to save—

I'm just supposed to smile when he turns his back on me?

And he *will* turn his back on me. Our crew lives by a single motto. *Lie and Die, Betray and Pay.* When my association with Anima was first found out, protocol demanded River feed me the barrel of a .44. He kicked me out instead, still in protector mode, I suppose.

"You won't know anything is wrong with me," I say on a trembling breath. I'm needed, and there's no way I'll let anyone else down just because I'm cut to ribbons inside.

"I won't know anything is wrong with you...but something *will* be wrong with you." The words should be a question, but he's made them a statement. "You can't... You shouldn't..."

He jerks a hand through his hair. "Damn it. You're twisting up my guts. Stop."

"How am I twisting—"

"Stop."

Fine. Whatever. I answer his nonquestion. "I can't control what I feel, but I can control how I react to those feelings."

"And that makes your pain any less real?"

"No, but feelings change all the time, for a million different reasons. They're unreliable and therefore inconsequential in the big scheme of things. Why give in to the worst of them?"

His lips purse. "What about love?"

It's a very personal question, but I find myself saying, "Love is a choice, not an emotion."

He's shaking his head before I've finished speaking. "You're telling me a man and woman should decide to be together, rather than waiting to fall for each other?"

"I'm talking about love. You're talking about chemistry."

"I love Kat. I don't chemistry her."

I don't know why, but hearing him say he still loves the girl who continually tells him to date other people is worse than River's potential rejection. "Real love never fails, never fades, and the greatest expression of it is giving."

"I give—gave—her everything."

"Did you really? Did you give her your time and attention when you were busy with other things? Did you put her happiness before your own? Did you give her what she needed or what she wanted?"

A muscle jumps beneath his eye. "I'm done with this conversation."

Well. Score one, Milla.

He turns onto a redbrick road, where a towering, intricately twisted wrought-iron gate blocks our entrance. As we slow, that gate opens automatically and we're able to cruise down the drive and park in front of...a hotel?

No, I realize. This is Reeve Ankh's new house. A massive plantation with white shuttered windows, massive columns and a wraparound portico. Pecan and apple trees intermingle along the front of the property, a display of nature's best. To the left are strawberry and blackberry vines, and the sweet fruits scent the air.

"While we're here, you stay by my side," Frosty says as we climb the porch steps. "Got it?"

"Sir, yes, sir. Do you?"

"I won't try to ditch you, if that's what you're hinting at. Not here, at least."

His determination to keep me in his sights gives me pause. Usually he can't wait to ditch me. Why would he—

The truth hits, and for a moment, I'm blindsided. After all the time we've spent together, he doesn't trust me. Not even a little. He thinks I'll sneak off, maybe try to destroy the security system or something equally disastrous.

I don't know why I expected better. He's giving me what I deserve. What I will always deserve. I need to take my licks like a big girl and move on.

Feelings are inconsequential, right?

"We'll get Reeve to run those tests before we leave," he says. "I want to give the newest dose of antidote time to do its thing first."

"Pleasure before business. Got it."

The moment we reach the tall, arched front doors, they

open from the inside. The reason pats Frosty on the shoulder. Justin Silverstone.

I wish I could hold out hope for the same forgiveness he was granted after working with Anima, but I know better.

"Hey, man." Justin clasps hands with Frosty and the two perform some kind of manly chest bump. With his dark hair and even darker eyes, he's a big ole bowl of puppy-dog cuteness.

Frosty scans the open foyer, which is currently devoid of furniture. Are Cole and the others afraid something will happen to this new place, so don't want to bother decorating? Or did they just not have time?

"Cole and Ali still around?"

"Yeah. Everyone's in the gym." Justin gives me an appreciative once-over. "You're Milla, right?"

"That's right." If he insults me, I'll...take it.

"Sweet." He slings his arm over my shoulders to urge me forward. "You, lucky girl, are getting a personal escort." When we're several feet ahead of Frosty, his tone goes low and quiet. "I heard you switched to Team Awesome. Congratulations."

"Actually, I like to think I never really switched." I match my volume to his. And then I offer him more than I've offered anyone else, the words bottled inside me for far too long. Maybe because he's the one person in the world who will understand. "I somehow convinced myself it was okay to do the wrong thing for a very good reason." Maybe, if I'd gone to my brother, told him what Anima had said, we could have come up with a plan to protect him *and* bring down the company, without putting anyone else in danger.

Frosty remains behind us, but follows close to our heels. "What are you two muttering about?"

"If it was any of your business, we'd talk louder," Justin says without looking back. Going quiet again, he adds, "Don't worry. I've been in your outcast shoes and I know how difficult it can be, but it doesn't last forever."

I rub at *Betrayal*. "How did you win everyone over?"

"Time. Action."

I sigh. "An eternity wouldn't be long enough for me." People died because of me. Innocent people. I deserve a dagger, not a welcome-back party. "But I'll make things right, no matter what."

"Hey, we all make mistakes. The others *will* remember that fact."

I don't believe him, but I offer him a smile of thanks anyway. He's trying to make me feel better and I'm grateful.

As we enter a spacious room filled with workout equipment and a boxing ring, my brother comes into view. I trip over my own foot. Frosty grabs a fistful of my shirt, yanking me back so that I never actually fall.

"Thanks," I mutter, watching as River laughs and enters the ring with Cole. Like me, my brother has a body covered in scars and black-and-white tattoos.

Black and white. Right and wrong. Nothing in between.

My heart swells with different emotions. Love. Joy—he's here, he's safe. Regret. Remorse. Happiness. Sadness. Anticipation. Dread.

Cole is shirtless and sweaty, muscled and just as heavily tattooed. He bears names and symbols to honor the loved ones he's lost—and those he just plain loves. Like Ali.

With his black hair and violet eyes, he's more beautiful than any other boy I've ever seen—with the exception of Frosty. I once tried to pick him up. Not because I'm attracted to him but because I hoped to use him against Ali. Anything to push her toward Anima.

Now, shame stabs at me.

Both boys are expertly skilled at combat, and it's clear they know each other's habits. When one swings, the other ducks. When one kicks, the other jumps.

"You on your period again?" Cole asks.

"Your mom is on her period," River responds.

"No mom jokes," Ali calls from the sidelines. "Or I'll punch you both in the ovaries."

"No girl jokes," Cole tells her.

"Fine. I'll punch you both in the apple bags," she amends.

"Apple bags?" River laughs. "My new favorite phrase."

"My girl gives good poetry." Cole smiles fondly, then nails River in the jaw with a hard right cross. "I give good aneurisms."

"You aren't the only one." River lands a punch of his own before spinning out of range to avoid Cole's retaliation. He stills, but his gaze keeps going, moving through the room. Always check your surroundings. You never know who's trying to sneak up on you.

He stops on me, and a humiliating whimper escapes. He loses his smile, regret pulsing from him. For a single heartbeat, at least. Does he miss me? He must. Then his expression shutters, and he nods a greeting to Justin and Frosty.

I am not a slave to my emotions, remember?

But...I think my heart is actually breaking inside my chest.

That's okay. I'll heal. Failure isn't the end; it's just a delay.

"Come on." Justin tugs me forward. "I'll introduce you to our new recruits."

I dig in my heels, staying in place. "Frosty?" I haven't forgotten my promise to him.

"Go on. But stay nearby. I mean it."

"We will, Dad." Justin flips him the bird. "We'll be in the room next to this one. Happy?"

"Only when my fist goes through your chest cavity, douche-purse."

Douche-purse. The entire crew has always loved to tease Ali about her grandmother's attempt to be cool. "Be careful," I mutter to Justin. "I've seen him do the chest cavity thing."

Justin flashes me a wicked grin. "If you think I lack the skill to protect myself, you just haven't seen me fight."

Poor, deluded boy. Frosty will wipe the floor with his face. Frosty can beat *anyone*.

"Come on." Justin gives me another tug.

This time, as I allow him to lead me away, I glance back at Frosty. One last glance because…just because. I expect him to be locked in a conversation with one of his friends. Instead, his eyes are glued to me, his hands clenched at his sides.

He's angry? Why?

When Justin punches the security code into the back door, I force my attention to my feet. I didn't mind spying on Frosty when I thought he would try and hurt me, but I'm not being threatened right now and I don't want the ability to go places I'm not invited. Not here. Why flirt with temptation? Why make these people suspect me of wrongdoing? Well, more than they already do.

The new room is just as spacious and filled with even more equipment. Besides a punching bag and boxing ring, there's a row of treadmills, stair-steppers, elliptical machines and stationary bikes.

Love, Gavin and Jaclyn are instructing a group of eleven people to run the treadmill at top speed for two minutes, then move to the stair-stepper for another two, then the elliptical for another two, then the bikes. Then they have to do it all over again.

The recruits range in age from older teens to men and women in their midthirties. But no matter the age, these people have clearly never trained before, their stamina seriously lacking. The majority of them look as if they're about to go into cardiac arrest.

How did Cole—or whoever—find them? River and I used to hack names from databases in mental institutions, searching for anyone who sees monsters the rest of the world is too blind to notice.

Love smiles and waves at Justin. When she spots me, all hint of friendliness vanishes.

She's a beautiful girl with curly dark hair and brilliant green eyes. No wonder Chance is into her. Not that the two are officially dating, but really, it's only a matter of time. Chance has never chased after a potential conquest, or hung around an *actual* conquest this long. Love 'em and leave 'em, that's his usual style.

I should know.

I look at Justin. "Why did you bring me in here?" Not to introduce me to the recruits, that's for sure.

"I've been in your shoes, remember? I know you need to

burn off some dark emotion, and this is the perfect place to do it."

"Take five," Love announces, the recruits practically falling off the bikes. "What's she doing in here, Silverstone?"

I bristle, even as I wither.

"She's on our side now." Justin steps in front of me. "Cage the rage."

The recruits stare at me with open curiosity.

"Bathroom," one of the girls calls, disappearing into what looks to be a locker room. I catch the barest glimpse of her hair—jet-black, straight as a pen—swishing from a ponytail.

My heart skips a beat. Why such an extreme reaction?

Love growls, "Don't be a fool, Justin. She's here because she has nowhere else to go. The moment she gets a better offer she'll take off. *If* she survives the day."

"Is that a threat?" I ask.

Gavin crosses his arms. "Out," he barks at the recruits, and they quickly scurry from the room, following the same path the dark-haired girl took. When our group is alone, he points to the boxing ring. "Justin suggested you cage the rage, and I agree…only, I want you to do it in an actual cage."

I blink at him, incredulous.

Love rubs her hands together with glee. "Yeah. That's a very good idea."

"Ladies." Gavin waves to the ring. "If you'd be so kind as to climb inside, you may pummel each other to the death while the rest of us watch…and take bets on the winner."

11

Frosty

BE AT PIECE

I'm not sure what's wrong with me. I'm not Justin Silverstone's biggest fan, but he's not a bad guy. Despite the mistakes he made in his past, he recently helped us destroy Anima from the inside out. He's proven himself. And yet, the moment he put his arm around Camilla and turned on his megawatt smile, I've wanted to open him up from navel to nose, just to play Operation. Same way I reacted when the waiter touched her.

I think I'm on my period.

I stride to the ring where Cole and River are still hammering at each other. I remove my shirt and drop it on the floor.

"Woo-hoo," Ali calls. "Take it all off."

Ha! Looking at Cole, I hike my thumb behind my shoulder. "Out. It's my turn."

He struts over, pats me on the back. "Go easy on River. He's delicate."

River wipes a streak of blood from his cheek. "Last night I didn't go easy on your—"

"No mom jokes!" Ali shouts.

"Dad," River quips, and everyone snorts with laughter.

A side door opens and in strolls an older woman with silver-streaked black hair and kind brown eyes. Ali's grandmother. Everyone calls her Nana. She's carrying a tray of cookies and small plastic cups of milk.

"All right, everyone. Recharge with a snack," she calls.

"Are those chocolate chip?" Cole reaches her first and claims one.

"Oh, my goodness." Nana sets the tray aside and coos at the guy. "Cole, dear, you have a boulder-size knot on your jaw."

"River did it." Cole smirks at the guy. "And he insulted my mom. And my dad."

"River Marks." Nana shakes her head, as if her heart is actually breaking. "How could you be so rough? And so insensitive!"

River glares at Cole before bowing his head. "I'm sorry, Nana."

"The human body is like a flower. Treat it well, and it will bloom." She approaches the ring and extends two cookies. River and I accept with eager thanks. "Let's be kind to each other and keep our punches away from the face and groin."

"Yes, ma'am," we say in unison. Then, of course, we devour the offering as if we've never tasted sugar.

"Good, good." She brushes the crumbs from her fingers. "I'll leave you kids to your practice." She kisses Ali, then Cole, and leaves.

"Are you a rose?" River sneers at Cole. "Or a lily?"

"Orchid. And your jealousy is showing," Cole responds.

"I'm a weed." I crack the bones in my neck, then my knuckles. With as much pent-up aggression as I'm dealing with, I need an opponent that will fight as dirty as me. River fits the bill. I also have an urge to hurt him for hurting Camilla.

Dude. I shouldn't even like the girl, and now I want to defend her? Protect her? *Avenge* her?

"You ready for—" River begins.

I pop him in the mouth before he can finish his sentence. His lip splits in the center and blood trickles down his chin. He wipes the drops away and smiles with relish. A smile that only whets my appetite for more. More pain, more violence. I take another swing at him, but he's ready this time and ducks, coming up to nail me in the stomach. Air explodes from my lungs, pain shooting through me. When he draws back his elbow to take a double jab at my kidneys, I spin to the side... behind him...and elbow him in the spine. As he stumbles forward, I turn the rest of the way and kick him from behind.

Yeah, I'm that guy.

He lands on his face, but rolls forward and comes up to meet my new approach with a roundhouse kick, Chuck Norris style. Impressive. I'm the one who lands on my face this time, but like River, I don't stay down long. In a blink, I'm up and slamming a fist into his sternum. I think I hear bone crack.

"Man-meat in action!" Ali calls. "Hurt him! Hurt him so bad!"

I'm not sure which of us she's cheering for.

River circles me, his expression no longer tolerant and eager, but tense and dark. "You shouldn't have brought her here."

I don't have to ask who "her" is. "Oh, you claim her now? A minute ago, you looked through her as if she didn't exist."

His eyes slit, his black lashes practically fusing together. "She betrayed me, betrayed us all. What kind of leader would I be if I showed her favoritism?"

"Maybe she doesn't want a leader. Maybe she just wants a brother." And damn it, I'm not doing this. I'm not pushing her brother to forgive her when I will forever hold a grudge.

I nail him in the cheek, and his entire body rotates with the blow.

"That all you got?" he taunts.

I nail him with my other fist, sending him flying in the other direction. The dual forces make him dizzy, and he shakes his head. I use his distraction to my advantage and throw another punch. But he's expecting it, and he uses my own move against me, spinning to come up to my side...behind me...and elbowing me in the spine.

Adrenaline prevents me from feeling the pain—right now—but doesn't save me from a fall. My hands absorb my weight as I kick back with both my legs. Contact! River stumbles backward, hitting the rings. He bounces forward. I meet him in the middle, throwing a punch while winding my foot behind his ankle and tripping him.

"Not even close," I say.

He goes down, and I use my knees to immobilize his shoulders. He isn't so easily subdued and quickly bucks me off. I land on all fours. Outside the ring, I catch a glimpse of Ali standing beside Kat and a little girl I recognize only from pictures—Ali's dead sister, Emma. The three are talking, and none are smiling.

River drills a fist into the back of my head. As I go down, stars wink through my vision. I come up swinging, popping River so hard I'm pretty sure I break his nose. Oh, well.

Blood pours down his lips and chin, and his knees buckle. He howls in pain.

"Have Cole use *dýnamis* on you, and the injury will heal in minutes." Or a few days. Whatever. He'll heal faster than usual, and that's good enough.

"Kat." I jump over the ring, lowering the top rope with my weight while allowing my legs to soar over. "What's wrong?"

She wrings her hands as she focuses on me. "I just… I'm feeling guilty. Emma found out about— Well, she pointed out that doing to your enemy what your enemy did to you makes you a hypocrite. And she's right. I know the devastation such an action causes, and yet I'm doing it anyway."

"I don't understand. Doing what?"

"Anima…betrayal…"

I'm still lost. Feelings of guilt…taking a play from Anima's book… "Have you lied to me about something?"

"No. I've told you the truth."

"Are you worried about the company?"

"In a way. In the vision, Camilla saves you from a person, not a zombie. Why would a person unaffiliated with Anima attack you? They wouldn't. You're awesome."

"I hate to be the one to shatter your illusions about me, but I'll never be voted most likable. Lots of people unaffiliated with Anima would pay huge stacks of cash to hurt me. Plus, there could be a newly formed antislayer group. Or a previously unknown group. The government. Military. Or anyone, really."

"Well, it's still logical to consider the possibility that some part of Anima is still in business."

Emma clears her throat. "You're digressing, Kitty."

Hearing such a little girl use such a big word—*digressing*—is weird.

Kat shoos her away. "*Anyway.* You'll be voted whatever I want you to be voted. Nothing else. Meanwhile, wipe your face. You're bloody, and it's gross."

Before, whenever she called me gross, I yanked her against me and planted kisses all over her face. She squealed and I laughed. Now...the urge just isn't there. I think I've grown used to *not* touching her. Used to being kept at a distance and told I'm just a friend.

I love her, I'll always love her, but the intensity to be with her is gone.

The knowledge rips through me. I'm moving on. Starting the next chapter of my life. A chapter I never expected to start, and it's bittersweet.

"So...how are things with Camilla?" she asks, her tone light. Too light.

"She's not as bad as I thought." I won't mention the moments of attraction and jealousy. No good can come of it.

"Well, she's sucking at her job right now." Kat scans the room. "Where is she?"

Good question. At least half an hour has passed since she took off with Justin. I should probably go check on her.

When River opens the door that separates this room from the one holding Camilla and Justin, cheers ring out. Ali and Cole share a confused look before following River inside. I take a step forward to do the same, only to stop.

"Go." Kat waves me away. "I'm due back at court."

I don't say *I love you*. I just nod, and she's gone, that sense of bittersweetness only growing.

I barely make it through the door, which locks automatically behind me. Mental note: learn the codes.

Kids I know and kids I've never met surround a ring just like the one River and I used. As the cheers intensify, I scan the heads for familiar platinum and come up empty. Damn it, where is she?

"Kill her!" someone yells. "Make it hurt!"

Bets are flying. Five on Love...ten on Love. Five on Camilla.

What the hell?

I push my way through the crowd and curse. She's in the ring with Love, the two punching and kicking each other, and there's nothing catlike about it. There's no scratching, no hair pulling. Just sheer aggression. A battle for domination.

Both are bruised and bloody, but still steady on their feet, still throwing punches, ducking, throwing more punches. The problem is they aren't just fighting physically. After Camilla nails Love in the jaw, she pushes her spirit out of her body and punches *through* Love's jaw, hitting the girl's spirit. Love recovers fast and pushes out her own spirit to block Camilla's next blow. But Camilla is already back inside her body, throwing another punch.

I'm impressed. And maybe I'm a little proud—something I don't like. Love is my friend. Her defeat should not give me a thrill. "Twenty on Love," I call.

Camilla must hear my voice over all the others, because she stiffens and hesitates to make her next blow, allowing Love to land a double jab to her side. As Camilla gasps for breath she no longer has, I tighten my hands on the ring, fighting the urge to jump inside...and help her.

I don't know who I am anymore.

Gavin comes up beside me and grins a toothy grin. "Sweet, huh? I sent the recruits away, but they heard the commotion and begged for the opportunity to watch."

"You're an ass," I growl.

"That's not exactly an insult. A great ass is something *everyone* wants."

An alarm suddenly rings out, assaulting my ears. I cringe, everyone around me going still and quiet as they look around. The recruits begin to panic, spinning in circles. Trying to decide where to run?

"I'm going after Nana and your dad," Ali shouts to Cole.

He nods, knowing what I know. Someone tried to open a door they shouldn't. Everyone we trust already has access.

He throws orders at the others. I can't make out every word, but I get the gist. He wants some of us to escort the recruits to a safe room and the rest of us to search the house for an intruder.

Gavin and Jaclyn start gathering the recruits, pushing them underneath the ring, where there is, apparently, a trapdoor leading to a secret room in the basement.

My first thought is: *get to Camilla.* But as I step into the ring, I realize she's no longer there. Scanning the room, I see her race through the open door in back. To search for the intruder?

I take off after her, growing madder by the second. Waiting for backup can mean the difference between life and death.

I lift a revolver from a table of weapons and burst into—a hallway. The lights are out, the windows covered. Darkness greets me, but I never slow my step.

"Camilla," I shout.

"Cemetery girl…stop her…"

I can barely make out the words.

"Camilla," I shout again, increasing my speed. I pass through another door and grind to a stop. Damn it. I'm in a large ballroom that has eight other doors.

When I find her…

There's going to be trouble.

12

Milla

THERE WILL BE BLOOD

The girl who darted me at the cemetery is also a recruit. AKA the girl who went to the bathroom.

When she returned to the gym, she hung back in the doorway. Just in case. Our gazes locked, and when I gasped, she knew I knew her identity. I would have recognized BG's blue-black hair and freckled face anywhere.

That's when she pulled the alarm.

I almost ran her to ground a few minutes ago, but Frosty's first shout distracted me and she gave me the slip. And since she's been living here as a recruit, she knows what I don't—the layout of the house. Now all I can do is chase her shadow.

She makes it upstairs and hurries around a corner. Pursuing her, I end up in another hallway, this one a smorgasbord of doorways. Twelve in total, each one closed. My heart pounding as I stop, and my ears twitch as I listen.

"Camilla!" Frosty's voice echoes in the distance.

He sounds worried, but I know better. He wants to ensure I'm not planting bombs or selling secrets. Still, part of me longs to call out, to let him know I'm okay. But I don't. I don't want BG to pinpoint my location, and I don't know what BG will do now that she's been found out. Attack? Even dogs fight back when they're backed into a corner. I won't put Frosty at risk. I won't be the reason he's hurt.

As I move forward slowly, I keep my gun raised and my finger on the trigger. Hinges whine when I open the first door. I don't enter the room, just reach inside to flip on the light. An unfurnished bedroom, dust on the floor. No sign of footprints.

I continue onward, opening door after door, finding no sign of entry. Where the hell—?

A clatter of noise erupts at my left. I turn. A mistake. At my right, I catch a brief glimpse of a sweat-dampened face and dark hair—Bathroom Girl—before I feel a sharp sting in my neck. Suddenly I'm falling backward, falling down...landing with a hard thump and gasping for breath I can't quite catch. Warm liquid spills over me, soaking my shirt.

I drop the gun and reach up with hands now cold and shaking. They're instantly drenched by something warm and wet. My throat has been...cut?

Hurried footsteps cause the wood beneath me to vibrate. The slam of a door registers, as does realization. BG left me here, alone, to bleed out.

My lungs burn for air, any bit of air. I'm going to die, even though I've never really lived. It's the very fate I almost delivered to Ali, and I deserve it, I know I do, but I'm not ready. Not here, not now. Not like this. Not before I've saved Frosty.

Panic hits me, but it only makes my bleeding worse. Frosty could be… Fog drifts through my mind… Could be hurt… hurt, yes…oh! The pain. The burn. Hurt… I need to warn the others of the threat, but…but… And if I have any hope of survival, I need help, too. Help, yes… The fog is growing thicker by the second… Think, think…

I need…Frosty.

Yes! Frosty! He still hates me, but he wants me well so that Kat will continue to visit him. He's the only person who won't look at me and think "good riddance."

No, no, not true. Justin. He'll help me.

But I want Frosty.

As my strength dwindles and the burn rages on, I pat the ground for my gun. As soon as my fingers curl around the handle, I aim the barrel away from my body and squeeze the trigger. *Boom!* I try to fire again, but the muscles in my hand go lax.

A moment passes as I wait, an eternity.

Darkness begins to descend. I fight to remain conscious. This isn't the way it's supposed to end for me. Right? If I'm dead, how will I save Frosty? What will happen to him?

"Camilla!" Suddenly, frantic hands are pressing something, a cloth maybe, against my wound. "Who the hell did this to you?" He shouts for Cole… Bronx.

Bathroom Girl, I try to tell him, but no real sound emerges. I wish I could open my eyes, but I don't have the strength. *Cemetery. Darts.* Again, no words escape. Blood bubbles up my ravaged throat and gurgles from the corners of my mouth.

Frosty curses with a violence that might have made me grin in any other situation. A moment later, the cloth is gone.

"This is going to hurt," he says. "I'm sorry."

Behind my eyelids, I can see a sudden blaze of light. Heat wafts across the air between us. He's just summoned *dýnamis*?

Oh, yes. He has—and now he's pushing a part of his spirit inside my body, the way he does with zombies, letting the flames devour my heart. My lips part, a silent endless scream unleashed. My back arches, the fire blistering through me, charring everything. The pain…the pain…utterly unbearable, worse than anything I've ever endured. And I've had my throat slit! I'm melting. I have to be melting.

"What the hell happened?" Cole demands.

"I don't know," Frosty snarls. "Help her. The *dýnamis* has stopped the bleeding, but she's lost so much blood…too much. And damn it, the wound hasn't closed."

"Good glory no, no, no," Ali babbles. "This can't be happening. She's not supposed to die yet."

Yet?

Doesn't matter. What I considered unbearable a few seconds ago? I'm soon taught differently. The others push fiery hands into my spirit, and it's too much. The darkness covers my mind and I know nothing else…until strong arms slide underneath my shoulders and knees, lifting me.

The burn is gone, my body now boneless. I have no control as I float a thousand miles, the journey bumpy. I'm cradled against something hard and hot—Frosty's chest. I can feel the swift drum of his heartbeat, smell the deliciousness of his scent… Wait. I can smell! I'm breathing.

"This way." A girl's voice, familiar to me. Reeve, maybe. "Gently…yes, like that. Careful!"

More jostling.

"Milla? Milla!" River's voice now. "Damn it! Let me have her!"

The jostling stops, but the lack is jarring and my head wobbles, pulling at the skin on my throat. I whimper.

"Get out of my way," Frosty says.

"Give her to me," River demands. "Now."

"Get. Out. Of. My. Way." Frosty at his meanest. Most people would crap their pants in fear right now, but my brother isn't most people.

"I like you, my friend, but I will kill you to get to my sister."

"You won't live long enough to kill me," Frosty says. "Move or die. I'm going to save her, and you're in the way. Last chance."

The pain only increases as another warm gush of liquid trickles down my chest. I'm bleeding again, fog rolling back in, darkness on its heels, throwing me out of the present and into a hidden corner of my mind, where I've stored the worst of my childhood...

"You think you see monsters, little girl? I'll show you a monster." Spittle sprays from Daddy's mouth. He unbuckles his belt and slowly draws the leather from the loops. I know he's taking his sweet time on purpose, giving panic time to settle deep inside me.

When he finally takes his first swing, he ensures the buckle slams into my hip. Screaming, I scramble away from him, but he follows me and the blows just keep coming. Skin and muscles tear. Bones crack. As much as I hate this—fear this—I'd rather he hit me than Caroline. My twin. My love. My life.

She's weaker, and takes far longer to recover. Not just physically but mentally, too. I'm afraid her mind will one day break.

Just as my father draws back to deliver another blow, the scene morphs, and I'm suddenly trapped in a closet so dark I can't see my hand in front of my face. But it doesn't matter; I have to stay still and quiet. River said so, right before he rigged the handle so no one could open it without a fight. Through the door I hear my father screaming at my brother, calling him terrible names, demanding to know where I am. Caro's dead, and he wants me to take the blame. I'll spend a little time in juvie, he said, but if he's blamed, he'll spend the rest of his life behind bars.

I want him behind bars. He did it. He did it, he did it, he did it, and I hate him. I hate him so much I'm choking on it. And in that moment, I hate Momma, too. She left us to save herself, making everything worse for us.

She's as much a monster as Daddy.

Without her, Caro and I were supposed to be the women of the house. We're responsible for Daddy's breakfast, lunch and dinner. But Caro is a terrible cook, so I've been preparing the meals on my own. Problem is, we stayed in the park longer than I intended, waiting for the creatures from my nightmares to appear. I want Caro to see them, just once, so she'll know River and I aren't crazy, so she'll listen when we tell her to run and hide.

River even asked around town and met another boy—Mace—who told him we don't have to be afraid anymore, he can teach us how to fight.

I want to fight. No more helplessness. No more fear.

I just... I want to start this day over. I want to save Caro.

A crash shakes the foundation beneath me. I hear a thud, a whimper. The closet door is wrenched open, hinges broken, wood shards raining all around me. Light floods inside and my eyes tear against the brightness. Suddenly my father is standing before me, his features twisted with dark rage. I cower back, trying to hide behind the winter coats, but he finds me…and he grins.

"You can't hide from me, little girl."

"I'm not gonna do it." I crawl to the side. "I'm not gonna say I hurt Caro."

"You will."

I look away, not wanting to watch as he removes his belt. I see River lying on the floor. His eyes are closed, his lip split. There's a lump on his jaw. He's curled around Caro protectively, and he's still, so still. Is he dead, too?

Rage bubbles up inside me. Daddy killed my sister and maybe my brother. I hate him, I hate him, I hate him! Now, *I'll* kill *him*.

With a screech, I launch at him. I hit him with every bit of strength I possess, but it's not enough. He laughs and swings his fist at me.

The scene morphs, but this time, I'm not stuck in the past. The pain is gone. The fear is gone. I'm standing in an open field of light, surrounded by puffy white clouds. A sense of peace wraps around me, welcoming me. I breathe deeply, and oh, wow, the air is scented with spring rain and summer flowers, and it's a heady combination.

I'm… I frown. I'm connected to some sort of power grid, a million different thoughts seeming to stream through my mind at once. Thoughts I can't fathom. There is no begin-

ning and no end. There was, there is and there always will
be. Light triumphs over dark. The battle is already won, and
yet, the final battle hasn't even been waged. Present is one
with the future, and the past is wiped away. I have a purpose,
a destiny, but I've allowed petty emotion to block my way.

What *is* this place?

Kat appears in front of me, and she's shaking her head, adamant. She's no longer wearing the shirt and shorts I've seen
her in every time she's visited Frosty. Now a long white robe
drapes her short frame.

"No," she says, still shaking her head. "Your entrance is
denied. It's not yet your time."

Yet. There's that word again.

"Fight, Camilla. Fight." She shoves me backward, and we
actually connect. Her hands against my shoulders are solid. I
fall backward, losing the connection to the grid, the endless
stream of thoughts ceasing, the peace leaving me, the pain
returning, until my mind goes blank once again.

13

Frosty

EVERY END IS A NEW BEGINNING TO A NEW END

The panic I experienced when I found Milla…it's nothing compared to the panic I feel *now*. She's so pale, so still. Blood is splattered over her face. It soaks her neck and chest, and the sight of it brings back my worst memories.

I watched Kat die. I won't watch Milla do the same.

I've spent nearly a month with her. Every day. No exceptions. She's there when I wake up and she's there when I go to sleep. I've watched her interact with others and I've watched her fight zombies. She's strong. Amazingly strong. But like everyone else, she's fallible. Seeing her on the floor, cut open and bloody… Something inside me broke. The anger I've harbored toward her, maybe. Or what remains of my hate. All I felt was fear and desperation.

I haven't shaken either one.

When I get Milla into bed, the four people with me—Cole, Ali, Bronx and River—light up and push *dýnamis* into different parts of her body. Usually the pain of this rivals the pain of the wound, as bone, muscle and flesh weave back together, but Milla gives no reaction and my mouth goes dry.

She's still breathing. That's all the matters. Right?

"Our turn," Reeve says, and we back off. She and Dan Weber—a fortysomething surgeon who used to work with her dad—examine the wound and check Milla's vitals.

We opt not to take her to a hospital for several reasons. One, our fire is of more benefit to her than any medicine, whether it seems like it right now or not. Two, we can't risk the cops being called, and Milla being questioned about what happened. Three, what will the doctors do when she heals faster than humanly possible? Test her? Submit her name for further study? Four, we can't guard her the way I want her guarded anywhere but here.

"To borrow the word I've heard both of you use, *dýnamis* has already repaired her larynx," Reeve says, her relief palpable.

The surgeon, who is stitching Milla's throat, nods his agreement. "It's nothing short of miraculous." When he ties off the last stitch, he looks to River. "Do you have the same blood type as your sister?"

"Yes."

"Good, that's good. Siblings often do." Weber bustles around the room, gathering the supplies he needs. His hands are steady, his expression impassive.

Cole and Bronx carry a cushy chair into the room, and River sits. Weber sticks him with what looks to be an IV needle, but the tubes are then connected to a needle in Milla's arm, and blood is poured straight into her veins.

"Take as much as she needs." There are tears in River's eyes.

I think there are tears in mine.

"I'll take what's safe for you," Weber responds.

"No," he snaps. "You'll do what I tell you and take whatever's necessary."

Weber, like the rest of us, knows he's lashing out because of fear and offers no further comment.

Reeve checks everyone else's blood type, but only Ali is compatible. If necessary, I'll steal bags of O negative, the universal donor, from nearby hospitals.

"Get some rest," Weber tells River after he removes the tube. "I'll need you again once you're recovered."

"I'm not going anywhere," he says, the words slurred. His eyes are rolling around in his head, and I wonder if Weber gave him a sedative, or if the blood loss is to blame.

Reeve shoos away Ali and Cole. "Let's give the girl some space."

"I'll be in the hall," Bronx says, refusing to stray far from his girl.

She kisses his cheek, then looks me over, her brows raised. "You, too, Frosty. I'll monitor her and call you if there's a change."

I cross my arms over my chest. It'll take a crane to get me out, and even then it's iffy. Milla got hurt on my watch. I'm not letting anything else happen to her.

"Well, all right, then," she says with a sigh.

I'm not sure how much time passes before Milla begins to stir. Reeve and River are asleep, despite the frenzied beeping from the heart monitor.

"Caro," Milla whimpers. "So sorry. Should have... couldn't... I'm sorry."

River's eyelids pop open and he jolts upright.

Who is Caro?

I reach out to rub Milla's hand in comfort, but she screams and jerks away, severing contact.

"Don't touch her." River rushes over to draw me back. "Not when she's like this. It only makes the memories feel real."

Memories, not just nightmares.

Her head thrashes from side to side as she gasps out, "Daddy, no. Please, no. I'll be good. I swear I'll be good."

Sickness churns in my stomach. "She was beaten by Daddy Dearest, wasn't she?" She'd once alluded to it, but now I know for sure.

River tilts his head sharply. "He used to beat the shit out of us."

"And Caro?" I ask.

"Milla's twin, killed by our father. Don't ask either of us for more details. Just...don't."

She had a twin. A sister, loved and lost in the worst possible way. I can't even... Hell. No wonder she hangs on to River so staunchly, determined to keep the guy alive, whatever the cost. Having lost Kat, I'd do anything to save the loved ones I have left. Things I wouldn't have considered before.

I scrub a hand down my face. I've been the worst kind of hypocrite. Milla deserves far better than what I've dished to her.

"Is your dad still alive?"

"No." River combs a hand through his hair. "I'm going to find out who did this to my sister, and I'm going to make sure the body, when I'm finished with it, is never found. If I'm needed, call me and I'll return."

"You have my word. But I expect *you* to call *me* if you find the culprit. I'll help. Or I'll be your alibi."

Over the next handful of days, we're treated to many more screaming episodes from Milla and all but one revolves around her father. The other is about some guy named Mace. She sobs over him as if he ripped out her heart and stomped on it with cleats.

I want Mace to occupy the same grave as her attacker.

I hate that she's trapped in such a terrible past, but at least she's on the mend.

Cole comes by at least once a day to speak with me. He's locked up the recruits who weren't in the gym when the alarm went off. He's questioned them, but each passes a lie detector test. We have no clues, nothing to narrow the list of suspects. The mystery is driving me to the brink. Who did this to Milla, and why?

During the chase, Milla mentioned "cemetery girl." How would the girl who'd shot darts into her get inside the mansion without being a recruit? *Is* she a recruit, or are we chasing the wrong lead?

I trust my friends and no one else. I've left Milla's side only long enough to shower and snack. And only while a guard is stationed at her bed.

Kat has visited me every day, but I've been miserable company.

"Do you care about her?" she asked just this morning. "Her life matters to you?"

"I don't want her dead." It is the truth, and yet, it isn't the full truth. I'm not sure how I feel about Camilla anymore. "It's hard to hang on to anger when you learn the nuts and bolts that make her tick."

Kat stared at her feet, saying nothing, radiating guilt... Why?

"Her twin...Caro...is she a witness?" I asked.

"No. Caroline chose to leave the holding zone years ago and step into the Rest."

So. Milla wouldn't receive any comfort on that front. "What about her father?"

"He didn't go up."

"I'm happy to say Milla is going to make a full recovery," Reeve announces, pulling me from my thoughts. "The drugs will leave her system in a day or two, and she'll wake."

I'm in the chair beside the bed, and Reeve is standing on the other side. Sweat is beaded on her brow, and her usually brown skin is chalk white.

"You don't look one-hundred-percent convinced of what you're telling me."

"How I look has nothing to do with Camilla. I'm just not feeling well. The flu is going around."

"Maybe you should go lie down. And not touch the patient. If she gets sick while she's in this state..." I'll be ticked.

"I'm wearing gloves. See?" She waves her latex-covered hands. "I just... I want to help her. I know she did some bad things, but after hearing her beg her father not to hurt her, after seeing her scars, I just want to make things better for her."

"Yeah." I know exactly what she means.

"We should—oh, crap." Her eyes go wide as she clutches her stomach. She darts to the wastebasket and vomits breakfast.

Gloves can't stop the spread of airborne germs. "Get out. Now." I'm done being nice about it.

I'm pushing to my feet as Bronx rushes into the room. Anytime Reeve is in here, I can count on the fact that he's in the hall. He's always been protective of her, but because she's treating Milla, he's been taking it to the extreme. I get it, I do, but I'm suddenly irritated by it. Milla is practically in a coma. What harm could she really do?

"You okay, baby?" He looks as sick as Reeve as he winds his arms around her.

I— Damn. A heat wave washes over me, and I shift in the chair. Did someone screw with the thermostat? A moment later, I'm so dizzy I nearly topple to the floor. My stomach flips over, waves of acid eating at the lining.

"You caught it," Reeve manages to say.

"We all have," Bronx replies. "Cole and Ali have been hunched over a toilet for the past hour."

"Out," I say. "Get out, and take the vomit basket with you. We shouldn't be in here, exposing Milla." Though my strength is hemorrhaging at an alarming rate, I get the pair into the hall and shut the door, sealing Milla inside the room and our germs—hopefully—outside it.

Milla

DEATH, INTERRUPTED

A sharp sting accompanies the searing pressure on my neck and my eyelids pop open. I'm in a small room, surrounded by medical equipment. I'm lying on top of a gurney, sweating, panting and aching.

"Don't move," Ali says with a rasp I've never heard from her. "I'm just checking your progress." She finishes peeling back the bandage and nods with satisfaction. "You're healing nicely."

I remember the slash of Bathroom Girl's blade and cringe. "Frosty," I say. The vibrations hurt my throat, but it's a pain I welcome. It says, *You're alive.* "He's okay?"

"Yeah. He's fine. He saved your life. Used *dýnamis*—cool word, by the way. We all used it on you, actually."

Yes. I remember that, too. "Was anyone else hurt?"

"No. Only you." She carefully slathers ointment over my wound. "Cole's dad took my grandmother on vacation. We're not exactly one-hundred-percent sure what's going on, but we're not taking any chances with her life."

I frown. Not only is Ali's voice jacked up, but she's also pale and her cheeks hollow, as if she's lost weight. Her hair is limp and tangled and in need of a good wash. "Something happened to you."

"The rest of us have been stricken by some kind of flu, but we're finally on the mend."

"I think you left your sickbed a little too soon."

"Well, I knew you'd be waking up and I wanted to talk to you."

"About?" I ask.

"Do you remember that coded paper I once translated for you?"

"Yes." I got it from Anima. Stole it, actually. At the time, I was doing everything they asked of me, while still working to take them down. I'd gone in to give a report of my progress—the higher-ups believed face-to-face meetings would scare me and keep me in line—and I'd seen a stack of papers covered in symbols. Judging by the notes made in the margin, the employees were trying to translate and failing.

I hid as many sheets as I could under my clothing, but I had no luck translating the code, either. Then Ali came along. She and Cole had answers in minutes. Apparently they had an entire book filled with the same code. A journal written by Ali's however-many-greats grandfather, a slayer who'd seen into the far distant future.

"Well," Ali says, "the journal has fifty-three blank pages— used to be a hundred, but every so often, new passages just appeared. We think we see only what we're ready to see. Anyway. While you were recovering, a new passage appeared, and I think it applies to you."

This could be good. Or this could be very, very bad. "What does it say?"

She closes her eyes and recites, "'Two fires burn. The light and the dark. One purifies, one destroys and the two never coexist in harmony. One is truth, and one is lies, lies, the darkness lies. But it's not too strong, never too strong, for light cannot be extinguished by dark, only covered, covered, covered, but dark can always be chased away by light. Look inside...look inside.'"

She opens her eyes. I wait for her to say more. She doesn't.

"Well. That's not cryptic *at all*."

"Frosty told us about your nightmare. The red flames. Red must represent the dark, the destruction, while white—*dýnamis*—represents light, the purification."

Light cannot be extinguished by dark, only covered, covered, covered. "Why repeat different words?"

"Another excellent question."

With no real answer apparently. "This is a lot to take in." Especially now, when I'm so unsteady. "As fast as my mind is whirling, I'm almost afraid I'll pop a vessel."

She takes pity on me and says, "We'll put this on the back burner for now and move on. Did you see who did this to you?"

"A girl. The one I saw in the cemetery. The one who went to the bathroom after bicycling. Gavin and Love will know who I'm talking about." My stomach rumbles, and I use what little strength I possess to rub away the hunger pangs. "She has blue-black hair. It's long, reaches her waist. Her skin is freckled and her face—"

"Yeah. I know who you're talking about." Ali adheres a new bandage to my neck. "Tiffany Reynolds."

I arch a brow in question. "You can't leave it at that. Tell me everything about her, everything that happened."

"Okay, so, there's no area outside this compound without a camera. Bronx checked our security feed and discovered no one had snuck in. We figured this had to be an inside job. We ruled out the kids who were underground with Gavin and Jaclyn. That left eight others. We kept those eight sequestered as we waited for you to recover."

Smart. I would have done the same.

"Two days ago, we made the announcement you would recover fully and Tiffany sedated the guards—Justin and Gavin—and snuck out. Apparently she'd hidden syringes full of different kinds of drugs all over the house. Anyway, the rest of us were too sick to stop her. In fact, she's the only one in the house who didn't get sick, which makes us suspect we didn't have the flu, after all, that she drugged us."

"She knew I could identify her as Cemetery Dart Girl. But why shoot me up with mutated zombie toxin in the first place?"

Ali sighs. "We don't know. We can only guess. Revenge, maybe. She could have worked for Anima once, or known someone who did and lashed out at you to even the score."

"Why try to kill me specifically, though? Why not go after the rest of you while she had the chance?"

"Believe me, I've asked myself those same questions."

I get more comfortable against the pillows, though my stomach is still rumbling, and look myself over. I'm wearing a loose-fitting T-shirt and I'm braless. Under the covers, my legs are bare. I won't ask who changed my clothes. And I seriously won't ask who inserted the catheter and got an up-close-and-personal glimpse of my lady bits. Not to mention my scars.

"How did you recruit Tiffany?"

"We took River's advice and trolled online message boards looking for people who claimed to see ghosts and monsters. There were more than we ever imagined, and once we had names, we were able to do background checks. We approached the ones we liked."

I wait for more details.

Ali doesn't disappoint. "Tiffany is seventeen and lives with her mom. Low income. Her dad took off a few years ago. She's homeschooled and a straight D student. Antisocial most of her life, but never in trouble with the law."

I want to hate her. But do I have the right? She tried to kill me, and I once tried to kill Ali.

"I'm so sorry," I say. "For what I did to you... I was wrong in every way."

She studies my face and whispers, "I believe you, and I forgive you."

That easily? I'm not used to such understanding, and it throws me.

"There's something I have to tell you, Camilla."

"Milla," I counter. The day we met, she'd called me Milla, and I'd nearly snapped her head off. A nickname reserved solely for my friends, I'd said. I could so-o-oo kick my own ass.

She nods. "Milla. There's something I have to tell you about the vision I had. I promised Kat I wouldn't talk about it, and I never break my promises, but I shouldn't keep quiet. Should I? Emma doesn't think so. But good glory! This is tough. A rock and a very hard place."

"Just say it," I tell her. "It'll be okay, whatever it is."

She licks her lips. "I've only seen bits and pieces of this particular future. A woman aims a gun at Frosty, just like I told you. I don't see her face, only her hand."

"Kat already gave me those details."

"Yes, but—"

A knock sounds at the door, and Frosty sticks his head in the room. "May I come in?"

My heart immediately speeds into a wild gallop. A fact the monitor attached to my chest embarrassingly proclaims. As my cheeks burn, I reach up to smooth my hair into place. When I realize I'm primping for him, I stop and frown.

"Do you have food?" I ask.

He gives me the barest glimpse of a smile before fully entering the room. "Some people would say I'm man-candy."

My heartbeat increases. With a screech, I rip the electrodes off my chest. "Some people...or you?"

Ali pats my hand. "We'll continue our conversation another time." She stands a little too hastily, and she's out the door before I can stop her, leaving me alone with the boy who saved me even though I ruined his life.

My crush.

I like him. The truth is suddenly undeniable. I *like him* like him. A lot. He's pretty and he's strong. He's smart and he's witty. He's charming when he needs to be and violent when he has to be. He's honorable, and when he loves, he loves with his entire heart.

To find the right person for you, you have to be the right person. I am not that person. Could I be any stupider? To him, I'll never be anything more than Kat's killer.

I study him. His dark blond hair is unkempt, a wild tangle around his unshaven face. Golden stubble dusts his jaw. His clothes are clean but wrinkled.

"I'm glad you're here," I say and blush. Wow. Talk about lame.

"Me, too," he replies, sitting in the chair Ali vacated. "How are you feeling?"

"Better." I nibble on my bottom lip. "Thank you for saving me."

He shifts, clearly uncomfortable. "You were dumb, chasing after a stranger in a strange place on your own."

O-kay. Not going to pull his punches. Got it. "There wasn't time—"

"There's *always* time. Safety first, everything else second. Your life is—" He stops.

Silence crackles. "Is…?" I prompt as my stomach twists nervously; I know the direction he's headed, but some part of me hopes for something better.

"Needed," he says, and I'm deflated.

He saved my life because I'm needed. Because I'm a means to an end.

As suspected. Nothing's changed between us. Nothing ever

will. Except…the way he's looking at me right now, with relief and something else, something I can't name. "Why are
you here, Frosty?"

"To talk. So let's talk."

15

Frosty

A SERIES OF UNFORTUNATE EVENTS

She looks good. Color has returned to her cheeks. The *dýnamis* I fed her spirit every day before getting sick sustained her spirit, soul and body, thank God, keeping her from wasting away.

A white bandage stretches from one side of her throat to the other, a stark reminder of the open, gushing wound that would have killed anyone else. Had I found her a few seconds later, she *would* have died.

"What do you want to talk about?" she asks.

"Did I say talk? My bad. I meant threaten. If you ever again run off on your own, I'll put you over my knee and spank the bad decisions right out of you."

Her eyes narrow to tiny slits. "If you ever threaten me again, I'll hollow out your liver and fill it with rocks."

I smile. "Nice." This is the most relaxed I've been all week. I haven't been eating, haven't been sleeping. I've just been worrying that the girl placed in my protection wasn't going to live to see another sunrise. "But you know rushing off is a habit, and it needs to stop."

She opens her mouth to reply, but I shake my head, adding, "Just zip it and enjoy your lollipop." I pull the candy from my pocket. "Or maybe you'd rather watch *me* enjoy it?"

She licks her lips, the sight of her little pink tongue causing something to clench low in my gut. "Gimme."

I've been carrying the stupid thing in my pocket for days, desperate to give it to her. As a kid, Cole had given me a piece of candy anytime I'd gotten hurt. Funny thing. I always felt better.

"You were a good patient, healing like you were told—" I toss her the treat "—and you deserve a reward."

I just wish her inner wounds had healed. I ache for the little girl she was and now I understand the woman she's become. A woman willing to do anything to protect her brother. As children, they'd had each other, no one else. Part of them still had to feel that way.

As her tongue flicks over the candy, her eyes close in surrender—and I discreetly adjust my pants.

"This has to be the best thing in the entire world," she says.

"Did your mom ever give you a lollipop to make you feel better?"

"No. She didn't do anything without my dad's permission, and he considered candy a privilege we hadn't earned."

I'm suddenly thankful for what little time I had with my adoptive parents. I might have felt like the odd man out, but I always knew they loved me. They kissed and hugged me anytime I cried—not that I cried, because I was manly, even back then. They gave me a warm bed to sleep in, clean clothes to wear and always helped me with my homework. I had a safe place to go.

Safe. The word echoes in my mind. "Milla…I'm sorry," I say, the words bursting out of me. "I'm sorry I brought you here and failed to protect you."

She smiles at me, and it makes the clench in my gut a thousand times worse. "I'm here to protect you, remember? Not the other way around."

"I can take care of myself."

"Yeah, well, so can I."

I wave a hand to indicate the medical equipment surrounding her. "I won't state the obvious."

She flips me off, a double-birded salute. "Doesn't matter. You're proving my point for me. If *I* need help occasionally, when I'm a way better fighter, you *definitely* need help."

"Well, well, aren't you a little ray of sunshine," I say with a wink.

She gapes at me, as if she can't believe what she's seeing. "*Anyway.* I remember hearing my brother's voice. Is he waiting to see me?"

I don't know how to soften the truth, so I give it to her point-blank. "He left." I would have joined him, but I took up the mantle of guard, just in case Tiffany tried to come back to finish what she started.

She withers against the mattress. "Of course he did."

"It's not what you—" If she learns River is hunting Tiffany, she'll try to leave her sickbed before she's ready and go after him. "He loves you. He'll be back."

She gives me a sad smile while stroking her Betrayal tattoo, and damn if it doesn't break my heart.

I switch gears. "I saw you with Love. You're pretty good with your fists."

"No. I'm *great*," she says. "I let her get in a few knocks because she had some anger to exorcise, but any other time, I would have laid her flat without taking a single blow."

"Confident."

"With reason."

"Or just plain cocky."

"Well, why not?" she says. "It's not bragging if it's true."

A point I can't refute.

"What's happened while I've been out?" she asks. "With zombies, I mean. Any sightings?"

"A patrol went out every night except the past three. We were all too sick to leave the house. No zombie clouds and no zombies." I reach over before I realize I've moved and squeeze her fingers. "I'm glad you're okay."

Frowning, she stares down at our hands—I love the contrast of my deep tan against her light bronze. "I know why you saved me. Kat. But she's not the reason you're here right now, offering me candy and chatting me up like we're old pals. What's going on with you, Frosty? You're being nice, and I'm not sure I like it."

"Look," I say and sigh. Why not put it all out there? "You made a mistake in an effort to protect your brother. You're not a bad person, and you're trying to make up for the pain you caused us. I respect that. You aren't my favorite person, but I don't hate you."

"Do you…?" She twists the covers, suddenly nervous. "Do you want to be my friend?"

I tilt my head to study her more intensely. "I don't know." Is friendship possible for us?

I learned a lot about her while she recovered. She's strong yet vulnerable. She's hard as stone yet tenderhearted. She's supersmart yet blinded by love. She's whole yet broken.

She's a walking contradiction—and I'm utterly fascinated with her.

Unlike Kat, she hasn't yet learned her worth. I haven't helped with that. None of us have.

Hell, maybe I do want to be her friend. "How about we give it a try, see how it goes?"

"I'd like that," she says softy. A beat passes in silence as she peers over at me. "And Frosty? Thank you. For everything."

"You would have done the same for me." I rub the back of my neck, uncomfortable by the turn of the conversation. "Before I forget, I should warn you. While Ali and Cole have learned to control what abilities they share, I haven't. I'm sure I passed different things to you—like a spiritual STD. I don't know what, and I don't know how or when the abilities will manifest."

Her jaw drops. "You're saying I might be able to cast zombies in the air with a bolt of energy? Or cover other people's memories? Or heal from Z-toxin without the antidote? Seriously?" A grin spreads from ear to ear. "Talk about a silver lining to almost dying."

Actually, she *did* die. Her heart stopped, and I broke her sternum while performing CPR. Thankfully, the fire healed that, too. "It's not exactly a fair trade-off."

"Agree to disagree. Whatever makes me stronger, faster, *better*, I'll go to hell and back to get."

I can guess why. Helplessness is her kryptonite.

Great. Now I want to hug her. I stand instead. "I've bugged you enough. I'll let you rest." I stalk to the door, only to pause. "Hey. Can I ask you a question?"

"You just did."

"Ha. Funny." I rub the back of my neck, realize I'm doing it and frown. It's a habit—a tell—I picked up from Cole. Uncomfortable, rub. I don't face her. I don't want to watch her expression change. Don't want to ache anymore. "What happened to your dad?"

Silence.

Then… "Why?" Her voice is heavy with tension.

"River told me he's dead. I'm curious about the details."

"River told you… Well. He doesn't share even those details very often. Or ever. Dad was…he was murdered."

By who? River? Or maybe Milla herself? Did their abuser finally push them too far? I want to ask, but I'll be delving into extremely personal territory. Hell, I already have. But the further I go, the more answers I'll owe her about my own life. I can't give her what I've only ever given Cole and Kat. I just can't.

"Your weapons are on a tray beside the gurney. There will be a guard I trust outside your door at all times, and I'll make sure you're given a phone. Call me if you need anything."

"You're leaving the mansion?"

"Yeah. There's something I have to do." I place my hand on the knob, but once again I stop. I have another question, and I don't want to leave until I know the answer. "In your sleep you said a name. Mace."

She sucks in a breath, hurt she can't hide suddenly gleaming in her eyes.

"Who is he?"

"The only boyfriend I ever loved," she says quietly, and something dark curls through me.

"Where is he now?"

"Dead. Like Kat." She smiles at me, but the expression lacks any kind of humor. "You and I have something in common. We both lost our happily-ever-after."

I want details. I have to know everything. It's suddenly a compulsion, an obsession I can't explain. But when I open my mouth to ask, she whispers, "Just go. Please."

I've stepped on a land mine of bad memories, and she's done hurting for me. If we were together I could keep pressing; I could carry some of the hurt for her, could help her heal. But we aren't, and I can't.

I leave her then, and find Cole waiting in the hall. "Ali wants to talk with you about the vision she had involving Milla."

"Something change?"

"I'm told you may get hurt even if you're saved."

Physical pain? Big deal. "A chat will have to wait. I'm about to arm up and head out."

"Fair enough. Need anything?"

"Yeah. Do me a solid and station Bronx at Milla's door. And if you have extra cell phones, give her one and text me the number."

He grins at me, slowly, slyly. "It's nice to see you again, my friend. Very nice."

"What does that mean? You've seen me every day for a week."

"Yeah, but this is the first time I've seen *you*. Also, I approve of your hunt for Tiffany." Cole knows me well. "I've been in contact with River. He's staked out in front of her house. She hasn't visited her mom since she escaped, but..."

A dog never strays too far from home.

"We'll take care of her," I say, relish in every word.

16

Milla

COFFIN FOR THREE, PLEASE

I throw my legs over the side of the bed and stand. My knees shake—a ten on the Richter scale—but I manage to remain upright. Another day has passed. Eight in total that I've been stuck flat on my back, and I'm not spending another second that way.

Earlier, Reeve removed the tubes and ran more tests. No matter how much antidote she introduced to samples of my blood, the zombie toxin remained. Except, I'm not rotting. I'm not changing. She's not sure what's happening to me exactly, which makes me think the toxin is working on a spiritual level and the changes simply haven't manifested physically. Yet.

It worries me big-time, but I won't let myself wallow. There are things to do and people to save. Whatever happens to me, well, it happens.

As soon as I'm steady, I release the bed rail. I stay on my

feet and even manage a shuffle-walk to the bathroom. Win! There's a pile of clean clothes resting by the sink, and for a moment all I can do is gape. Someone anticipated my needs and cared enough to follow through.

These slayers...they really are good people. The best. I never should have betrayed them.

A hot shower invigorates me, and by the time I step out to dry off, I feel human again. I dress in a T-shirt that reads Wanna Taste? and a pair of shorts with pockets deeper than the hemline.

I exit the bathroom on a cloud of fragrant steam and find Ali and Kat perched on my gurney, a dark-haired little girl dressed in a pink tutu twirling in front of them.

The ballerina stops when she notices me. "Hi." She smiles. "I'm Emma."

"My little sister, in case you didn't know," Ali says. "She's a witness, like Kat."

"Actually, I'm the *best* witness." Emma performs a pirouette.

"Sorry, Em, but I held a vote." Kat stands and anchors her hands on her waist. "I won by a landslide. You need to accept it."

"We tied, *Kitty*. You voted for you, and I voted for me."

"Right, but as the adult, I had to break the tie. After a completely unbiased deliberation, I had to go with myself."

"Anyway," Ali says with a fond smile. "We heard you stirring." There's more color in her cheeks today, but she's still paler than usual. "You shouldn't be up and about yet."

"You probably shouldn't, either, considering you've been sick, and yet here you are."

She sighs. "Yeah, that's what I thought you'd say. Here."
She holds out a cell phone. "Frosty wants you to have this."

I accept the device, my heart picking up speed. There's a
text from Frosty waiting for me.

Stay in bed & see my smile. Get up & see my wrath.

I smile. I just can't help myself. My fingers fly over the tiny
keyboard before my brain registers I'm messaging him back.
Show me UR smile & I'll show U mine. Show me UR wrath &
I'll break UR face.

Send.

His reply comes a few seconds later. Still hoping 2 knee my
balls in2 my throat, I C ;)

I snort. Not because of what he said, but because Frosty
the Ice Man just winked at me via text.

"What?" Ali asks, and I jerk guiltily.

"Oh, uh, nothing. What were we discussing?"

There's a knowing tightness around Kat's eyes, and I understand. I do. She might be pushing Frosty at other girls,
random girls, but she'll never push him at me.

"You've healed even faster than abnormal," she says.

I'm about to reply to her when a vague recollection of
standing in front of her flashes through my mind. I frown.
"Did I go to heaven...and did you shove me out?"

Emma jumps up and claps. "Sweet! You remember. Did
you see me? Huh, huh? I was there. I got to watch."

"You were in the holding zone, and yes, I shoved." Kat flips
her dark hair over her shoulder. "You're welcome."

"I liked it there," I admit.

"Too bad. It wasn't your time."

Interesting. "Are you saying everyone has a fated time to die, and nothing and no one can change it?"

"No way, no how. Free will…disease…mistakes…bad judgment and a thousand other things can kill a person long before their time. But I'd already petitioned the court for your life. And before you ask, time is different up there."

Petitioned? Court?

"One day can equal a thousand years," Emma says, "and a thousand years can equal a day. Go ahead, try doing the math. I dare you."

A bazillion more questions fill my head.

"Milla," Ali says, "if you're up for it, I'd like to teach you how to use and control whatever new abilities you've acquired."

There's a vibration in my pocket, and I know Frosty just responded to my last text. I want to read the screen so badly I can taste it, but I don't. Not here. Not now. Not until the urge to flirt with him has faded.

"I'm on board. Thank you."

"Uh-oh." Kat tilts her head, her hazel gaze far away. The same transformation overtakes Emma. "I'm sensing something *not fun* on the horizon. I'm gonna go check it out."

The two spirits are gone a second later.

"Come on." Ali waves me over and opens the door.

I grab a blade from the nightstand before I trail after her. I'd rather go naked than go without a weapon. "I wonder what they sensed."

"Could be anything from one of us breaking a finger to

all of us dying. We won't know till we know, so until then, there's no use fretting about it."

Bronx is waiting for us in the hall, and without a word, he tracks after us.

"What's with the shadow?" Is the threat level so high that Cole wants his Ali-gator guarded at all times?

"Before Frosty left, he asked Bronx to look after you," Ali says.

Pleasure warms me—I'm not just a means to an end, I can't be—only to dissipate. He's a good guy, and I can't read more into his actions. He hated that I got hurt on his watch, in a place he brought me, and he's taking measures to ensure it doesn't happen again. That's it.

I glance back at Bronx. "You're dismissed, soldier." I don't want Frosty receiving a report of all the things I do wrong. "Your services are no longer needed."

He doesn't glance at me, and he doesn't reply.

Great. We're playing Milla Is Invisible.

Ali laughs as she tugs me down the stairs. "When I first met Bronx, he didn't speak to me for several months. This is his observe-and-learn stage. Just let him do his thing, and you'll be better for it." She stops in the gym reserved for recruits, the one with treadmills and stationary bikes. Right now, however, we're the only people— Oops, spoke too soon.

Gavin has Jaclyn pressed against a wall in a shadowed corner. They're kissing as if the world is set to end tomorrow. As if they're starved for each other. The way Frosty used to kiss Kat.

The way I've *never* been kissed, not even by Mace. I loved that boy with every fiber of my being, and he loved me, too...

or so I'd thought. He used to tell me I was so young, only fifteen to his nineteen, we needed to keep our relationship a secret. Not long after his death, I learned he'd loved other girls in secret, too. A lot of other girls.

Now, looking back, I can see my feelings were more about hero worship than love. Mace taught River and me how to fight zombies—and our dad. How to do whatever was necessary to survive the streets and thrive.

I didn't lie to Frosty about believing Mace was supposed to be my happily-ever-after. I believed it the day I met him up until the day he died. It was the day after his death that I began to suspect the truth: I'm supposed to end up alone.

Since Mace, my handful of boyfriends were more concerned with leaping straight into sex than any kind of relationship, and I let myself get caught up in their haste because I wanted to be wanted. And for a little while, I was. It felt good. But then the sex ended, and the guys took off, and I was left hurting even more than before.

Now a pang of longing cuts through me. I want to be kissed like Gavin is kissing Jaclyn. I want to be cherished. I want to be someone's treasure.

I want to be something worth fighting for.

"Seriously, guys," Ali calls. "We're supposed to be examples, not reenacting porn."

The two leap apart. Jaclyn even slaps Gavin across the face, though the action lacks any kind of force. "Pervert! Don't come near me again."

"Don't worry," he sneers, rubbing his cheek. "I'll wait until you beg me for it. Again."

"You'll be waiting forever." Jaclyn storms out of the room.

Gavin glares at Ali. "As usual, cupcake, your timing sucks." He walks over and bumps fists with Bronx, who then takes a post against the wall, arms crossed over his chest. "You can make everything up to me by telling me you and princess are about to oil-wrestle."

"How about I tell you the truth instead? After Milla runs the treadmill for half an hour, you're going to be our test dummy and she's going to practice using her new abilities. Congrats!"

"I'm not sure how we're still friends." He sets one of the treadmills to the highest incline. "But at least I'm your favorite."

"I don't have a favorite man-friend." Ali smiles sweetly at him. "I dislike you all equally. Now hush."

I snicker, liking this girl more every time she opens her mouth.

Gavin focuses on me and arches a brow. "You got something to say to me, princess?"

"Yeah. Why did I get the name *princess*? And do you realize you're a douche-canoe?"

He waves his arms in the air, as if he's the last sane man in the universe. "What's with the chicks in the place, man? They spit on my best moves."

"These are your best moves?" I climb onto the treadmill. "How sad for you."

His eyes twinkle merrily as he presses the on button. "I hope you enjoy this. I know I will."

The machine lifts to its highest incline, the belt at my feet churning faster and faster, until I'm sprinting. Soon sweat is beading over my entire body, my chest and thighs burning.

But it's a burn I welcome. I'm used to working out daily. Before saving zombies became a thing—a practice I'm not sure I'll ever willingly support—an out-of-shape slayer was a dead slayer.

"By the way. I'm making you run for a reason." Ali moves beside the machine. "I want to exhaust you so that only the barest power remains active. That way, if any of your new abilities go haywire, you'll cause less damage to yourself and others."

Makes sense. Normally I can run at this speed and this incline for an hour and still do a few victory laps around the room. Today, not so much. By the end of the half hour, I'm drenched in sweat and shaky, wheezing for breath.

Ali throws me a jug of water. I reach, but I'm as slow as molasses now and it soars past me. Dang. I give chase and drain the contents, the cool liquid heaven to my abused body.

"All right. Phase one complete. Time for phase two, where we kick things up a notch. Gavin, Milla, climb into the ring and stand there and there." Ali points to two spots on the matt. "Gavin, you're going to play the part of mindless zombie, so just act like yourself." Looking at me, she says, "Milla, you're playing the part of determined slayer. Run to him and light up."

Run? Moaning, I set the empty water jug on the bench next to the row of lockers. My legs scream in protest as I climb over the ropes to join Gavin inside.

"Shouldn't we take a cookie break first?"

"What are you waiting for? An engraved invitation?" He waves his fingers at me. "Let's do this."

"Stop using words. Mindless grunts only," Ali calls.

"Bra-a-a-ains," he says in a singsong voice.

"Better." I jog toward him—it's all my thousand-pound limbs can manage—and push my spirit out of my body at the halfway point. I summon *dýnamis*, something I've done a million times, even while exhausted, but nothing happens. Not even a flicker.

He tsks. "If I *was* a zombie, you'd already be dinner."

I check my internal faith-o-meter. It's full. I know I can do this. So...what's the prob?

"Come on. Do it again," Ali commands.

I turn my hands over in the light, part of me expecting to see the flames I don't feel. If I can't fire up, I can't kill zombies. If I can't kill zombies, I might as well curl up and die. It's all I'm good at—all I'm good for.

Okay, so maybe my faith-o-meter isn't actually full. Fear is a drain and it can empty an ocean of faith in seconds.

"Again," Ali repeats.

I'm fighting for breath as I backtrack. *Calm. Steady.* I can do this. I know I can do this.

Again, Gavin waves his fingers. I jog toward him, every cell in my body willing *dýnamis* to come...but once again the flames fail to appear.

"Again."

I remain in place. What's wrong with me? Why is this happening? I'm the same girl I've always been. The only difference is the toxin now swimming through my—

The toxin!

"Tiffany!" A bomb of rage detonates inside me, just boom, and bolts of emotion explode *out* of me. I stumble back as if I've been pushed, heat consuming me in an instant.

"Milla," Gavin shouts. "Enough! You have to stop."

His voice sounds as if it's being filtered through a long tunnel. I turn toward him, but he's not standing where he was—because he's not standing at all. He's floating in the freaking air. I can't make out his features; his image is too distorted through the flames. *Red* flames. Deep, angry red. The color of congealing blood. The color of my dreams.

Only, this is real and I'm not dying.

Am I? I'm weak, so weak, and only growing weaker.

Crap! Crap, crap, crap. What did the journal passage say before? Two kinds of fire. One destroys, one purifies. Obviously, the red destroys. But what else, what else?

Covered, covered, covered. Yes. Right. Darkness can only cover light. So, if red represents dark and white represents light, *dýnamis* might still be inside me, simply covered. If I can uncover it, I can stop this.

My limbs shake as more and more energy seeps out of me. Just how am I supposed to uncover the white flames?

Frantic, I try dismissing *thánatos*…it crackles, spreads and sings, soon blistering every inch of me.

"Milla!" Ali's voice is filtered through the same tunnel. And like Gavin, she's floating several feet in the air. She's curled into herself and clutching at her ears, as if she's battling the worst kind of pain.

I'm doing this? I'm hurting her? Hurting Gavin?

Crap! There's a third body in the air. I'm hurting Bronx, too?

I have to stop, now, now, freaking *now*, but the more I fight the flames, willing them to go away, the hotter and higher they grow. What should I do? What the hell should I do? I stumble to my body to brush spirit against flesh. In an instant, the two halves of me are joined—but it only makes things worse. My body goes up in flames, too. My skin remains unharmed but my clothes burn to ash, leaving me bare-ass naked.

The cell phone flops to the ground, the plastic already charred, the screen melted. I whimper. Now I'll die without knowing what Frosty said in his message.

And oh, wow, that's my first thought? Really? I'm freaking naked! Hurting people.

I'm so messed up. A menace of the highest order. "Help," I shout. "Help!"

Wait. What if other slayers come in here, and I hurt them, too?

"No! Don't help!"

"What's going on?" a new voice proclaims. Jaclyn maybe.

"You have to leave," I scream at her. "Please. I can't control it."

Bees sting my neck. No, not bees. More darts? A cool rush of liquid spills through me, fatigue fast on its heels. My knees tremble and collapse, but even when I land, I don't have the strength to remain upright, so I pitch forward.

Three heavy thuds echo, followed by three grunts of pain.

"How did she do that?" Gavin demands through panting breaths. "*What* did she do?"

My eyelids weigh ten thousand pounds and I can't open them.

"I don't know, I don't know," Ali says, sounding worried. "I lift zombies with my energy. No one has ever lifted slayers."

"I'll get Cole," Bronx says.

"Gavin," Jaclyn gasps. "You're bleeding from your eyes, ears and nose!"

"This is bad," Ali says. "This is beyond bad."

I *did* hurt them. And I did it while I was exhausted. What would have happened if I'd been at full strength? Would they have ended up in bits and pieces? Would I have made them explode the way Ali has made zombies explode?

I can't stay here, I realize. I can't stay with Frosty. He'll be safer without me. They all will.

17

Frosty

DEAD AND BREAKFAST

Something I learned last night: another name for *stakeout* is *torture in a hot box.*

We don't have Tiffany's GPS coordinates, but we have her home address, so River and I parked our car down the street to watch the house...and watch and watch as nothing happened.

Tiffany is still MIA. But the would-be murderer is only seventeen with a worried mother who's placed missing-person posters throughout town. If the girl hasn't left town—hell, even if she has—she'll return sooner or later. Or, at the very least, call.

One call. That's all we need.

River slams his fist into the steering wheel of the old beater that blends in well with the rusty death traps parked in front of the dilapidated houses along the pothole-infested street. Graffiti decorates many of the curbs, and most of the streetlamps have been busted.

A MAD ZOMBIE PARTY

"The longer this girl makes me wait," he says, "the worse it's going to be for her."

I agree. "For someone who disowned his sister, you sure do seem upset that someone hurt her."

"Back to this?" He flicks me a narrowed glance. "I love her. I've never stopped loving her, never will."

"And yet you abandoned her."

"Did I?" His eyes narrow. "I've kept tabs on her this entire time. I've seen her trailing you. At first I thought the two of you were dating, but the way you treated her... I've wanted to kill you a thousand times over. So don't try to tell me *you* give a shit about her."

"What I give or don't give is my business. She's under my protection." I say the words, and I mean them. I'll protect her with my life, if necessary. Because it's the right thing to do.

He turns in his seat to face me head-on. "Since when?"

"Since Ali's vision."

"A vision no one will talk about with any kind of detail. *When* is Milla supposed to save your miserable hide?"

"Visions never come with a 'save the date' card." I should know. Before Kat's death, I'd begun having visions with Bronx. Visions of battles and blood and pain. After Kat's death, I couldn't stand the thought of seeing a future without her. Thankfully Ali and Cole had learned how to control their visions by that point; they taught me. Mind over matter. I haven't had a vision since.

River runs his tongue over his teeth. "My sister's actions led to your girlfriend's death. You're not the kind of guy who forgives and forgets, even to save his own skin. You're the type who will go down with a ship if it means you can hold your enemy's head under water."

He's right. "Milla isn't my enemy. Not anymore."

"What is she then?"

"A friend." On a trial basis. At least, that's what I told her. But I think we're already past that. I trust her to have my back.

"A friend. Please." River grabs my collar and yanks me nose-to-nose with him. "She's had a shit life, and the few times she's lowered her guard and allowed someone in, they've cut and run. She doesn't need you to make everything worse."

I wrap my fingers around his wrist and shove him back. "I won't touch her. I don't think of her that way."

That's a lie. I know it the moment the words leave me. I've thought about her *that way* plenty of times.

A growl rises from low in River's chest. He knows it, too.

"I won't touch her," I repeat. Trying for more than friendship…a romantic relationship, or even just sleeping together… no. Not gonna happen. No matter how many times I picture her naked.

The *briiing-briiing* of a phone drifts through the speakers of one of the many devices River has stored in the car, a welcome distraction. The dude is no newbie to hunting humans and somehow hacked into the mother's phone, allowing him to listen to every ingoing and outgoing call from a distance. This is the eighth call of the day, and I'm losing hope.

"Hello," the mother says.

"Missing-person posters, Mom? Really?"

"Tiffany?" A whimper of relief crackles over the line. "You're alive!"

River and I go still. *Finally!*

He works his fingers over a small keyboard connected to the device.

"Where are you?" the mother demands. "Where have you been?"

"That doesn't matter. All you need to know is that I'm fine, and you can call off the pigs."

"Must you be so disrespectful? And you're fine? Really? You're *fine*? That's what you have to say to me, after all this time? Well, I'm sorry, but that's just not good enough. I've been worried sick about you. My ulcer has flared up."

"Your ulcer always flares up. Don't pretend you care about me," Tiffany snaps. "You think I'm crazy. Well, guess what? I'm not. Zombies are real, and I'm not the only one who sees them."

The two argue about truth versus fantasy—mental instability—about Tiffany going to see her shrink, about the bag of money the mom found in the girl's room, before the mother finally begs her to come home.

"She's not even trying to jack her signal," River says. "I'll have her location in three...two....bingo." He tosses the little machine on the floor and starts the car. We're flying down the road a few seconds later.

"Where is she?" I ask.

"A Taco Bell about five minutes away."

A public place. We'll have to be careful. Nowadays everyone has a camera on their phone. If we're filmed grabbing a teenage girl, we'll be sent to prison on kidnapping charges.

Or maybe not. There's a detective who might step up and help us. She's a civilian and she can't see zombies, but when she investigated the deaths of six of my friends, including Kat, she had to accept the fact that there's an unseen evil out there and slayers protect the rest of the world from it.

Our tires squeal as River parks like a stunt man in an action movie, the car spinning into an open corner slot in front of Taco Bell. I'm racing inside the building before he's even opened his door. I've seen Tiffany's picture. Black hair, brown eyes. Freckles. I've read her stats. Five foot six. One hundred and sixteen pounds. I scan the faces before me. An older couple. A teenage girl—a blonde with too much makeup, zero freckles and a red, angry gash across her jawline. A group of construction workers.

My gaze flips back to the blonde. I compare her face to the picture of Tiffany stored inside my mind. The two have the same bone structure.

Makeup can hide freckles. Bleach can lighten hair.

It's her. Has to be.

Rage takes a few swings at me. This girl callously and coldly sliced open Milla's neck and left her to die.

This girl will pay.

Tiffany spots me and gasps. As she jumps to her feet, her chair skids behind her, its legs scraping over the tile like fingers over a chalkboard. The rest of the diners grimace and either glare or frown at her.

If she was smart, she'd tell everyone the boyfriend who hurt her is back to finish the job. In seconds, she'd have a roomful of rescuers. And maybe that's exactly what she plans as she opens her mouth. But a slight whistle of wind passes me, and she snaps her mouth closed. Her eyes go wide, and she pats at her neck.

Satisfaction cools my rage. River just darted her the way she once darted Milla. Only he used a tranq.

As her knees give out, he rushes over to catch her before she falls. He eases her into the booth and slides in to sit beside her. Her head rests against his shoulder as he casually eats the rest of her burrito.

"I'm so happy to see you again, sugar." He kisses her temple. "Hungry?" he asks me.

Why not? I take a seat across from the pair and select an unwrapped taco. "You came prepared."

"Always do. Now we need to figure out how to get her to the car without looking like we're planning a gang bang or date-rape."

"Please. That'll be easy." I finish the taco, drain what's left of her soda. "Watch and learn." I reach out and rip out a row of Tiffany's stitches. Her wound opens, blood pouring down her chin. "She's bleeding," I announce. Too gleeful? I try for a more concerned tone. "We have to rush her to the emergency room, like, now."

I stand. River is fighting a grin as he follows suit and gathers Tiffany in his arms.

"Poor girl," someone says.

"I hope she's okay," another whispers.

River climbs in back of the car, keeping Tiffany in his arms. As I settle in the driver's seat, he tosses me the keys.

"Way to keep us under the radar," he says.

"Hey. We're not potential date-rapers right now. We're heroes."

"Yeah, but what you did was pretty cold."

"You complaining?"

"Hell, no. I'm impressed."

I snort.

At the first red light, I whip out my phone to text Cole and let him know we're on our way. I expect to see a message from Milla. Earlier, she told me she would break my face if I showed her my wrath and for some dumb reason, I thought it would be a good idea to tell her she needs my face intact more than I do, that she's the lucky one who gets to stare at it. In other words, I flirted. But she hasn't responded, and I'm glad. Really.

Caught Tiff. On way. Need room 4 interrogation.

His response arrives after the light turns green, so I have to wait until I hit the next red to read it. Yeah, I'm responsible like that.

Room ready. But U should know—we had prob w/Milla. Get here ASAP.

The light turns green. I don't care. I type, What kind of prob?? Is she hurt?

I press Send and stomp the pedal to the metal, breaking speed records.

"Slow down," River snaps. "We get pulled over, we'll lose our prize. Not to mention the stint we'll do behind bars."

"Something happened to Milla. A *problem*."

He sucks in a ragged breath. "Hell. Why are you driving like my grandmother? Go faster."

I take the next few corners so fast, I leave rubber and

smoke in my wake. Eight minutes and thirty-three seconds later, we're parked in front of the mansion and running inside. When we pass the door, I notice Gavin coming down the stairs.

"Milla," I say.

"Back in her room. But I don't recommend going inside."

River tosses Tiffany at him. "Do me a solid. Tie her down and lock her up. Put a guard at her door."

Gavin doesn't catch her, but then, he doesn't really try. "Oops." He picks her up none too gently. "Consider her restrained," he says, relish in his tone.

I take the stairs two at a time and rush around the corner. Ali and Cole are standing in front of Milla's door, arguing about what to do.

"—need to put another tranq in her," Cole says. "She shouldn't have recovered so quickly from the first one."

"I'm telling you, she didn't hurt us on purpose. Trust me on this. We all just need to sit down and talk about what happened. Okay? While we do, Reeve and Weber can run some tests."

"Talking isn't going to solve this, Ali-gator. And how many tests has Reeve already run? And how the hell do you know Camilla didn't hurt you on purpose? For all we know, she and Tiffany are working together."

"But why would she allow her throat to be slit?"

"Because she knew we would use *dýnamis* on her, sharing our abilities with her. Because she plans to wipe us out by using our strengths against us."

"*She* can hear you," Milla screams through the door. "FYI, she thinks you're an idiot!"

My hands fist. "You *are* an idiot," I say to Cole. "She couldn't have known we'd reach her in time to save her. And there were better, far less painful ways to hurt herself and gain our sympathy."

"And," Ali says, "none of us knew how she'd react to our fire and our abilities."

"How *did* she react?" River demands. "Is that the problem?"

"She hurt slayers rather than zombies. Me, Gavin and Bronx." Ali chews on her bottom lip. "She somehow tossed us in the air and held us there while squeezing us as if we were inside a trash compactor. I've never experienced anything like it."

And now, knowing Milla, she fears she'll hurt others and become an outcast all over again.

"Milla...we have to know. When you worked for Anima," Ali calls, "did they do anything to you? Experiment on you?"

"No. Never."

"Are you sure?"

"Yes! That's something I'd remember. This is Tiffany's fault. Her toxin somehow screwed me up and now I can't be fixed. If I could, your fire would have done it already."

River knocks on the door. "Let me in."

"No. Stay out. Stay the hell out. Don't you dare come into this room. You do, and I will shove my dagger so far down your throat you'll be shitting metal for days."

Creative.

He hesitates and I push him out of the way. "I'm coming in, Milla. Just remember you're supposed to save me, not kill me."

"No! Don't you dare come in." She's even more frantic now. "Stay out, Frosty. I mean it. Stay away from me."

I pick the lock and twist the dooknob.

18

Milla

BALLS AND CHAINS

I'm cramming my weapons into a black duffel bag when Frosty enters the room. "You're brave, I'll give you that much," I snap. I don't turn to look at him. The thought of harming him or my brother—or anyone!—scares the pee out of me. Staying in the mansion is no longer an option.

"Well, *you* are a coward," he says. "You had a bad experience with your new abilities—your first time, no less—and you're throwing in the towel?"

"Yes! You weren't there. You didn't see the damage I did to your friends." Humiliating tears leak from my eyes.

He's in front of me a second later, cupping my face in his big, rough hands. His thumbs tenderly brush the tears away. "You're crying," he says, and he sounds amazed. Something changes in his expression, a lingering hardness finally going soft. "You care about us."

"Of course I do." I wrench free of him, his kindness more than I can bear. "You guys are great."

Gently, so gently, he says, "You'll practice. You'll get better. I'll help you."

"You don't get it. If I practice, I *hurt* people." There's a minicrossbow in the pile I've created, but it's not mine. It's something Cole favors, which means it's most likely his. Whatever. I pack it anyway. I'm going to be on my own. I'll need all the help I can get.

"What about Ali's vision?" Frosty asks.

Argh! Why isn't he yelling at me for harming his friends? Why isn't he grabbing my arm and dragging me to the front entrance, giving my ass a kick for good measure before slamming the door in my face?

"Maybe Ali got things wrong. I mean, I've been with you for a month and nothing's happened. Maybe the vision is merely symbolic. Maybe I save you by not being near you."

"Symbolic? Really?"

"What? I'm dangerous now."

"You've always been dangerous."

"To zombies, yes, but not to other slayers."

He barks out a laugh.

Yeah. Okay. I was dangerous to other slayers before this. And not just because of my ties to Anima.

"I couldn't control the ability, or whatever the hell it was. The *dis*ability." I'd been hoping for something great to happen to me. The break I so desperately wanted. Instead, I got this. Something worse. My shoulders sag. "Red flames consumed me, just like they do in my nightmares, and I tossed three powerful slayers into the air without lifting a finger. Energy poured from me, wrapped around them and squeezed.

They bled from their eyes, nose and ears. I wanted so badly
to stop, but I couldn't."

"You'll practice," he says again.

He still doesn't get it. "No. I'll put others in danger. I'd
rather die." Lack of control is an excuse I can't abide.

I'm sorry I hit you, honey. Daddy lost control of his temper.

"Milla," Frosty says, realization suddenly as sweet as it is
shocking.

Ever since I woke up from the attack, he's been calling me
Milla. Not Camilla. Not "hey, you." Not "bitch." But Milla.
As if I'm his friend rather than his enemy. My eyes go wide,
and I pivot on my heel to face him—

—in a blink, the entire world stops spinning. The walls
of the house fall away, and I'm running as fast as I can, Kat
clutched close to my chest. Her collarbone is broken, the edge
peeking out of her skin. She's cut everywhere and bleeding.
Judging by the way Kat is wheezing, I know one of her lungs
has collapsed. She'll die if she doesn't get help.

But she needs antidote more. She's been bitten by a zombie, and the clock is ticking. Damn it! She can't die, can't die,
can't fucking die. She's my life. My everything. But shit, shit,
there are zombies hot on our trail, and each one has a bomb
strapped to his neck.

I veer to the right—a mistake. More zombies glide from
between the trees.

Boom!

The ground shakes. I lose control of my left arm, which
was broken when the house collapsed, but somehow I maintain my grip on my girl. *Can't drop her, can't drop her.*

Shadows twist at my left, so I make another right turn and

catch sight of a dozen Anima agents plowing my way. Damn it! Where can I go? The agent at the helm raises a pistol, aims at me—at Kat. I have no other choice. I go left.

Pop! Pop!

I curl inward as best I can, trying to wrap myself around my girl, and I end up taking the bullets in my upper arm. My broken arm. The increase in pain is incredible, but it's nothing compared to my determination. Except I've turned us into another hail of bullets.

Pop, pop, pop!

Kat is hit, hit, her body jerking. No. Hell, no. Rage, frustration, desperation—each chokes me.

"Go!" Cole shouts. "I'll hold them off." He's got two semi-automatics in hand and as he sprays the agents with metal I beat feet in the opposite direction, going back the way I came. He'll be okay. He has to be okay. "I'm sorry, kitten. I'm so sorry. I'll get you out of here, I promise. I'll get you somewhere safe, and I'll take care of you. You'll heal. You have to heal."

Pop, pop, pop!

More gunfire sounds in the distance, and panic infuses every cell in my body. Agents race from the left and right, their weapons already trained on me. I have nowhere to go.

Damn it! I have a split second to decide what to do. Keep running and pray they miss, or set Kat down and fight, wasting precious time.

Ali rushes around the bend, and she's headed straight for me. Her eyes are wide, and I know. It's already far too late for option two. I'm going to have to take the gunfire—risk *Kat* taking the gunfire.

I pick up the pace and once again contort my body around Kat's in an attempt to shield her.

Pop, pop, pop!

A bullet slams into my thigh, followed by another, and my leg just…stops…working. As I stumble forward, the rest of my limbs go lax. I can't right myself, can only fall, fall. I twist midway to absorb the brunt of impact, but when we hit, Kat rolls from my arms.

Tears sting the backs of my eyes. I somehow crawl to my feet, the pain, the pain. But it's nothing. She's everything. As I reach for her, another stream of bullets sprays, and I'm nailed in the chest. I fly backward, away from her.

"No! Kat!"

Her gaze finds me. She offers me a sad smile. As I stretch out my hand, her lips part. I think…I think she just took her final breath. Her chest stops rising and falling. Her eyes dull.

"No! No, no, no."

Darkness descends over my mind, but only for a moment. Light returns, and with it, a new scene takes shape.

I'm lying on a tiled floor, surrounded by a pool of blood—mine, River's and Caro's. I hurt. I hurt so bad. I'm certain death has sunk his claws deep, deep inside me, determined to rip my spirit out of my body. I'm having trouble breathing. Every time I try to call for help, blood trickles from the corners of my mouth, choking me.

Though my vision is hazy, I know my father looms above me. He's hit me so many times I've already lost count—but he isn't done.

Right now, I have a reprieve as he screams at me. My ears are ringing, but I can make out most of the words. *You're use-*

less. You're worthless. I wish you were never born. You can't possibly be my kid. Your mother must have slept with someone else, the whore. I busted my knuckles, and now I'm going to use a baseball bat.

All this, because I refuse to accept blame for Caro's death. Caro, my other half. My better half.

I never should have kept her out so long. I should have returned her hours before. But I didn't, and Daddy's dinner wasn't ready on time. I took full responsibility, but he blamed her. *You're crying. Only guilty girls cry.*

I tried to shield her, to take her blows for her, but he just kept shoving me aside. By the time River got home, it was too late. Caro's body…motionless…

Me, broken and bloody.

At least River was able to rip the baseball bat from Daddy's hands.

Daddy turned on him, hitting him in the stomach until he vomited blood. Even still, River was able to push me into the closet and lock the door. But it wasn't long before Daddy killed River, just like Caro, and busted down the door.

He's yelling at me again. It's my turn to die, and I'm glad, but I don't want to go without taking him with me. I crawl to the stove, where pots have fallen.

I swipe up a cast-iron skillet and slam it into his leg with what little strength I have left. I only make him madder. For once, he isn't concerned about hitting me in places no one will notice. It's open season.

Daddy kicks me in the stomach. I curl into myself, gasping for breath I can't catch. He kicks me again, and stars burst over what little of my vision remains. My lungs burn as if they've been bathed in acid, that acid rising…rising…spewing out of my mouth.

Blood. So much blood. I'm not going to be able to take Daddy with me, am I?

I'm so sorry, Caro. I'm so sorry, Riv.

I'll be with them soon. The pain will end, and we'll be together again. That will have to be enough.

Black spiderwebs weave through my mind, but I fight to stay awake. Gotta prepare for the next blow. But…it never comes.

I'm not sure how much time passes before the spiderwebs thin and I'm able to blink open my swollen eyes. My father lies on the floor in front of me, his face turned in my direction, his eyes wide and glassed over, his mouth hanging open. River stands beside him, a bloody kitchen knife clutched in his hand. He stares at the weapon as if he isn't sure how it ended up in his possession.

"River," I gasp, but no sound emerges. My ribs are broken, muscle torn—

—a knock echoes, and the scene vanishes. I blink, and I'm back inside the bedroom at Reeve's, standing in front of Frosty.

He's pale, waxen, and he's staring at me with horror.

"Wh-what just happened?" I ask.

"I think we had a vision," he rasps. "Two of them."

Another ability passed on to me? Yes, of course. Only, I didn't see the future, like Ali. I saw the past.

And Frosty saw it, too.

Oh…no, no, no. He knows my deepest, darkest secret now.

He'll treat me differently. He'll feel sorry for me. But I don't want his pity. Yes, I've suffered. But we've *all* suffered.

"I didn't… I don't… Milla, I'm so sorry."

That. I don't want that. He owes me nothing. I owe him everything.

I turn away, not wanting him to see the emotion in my eyes—or the fresh flood of tears.

I suppose I should be glad that I saw into his past, the way he saw into mine. The very moments that define the people we are today. And maybe I *would* be glad, if I'd seen something else. But Kat's death? Feeling his desperation and pain? His unending agony? Agony I helped cause. No. Guilt eats me up, the bites bigger than ever before.

The knock comes again, and River steps inside the room. I'm emotionally raw right now, and seeing him pushes me over the edge. The tears trickle down my cheeks, burning my skin.

"You guys have been quiet for a while." He looks between us and frowns. "What's going on?"

Frosty shakes his head and backs out of the room. He kicks the door shut behind him, the loud *thud* jolting me. I stumble back as if pushed, my knees catching on the mattress. I land, bouncing up and down until finally stilling.

"Milla." River strides across the room to crouch in front of me. "What happened? Talk to me."

I begin to shake. "I didn't…I didn't know Anima would do what they did. I thought they would do as promised and sneak in, grab Ali and leave. But that's no excuse. I'm at fault. I knew Anima lied and tricked. I should have been prepared. I should have double-crossed them. But I didn't, and I ended up hurting Frosty so deeply he'll never recover. I took the most precious part of his life, the treasure he cherished above all others, and I'm a horrible person."

Torment ravages my brother's eyes. "Milla, don't do this to yourself. You can't—"

A sob splits my lips, and I fall against his chest. After that, the sobs just keep coming, until I'm practically dry heaving. I *am* a horrible person, and these new abilities are my final punishment. Exactly what I deserve.

"I've been following you off and on for weeks," River admits when I at last go quiet.

A few times I'd *felt* someone was watching me, but... "If that's true, why didn't you help me the night hordes of zombies attacked me? I would have died if Frosty hadn't stepped in."

He closes his eyes for a moment. "That was one of my nights off, and I'm sorry for it. I had no idea—" He goes quiet, as if he can't bear to finish.

So...who had watched me that night? Tiffany?

"I love you," he says, "and I couldn't stay away. Even as furious as I was, I couldn't *not* check on you. I know you only did what you did because you love me, too, and you hoped to protect me the way we failed to protect Caro." He strokes a hand down my back, the way he used to do when we were children, gentle, so gentle, always careful of my bruises. "You're carrying a lot of blame around. What you did for me. Kat. Even Caro. But it's time for you to let everything go."

I'm so tired I shake my head in negation rather than voice a response. Letting go of the guilt won't do me a bit of good. It has claws, and they're buried deep in my heart.

"Seeing you covered in blood… I remembered how quickly life can be snuffed out. I don't want to waste another moment apart from you. I forgive you for working with Anima. All right?" His arms tighten around me, and he kisses my temple. "I've missed you. I've cursed myself for sending you away. I've hated myself, and yelled at everyone else. And you know how I feel about losing my temper."

Yes. Like me, he would rather lose a limb than act like our father.

"I want you to come back with me," he says. "There will be problems at first, but we'll get through them together."

I shake my head, adamant. No way I'll put his crew at risk. And his reign in jeopardy.

"Milla," he says, "I talked to Ali, and I know you're scared about the new ability, but if you do nothing, you'll always be scared and you'll always be a danger to those around you. You have to learn how to use it to your advantage."

I give another shake of my head, but this time, I'm not as confident.

"You know I'm right," River continues. "If you don't control your emotions, your ability—your *whatever*, just go ahead and fill in the blank—they'll control you."

"Damn you," I whisper, finally finding my voice. He's right. I have to do this. I have to learn control, or I will be controlled. There's no middle ground. "You never give up, do you?"

"A trait we share." He smiles fondly. "Don't worry. I'll come up with a way for you to practice without putting anyone in danger. I swear it."

"I can't imagine a scenario where that's possible."

"Just give me time to think. Despite rumors, I'm only a man, not a god."

"Rumors suggest you're a devil, but fine. Okay. Take a few days."

"And then we'll go home—"

"No. I'm staying here." I won't be an anchor around his neck, dragging him down. No matter how much I miss him. "I promised Kat I'd guard Frosty, and I *will* keep my word."

I might have thought about abandoning ship, but once I calmed down, I would have come back. I see that now.

River rubs his knuckles into the crown of my head until I bat his arm away. "How about a bit of good news?"

"Yes, please."

"We caught the girl. Tiffany. She's locked up in the basement."

A thousand emotions hit me at once. Rage—the one who tried to murder me is here. Satisfaction—I can hurt her, like for like. Sadness. I don't know why. Relief. Hope.

"I want to be the first one to talk to her." I clutch the sleeves of his shirt. "Okay? All right?" The wrong interrogation technique could cause her to clam up. "Will you make sure? I just... I'm not ready to deal. Not right now." I'm still too raw.

"I'll make sure," he says with a nod.

Cole bursts into the room, his features dark with concern. "Your panic attack has to wait. Bronx was out on patrol, found a zombie and let himself be bitten. But the toxin wasn't cleansed and Bronx didn't recover on his own. Love was with him and tried to heal him, but she couldn't summon *dýnamis.* Now there are more zombies. We need everyone out there, and we need massive amounts of the antidote. Now."

"Go." I give River a little push. "I'll be here when you get back."

Cole's freaky violet eyes lock on me. "You're on your feet. You're coming, too."

19

Frosty

YOU ARE WHAT EATS YOU

At my apartment, I drink and I pace. No matter how much alcohol I pour down the hatch, no matter how many times I stomp my feet into the carpet, I can't block the memory of Milla's beating. She was covered in blood and bruises, different parts of her face swollen, her wrist bent back at an odd angle. A bone in her leg peeking through skin. I'd felt her pain, her all-consuming despair. I'd heard her thoughts. Beatings were a way of life for her and her siblings.

Whatever ill feelings I still harbored toward her died a swift death today, bludgeoned with a baseball bat, just like Milla herself. Resentment no longer clouds my thoughts, and I see the truth. She's been hurt enough. I want to comfort her, not hurt her—never hurt her—and I want her to comfort me. I'm unmanned. And I get it now. *Of course* she helped Anima when her brother was threatened. He was all she had left. Her only family. Her hero.

How did we have visions of the past? Why?

I throw the bottle of whiskey against the wall, glass shattering in every direction. I stop, just stop, and sink to the floor, my back pressed against the couch.

"Dude. Miserable is so not a good look for you."

My gaze locks on Kat, who is standing a few feet in front of me. As usual, she's wearing the T-shirt and shorts she died in. At this point, I think I'd rather see her in a burlap sack or a Mr. Potato Head costume. "Can't help it," I croak.

"Well, you're gonna have to try. You need to arm up and head to Shady Elms. Five minutes after you left the mansion, Cole started texting you. Bronx is in trouble, and all slayers have been summoned for a battle royale."

"They'll be fine without me."

"Cole insisted Milla go, even though she's—"

"Damn him!" I jump to my feet. Milla is weakened, emotional and probably easily distracted right now.

Kat watches me with sad eyes as I gather an arsenal. "I'll be rooting for you. And of course, I'll critique your performance later."

"Bonus points for every kill?"

"Please. That'd be too easy. You'll get bonus points for every un-kill. Reach a hundred, and you'll earn a prize."

"Right. The new 'save 'em' ability."

"Yes," she says. "Although that particular ability didn't work for Bronx tonight."

Well, well. I might get to kill, after all. "The prize?" I cram four extra clips into my pockets. If I have to save zombies, fine, I'll save them, but there's no way in hell I'll let them bite me. I'll disable, capture and find another way.

"The prize," Kat says, "is that I'll finally forgive you for riding across a rainbow with another girl on the back of your unicorn."

"My dream-crime record finally expunged. Nice."

"Pain is pain."

I flash her a grin, but she's already gone.

I rush out my front door—I'm in a T-shirt and jeans, with combat boots on my feet—and slide into my truck. Night has fallen, and shadows are thick. Stars dot the sky, but they're smeared with dark gray rain clouds that are threatening to overflow.

I break every speed law and soon close in on Shady Elms. Lights blink up ahead—headlights? Yep. Smoke curls from the crumpled hood of a van. My friends crashed? I park and jump out. I run...only to tumble to the ground, tripped by... I don't know what. I land, dirt and twigs filling my mouth. A bright light suddenly shines over me. Motion-activated? Or controlled by a human hand?

Human hand. Definitely. A gun is cocked. I roll out of the way just as—

Pop, pop, pop! Bullets spray the spot I just vacated.

I come up firing a gun of my own. A grunt echoes, the scent of blood saturates the air. Whoever shot at me is wounded. I stomp forward, remaining low just in case. The light is still shining and reveals the glint of another trip wire. I cut it and turn the source of the light—a lamp that's been anchored into the ground—to illuminate the opposite direction. A man in bodily form is slumped over a rock, a deep gash in his neck.

I don't know him. He isn't a slayer.

Keeping my gun trained on him, I feel for a pulse. He's dead.

Who is he? And why did he attack me?

Are there others nearby, waiting to pick off slayers when they return to their bodies? But...why not strike now?

The answer becomes clear a moment later. My friends killed the others...and a new crop of enemy soldiers has just arrived.

I hear car doors slamming in the distance. I sneak through the bushes—three black-clad men stand beside a van, checking their weapons, while a fourth gives the pre-war speech. "Kill or be killed." There's a wrecked sedan next to the van, four motionless bodies inside it. The people my friends killed. Go team.

The newcomers got something right. It's kill or be killed. I nail them all with a bullet between the eyes.

I wait for a minute...two...but no other vehicle arrives. I return to the van my friends used. A more in-depth search reveals tires shredded on both sides and part of the hood embedded in a tree. The bodies—empty shells—of slayers surround the vehicle, each one bloody and bruised.

The gash on Milla's forehead has leaked crimson all the way to her chin.

Furious and frantic, I push my spirit out of my body and follow the sounds of battle, the smell of rot. As a handful of zombies lurch into my path, I crisscross my arms, my semi-automatics, and shoot each creature directly in the mouth, shattering jawbones and teeth.

Bite me now, assholes.

I sprint forward, every second now an endless eternity as those blinking headlights illuminate sheer violence...just before darkness descends.

Light. Bronx and Love are on the ground, both twitching

and jerking as if seizing. Milla crawls toward them, her hands engulfed by red flames.

Darkness.

Light. Milla touches Bronx, the crimson flames crackling over his chest. His back bows, his cry of agony echoing through the night.

Darkness.

Light. A zombie has snuck up behind Milla, who is distracted as she patches a wound on Bronx's chest—a wound that now appears bigger. Sharp, yellowed teeth sink into her shoulder and she screams.

"No!" I pick up speed.

Darkness. Crimson flames burst from her and lick at the creature.

A creature who latches on harder and shakes his head, like a dog with a bone.

Almost there...so close...but not close enough.

Light. Ali yanks the zombie away from Milla and holds out her arm, clearly expecting *dýnamis* to appear—it doesn't.

Darkness. *Come on. Faster.*

Light. Cole kicks the zombie in the face. Something bad must have happened to Ali, because she's on the ground, writhing in pain.

Darkness.

Light. Milla crawls to Ali's side, and with a *jab, jab, jab* she injects her, then Bronx, then Love with...antidote? Yeah, has to be. All three go still.

Finally! I reach the edge of the battlefield.

I aim and fire, putting a bullet between the eyes of all three zombies sneaking up on Milla. She glances up. Our gazes meet. A profound wave of relief sweeps through me when she lumbers to her feet. She's okay. Then the headlights go out. By the time they come back on, she's back in the fray, her short swords swinging with expert precision.

I sheathe my guns and withdraw my own short swords. With purposeful flicks of my wrists, I remove any zombie hands, arms or heads that move into my path. Body parts pile up around me. Black goo sprays, burning me.

As the horde begins to thin at last, I see the other slayers fighting around me. Not just Cole and Milla, but River and Love, who is back on her feet, as well as Chance, Gavin and Jaclyn. Some are more injured than others, but all are bleeding profusely.

"Jaclyn! Your six!" As Gavin reaches for her, a single white flame springs to life at the end of his hand...only to die a second later. The lack costs him. A horde converges, ripping hunks of skin and muscle from his arm. He fights his way free and hisses in pain. "I'm not healing, and they're not being cleansed."

A mad fury overtakes Jaclyn, who has successfully disabled the zombies sneaking up behind her thanks to Gavin's warning. She drops her daggers and withdraws two .22s.

Boom! Boom! Boom!

Zombies drop, creating a pathway, allowing Milla to work her way to Gavin and inject him with antidote.

"Stop trying to light up," Cole shouts. "Disable as many Zs as you can."

Milla fails to notice the fiend lying on the ground, reaching for her—

"Milla!" I shout.

She looks up at me, but it's too late. The creature latches on to her ankle to yank her calf toward his chomping teeth. I act on instinct, diving down and shoving my hand between her leg and his mouth. The burn is instantaneous and utterly incapacitates me. I collapse, unable to move...unable to breathe.

I've been bitten before, and it hurt like hell, but it didn't hurt like *this*. Didn't affect me like this. Before I retained control of my body and lost control of my mind, the urge to eat, to kill, overwhelming me. Now, the opposite is true.

"Frosty," Milla shouts.

I can't respond.

There are severed heads all around me, those with teeth snapping at me. One of the slayers steps forward to slash at a still-standing zombie and inadvertently kicks one of those heads toward me. Still, I can't move.

"Frosty!"

A second later, the foundation vanishes from under me. No, no. That's not true. I've been tossed into the air, where I hover like a balloon on a string.

Pressure crushes me at every angle. Even as warm blood leaks from my eyes, I'm able to see that the other slayers are right beside me. All but Milla. She stands on the ground, her hands raised.

"Throw...us," Ali calls. "Throw...with...your...arms."

Milla has seen Ali in action and understanding quickly dawns. She jerks her arms to the side. Suddenly I'm flying, flying...slamming into a tree a good distance from the zombie horde. I flop to the ground and someone lands on top of me, grunting and rolling off, but it doesn't matter. I can't breathe with or without the added weight.

River rushes over and slams a needle deep into my neck. "You're welcome." The antidote flows through my veins, cool and soothing, and my muscles begin to unlock from my bones.

"Milla," I say. "We have to help her."

"On it." He pulls me to my feet and takes off.

I stumble after him, dizzy but fighting it. I *will* help Milla.

I withdraw my semiautomatics, reload and fire at every zombie I come across. When I'm out of ammo, I use the axes anchored to the handles, soon clearing the immediate path and buying myself a few seconds to replace the clips. As I aim and shoot, aim and shoot, rotted brain matter splatters. Bone shards rain. Teeth fall to the ground like discarded pieces of candy.

Where's Milla?

I scan...scan...there. She shoves a zombie to the ground and follows him down. After jamming her knees into his shoulders, she uses her swords like a pair of scissors and lops off his head.

Good girl. But another zombie plows into her from behind, throwing her down. Upon impact, red flames erupt from her hands, chest and feet.

Her nightmare has come to life.

Panicked, I run to her. Is she dying? Burning to death? I summon *dynamis*—fight fire with fire—but in an instant, I'm consumed by fear. It burns my mind, brands my heart, makes my limbs tremble. This isn't... I can't... *Helpless, so helpless.*

The thought overtakes my mind. I don't understand what's happening, and it takes everything I've got to shake the fear. Even still, the flames never come.

I reach Milla as she stabs the zombie in the mouth and

stands. She's panting, the red flames growing stronger, wafting smoke in the air. Every other zombie focuses on her, moving closer to her, ignoring the other slayers.

I join River, Cole, Love and Jaclyn to slice and dice our way through the masses while Ali, Gavin and Justin do the same on the opposite side. But we're all too late. Milla releases an ear-piercing scream. I stop fighting and run, just run. If I get bit, I get bit.

I reach the front unharmed. But…Milla isn't being eaten as I feared. Her eyes are as red as the flames, and they are bloody pools of hunger.

She rips out a zombie's throat while her attention is locked on me. She licks her lips, even bares her teeth and steps toward me.

I'm on today's menu?

River whizzes past me to jam a needle into her neck. But *he* is the one who bellows in pain, those crimson flames brushing over his skin.

At last the red fades from Milla's eyes. I whip off my shirt to pat her down. The flames die—on her, on her brother—and the siblings collapse.

I gather Milla close and scan the area. Cole and the others have finished off the rest of the zombies. Easy to do, really, considering the meat bags stopped fighting us.

Milla moans. "Frosty…"

"You're okay. You're okay now."

"The flames—"

"I know. They're gone."

"The flames." She clutches my shirt. "The flames…"

"Shh, shh. They're gone. I've got you, and I'm not going to let anything happen to you."

Her eyes close and she goes limp. I hold her closer.

A few feet away, Cole barks, "We need a new van and a tow." He's holding an unconscious Ali in his arms, a phone pressed between his ear and shoulder. "And hurry."

"What the hell just happened?" River demands. "When I tried to light up, I got hit with a blast of fear instead."

A chorus of "Me, too" rings out.

"And Milla," he adds, "her flames were red. I'm not the only one who noticed it, right?"

"Whatever Tiffany did to us," Cole says, his voice tight, "I think this is the result."

Bronx scrubs a dirt-smudged hand down his face. "Fear is the opposite of faith, and faith is our source of power. Without it, we lose. Every time."

"Why wasn't Milla affected the same way?" I ask.

River shrugs. "Maybe those red flames protected her from whatever was done to us."

Right thought, wrong direction. "I don't think *thánatos* protected her so much as itself." In her nightmares, the flames kill her. Predator versus prey.

"Head to the car, everyone, and join your body." Cole motions to the left. "Justin's on his way."

"Call him back and tell him to be on the lookout. Zombies aren't the only evil on the prowl tonight." I shift Milla in my arms and stand. "Someone set a trip wire at the west side of the cemetery and tried to put a bullet in my brain while I was down. He missed and I shot to kill."

"You see any others?" Cole asks as he dials.

"Yes. Three. They received the same treatment."

"I'll hide the evidence and meet you back at the house." River doesn't wait for permission, just takes off.

"Someone help me with Gavin." Tears spill down Jaclyn's cheeks as she tries to pull him up one-handed, her other hand tucked against her middle to protect a swollen wrist. "He's too heavy for me to carry."

Like Ali and Milla, Gavin is unconscious. Bronx and Chance heft him up, each using a shoulder as a crutch to keep him vertical. Together, we make our way to the vehicles. We're a ragtag group, but we're alive. I tell myself that's enough. For now.

Milla

BLOW OUT THE CANDLES ON YOUR GRAVE

When I open my eyes, the first thing I see is Frosty. His face hovers just above mine. Sublime heat envelops me, saturating me with his scent. His heartbeat drums against my temple.

We're outside, the night dark. He's walking...carrying me. I smile...until memories swamp me. We just had our asses handed to us. On a silver platter. With a side of pork rinds. The servers of this ass-handing? Zombies we killed once before.

How?

I have a thing for faces and clothes. Even undead faces and clothes. The people I meet become photographs inside my mind—maybe that's a slayer trait, maybe not. Tonight I was able to pull the photographs from the last battle and play match. Vintage suit with stains on the tie—match. T-shirt with I'm Kind of a Big Deal stitched across the breast—match. Purple jogging pants—match.

We ashed those zombies a month ago and now they're back? *Impossible.*

That's not even the worst part.

When I was bitten, the red flames mixing with a fresh dose of zombie toxin, I became aware of every slayer within my vicinity, and even a few beyond the graveyard. I lost track of everything else, blindsided by a hunger I couldn't fight.

I wanted to eat. To gorge.

"I'm awake," I whisper, doing my best to hide my horror.

"How do you feel?" Frosty sets me on my feet.

We're at the entrance to the cemetery, where the van is wrecked and Frosty's truck awaits. "Sore, but grateful I'm alive."

Our bodies surround the vehicles, and one by one, we join up.

Justin arrives with a new van, and we pile inside. Everyone but Frosty.

"Where—" I begin.

"I'm staying to help River," he says.

"I'll stay, too," I say. I don't want to be parted from him. He's injured.

"You haven't seen yourself." He gives me a half smile, reaches out and squeezes my hand. "You need medical attention."

"So do—" But he's already walking away. "You," I declare lamely.

Justin whisks us to the mansion, where the recruits help us into the former ballroom on the bottom floor, which has been transformed into a makeshift hospital. One of the recruits is in medical school, another in nursing school, and

Weber barks orders at them. We're examined one at a time, those in the worst condition first.

Once Gavin and Ali are doctored, Weber focuses on me. I'm bandaged up and deemed "on the mend," but I'm unable to catch my breath until Frosty walks through the door.

He scans the room and stops on me. My heart skips a beat as he closes the distance. Though I'm in pain—I refused painkillers, not wanting to be weakened or fall asleep—I stand and motion to the gurney.

He sits without a word of complaint.

"Where's River?"

"Once we had the bodies loaded, he took off."

"Serves you right. Now don't you dare move," I say. "I mean it."

"Trust me. I'm not going anywhere."

I gather the cleaning supplies I think I'll need. I'm as gentle as possible as I wash the blood from his face. He must have had a shirt stored in his truck because he's wearing a new one.

"Any injuries I can't see?" For some reason, the question makes me blush. I *never* blush.

"I have a few under my shirt." He doesn't move, just sits there, his gaze glued to me and so intense it's as if he's seeing past flesh and bone.

I gulp. "What are you waiting for? Take it off."

"If you insist." He grips the shirt by the collar and tugs the material over his head.

Is my tongue hanging out? Am I drooling?

Cord after cord of strength greets me. And his tattoos! *Mercy. I beg for mercy.* In the center of his breastbone, there's a human heart pierced on the bottom by numerous daggers.

On the handle of each is a name. Boots. Ducky. Ankh. Trina. Haun. Cruz. Willow. Roses grow from the top of the heart, the stems twisting and twining all the way to his shoulders, where the buds are in bloom. A curtain of mist floats between the thorny foliage, and in the midst of it is the name Kitten.

I clean him of dirt, sweat, zombie goo and blood, my blush heating a few thousand degrees. Trembling, I turn my attention to his arms, a much safer area, and the bands tattooed around his wrists. There are three Z-bites, raw and angry, and I slather each with salve before adhering a bandage.

I step behind him to finish up and have to swallow a whimper. There's an etching of hands in the center of his back. They are joined together to form a steeple, the Lord's Prayer scripted around them. Some of the words cover scars—*name, kingdom, deliver*—making them stand out as if they are alive with power.

"You're good at this." His voice is tight with...I'm not sure what. "At playing doctor, I mean."

"I should be. I spent the first part of my childhood acting like a nursemaid." It's something I wouldn't have said to anyone else, but Frosty knows about my past. He's seen it.

The muscles between his shoulders knot. "Is that what you'd be if you weren't a slayer? A nurse. Or maybe a doctor?"

"A doctor. Maybe."

"Any plans for college?"

"I wish, but I barely graduated high school because I missed so many days." And it isn't like I could afford college, even with loans. Loans have to be paid back. Anyway, who's going to hire the girl always covered in bruises? "What about you?"

"I'd like to be a homicide detective. Take down human bad guys for a change."

Admirable. "The streets will definitely be safer with you on patrol." I grab a clean rag, dip it in a bowl of soapy water, wring it out and gently scrub the scratches along his spine.

"You're not going to tell me it's too dangerous?" There's true curiosity in his tone. "That maybe I should be a mail-man or something?"

"Uh, I've seen you fight zombies, remember? Nothing's too dangerous for you." But *he* is too dangerous for *me*, there's no doubt about that. I'm basically petting him right now. "Well. Nothing seems to be broken and the bites have already scabbed. You should make a full recovery."

I toss the dirty rags into the laundry basket beside the gurney and hand the bowl of soiled water to a recruit with an order to drain it. Then I stand there, unsure what to do next. I don't want to leave Frosty, but I don't want to embarrass myself, either.

He takes hold of my wrist and draws me closer...closer still...until I'm standing between his legs. I can only blink up at him as my trembling renews and redoubles.

"Let me see *your* injuries."

"No need, they're—"

"I wasn't asking." He gently peels back the bandage on my forehead to study the slash. Well, okay, then.

"I hit the window when the van crashed," I say.

"No stitches."

"It wasn't deep. It might scar, though."

"You worried?"

"No. Yes. Maybe. Maybe I'll cut bangs."

"Why? You're beautiful the way you are," he says. "With or without a scar."

My mouth falls open. I...have no idea how to respond.

"Don't even think about accusing me of lying." His gaze heats as it studies mine. "I don't lie. Ever. I don't need to, because I don't care if I hurt anyone's feelings. The truth is the truth, forever unchanging, and it's better than a lie any day of the week."

Dang. My crush on him soars to a new level.

"Scars speak for you," he adds. "They say you're strong, and you've survived something that might have killed others. To me, there's nothing sexier than strength."

"I agree," I whisper. One hundred percent. As slayers, we've lost friends, family, homes. At times even our sanity. We know the weak fall and never get back up.

We can't afford to be weak.

And oh, crap. I want to throw myself into his arms. Instead, I change the subject...fast. "Did you notice anything weird about the zombies tonight?"

"Weird...how?"

"They looked exactly the same as the last batch we fought."

"Twin zombies are as likely as twin humans, I suppose."

"Yeah, but *all* of the zombies were familiar to me."

He frowns. "I didn't notice, but then, I'm a guy. I usually only notice short skirts and see-through shirts."

I smile, and his gaze falls to my lips. The way he stares... My heart hammers in my chest, my blood heating. Awareness crackles inside me.

"All right." Cole's voice booms through the room, startling me, and I leap away from Frosty as if pushed. I keep my back to him, not wanting to see his expression darken with disgust as he remembers who and what I am. "We need to talk about what happened tonight."

In a snap, the room goes quiet.

Cole moves to the center, ensuring he's the sole focus of the occupants. "Was anyone able to use *dýnamis*?"

"No."

"Nope."

"Not me."

Not a single affirmation comes.

"What about your abilities?" Cole asks.

"I wasn't able to do *anything*," Ali says, and nods of agreement follow.

I'm the only one who maintained the status quo. Too bad my status quo sucks. "*Thánatos* seems to make zombies hungrier. It surprised me. I wasn't prepared for that."

"When you touched your brother, the wound on his chest *worsened* rather than healed." Ali tilts her head, thoughtful. "Light is purification. Dark is destruction. They are opposites."

Wait, wait, wait. I hurt *River*? My stomach curls into a ball and drops to my feet.

"Covered, covered, covered," Ali says, her eyes glazed as she remembers the journal passage. "Look inside."

Inside what? Myself? Well, I have!

"Our only defense—hell, our only real weapon—has been stripped from us." Bronx bangs his head into his pillow. "We all suspect Tiffany is the culprit. Let's find out what she did to us and fix it."

"I'll question her," I announce. "I'm good at getting answers." And it's time.

Cole shakes his head. "My house, my interrogation."

"Tiffany slashed Milla's throat." Frosty places his hand on my shoulder, squeezes. "Give her a chance."

I still don't turn to face him, even though I want to look into his eyes more than I want to take my next breath. His support is...well, it's miraculous and wonderful and completely unexpected.

River strides into the room. "I second that." His pale hair sticks out in spikes. Crimson splatters mar his cheeks and arms, his clothes are ripped and dirt-streaked, his boots caked with mud. "You haven't seen my sister in action. You're in for a treat."

"It's true." Sometimes a girl has to toot her own horn. "When you're good, you're good. When you're me, you're better." *Toot, toot.*

"Let her try." Ali bats her lashes at Cole. "Please, Coley Poley."

I snicker. Coley Poley?

After a moment of hesitation, Coley Poley gives a stiff nod. "Fine. Do it."

Relief spears me. "I won't let you down. You have my word."

River spits out every bit of information he has on the girl. The more I know, the better prepared I'll be.

"I'm going with you," Frosty says. "I'll make sure nothing happens to you."

First he talks and jokes with me. Then he touches me of his own free will. Now he's *worried* about me? *Me?*

Am I being played?

"Sometime today," Bronx says.

"Right." Blushing—again—I stride from the room, Frosty close to my heels.

Tiffany is locked in an eight-by-eight cage in the basement. A cross between a prison cell and a kennel for large dogs. How appropriate. She's unarmed and by now, she's malnourished and weak.

I scan her new living quarters. Dim and dark, though spacious. Very little furniture, only a table and a few chairs scattered about. There are other cages lined against the wall, but they're currently unoccupied.

Tiffany's cage is the only one with a toilet, which is out in the open. Cameras are mounted in every corner of the room, allowing us to watch her from the safety and comfort of the security room, where numerous monitors are located.

Noticing us, Tiffany scrambles to the back of her cage. Her hair, now bleached to a yellow-white, is matted, her eyes wild. One is brown, one is blue because of a contact. Some of her makeup has been washed away by sweat, revealing freckles. Blood is crusted underneath a gash in her chin.

"You," she snarls at me. She's frightened. She's angry. And she blames me for her predicament.

My gaze remains on her as I say to Frosty, "Get her out and put her in a chair." The key to any interrogation is confidence. The moment she realizes I have nothing to lose and she has everything to gain, she'll settle.

To my surprise, Frosty obeys without hesitation and wrenches the girl from the cage.

"Gently," I say. Kindness goes a long way in a situation like this. "Please... Saucy Frosty."

Hearing my choice of nicknames, he flicks me a wry gaze. I shrug. It was worth a shot. He forces Tiffany to sit—and no, he still isn't gentle. As I scoot a chair in front of her, he remains behind her, his arms crossed over his chest. When Tiffany attempts to stand, he shoves her back down.

"Normally," I say, "I would beat you with a hammer before asking my questions. Why don't we skip that part and get straight to the Q and A? I've mopped up enough blood for one day."

She spits at me. "I'm not telling you shit."

With the distance between us, the glob of grossness lands to the right of my feet. I hold out my hand. "Napkin," I say to Frosty.

He tosses me his shirt.

Do not focus on his chest.

I wipe up the spit, and stand in front of Tiffany. She glares at me, even as she flinches back. I lean forward. She tries to push me, tries to kick me, but I slap her arm, bat her leg away and climb onto her lap, penning each of her limbs beneath my thighs.

I grip her by the jaw, forcing her to face me, and clean her eyes with Frosty's spit-dampened shirt. A creepy move, and yet also gentle, hopefully confusing her.

"Such spirit. Such stupidity." I pat her cheek before I return to my chair. "Did you know Anima once captured my brother?"

"I don't ca—"

"I went to rescue him and got trapped myself. I was surrounded by agents, disarmed and threatened. I couldn't fight, so I relied on bravado." I laugh without humor. "For my efforts, I was forced to watch as my friend—the one I convinced to help me—was stabbed repeatedly in the chest."

Tiffany pales. Frosty stiffens.

Ignore him. "Do you know who and what Anima is, Tiffany, daughter of Hannah Reynolds?" I state her address, one of the facts River gave me, letting her know I can easily turn my sights on her mother.

She pales. "Is it a cartoon?" Her tone is snarky, but she refuses to meet my eyes.

"Anima," I say, "is a company responsible for the deaths of many of my friends. They captured and experimented on zombies for their own personal gain, and they didn't spare the humans who got in their way. Male, female, young, old. It didn't matter. What you did to me—injecting me with toxin—that's something an Anima employee would do, but the company has been destroyed…which makes me wonder why you did it."

"I don't like you. Maybe *that's* why I did it." She realizes her mistake and scowls. "Not that I did anything."

I smile at her, but it's merely a cold baring of teeth. "You'll be honest with me, or you'll go back in the cage. I'll be sure to turn off all the lights on my way out."

"Bitch." She tries to stand, but again, Frosty pushes her into the chair. "I'm not scared of you, and I'm not afraid of the dark."

"You will be…but you didn't let me finish. Do you really think I'd put you back in the cage alone? Oh, sweetheart, you don't know me very well. My brother has a crate full of zombies just waiting for their next meal."

This is true—because River always has a crate full of zombies somewhere.

She licks her dry, cracked lips. "I don't know who Anima is, okay, and I didn't do anything to you. You've made a mistake. Got the wrong girl."

"Liar!" I bang my fists against the arms of my chairs. "I'll give you one more chance, and then I stop being nice. Why did you cut my throat? What did you inject me with at the cemetery? Did you do something to the other slayers, something to negate their abilities? Tell me."

She gulps. "I'll tell you everything. But you have to give me something in return."

She's an opportunist. Got it. I smile slowly. "For starters, I'll allow you to live."

She shakes her head.

"And," I add, "from this moment on, your responses will purchase your privileges. The lights…the food…a bed in your crate. A blanket. Water to bathe. Towels. Clean clothes."

She glares at me but says, "I don't know what was in the darts I used on you. I really don't. They weren't meant for a slayer."

My stomach twists. "You'll get to keep the lights on. Now. For whom were the darts meant?"

She presses her lips in a firm line.

Fine. "No dinner tonight. Would you like a bed?"

Her breath hitches. "Wait. I'd rather have dinner."

"Sorry, but that opportunity has passed. Maybe you'll earn your breakfast. Last chance to earn that bed."

"Zombies," she rushes out. "I was supposed to inject zombies."

A lump grows in my throat. "Why?"

"I don't know," she says with a stomp of her foot. "I was told what to do, never why."

That, I believe. Her frustration is palpable. "You want breakfast? Tell me what you did to the other slayers."

"I put something in their food. A white powder. I don't know what it was."

I believe that, too. She isn't bright enough to have masterminded this kind of destruction. "Why did you try to kill me?"

"I wasn't supposed to harm anyone, but you saw me there, at the cemetery. You recognized me and would have ruined everything. You ruined everything anyway," she adds bitterly. "I thought if I got rid of you, I could stay here."

I arch a brow. "What did I ruin, exactly?"

"As long as I was on the inside, I got paid to report whatever I learned. The moment I got kicked out, the cash stopped coming."

So. I almost died so that she could collect a check. "Who paid you?"

"Who do you think?" With a smile, she throws the name at me as if it's a weapon. "Rebecca Smith."

21

Frosty

DEATH BECOMES HER

Rebecca Smith. A woman I hate with every fiber of my being. The former leader of Anima, and a bitch of the highest order.

Four months ago, we had her in our possession. Had I made the call, she would have left us in a body bag. She's the one who blackmailed Milla. She's the one who attached bombs to collared zombies. She's the one who destroyed my home, sending her hazmat-protected agents in to kill our group with bullets when the blasts failed to do the job.

She's the one who orchestrated Kat's death.

Ali used her slayer ability to conceal Ms. Smith's memories, essentially making the woman's mind a blank slate. Ms. Smith once did the same to Ali, after all. But with a little help from Cole and Helen, Ali was able to regain full access to her memories. Someone must have helped Ms. Smith. And she must have hidden resources we know nothing about. How else would she have drugs to negate our abilities? Serums to clone zombies, if Milla is right about seeing familiar faces. A potion to turn *dýnamis* into *thánatos*—or cover it. Isn't that what the journal said? *Cover, cover, cover.*

Milla and I return the ballroom, but I barely have my rage under control.

Everyone else radiates different degrees of shock.

"Do you believe Tiffany is telling the truth?" Cole asks, his voice tight.

"Yes." The response comes from Kat, who appears in the center of the room. Tutu-clad Emma stands beside her. "Rebecca Smith is alive, and her memory is back."

I nod a greeting at Kat, like I do with all my friends, and for once, there's no desire to do more. No desire to close the distance and draw her into my arms. No desire to hug and kiss her or whisper inappropriate things in her ear.

Maybe my emotions are too dark. Maybe…

I've finally moved on.

She's a part of me. She owns a piece of my heart, and she always will. I'll always love her. But I won't—don't—need her anymore.

The truth hurts me. It also frees me. I can survive without her.

She returns my nod with a sad smile, as if she can read my mind.

"We just found out." Emma wrings her hands together. "And only because Rebecca's witnesses took us to court. They requested a second chance to make her realize she's headed down the wrong road."

Ali sucks in a breath. "*Is* she protected?"

"Right now, yes. Which means her location is hidden from us." Kat's shoulders stoop. "I'm sorry."

"We should have killed her when we had the chance," I say.

"I get killing in the heat of battle," Milla says, her tone soft. "But she's never part of the battle. She's a coward in that regard. If we'd killed her, it would have been in cold blood, simply to make our lives easier." She places her hand over her heart. "Honestly, I'd rather die before my time knowing I did the right thing than live a long life knowing I did the worst thing."

Wise words, and damn it, there's no refuting them.

"I'll call Detective Verra." Cole palms his phone. "I'll let her know what's going on."

"Meanwhile we'll keep petitioning for answers." Kat links her fingers with Emma's. "Helen is still in court, requesting the recipe for an antidote to counteract whatever Rebecca did to you. All of you," she adds with a glance at Milla.

Bronx wraps an arm around Reeve's shoulders. "I'll program home-security alerts into each of your cells. If Rebecca sends her agents, you'll know the moment a single perimeter is breeched."

"Meanwhile, we need to rest. Right now I'm not capable of fighting bedbugs." Gavin wiggles his eyebrows at Jaclyn. His patented move: joke to lighten tension. "Stay in my room and fight them for me?"

Justin walks over and slugs him in the arm.

"Ow." Gavin frowns at him. "I didn't ask her to fight them naked, now, did I?"

Jaclyn looks ready to fall over with fatigue. Hell, all of us do.

"Gavin's right," I say. "We need rest."

Cole nods. "I'm ordering each of you to stay in bed for at least eight hours. We'll reconvene at noon tomorrow and decide what to do about Ms. Smith."

Emma blows Ali a kiss and disappears. Kat gives me another one of those sad smiles before she, too, is gone. Despite everything, I hate the sadness and I hate to see her go.

Cole takes Ali's hand and leads her out of the room. Gavin arches a brow at Jaclyn, and she gives an almost imperceptible nod. I'm pretty sure I just witnessed a silent invitation to hook up...along with an acceptance. The two shuffle out of the room, Justin not far behind.

River steps in front of Milla and says, "You came after me."

She looks away from him. "It doesn't matter."

"You came after me, faced Rebecca, and I flayed you for it."

"Don't. Seriously. It's over and done."

"You're wrong. It'll be over only after I've spent years making it up to you." He holds out his hand. "Please, Milla. Come home with me."

A very dark curse explodes from me.

She frowns at me, then says to her brother, "I told Kat I'd sleep with Frosty." Her cheeks brighten to an adorable pink, and I relax. "I mean, not sleep with him, but sleep in the same room with him."

"Sorry, but there's no way in hell I'm allowing that." River shakes his head, adamant.

Smiling, she pats his cheek. "You're so cute when you try to boss me around." To me, she says, "Take me to your room."

"I don't actually have one." I've spent many nights here, but only in her sick room. "We'll have to pick one."

"Well, all right then." She rubs her eyes. "Let's pick one. I'm not sure how much longer I can stay on my feet."

"Fine. Stay here. But I'll be sleeping in the room next to yours," River mutters. "And by sleeping I mean listening through the wall, ready to gut a former friend for trying something he shouldn't."

"Don't worry," Milla says, her gaze swinging in my direction, only to pass over me. "Frosty and I aren't like that. We'll never be like that."

The words are true, and yet I'm frowning as I lead the pair to the west wing of the house, where all the bedrooms are fully furnished. Most of the doors are shut and locked, couples already inside, doing things I won't be doing to Milla.

Kissing…touching…

My hands clench at my sides. There are three open doors in back, and I claim the first, not caring if I find a princess paradise or a man cave. Like Milla, I'm not exactly steady on my feet.

Out of habit, I memorize my surroundings. Just in case I have to find my way around in the dark. Or fight an assailant during an ambush. King-size bed with mint-green covers. Two intricately carved nightstands and two navy leather chairs in front of a marble fireplace that has veins of pink and gold running throughout.

Milla says, "Good night, Riv," and shuts the door, sealing us inside. Alone. My mouth goes dry.

"Mind if I take the first shower?" she asks.

"Go ahead."

She shuts herself in the bathroom. A few seconds later, water is raining on porcelain. The pitter-patter should be soothing, but it only revs me up. Milla is wet and naked. How easy it would be to join her, how sweet to wash her back the way she washed mine earlier.

Frosty and I aren't like that. We'll never be like that.

I stomp to the dresser, where I find garments of every size. T-shirts, sweatpants, jeans, socks, panties and boxer briefs. I dig out what I need, choose a few things for Milla and pick the lock on the bathroom door. I'm playing with fire, and I know it, but I'm determined to win our game of B & E.

My blood heats as I step inside, and the thick, mint-scented steam doesn't help. I'm quiet, but the shower curtain suddenly whisks open at one side, just enough for a grinning Milla to stick out her head.

"Caught you." Water droplets cling to her lashes and glisten on her lips.

Again, my mouth goes dry. I crave a taste of—

Nothing. "Hate to break it to you, Mills, but it's easy to catch me when I want to be caught."

"Mills?"

"Would you prefer Sweetness?" I drop the clothes as my gaze slides down...down, my mind willing the curtain to fall. I want to see more of her. Want to see *all* of her.

Her cheeks flush. As tough as she is, she's also shy, a little vulnerable. Too damn adorable.

She clears her throat and retreats behind the barrier. "Well. You should probably go."

Yes, I probably should. But I don't. "You did good tonight. With Tiffany *and* zombies."

"Thank you. You and River were right, though. I need to

practice using my new ability. At least now I know I can use it without killing everyone I love."

Love?

"By the way," she says, "I'll need a new phone. The red flames fried my old one."

"No problem. There are plenty of extras here. We'll get you one in the morning."

"Thanks."

I take a step toward the stall. "Milla?"

"Yes, Frosty." There's a tremor in her voice.

What the hell am I doing? "I'm going." I leave at last, before I do something we'll both regret.

A short while later, she emerges. Her hair is damp and wavy, the T-shirt and shorts I selected far too small for her. Oops. My bad.

"I thought guys like you could take one look at a girl and guess her size." She tugs at the hem of the shorts. "You failed."

"Actually, I succeeded." I grab the clothes I intend to wear. "I needed me some eye candy."

A twinkle in her golden eyes. "How about I pick *your* outfit?"

"Like you'd really give me clothes. You prefer me naked, and you know it." I'm flirting—again—and I have to stop.

I don't want to stop.

The twinkle intensifies. Her cheeks burn with rosy color. Color that spreads lower and lower... And her lips...those plush, red lips...

Yeah. I gotta stop looking at them. I'm becoming obsessed, and it's putting me in the middle of a tug-of-war I can't win.

Want her, don't want her. We can do this, we can't do this. We should try, we shouldn't try.

I retreat into the bathroom and take a very long shower. So long she has to wonder what I'm doing. So long my skin prunes. After I change my bandages, I dress in a T-shirt and shorts that actually fit me. By the time I emerge, Milla has made a pallet on the floor, and she's buried under it, pretending to be asleep, clearly expecting me to take the bed. Hell, no.

"Get in the bed, Milla."

"I'm fine here. Really. I've slept in worse."

I hate reminders of the crap life she's led...not to mention the horrible way I've treated her. But I'm not going to argue with her. Not this time. She has a terrible habit of winning. I march over, scoop her up and throw her on the mattress.

Before she's finished bouncing, she grabs me by the nape and yanks. I perform a very undignified face-plant. As fast and wily as she is, she's on top of my back, her knees digging into my shoulders before I can sit up.

I grin. "Good move, sweet pea, but to keep me down, you'll have to learn to fight dirty."

Without any more warning than that, I reach around to clasp her arm and jerk her forward, using the counterforce to turn myself. She ends up sprawled across my chest. I roll before she can regain her bearings and trap her with my weight.

She's far from daunted. "Sweetness... Sweet pea. Not exactly the nicknames I expected from you." The twinkle returns to her eyes, and I want to look away—I have to look away if I'm going to walk from this encounter unscathed, but all that glittering gold...it's like champagne, intoxicating me, until I'm falling deeper and deeper into their depths and happy to drown.

"For your information," she adds, "if I decide to fight dirty, you'll end up having to scoop your intestines off the floor."

She's teasing me, but my humor has fled. I'm too tense, too achy, truly alive for the first time in months. The hardest parts of me are aligned with the softest parts of her; we are two puzzle pieces and we fit together perfectly. Blood rushes through my veins, an awakened river that had burst from a hot spring. My heart pounds against my ribs.

"Frosty." She flattens her hand on my chest. She's trembling now.

The air heats and thickens as I slide my hands into her hair and fist the strands. I can't stop the action. I don't want to stop. I just want her.

"What are we doing?" she asks softly.

I don't know. Going crazy? Celebrating life while we can? "Making each other feel good?" I rub my lower body against hers and she gasps. So I do it again, and again. "Yeah...that certainly does feel good."

I tell myself my desire for her is natural. She's a beautiful girl, and a hard-on doesn't mean anything. I can be with her and scratch an itch. Then we can move on. Pretend it never happened and remain friends.

But I'm not that guy, I remind myself. Not anymore. I stop and roll away from her.

She stands on unsteady legs and stares down at me. "There's something you need to know about me. It's personal."

"Tell me."

"I've had boyfriends. A *lot* of boyfriends. Actually, no. I haven't. They don't qualify as boyfriends. Most had their fun and took off, leaving me to wonder what I did wrong, what was wrong with me, why they could commit to anyone but me, and I'm not going through that again." Her tone acquires an edge of bitterness. "Especially with you. You're still in love with Kat."

"I'm not." The girl I once thought I'd marry is now a friend, nothing more. I let her go, just the way she wanted.

She tried to tell me that we were never meant to be. At the time, I didn't believe her. Now? My blinders are off, and the truth is undeniable. A punch of ice.

She used to make me laugh, and she used to make me hot, but she never accepted the slayer part of my life. Anytime we spoke of college and getting a "real" job, she begged me to consider accounting.

"Being a cop…it's too dangerous," she said. "Be safe for once."

Milla—surprisingly sweet, amazingly sensitive Milla—gets and accepts the danger I face. She stands by my side, protects my back.

Another punch of ice. The girl I once hated understands me in a way my girlfriend never did.

"Come here," I say. "Please."

Milla lies beside me and tentatively links our fingers. It's a gesture of comfort. One I welcome.

"Tell me about the girls you've been with, other than Kat," she says. "Anyone special? Anyone you miss?"

"No. Kat was my first. After her, I wanted to escape my life, just for a little while, and sex with strangers allowed me to do that."

"But pleasure doesn't last, does it." A statement rather than a question.

I answer anyway. "Not that kind, no." It's a reminder I need right now. I want this girl, but I'd only treat her like the others, and she deserves better. "You can trust me. I'll never hit and run with you."

"Hit and run. Nice."

"I'm a warrior poet. What can I say?"

"If you tell me you respect me too much to sleep with me, I think I'll go ahead and spill your intestines."

"Please. You'd have to break your famous control for that."

She curls onto her side to face me—but she doesn't relinquish my hand. "Famous? Do tell."

"You're a legend. Everyone watched you with Tiffany, knew you wanted to lash out at her, but you kept your cool and asked your questions in a calm, serial-killer kind of way, always rolling with the punches."

"Well, I learned from the best. My father was a different man for different people. His way of ensuring everyone loved him, I guess, and gave him whatever he wanted. No one saw the monster lurking under his smile." She traces her thumb over my palm. "You're good at what you do, too. And vicious. You go for the kill shot every time, without hesitation. It's poetry in motion."

"Yeah, well, you do this cool wrist thing that turns your swords into a pair of scissors. Your every motion is fluid. I do it, and I look like a three-year-old trying to cut along the lines."

"You never miss a shot," she says. "Sometimes I have to readjust my aim."

"You aren't afraid of needles. I see one, and I start crying like a baby."

"I've never seen you cry."

"It's on the inside."

She rolls her eyes. "Well, your tattoos are awesome."

I rub the one in the center of my chest. The heart I continually add to as my friends die. "Your tattoos far surpass awesome. I know you did the compass, but what about the others?"

"I did the ones I could reach. River did the rest."

Dude. "I know who will be giving me my next one. Hint— her name starts with Milla and ends with Marks."

"No way. The only other person I've ever tattooed is River, and only because he can fix everything I mess up."

"Flaws are human," I tell her. "I like flaws."

Her smile returns, slow and bright. "I always liked to draw, and one day River decided he wanted a tattoo. He stole the equipment and had me practice on oranges. When he decided I was good enough, he asked me to cover some of his scars."

Scars caused by their shit excuse for a dad. "Why Betrayal?"

She hesitates. "It's a reminder that the cost of betrayal is far too high."

Yes. Always. "Why the pink ribbon on your foot?"

An air of sadness overtakes her. "As a little girl, Caro and I… We…" Her chin trembles. "I loved to dance."

Treading carefully, purposely keeping my tone light, I say, "You can talk to me about her. I'll never use her against you."

She stiffens, sighs. "I forget you saw her death. But it's hard, you know. I want to honor her, but even saying her name fills me with guilt and regret. I didn't protect her."

"You were a child."

"I could have told someone what was happening."

"You were scared."

"And that fear cost me dearly. When she died, a part of me died with her. The best part. Her part. She made me whole. Now I'm only half a human, if that makes any sense."

"The guilt and regret belong to your father, sweet pea, not you."

"Easy to say, harder to accept."

I tighten my hold on her hand, letting her know I'm here, I'm not going anywhere.

"We wanted to be ballerinas, but we couldn't afford lessons. And even if we could, we couldn't have gone because, from the shoulders down, we were always covered in bruises. The pink ribbon reminds me of her, of our dream. To always hope for something better."

I smooth the hair from her cheek. "No one ever noticed, stepped in and tried to help you?"

"We moved around a lot. Mom homeschooled us until she took off. And we wore long sleeves all year round, even during the hottest part of summer. No one ever asked why."

I'm a no-good piece of shit. This girl has been to hell and back—multiple times—and I have only ever added to her problems.

"Why a compass?" I run my thumb over her wrist, surprised when her pulse jumps up to greet me. "To find your way?"

"Exactly."

I trace my fingers over a beautifully detailed dove. "And this?"

"You're familiar with Scripture, I'm guessing. You wear the Lord's Prayer."

"I am, and I do." Before she died, Cole's mom took us to church every Sunday. I saw—see—so much of myself in our lessons. Good versus evil. Dark versus light. Hope versus defeat. Forgiveness versus resentment. "The dove represents love, joy, kindness, patience and peace."

"That's right. I thought if I couldn't have those things in real life, I could have them in my skin." She scoots a little closer. "What about your parents?"

"I don't know my biological parents. I was adopted as a kid, and my parents loved me, they just weren't equipped to deal with someone like me. A little wild—"

"A lot wild."

I grin. "A fighter. Ornery. A sass mouth, my mother used to say. She and Dad were killed by zombies. We knew nothing about Blood Lines, and three undead were able to enter our home. They sensed me, but reached my parents first. I heard screams and raced into the living room. My parents didn't know why they were in pain, patches of their skin turning black, but I did. I could see the monsters. For the first time, my hands lit up, which is the only reason I survived."

"I'm sorry for your loss."

"Thank you. My aunt and uncle raised me after that, but they were even less equipped to deal with someone like me. An outsider. A weirdo. And wow, look at me, complaining. I was never beaten."

"Like that matters. You shouldn't compare your pain to mine. You suffered, plain and simple."

I trace the shell of her ear. "You make me wish…"

A shiver dances over her. "What?"

I caress her jawline, the line of her neck, the rise of her shoulder, reveling in the softness of her skin. The goose bumps rising in my wake entrance me—and once again I'm hard as a rock.

"What?" she repeats softly. "What do you wish?"

Not going to hit and run, remember? I force my arm to my side and roll away from her. "Nothing. I'm tired. Good night, Milla."

There's a slight pause, a crackle of disappointment before she responds. "Good night, Frosty. Sweet dreams."

22

Milla

BLEED ME A RIVER

Awareness erodes my delicious lethargy, and I blink open my eyes. I'm warm, toasty and relaxed…and I'm in a room I don't recognize. Before I can work up a good panic, memories flood me. The Z-battle and near defeat. Tiffany. Wrestling with Frosty—being caressed by him, sharing stories with him. Sleeping next to him.

Tingles raze each of my nerve endings. As I scan the layout of our bodies, I realize I'm not next to him anymore. I'm freaking on top of him!

His heart thumps against my temple, and his luscious heat envelops me. One of his arms, firm and sure, drapes my lower back, while the other nestles in my hair. My legs straddle one of his. Hello, Seabiscuit.

I've never woken up with a boy. Mace always took off before sunrise, not wanting River to see us together "until we're ready to share our love with others." Liar! The rest of my losers took off soon after they'd gotten what they wanted, leaving me confused and just plain sad.

I like this. I like it more than anything ever…which is the very reason I gather the strength to stand and tiptoe to the bathroom.

Sore muscles scream in protest as I brush my teeth and hair and take care of business. When I exit, Frosty is still sleeping, thank God; I'm able to sneak out of the bedroom undetected.

I take a few wrong turns and end up back where I started, bumping into Chance as he quietly shuts Love's door. Of all the people in all the mansions in all the world…

I sigh. "Kitchen?" I ask, not really expecting an answer.

"This way." He waves me over, shocking me to the depths of my soul when he wraps an arm around my shoulders. "Thank you. For what you did last night. Without you, Love would have died."

I stop, utterly floored. "You really care about her. Like, seriously care."

I didn't ask a question, but he stops, too, and gives me a nod.

"But why…?" Am I really going to do this? Put myself out there? Make myself vulnerable to a guy who hasn't spoken to me in four months? Who has every reason to spurn me? Whom I have every reason to spurn? I might have put him in danger by working with Anima, but long before that, he hurt me by leaving me the morning after we hooked up. "Why didn't you care about *me*?" Yes, I'm really going to do this. I deserve answers. "Why did you cut and run after one night?"

Remorse darkens his eyes. He presses his forehead against mine, an action I've missed, something he did long before hooking up with me. "I wanted it to be you. My forever. But wanting something doesn't mean it's right for you. And yes, I should have talked to you about it, should have opened up, but I took the puss way out and I'm sorry."

That's something, at least. An answer. "I guess I forgive you," I say, remembering the way Ali forgave me. Can I do any less now? Besides, Chance wants what I want. A love to last the ages. Something powerful and unstoppable.

What Kat and Frosty had.

Frosty claims he doesn't love her anymore. Is he just fooling himself?

Could he ever love me?

Do I want him to?

"Enough mush. Let's get some breakfast." Chance urges me forward. We're about to snake the corner when Frosty's voice snaps behind us.

"Milla."

Chance and I turn in unison.

Frosty is scowling, but—shocker—it's not directed at me. "Here's your new phone." He tosses the device at me, but his aim sucks and I have to dive to catch it. "Don't leave the house." He slams the bedroom door, and if there'd been portraits on the walls, they would have fallen.

O-kay.

"Well. That's new." Chance pulls me back into motion.

"Guys barking orders at me?" I snort and pocket the phone. "Hardly. But I think he dislikes you more than he dislikes me. What'd you do to him?"

He casts me an amused grin. "I'm surprised you can't guess."

"What do you mean?" What am I missing?

"Just...be careful with that one. He might have forgiven what you did, but he'll never forget."

A lump grows in my throat. After last night, I'm not just crushing on Frosty. I'm falling for him. Hard. I want him. All of him. The good, the bad and the ugly. I want to wake up in his arms every morning, and fall asleep with him every night. I want to fight for him and even with him, and then I want to make up with him. I want to guard his back and know he's guarding mine. I want to laugh with him and hold on to him when I cry. I want to know, finally, I'm someone worth *anything*.

But I'm not dumb. Not always. I know he'll never be able to give me those things.

The scent of bacon and eggs reaches me, and I latch on to the distraction as if my life depends on it. In the kitchen, Reeve stands at the stove, stirring a pot, while Ali sets the table. Bronx and Cole are squeezing oranges for juice; it's such a domestic scene, I'm momentarily speechless.

I take out my new phone, snap a picture and send it to Frosty: Breakfast almost ready. Bacon, eggs, biscuits & gravy.

His reply comes a few minutes later. I'd rather have chocolate cake.

I type, Well, then I guess the theme of the day is disappointment. Take what's here or starve.

As I'm sneaking a piece—or six—of bacon, Frosty comes down to join us. How does he feel about me? Our gazes meet, and for a moment, only a moment, the rest of the world ceases to exist—

—I'm in our bedroom...the bed...the two of us snuggled

close. Desire floods me, a tidal wave I can't contain, pulling me under, drowning me—

—but I'm back in the kitchen a moment later, my cheeks burning bright red. We just had another glimpse of the past, but this time, we experienced my longing for him. Now he knows how I feel. And that makes me wonder...

Why are *his* cheeks red?

"Frosty!" Ali rushes over, wincing a little with each step. She hugs him. "You're joining us for breakfast? Is it Christmas?"

He jumps up and down and claps like he's only five years old. "Christmas! Where's my present?"

"Right here." She pretends to unwrap her fist and extends her middle finger. "Do you like it?"

"Love it. But it's too much. I can't accept."

She holds the finger to his nose. "I insist."

"You are such a brat." He bats her arm away. "I'm not sure how Cole puts up with you."

"He realizes I'm the best thing that's ever happened to him." She fluffs her hair. "That's how."

Cole winks at her. "Took the words right out of my mouth, Ali-gator."

When the rest of the household wakes, we hold a meeting to decide what to do about Rebecca, and what to do with Tiffany. We can't reach an agreement about Tiffany—half of us want to keep her caged, the other half want to set her free and follow her, hoping she'll lead us to Rebecca, while two holdouts (cough, Frosty and River, cough) just want to kill her.

In the end, we decide we need a strong defense before we can even think about playing offense. Even if it means giving Rebecca time to plan her attack. So, we spend the first week fortifying security on the house. More cameras in and out, motion sensors, trip wires on every door and window, all of which can be activated with a single press of a button. We also pour Blood Lines around Shady Elms, trapping any surviving or new zombies inside a select area. Humans can still enter and leave at will. During the day, the zombies will seek shaded areas, leaving the humans alone. At night, nothing bad will happen as long as those humans stay away.

Also, we don't know which of the recruits we can trust, but we do know we can't allow Rebecca to swoop in and one, kill them, two, turn them into zombies, or three, use them as bait. So, River assigns his most trusted slayers to follow and guard them and continue their training, even though they aren't allowed back inside the house.

The next week, we practice fighting, trying to strategize around our lack of abilities, as well as deal with—and use— my *thánatos*. After my trial by fire, I had to admit there was no avoiding the ability. I quickly learn that keeping my emotions under control is the key to my success. When I'm angry, the energy that leaves me is sharp and cutting. When I'm frantic, the energy is choppy and shoots out in bursts. When I'm calm, the energy is less sharp, less cutting, and a constant flow.

Reeve and Weber create different serums, hoping something will spark *dýnamis* in at least one of us. So far, no luck. How are we going to heal from battle? How are we going to defeat Rebecca?

Finding out she's back in the game has jacked up my protective instincts to the max. I refuse to leave Frosty's side. I even follow him into the bathroom one morning—*you're wel-*

come, Ali. Yeah, he promptly kicks me out and slams the door in my face, but I stand guard outside. To get to him, Rebecca will have to go through me.

But while I'm more determined than ever to save him, he's more determined than ever to ditch me. The only time he seeks me out is at night, and only because we share a room. He no longer sleeps on the bed. He makes a pallet on the floor. We don't talk the way we did our first night here. In fact, we barely speak at all. We definitely don't look at each other. Too afraid of having another vision, I suppose.

The times he manages to lose me—like now—are agony for me. To be honest, though, that agony is nothing compared to what I feel whenever he's near. One glance, that's all it takes, and I'm solely focused on him, everything else forgotten. My skin pulls tight over my bones and I go liquid inside. I lose my breath. I ache.

I hate it. I love it.

At least Kat approves of my dedication to my job. She appears to me to tell me I'm doing such a good job it's almost like *she's* doing it.

I use the opportunity to question her. "Do you guys date up there in the holding zone, or whatever?"

"Yeah. People date, get married. All the good stuff."

"Are *you* dating anyone?"

Twin pink circles dot her cheeks, and I gasp.

"You are!"

"I'm not," she says, glaring at me. "I'm really not."

"But you're interested in someone. I can tell."

"Oh, just shut up! And don't you dare tell Frosty about this. I don't want him hurting any more than he already is.

Not that there's anything to tell him, because I. Don't. Want. Anyone," she snaps before disappearing.

Please. I could be water boarded, and I wouldn't tell Frosty about this. But knowing she has moved on and she's happy rids me of a lot of my guilt.

Soon after our exchange, Cole corners me in the locker room. It's just the two of us, and he looks ready to commit murder.

"What are you doing to my boy?" he demands.

"What do you mean?"

"The way he follows you and watches you… I'm not sure if he wants to choke you or screw you. If you're antagonizing him—"

"I'm not. And what do you mean, he follows me?"

"If you're teasing him—"

"I'm not!" I repeat. "Now, about him following me…"

He purses his lips and storms away.

After that, I keep watch for Frosty. Another week passes and I discover he *does* follow me. I confront him about it, expecting him to admit he hoped to catch me doing something wrong, but he is more embarrassed than angry—as if he watches me because he wants to, maybe even hopes to protect *me*.

I just… I don't know what to think anymore.

I'm running the treadmill to expel some tension and build my stamina when my phone beeps. I see Frosty's name on the screen and bite my lip to stop a grin of happiness. He's speaking to me again?

A treadmill expert, I don't have to stop the machine to read it—or reply. (Don't try this at home.)

Frosty: I'm hungry. Make lunch?

Me: Sure. I'll make U a sandwich. In never. Make sure U set UR watch

Frosty: It's set for Maypril 32nd, 1:63 a.m. But I don't want a sandwich, I want pizza.

Me: Name 1 thing wrong w/a sandwich

Frosty: It's not pizza

I snort. He's got me there.

Frosty: This is a special day. I'm officially a HS graduate. Shouldn't I get an award???

I'm proud of him. Graduating is a feat for anyone, but especially for a slayer.

Me: Yes! I'll give U award—1 sandwich coming up

Frosty: Cruel, Milla, Cruel. Where R U?

Me: Gym, why?

Frosty: Hoping U decided 2 go 2 kitchen & MAKE THAT PIZZA.

Me: No chance

Frosty: Speaking of, Chance w/U?

Me: No, WHY???

For some reason, Frosty's rage against Chance has only grown these past few weeks.

Frosty: What R U wearing?

Are you kidding me with this? He's been ignoring me all week, and now he's flirting with me?

Me: Were U hit in the head this morning??

Frosty: What? U don't want 2 coordinate outfits?

Me: I'm naked. Wear the same outfit & meet me in the kitchen 4 that sandwich

"I thought we agreed on pizza. And you are so not naked."

I jolt, the smooth huskiness of his voice a caress to my ears. I look over to find him standing in the doorway, his shoulder pressed against the frame, his arms crossed. The tingles and aches only he has the power to cause immediately start up, and the heat he always ignites quickly spreads.

"Congratulations on finally becoming a real man," I say.

"Thanks. It was a long time coming."

Could he be any more adorable? Longing sweeps me up and under. I want more from him. A lot more. I want to know everything. But I don't even know his real name.

Our gazes meet. I wish he'd tell me how he feels about—

—I'm standing in front of a swing set. The sun is shining so brightly, and I'm glad, I like the sun, but I don't want to be outside. The doors to the school are locked, though. It's recess, and I'm supposed to stay on the playground.

My aunt says recess is the best place to make friends. But I already made some. Cole, Jackson, Greg and Robert—everyone has a nickname.

Cole told me to call him Sir, but that's not happening.

Jackson is Bronx. Greg and Robert are Boots and Ducky. They're calling me Frosty.

They see monsters—zombies. To them, I'm not a freak. I'm normal. And they're teaching me how to fight properly!

I grin, but it doesn't last long.

My cousin Tomas told Aunt Reba that Cole is the one who punched me in the face. She told me I couldn't hang out with him, that he's going to end up in prison. She doesn't understand. I practically begged him to hit me.

A rock slams into my chest and I stumble forward, look-

ing up to see a kid at the top of the slide. He throws another
rock at me, but I duck and it sails overhead.

"Aston is a dumb name." He snickers. "Are you a dummy?"

The kids around him stop what they're doing to chant,
"Dummy, dummy, dummy."

A pat on my shoulder startles me. I turn to see Cole's purple eyes focused on me.

"Ready for another lesson?" he says.

"Yep. I am."

"Good. I call this one *mess with the bull, get the horns.*" He
climbs the jungle gym with an ease that amazes me and
reaches the boy who first called me a dummy. He pulls back
his elbow and, boom, drills his fist into the other boy's nose.

Blood sprays, and the kid drops, howling in pain—

—the workout room comes back into focus. My foot gets
tripped up on the treadmill and I propel backward. Frosty
rushes over, catching me before I crash. My heart thumps
wildly. I'm sweating again, and now I'm more than overheated. I'm breathless and wanting and desperate.

Want me the way I want you.

But he sets me aside and shoves his hands in his pockets.

I rock back my on my heels. "So. Your name is Aston,
huh?" What strikes me as strange? I wondered just before our
vision. Did *I* cause it to happen?

"Aston Martin, actually."

Like the car? "No way. Seriously?" I bark out a laugh. What
a perfect fit. Sleek, powerful and fast. But I don't want him to
get a big head. "No wonder you didn't want to share it with
me. I think I'll stick with Dijon."

"Sweet pea, I can have you screaming *Aston* by the end of the day."

I stop laughing in a hurry. He can. He so can.

The air thickens between us, something I'm growing used to, and I clear my throat. "If you're here to drag me to the kitchen—"

"No. Forget the food. I'm actually here to chat."

"About?"

He runs a hand through his hair. "I've been watching you practice. We'd already realized the white and red fires are opposites, but I've noticed your abilities—those that have remained—are the opposite of Ali's, as well."

I ignore a wave of hurt. "You mean she saves, and I ruin."

"I mean she controls zombies, and you control slayers. Her fire heals—or healed—while yours harms. But don't get your panties in a twist. I'm not blaming you. Rebecca Smith poisoned you, and for that, we'll make her pay. Until then... Cole, River and I have been talking, and we've decided to try filtering your blood."

They've been meeting in secret, otherwise I would have heard rumors. Irritation has me snapping, "Fine. Whatever. I'll shower and meet you—where?"

"The basement."

Where Tiffany has been living? Why let her know what we're up to? I open my mouth to protest, but Frosty is already gone. I hurry to our room, shower and dress in a tank top, leaving my arms bare for easier blood donation, then I make my way to the basement.

Frosty waits at the entrance. He stretches out an arm, offering me a hand. I'm so surprised, so uncertain about how

I'll react to contact, I hesitate before accepting, and his eyes narrow to tiny slits. At the moment of contact, I gasp, tingles sparking with new life, heat rushing through me.

Is this what Chance experiences every time he touches Love? What Cole experiences with Ali? What Frosty used to experience with Kat?

I try to draw my hand back. I hate the thought of being enraptured by him while he feels nothing for me. But he tightens his hold, surprising me further, and draws me deeper into the basement, a room that has been utterly transformed. Three plush black recliners surrounded by a vast array of medical equipment and several rolling trays.

Tiffany is strapped to one of the chairs and sleeping soundly. Ali rests beside her, wide-awake and without straps. Cole stands behind his girlfriend, an avenging angel ready to protect the reason his heart beats at any cost, and a pang of envy shoots through me. Reeve and Weber are here, too, arranging needles and vials on one of the trays.

"Here." Frosty leads me to the only available chair. "Reserved just for you."

"Thanks," I mutter, easing down.

He stays beside me, but he will no longer meet my gaze.

"What's wrong?"

"He doesn't want you to do this," Ali says.

I frown. "We're just filtering my blood, right? No big deal."

"It's a little more involved than that." Reeve putters around the equipment. "We know that what affects the spirit affects the body, so whatever is going on inside your spirit will manifest in your blood, even in the smallest way. So, we're going to put you on dialysis and filter out as much Z-toxin as possible and hopefully rid you of *thánatos*. Afterward, we'll inject you with a serum we've been working on, one that should strengthen *dýnamis*."

Should. My gaze slides to Ali. "Has the serum not been tested?"

"No. You and I are the lab rats."

"Something I object to," Cole says.

Frosty nods. "Agreed."

Too bad. "I'll go first." Let me suffer the effects if something goes wrong. "If I survive, and it works, Ali can be next."

"No," Frosty says, sharp and stinging. "Why don't *I* go first?"

"I'll go first." Cole crosses his arms over his chest.

Ali shakes her head. "You guys aren't the yin and the yang, so you can suck it. Us girls got this."

Before a word war can kick off, I ask, "Why is Tiffany sedated?"

"We took a sample of her blood, wanted to know if she's tainted like the rest of you. The results were inconclusive." Reeve taps the belly of a syringe and squeezes out excess liquid. "As for the slayers, everyone but you has lost every ability except the one to separate spirit from body. I blame whatever poison Tiffany used."

Anger rises—Tiffany!—but I beat it back. I don't want to accidentally unleash a stream of energy.

Cole meets my gaze. "You're one of us now, and if you don't want to do it, you don't have to do it."

I'm one of them? Seriously?

A smile breaks through, and I can't stop it. I catch myself

rubbing the Betrayal tattoo, not because I feel guilty but because the word has lost its power over me.

"I want to," I say. "What are you waiting for, Reeve? Let's get this party started."

23

Frosty

NOM NOM NOM NOM

I hate this. I hate this so freaking much I'm close to snapping. How can I stand here while Milla is turned into a test subject? What kind of man does that make me?

The kind who wants to save his friends, who knows this might be the only way to return them to their former glory.

Right. But is that a good enough reason?

I sweat bullets as Reeve pushes the tray closer to Milla then sits beside her. It's time for dialysis, and that's fine. People do that every day without complications. Kat did it four times a week. It's the serum I'm worried about. It's uncharted territory. Milla could be hurt. Or worse.

Panic nearly overwhelms me, but I remind myself Ali has gone through something similar. When she was infected with massive amounts of zombie toxin and the antidote couldn't save her, she was certain *dýnamis* was a cure-all. We refused to try. We'd never used our fire on another slayer, had only seen what it could do to agents—the same thing it does to zombies—and we didn't want to risk her life; she continued to grow worse until the zombie side of her completely took over the human side and only then, when faced with losing her anyway, did we relent. In minutes, it worked.

Had we used it in the beginning, we would have prevented months of suffering for Ali.

And yet, as Reeve ties the tourniquet on Milla's arm, I say, "I think we should come up with another plan."

Milla peers up at me with a hefty dose of confusion. She looks so tiny in the leather chair, so vulnerable and in need of a protector.

I have to step up and be that protector. I will.

In the past few weeks, I've learned so much about her. I know her in ways she may not know herself.

As a child, she failed to save her sister from her father's wrath. At least in her mind. Four months ago, she failed her brother, her entire crew. Now she'll do everything in her power to help—even if it means harming herself in the process.

"You aren't a lab rat," I tell her.

"I am today. If it hurts, it hurts. I can handle pain."

"You handle it better than anyone I know, but that doesn't mean you should have to."

She links her fingers with mine. "I want to do this. I have to. The problems started with me, and they'll end with me."

"Besides, there's not much risk involved," Ali says. "Because of the vision, we know Milla lives long enough to save you...which means she'll live through this."

Always we come back to the vision, and I'm sick of it. She might not die today, might only wish she did.

Milla releases me. "You heard her. I'll live."

There's a bitter quality to her tone I don't understand. Does she think I care only about using her as a shield? That the only reason I want to save her life is because she'll one day save mine? That has never been the case, and it never will. In the beginning, I tolerated her presence for Kat. But now... hell. I just don't know.

I don't know *anything* anymore.

Kat's death broke my heart into a million pieces. Her insistence that I date other girls broke the pieces. I had nothing, was nothing, and had to put myself back together; whatever mortar I used changed me. I'm not the same. I'm a different guy, with different needs...and different desires.

And right now those desires revolve around a punk-rock Barbie with a bad attitude and a heart of solid freaking gold.

"I don't care about my future," I say. "I care about yours."

Her eyes widen. She shakes her head as if she's certain she misheard. "You...you...what?"

Ali rubs the bridge of her nose. "Can't say I'm surprised by this. We've all noticed the vibe changing between you guys. And we need to talk about that, we really do."

"We really don't." My love life isn't her business.

"But whatever's going on," she continues, unabashed, "you can't stand in the way of answers."

I ignore her. "Milla, I would rather you—"

"No. I'm not playing *I would rather* with you," she says, her features soft and vulnerable, beseeching me. "I have to do this. We'll talk about the other thing later."

If I continue trying to stop this, she'll fight me, really fight me, and maybe even hate me. So I do the only thing I can. I step back, allowing Reeve and Weber to get to work. Milla is poked and prodded, her blood filtered for hours, and finally she is injected with the new serum.

We wait, tense, as one minute bleeds into another and she has no reaction. I begin to breathe again.

"I don't—" Suddenly she gasps, her back bowing. A scream rips from her. Then, just as suddenly, she goes limp and quiet, her head lolling to the side.

My panic returns. I kneel before her to gently tap her cheek. "Milla."

"Don't worry. This is normal." Reeve chews on her bottom lip. "I think."

"You *think*?"

Cole comes over to place a hand on my shoulder. "I wouldn't have agreed to this if I thought Milla would be harmed."

"Give her time," Reeve says.

"I know you've softened toward Milla." Ali meets my glare without flinching. "But she isn't right for you, Frosty. She—"

"This may come as a shock to you, but you don't get a vote about the way I live my life." My phone vibrates in my pocket. I check the screen, find a text from River.

Guess what I C in the sky? Rabbit cloud.

Attached is a picture of the cloud in question.

Well, well. A zombie nest is stirring.

Another text comes in.

& get this. There's a cloud shaped like a tombstone right next 2 it. I swear I see the letters RIP in the center

A tombstone…a hint that the zombies are stirring at a cemetery? Shady Elms, perhaps. I wouldn't be surprised.

"Zombies will be on the prowl tonight." I show the photo to Cole.

"Capture them," Reeve says. "I need to study them, find out if Rebecca altered them and if so, learn more about their new toxins. That way, if our serum doesn't work or if Milla has a relapse, we'll be better equipped to deal."

Cole arches a brow at me.

I nod stiffly. I never thought I'd reach this point. A desire to capture zombies rather than kill them. But for Milla's health…

Yeah. I'll do it.

"I've never tried to capture multiple zombies but River has," Cole says. "I'll get with him. The rest of you meet us in the gym at six. We'll head for Shady Elms when the sun begins to set at seven."

If Milla's awake this evening, she'll insist on going with us. I can't let that happen. She's been through too much today. "You got a sedative?" I ask Reeve.

"Of course." She digs through a drawer on the cart. "I don't think you need one, though. You seem calm now."

"It's for Milla. Later."

Bronx shakes his head. "Mistake, bro."

Better she's pissed at me than injured—or worse.

Reeve hands me a syringe, and I stuff it in my pocket next to my phone. I crouch in front of Milla, trace my thumb over the softness of her mouth. Her eyelids pop open and she jumps to her feet, gasping for breath she can't seem to catch.

"Hey. Hey," I say, straightening. "You're safe. You're all right."

"No." She shakes her head. "It's still inside me, and it kills me, *thánatos* kills me and, and, and—" She clutches at my shirt, frantic. "The serum didn't... It couldn't... Only made the flames stronger..."

"Hey." I comb my fingers through the silk of her hair. "I'm not going to let you die. You have my word on that."

As she sags against me, I wrap my arms around her and hold on tight.

"I'm sorry, Milla, but we need to check your blood one last time." Reeve approaches, empty syringe in hand.

Milla nods and I continue to hold her, unwilling to let go. I need her comfort as much as I need to give comfort back to her.

Reeve sticks her, fills the belly of the syringe. A few minutes pass as Weber readies the specimen and exams it under a microscope. I know it's bad news before the guy even speaks. I can see the disappointment shining from his face.

"Milla's right," he says. "The red fire has already contaminated the blood we cleansed. In fact, I can see the essence of the red flames in her cells, feeding off everything it encounters. This virus—or whatever it is—used the serum as a power source. And she's right. If she lights up now, *thánatos* could feed off her, too."

A tremor shakes her, but she remains quiet.

Enough of this. I lift her. "Let's get you to bed. When you wake up, I'll make sure pizza is waiting for you rather than some lame sandwich." I resort to humor because, if I don't, I'll rage.

She softens and curls against me, conforming to the hard planes of my body. "Frosty?" she whispers, and my hands clench on her.

"Yes." I climb the steps, careful not to jostle her.

"Do you believe we'll beat Rebecca this time? Once and for all?"

"I do. We'll do whatever proves necessary."

"Yes. Yes, we will," she says, and there's a note of finality in her tone I don't like. "Whatever proves necessary."

I expect Milla to *want* to rest. I should have known better. The moment I place her on the bed, she sits up and says, "You guys lost *dýnamis*, and I need to know if I lost it, too, or if it's still simmering inside me, just covered, covered, covered up by the red flames."

"You heard Weber. Those red flames could hurt you now."

"They're hurting me anyway."

A muscle ticks below my eye. "And just how are you going to tell if your *dýnamis* is covered by *thánatos*?"

"By looking with my spiritual eye, where the fire—fires—burn." She turns away from me. "I'm doing this with or without your approval."

Stubborn girl.

"Fine." But I'll be watching her. I'll step in if I detect the barest hint of unease.

I remain by the bed, on high alert as one hour bleeds into another. Milla hasn't moved from the bed. She's oddly relaxed, as if she's meditating.

I'm due in the gym in ten minutes. If I'm going to use the sedative on her, there's no better time. She's distracted.

I palm the syringe.

"You're making a big mistake." Kat appears at my side.

For the most part, she's stuck to her once-a-day visitation schedule, but there are times she's granted permission to pop in whenever she wants. I've found those are the days she's on a rampage about something.

"I've made a mistake before, kitten. The time I thought I'd made a mistake." I whisper, hoping Milla remains in her calm, unaware state. "What are you doing here?"

"Good news. I received permission to *fix* this particular mistake."

Milla opens her eyes.

Damn it!

"Mistake?" she asks.

"That's right." Kat anchors her hands on her hips. "Zombies will be on the loose tonight, but Frosty Dearest is planning to fight them without you."

"Zombies?" Milla throws her legs over the side of the bed and stands. She grabs her swords from inside our shared weapons case and straps them to her back. "I'm going with. Don't argue."

"What about checking for *dýnamis*?" I say through gritted teeth.

"Well, well. Someone certainly changed his tune." She flips her hair over her shoulder. "I didn't see it, but I'll continue my internal scan later."

I glare at Kat. "Thanks for nothing."

She blows me a kiss. "Also, Milla, he has a sedative in his

pocket, and he plans to use it on you." Her smile is pure evil. "I do whatever's necessary, too." With that, she vanishes, there one moment, gone the next.

"You *what*?" Milla reaches a hand into my pocket, yanks out the syringe and has the needle uncapped and positioned at my neck before I realize her intent. "Do you really want to travel this road?"

"A weak partner can get a stronger partner killed."

"I'm not weak. I'm ready. And when did we become part-ners?"

"Today." And partners do not sabotage each other. I glare at her. "Fine. I'm sorry. I just don't want you getting hurt."

Her features soften, but only slightly. She recaps the syringe and tosses it into the trash. "I can't make any promises." She pops a clip in her .44. "But I'll survive. I always do."

Good enough for now, I suppose. I tweak the end of her nose. "You're a brat, you know that, right?"

"Yeah, but you're brattier."

This is true.

We head to the gym, and though we're right on time, we're the last to arrive. Cole's in the middle of a speech.

"—River and Milla in the van with Justin."

"And me." Where Milla goes, I go.

Cole nods. "The rest of us will leave our bodies here and head to the cemetery on foot. We need to make sure Rebecca and her agents aren't hiding nearby. River, when he arrives, will be in charge. I expect you to obey his orders as if they come directly from me. And remember, the goal is to cap-ture zombies in one piece."

"But two halves will be accepted," Gavin says.

Chuckles sweep the room.

River spends a good chunk of time explaining his plan. Namely, he and Milla will bag and tag the captives. I don't like it, I don't like it *at all*, but protesting would embarrass Milla so I remain quiet. For now.

"All right." Cole nods. "Let's do this."

I climb into the back of the van and help Milla do the same. Justin takes the wheel and River the front passenger seat. Cole, Ali, Gavin, Jaclyn, Love and Chance leave their bodies behind, as ordered, and take off on foot.

As we speed down the road, I peer out the window. The moon is a hook. How fun would it be to hang a tire swing from it? The stars are absent, and there are only two clouds in the sky. The one shaped like a fluffy bunny, and the one shaped like a tombstone.

"When I'm a witness—" I begin.

"Finger crossed that doesn't happen anytime soon," Milla interjects.

"Like these zombies will get the best of me. Woman, you've met me, right?"

She flips me off.

"Anyway." I tweak her nose, a new, favorite habit. "I'm going to shape a cloud into a penis."

"Of course you are. Because you're the most mature person I know."

"Okay, what would you shape, Miss Prim and Proper?"

"An angel. Giving people the finger."

I chuckle.

We arrive at Shady Elms and discover the others are still searching the parking lot, surrounding streets and forest for any sign of Rebecca's agents. When they finish, declaring we're in the clear, we approach the cemetery's perimeter. Zombies are indeed out tonight. There are too many to count, a sea of rotted spirits that seems to stretch for miles.

None of the zombies are able to step past the Blood Lines we poured soon after our last battle, but that doesn't stop them from trying to push past the invisible wall.

"Don't you see," Milla says, pointing. "The same zombies. Look there, there and there. And there! Four versions of the same zombie."

Ali's eyes go wide. "But...that's impossible. Right?"

"Rebecca." Gavin says the name the same way anyone else would say *cancer*. "Every human has one spirit. Just one. Are these...I don't know...clones?"

"We'll find out." Cole looks to River. "You're up."

Milla

ZOMBIE SEE, ZOMBIE DO

Frosty takes my hand and gives a comforting squeeze. I'm irritated with him for even thinking about sedating me and leaving me behind, but I'm also amazed by the concern he keeps showing for me. Plus, I'm worried about him and River— about everyone. Old fears of losing the people I love dog me. And the dog has rabies.

"You'll want to help us," River tells the others, "but don't. Stay out here and wrangle the collared zombies we toss at you. If you're in there and you're bitten, the horde could be cleansed…as things stand right now, it's not likely, I know, but we can't risk the ruination of the samples Reeve needs."

I remove the metal collars from my backpack and hook them to my belt loops. Collars we stole from Anima because they place zombies under our control.

"Ready?" he asks me.

I nod. "Ready."

River hands Frosty a vial of Blood Line neutralizer. "Use this only if we get hurt and you have to swoop to the rescue."

"Won't we have to use it to get the collared zombies out?" Ali asks.

"No. Once they're collared, they're tangible and they can move past the Blood Lines just as we do while we're in bodily form."

Frosty kisses my forehead. "Be careful. Or I'll be pissed."

More concern from him. It's... I don't... Wow. "Ditto." It's all I can manage.

River nudges me, and I force myself to focus. Zombies. Battle. Collars. Nothing else matters right now.

"I hope you know what you're doing," he whispers, and it's clear he's not talking about our mission.

I pretend he is, though. "I do. Try to keep up."

"Milla—"

I surge forward. He isn't far behind. Because we're still in our bodies, we pass the Blood Lines, no problem. But the moment we do, zombies stop trying to claw their way free and turn toward us.

I slow. River steps out of his body—which the creatures will now ignore—and rushes ahead of me. *Pop. Pop. Pop.* One zombie after another drops, felled by a single bullet. A path opens up and I make my move, separating from my body while ripping a collar free. Spinning, I end up behind a zombie coming in hot and slap the metal around his neck. He goes still instantly, the electrical pulses in the metal disrupting his ability to function.

He's now tangible to those in the physical realm—not to

mention visible. If civilians show up tonight...well, I won't worry about it. Frosty and the others will take care of it.

After tagging four more zombies, I slip back into my body and drag the first to Frosty...who steps past the Blood Lines to help me. Does he never freaking listen?

"Take him to the van," I command before returning to my brother rather than the other collars. The horde around River has thickened and needs to be thinned.

We press our backs together, just like in the old days, and fight the fiends while guarding each other. I step out of my body to swing my sword, then spin back into it, only to step out again and spin in the other direction to chop, chop, chop at the creatures. Limbs fall around us. Heads roll. Black goo sprays. The scent of rot saturates the air, strong enough to gag me, but I've learned to ignore it.

Red eyes glow in a darkness illuminated only by Justin's supercharged headlights, and teeth snap at us. No matter how many creatures we fell, the mob never actually thins...until Frosty disobeys orders yet again and comes in guns blazing. He shoots until I hear telltale *clicks* to indicate he's out of bullets. But it doesn't matter. He twirls the weapons in his hands and ax blades suddenly glint in the moonlight. He uses them to slice through putrefied brains.

"I've got this," River says. "Tag the fallen."

I rip the rest of the collars from my belt loop and pick off the zombies Frosty has immobilized.

"Take this one past the line." I push one of my conquests Frosty's way and return to my post behind my brother. The process repeats three more times, the three of us like well-oiled cogs in a machine...until I lose my brother in the sea of undead bodies.

Where is he?

I search, and yeah, okay, maybe I'm a little too frantic about it, losing focus. Fingers tangle in my hair, jerking me backward. I don't fight the fall but arch my back so that I roll when I land, kicking my feet up, somersaulting backward and nailing the one who grabbed me in the chest. I jump to my feet and punch him in the eye—the eye pops out. Sometimes I fight dirty. Who am I kidding? I always fight dirty. I grab a dagger and stab him between the legs. A groin amputation. My favorite. I nail him with a collar, ending his fight.

"Remind me never to make you angry." Frosty confiscates my last collar and snaps it around the neck of the female he just gutted.

"Don't worry," I say. "Your precious is safe from me."

"Well. Maybe I can change your mind about that," he replies, and...and...

What! "Let's get our bounty out of here and find River."

We return to our bodies and pull the remaining collared zombies toward the Blood Lines. Frosty is strong enough to drag two at a time, but I can only manage one; we have to return for the others. On our second trip, we're beset by another starved horde. So many it's as if we've felled none. Arms reach for us, mouths chomp at us, and we have to be careful. These creatures can ghost through our bodies and reach our spirits; they can still bite and infect us.

A zombie who is lying on the ground, camouflaged by leaves, suddenly sits up and clasps Frosty's ankle, reaching past flesh just as I feared. Frosty trips, falls...lands on his knees.

Teeth…about to sink into his jean-covered calf. I act on instinct, pushing my spirit out of my body and diving on the zombie, stopping the bite from happening. I release a stream of energy, just like I've practiced, tossing every slayer into the air as the zombie and I crash into the ground.

Even as impact knocks the air from my lungs, I punch the bastard again and again.

"Milla!" Frosty calls in warning. "Behind you!"

I hear the approaching grunts and groans too late. A zombie has snuck up and now clasps my arm. He gnaws through my shirt, and a thousand pinpricks of pain spear me, each of my nerve endings suddenly scraped raw. Red fire erupts from my hands unbidden, quickly traveling up my arms…down my chest, and I can't stop it.

I might as well have rung a dinner bell.

Zombie after zombie falls on me, the next several seconds nothing but a feeding frenzy. I writhe and I scream, but it does no good.

"Milla!" Frosty and River shout in unison. "Milla!"

They're stuck in the air, and as my emotions go haywire, they're probably being suffocated. I have to release them. And I can. I can! I'm not helpless. I've practiced this, too. I simply have to take control.

I force myself to look past the pain, to look past the fear… to look past everything…and finally reach a place deep, deep, the center of hope, where I'm in Frosty's arms, and he's *worshipping* me. His hands and mouth go everywhere, no part of me taboo. And when he looks at me, he sees *me*, not a substitute for Kat.

"I'll be here in the morning," he says, "and every morning after." Because he can't get enough of me. I'm the most important part of his life.

As the heat plaguing my skin fades from my awareness, I hear a whoosh and multiple thuds. Thank God! It worked! The slayers are falling from the sky.

I gather what strength remains, which isn't much, to punch and kick away my tormentors. Dose after dose of toxin pours through my system. More than I've ever endured. More than anyone has survived, I'd guess.

"I've got her," Frosty says. "Clear the path."

"On it," River answers.

Tremors rock me so forcefully I have to be causing some sort of earthquake. *Hungry...* Mmm, something smells good, so good, and I want a bite of it now, now, now!

"This is the antidote, Milla," Frosty says. "The concentrated one. Don't fight it." A sharp sting in my neck, a cool rush of liquid flows through my veins.

The hunger fades until the only things I can smell are musk and sweat.

Frosty sticks me a second time, and the pain fades, too.

"Come on." He forces me to my feet and wraps an arm around me to hold me upright. He drags me forward. "Come on, come on, just a littler farther..."

We pass the Blood Lines.

"Now!" River shouts. "Now!"

The other slayers lob grenades into the cemetery. *Boom! Boom! Boom!* One explosion after another lights up the night. Flames lick at the sky, smoke rising like a giant black mushroom. Lights, flames and smoke only slayers and other spiritual beings can see. And feel.

I choke and cough as wave after wave of fetid heat washes over me. Soot burns my nostrils, coats my throat.

My knees give out, but Frosty still has his arm around me and makes sure I ease to the ground. He whips off his shirt and holds the material over my face; the cotton acts as an air filter. I'm too weak to fight him, to tell him to take care of himself not me—and then I'm too unconscious.

I wake up however long later in bed. I'm alone, the sun streaming bright golden rays through the crack in the drapes, highlighting the small mural of flowers I painted beside the bathroom door. The bowl of fruit resting on the dresser. The array of makeup scattered across the vanity. The faux fur throw cascading over the edge of the bed.

A stack of clean clothes rests beside me, a note waiting on top.

Sweet pea,
Everyone made it home safely. The collared Zs are in a cage in the basement, hungry for a Tiffany dinner, which is probably why she's ready to sign over rights to her soul if only we'll let her go. (Guess what my answer is.) Oh, and just so you know, I was tempted to give you a shower while you were out—wait till you see yourself. But then I remembered the way you de-nutted that zombie. I decided I wanted to keep mine (they're bigger) and let you do the washing yourself. You're welcome.
Frosty

I can't look that bad.

I march into the bathroom, catch a glimpse of my reflection—and a small scream escapes. I'm not that bad. I'm worse. Mascara coats the underside of my red-rimmed eyes. There are black streaks at the end of my nose and around my mouth. My hair sticks out in tangled spikes, and several bites are scabbed over on my neck and arms.

Dude. I might not ever get clean.

I linger in the shower, giving the hot water and scented soap a chance to soothe me, at the very least. Rather than allowing my hair to dry naturally, I actually break out the blow-dryer and curling iron. Goodbye hideous hag. Hello femme fatale.

I do the makeup thing and dress. Of course, the clothes Frosty picked for me are, in a word, minuscule. A scrap of a tank. The world's smallest pair of Daisy Dukes. For once, at least, he included a bra and a pair of panties.

I exit the bathroom to find Frosty leaning against the door, his arms crossed, his biceps a thing of beauty. My heart nearly drops into my feet, and I'm suddenly wracked by tremors. He's taken a shower, too, his hair damp and darker than usual. His navy blue irises burn with savage masculinity, and they are pinned on me, devouring me.

He's so beautiful, and…still off-limits?

He looks me over slowly. "You are too damn perfect to be real."

This is a dream. This has to be a dream. "My boobs are too small." I realize what I've said and groan. I did *not* go there.

He smiles. "They aren't. Trust me."

Right. If my body isn't good enough for a boy, his brain isn't good enough for me. I know this. And yet I return his smile as if he's just revealed the secret to world peace.

"How do you feel?" he asks.

Pleasantries. Those, I can handle. "I feel surprisingly healthy."

"Good. I can yell at you without guilt."

"Yell at me?" I splay my arms wide. "But why?"

Eyes narrowing, he advances on me, a predator stalking prey. "I told you what would happen if you got hurt. Well, you got hurt."

Yes. He told me he'd be pissed. And clearly, he is. Far from cowed, I shiver. "You should make an exception. I got hurt *saving you*."

"Don't fool yourself. That zombie got the drop on me, yes, but I had an antidote in one hand and a dagger in the other. I would have been back on my feet in seconds, and he would have been in pieces."

"Oh."

"*Oh*, she says." He stops directly in front of me, pinches a lock of my hair between his fingers and sifts the strands. "You owe me an apology."

"Why? Why are you even upset about this?"

"Because—" His lips press together, a muscle ticking in his jaw. "Just because."

"Why?" I insist, and oh, good glory—to borrow a phrase from Ali—I'm breathless. He's so close to me. He's touching me. And he's so freaking *intense*. "Tell me."

"I'm upset because—" Again he goes quiet. His inhalations are as fast and shallow as my own. His gaze lingers on my lips, and when my tongue comes out to lick—desperate for a taste of *him*—his pupils dilate and like spilling ink, the black spreads over the blue. His grip on my hair tightens. "I hate what you make me feel." His voice lashes out only to crack at the end.

I fist the collar of his shirt. "What do I make you feel?"

Frustrating silence. Crackling tension.

A low growl causes his chest to vibrate. "I feel... Damn it, I feel..."

"Tell me."

"I feel like I can't get enough. Like I have to have more, will do *anything* for more. And damn it, I'm getting more." He cups my nape and yanks me against the hard line of his body.

I gasp. He swoops down, his mouth smashing into mine. His tongue thrusts past my lips, demanding entrance.

This is really happening? Frosty is kissing me? Then his tongue rolls against mine and the most intense pleasure consumes me, and I kiss him back with everything I've got, plowing my hands through his hair.

He tilts my head the way he wants it and takes my mouth deeper, harder. I whimper. I have wanted this, needed this, for so long, and now he's giving it to me and, and, and...

He anchors both hands under my bottom and hefts me up. "Wrap your legs around me."

The moment I obey, he walks me to the bed, every step causing us to rub together, creating the most delicious friction. He lowers me, settles his weight on top of me, and I realize he isn't the only one who needs more.

Heat wafts from him, enveloping me, and my blood turns molten; my bones liquefy. My body moves of its own accord, arching up, into him, grinding against his hardness.

He hisses. "I want you, Milla."

He said my name. He knows I'm the one he's with.

"Yes." *Oh, yes.* I pull at his shirt, but I can't get it off him while his hands are still on me. "Shirt. Off," I say between thrusts of our tongues.

He rips the material over his head and suddenly my nails are scraping over the tattoos on his back. I'm purring, and he's groaning.

"Your turn." A command.

I lift and he quickly divests me of my shirt and bra, leaving me bare from the waist up. He goes still, peering down at me with wonder.

"You're so beautiful, Mills."

The way he's looking at me, I *feel* beautiful...even cherished. "Kiss me, Aston." I use his name for the first time, and it tastes good on my tongue. "Don't ever stop."

His eyes grow darker as he dives back down, claiming my mouth in a kiss that sears even my soul. Our chests are skin-to-skin, and I want the rest of us that way, too. I've never felt anything so—

"Frosty?" Kat's voice intrudes.

"Kat?" Frosty wrenches away from me and stands. He's fighting for breath as he turns to face his ex-girlfriend, is paling as she backs away from him. "Kat," he repeats, taking a step toward her.

She disappears.

He takes another step, this one toward the door.

First, confusion hits me. He's leaving me? Then, horror dawns. He's definitely leaving me—for his ex.

Oh...hell. *He's leaving me for his ex.*

I sit up, scramble for my shirt and yank it over my head, desperate to cover myself.

"I'm sorry. I'm so sorry," he tells me, anguish in his eyes, dripping from the words.

Sorry isn't good enough. "Don't do this," I whisper. "Stay."

He scrubs a shaky hand down his face. "I'm sorry," he repeats. "I have to... I owe her."

What about me?

He strides from the room without another word...leaving me alone. Always alone. Never good enough. Never "the one."

He didn't bang me, but he sure did bail.

My heart breaks. All I can do is curl into a ball and sob.

25

Frosty

THE SCOURGE OF THE EARTH IS IN THE LOOKING-GLASS

I'm trembling as I shut myself in one of the empty bedrooms and shout for Kat. What she saw...

Witnesses aren't allowed to view romantic or intimate moments. When the screen—isn't that what she'd called it?—went blank, she must have come looking for me. What happened...hell, it never should have happened. I knew it then, and I know it now. And not because of Kat.

I've been a dead man walking since Kat's death, and Milla helped bring me back to life. I owe her, just like I'd claimed to owe Kat. But if we'd had sex today, would I have offered her more afterward? A happily-ever-after I've only ever imagined with Kat?

Probably not. Because, even though we're friends, I'm not falling for her. I *can't* be falling for her. Yes, she matters to me. Yes, I'm borderline obsessed with keeping her safe. Yes, I crave more time with her—to talk, because she's smart and funny. But I told her I wouldn't hit and run. And committing to her, just so I can touch and kiss her... I can't do it.

Are you sure? Temptation whispers. *You're still on fire for her, desperate to be with her. Only her.*

Shut the hell up.

If our history is our foundation, then our foundation is built on blood, guilt and sorrow. Whatever we manage to build will come crashing down during the first storm. I'll lose her, and I can't survive losing another girl.

Maybe I'd be willing to risk it, though—maybe I'd be willing to risk everything—if Milla put me first. I put my girl first, and I expect the same from her. But River is and will always be her top priority. With good reason.

"Kat," I shout. "Let's discuss this. Please."

She appears between one blink and another, tears streaking down her cheeks. "How could you kiss *her?*"

The first spark of anger burns through me. "You can't have it both ways. You can't cut me loose and act jealous when I'm with someone else."

She flinches. "I'm not jealous. I just... I told you anyone but her for *your* benefit."

I scrub a hand down my face. "I like her. She's a good person, and she's had a crap life. She's my friend."

"Do you usually suck the air from a friend's lungs?"

"That's no longer your concern, is it?"

"I know. I know." She draws in a heavy breath, holds it, and as she slowly releases it, her eyes beseech me. "I want you with someone else, want you happy...but you can't be with her, Frosty. You just can't. Pick anyone else, and you'll get my gold-star stamp of approval."

Over the years I've faced zombies, toxin, injury and the death of loved ones, but this...this might be worse. "I said I would love you forever, and that hasn't changed. I do, and I will. You're one of the best things to ever happen to me, but you're not my girlfriend. Not anymore. If I decide to be with Milla, I will. You don't get a vote, and your stamp of approval isn't necessary."

"Frosty." She clasps her hands together, creating a steeple. "Please, don't do this. You don't understand."

"Kitten—"

"You remember my cousin Teresa, right? She's smart and pretty, and she has—"

"Kitten," I repeat gently but firmly. "Enough."

"No." She closes her eyes, tears catching in her lashes. "She's going to... Frosty, Camilla is going to die."

"Of course she is. Death is hereditary."

"Yes, but her death will come sooner rather than later. Ali's vision..." Kat's voice goes soft. "Camilla will save you...but she'll die doing it."

The words reverberate inside my mind—*she'll die, sooner rather than later, she'll die*—and an unholy rage overtakes me. "Tell me everything you know about the vision. Every detail. *Now.*"

Kat flinches, but says, "You're inside a building. You're cut, bleeding. Cole, Ali and the others are lined up behind you. There's a gun trained on you, held in a very feminine hand. A series of shots go off. Camilla moves in front of you and takes the hail of bullets."

As she speaks, a thousand-pound weight settles on my chest.

"I never thought you'd grow to like her." Kat's eyes plead

with me to forgive her. "I thought she'd get what she deserves, and that would be that. I made Ali promise not to tell anyone, not even Cole, because I thought the end justified the means. I wanted you safe. More than anything I wanted you safe."

"So you did to Milla what we crucified her for doing to us? You decided to trade one life for another, Kat." Damn her! And damn the entire situation. "I can't imagine those higher courts would approve."

"They approve of sacrifice," she says haughtily. Then her shoulders droop and she adds, "When it's by choice."

"But you haven't given Milla a choice, have you?" My bitterness is like a train that's gone off the rails. A crash is inevitable.

"No," she admits, "and for that, I'll be booted out as soon as Camilla... When she's gone."

Gone. Dead.

I reel. I burn. "You need to go. Now."

"I'm sorry," she whispers.

"You're sorry? You're *sorry*? Do you think that makes everything better?" I don't give her a chance to respond. "Do you have any idea how badly I suffered when you died? I was *shredded*, Kat. For all intents and purposes, *I* was dead. Milla brought me out of the abyss. She showed me again and again how to live, how to move on, and now you're telling me I'm going to lose her, too. That I'm going to survive and watch, helpless, as another girl dies in front of me."

She wraps her arms around her middle. "If she doesn't take the bullets for you, *you'll* die."

"If you think I'd rather watch her bleed out, the way I watched you, you don't know me at all." I stride to the far wall, away from her—I have to get away from her. My hands fist and I throw a punch, cracking the plaster, and she gasps. I throw another and another, creating a hole.

The leash on my temper breaks, and I punch and punch and punch again, my skin splitting, my knuckles cracking and swelling, but I can't stop.

I'm not sure how much times passes before Cole grabs me by the wrist, preventing me from continuing.

"Did you know?" I demand, wrenching free.

"Not until two minutes ago." His features are hard, determined. "To be honest, I'm not sure I would have done anything different if I had. I would have thought you'd be relieved. When Kat approached her, Camilla was your enemy. You hated her. You wanted her dead."

"You know my feelings for her have changed. You all know."

"We guessed. You haven't been forthcoming with details. For all we knew, you were playing a game, hoping to break the girl's heart and punish her for her crimes." He adds, "Don't worry. I'll deal with Ali."

I scoff. "What? You'll spank her?" How am I supposed to cope with this? How am I supposed to go on my merry way, knowing Milla will one day die because of me?

Actually, no. I'm not. I absolutely refuse to let her die. If she isn't protecting me, she won't be in danger. She'll live. I'll die, but she'll live, and I'm totally okay with that.

I pinch the bridge of my nose. "I'm leaving, and I don't know when I'll be back. Don't follow me. Don't come after me."

"You'll get no promises from me. I'll do what I think is

best. But you better be careful out there. We don't know where Rebecca is or what she's planning."

Let her come after me. Let her feel the full brunt of my wrath.

"Do what you have to," Cole says, "but get yourself together. We're at war, and distraction can get you killed."

"According to the vision, bullets will do the job. But better me than Milla." I stalk from the room.

I'm being followed, and not by my friends.

The sedan with dark tinted windows has trailed me around several corners, making no effort to hide. Now the driver is even flashing his headlights at me, despite the glare of the sun.

One of Smith's guys hoping to chat? Well, fingers crossed.

I drive to a nearby shopping center, where fast food abounds and superstores flood the streets with traffic. At a green light, I slam on my breaks rather than speeding through the intersection, causing the sedan to bump into my tail.

I put the truck in Park, turn on my hazards and exit, my weapons hidden under my shirtsleeves.

"I'm fine," I tell the witnesses standing on the sidewalk, watching. "No worries."

A slender woman with milky-white skin and jet-black hair anchored at her nape emerges from the back of the sedan. She's pretty in a military-commander type of way. If the military commander in question is posing for a pinup. Her lipstick is bloodred, a perfect complement the tight black dress and six-inch heels she's wearing.

Rebecca Smith in the flesh.

Hatred mixes with glee, and I reach for a blade. *Slow your roll.* Witnesses equal cameras. Cameras equal jail time.

Okay. No flashing metal.

"You picked the wrong time for a meet-and-greet." I smile at her. "But it's nice to know you got your stupid back."

"We have a few minutes before the cavalry arrives." She drops her chin to look at me over the top of her sunglasses. "Do you really want to waste precious seconds exchanging insults?"

"I want you to die."

"And I want Tiffany."

"Aw. Look who's finally grown a heart. You normally don't give a shit about your agents." As long as I've known her, she's only ever used others as shields.

Kinda like what I've been doing with Milla.

I swallow a curse.

"Everyone in my employ means something to me right now," she says. "I'm rebuilding my business, and good slayers are hard to find."

"Still trying to unlock the secret of immortality?" My tone is as dry as a desert. The thought of someone like Smith, with no moral compass, having no expiration date—horrifying.

She tsks. "Go ahead. Continue to scoff. If I'd succeeded, your girlfriend would still be alive. But who knows? Maybe we'll save the next one."

I take a step closer, and she takes a step back.

She lifts her chin. "Look. These past few months, I could have killed you and your friends a thousand times over. Did I? No."

"Maybe because you've been too busy cloning zombies."

"Would you rather I make new ones?" She pushes her sunglasses up her nose. "I've been content doing my work and allowing you to do yours. I've kept my distance, only sent one agent into your midst and only so I could keep track of your activities and ensure you weren't coming after me."

"Tiffany claims you paid her to poison us. Oh, and did I forget to mention she slit the throat of one of my friends?" *My best friend.*

Smith blinks in surprise. Or what she wants me to believe is surprise. "Well, that certainly explains why the girl ran from me when she ran from you. I didn't tell her to harm anyone, and I'll punish her for acting out of turn."

"Taking you at your word isn't something I'm willing to do."

"As for the poison," she continues as if I haven't spoken, "that was payback, plain and simple. Ali took my abilities, so I took hers."

"And the red flames?"

She shrugs. "Tiffany acted out of panic. The serum was meant for zombies, to make them hunger for each other rather than humans, but Miss Marks gave chase and Tiffany hoped the serum would slow her down." One of her perfectly plucked brows arches. "See? I can be one of the good guys, too. If zombies only feed on each other, your precious humans are no longer in danger."

There's a catch. With her, there's always a catch. "You—"

"No more questions. Either you give Tiffany to me, or you go to war with me. Your choice."

"We're already at war."

Her lips pull back in a snarl. "You don't want to take me

on, Frosty." She hands me a business card. "I'll give you twenty-four hours to release her. You do, and I'll share the antidote to rid Miss Marks of red flames. You don't, and I will kill you all."

I get all up in her face.

"What are you going to do?" she taunts.

She's lucky I hear sirens in the distance. I walk backward, unwilling to give her an open shot at my back. I slide behind the wheel of my truck and peel out, spitting fumes in her face.

So much for taking a little time to think about the future. I rage the entire drive home. A home Rebecca Smith just threatened.

I may not trust her, but I do trust that she's evil and she'll stay true to her roots. She'll attack us, whether we relinquish Tiffany or not. She may or may not give us an antidote for *thánatos*. She may or may not even have one, might even give Milla something to make her worse.

No matter what Smith says, our group stands in the way of her ultimate goal. Eternal life. She'll do anything to stop us from stopping her. Lie. Distract. Destroy.

Turn around. Put a bullet in her brain now, before it's too late.

Temptation again.

You might spend the rest of your life in prison, but at least your friends will be safe.

Maybe. But for the first time, I get why Ali let the bitch go last time. Two evils do not make a right. If I kill Smith, someone else will simply rise from the ranks and take her place.

There has to be a better way.

Black and white, Milla once said. And she's right. In this, there are no shades of gray.

I reach the tall, wrought-iron gate at the front of the driveway and press my thumb into the brand-new scanner for a fingerprint ID. As the gate swings open, an alert is sent to the cell phone of every slayer in residence, including Milla. No one comes or goes without everyone finding out. Where is she? What's she doing? Hating me for abandoning her?

I park in the massive underground garage and storm upstairs to the kitchen, where Cole and Ali are waiting for me.

"I'm glad you came back." She wrings her hands. "We need to talk."

"We needed to talk weeks ago. Now it'll have to wait." My tone is sharp, cutting. "We've got bigger problems."

26

Milla

COWBOYS AND INTESTINES

Word of Frosty's encounter with Rebecca Smith spreads through group text.

Gavin: Anyone else listen in on Frosty's convo w/our Mom & Dad?? Yeah. Me neither.

Mom and Dad. Ali and Cole?

Love: Deets! Gimme!

Gavin: I don't like 2 gossip, so make sure U get what I'm saying the 1st time. Frost ran in2 Smith—there was epic battle w/words, promise of blood & gore. Looks like we're back @ war, folks.

Justin: We've been @ war. Dibs on Smith!

River: Fine but after U do her, I get 2 kill her.

Justin: My "do" is gonna involve knives. Tag team?

River: R U asking me 2 have a 3-way w/U? Always knew U had a crush on me. Alas, I must decline. I'm a lone assassin.

Justin: Screw U

River: So that's a yes to the 3-way???

Gavin: Can U make it a 4-way? The ice queen is giving me the freeze out & I could use a little warming up

Jaclyn: Say goodbye to UR penis, Gav.

Gavin: If U can't have it, no 1 can??

Love: Get a room! All this violent flirting is making me sick.

Gavin: We have a room, thanx. We're currently cuddling

Justin: My mind needs a bleach bath

Jaclyn: U guys suck—I'm nowhere near UR room, Gav & I never will B again. Every1, we need 2 prepare 4 Smith's strike.

Bronx: I'm always prepared 4 anything.

Reeve: That's no joke

I'm furious that Frosty had a semishowdown without me. I knew the moment he left the house, of course, an alert sounding on my phone. I should have gone after him instead of licking my wounds in our room.

He kissed me. I liked it. Actually, I more than liked it. I loved it. I wanted more and would have given him everything. But despite his promise, he would have bailed on me afterward, just like all the others. There's no doubt in my mind now. When Kat appeared, he couldn't get away from me fast enough.

Never good enough.

"Household meeting in the gym." Cole's deep voice echoes over the speaker system wired into every room in the house. "Five minutes."

I'm already dressed in a tank and jeans, and I stalk into the hall. River is at the corner, coming my way.

"Hey," he says as we head to the stairs together. "I've been looking for you, wanted you to know I called for reinforcements earlier today. Three members of our crew have already arrived."

Something about his tone… "One of them wouldn't happen to be a former *boyfriend* of mine, would he?" Though I kept my relationships secret, River always knew who slipped into my bed.

"Two of them, actually. You gonna be okay?"

My stomach twists, wringing out bile, but I say, "Of course." How much rejection will I have to endure in one day?

Well, we're about to find out.

Gavin is waiting at the gym doors. On the lookout for Jaclyn? When I pass by, he hooks his arm around my waist to draw me back. He mashes his fist into the top of my head. "Good work capturing those Zs."

"Thanks," I say, kind of loving the brotherly attention.

He lets me go when River tugs on my arm. We enter the room. Justin, who's sitting on the edge of the boxing ring, winks at me. Love, who is sitting beside him, nods at me. Cole and Ali stand in the far corner, talking quietly with Frosty.

My stupid heart skips a stupid beat.

Chance enters. Marty, Eric and Roger—the latter two the ones River warned me about—trail behind him. All three spot me and scowl.

"I've told them not to speak to you. Don't even acknowledge them." My brother leads me to Love. "Sit here."

Not exactly great planning on his part. Wherever Love is, Chance will show up.

An-n-nd right on cue, Chance locks on Love and stalks over with the three amigos in tow. Eric and Marty are actually vibrating with fury, I realize.

I lift my chin, refusing to fidget. They hate me for putting them in danger. They'll always hate me, and forgiveness isn't even a blip on their radar because I never meant anything to them.

Well, screw them. I'm worth something, damn it. I'm smart. I'm beautiful. Frosty said so. I'm strong, and I'm loyal. Loyal to a plethora of faults, yes, but I'm willing to die protecting the ones I love. How many can say the same?

Roger, staring at me, runs his tongue over his teeth. Usually an action of flirtation, he somehow makes it a physical threat.

Eric blows me a kiss, all teeth and bite.

No one notices. Or so I think.

Frosty strides over and drills Roger in the back of the head. As Roger crumples, Frosty slams a fist into Eric's nose, breaking the cartilage. A pained howl rings out.

"Anyone else want to try and make Milla uncomfortable?" Frosty glances around the room, tense and ready to throw down.

Silence reigns.

"Yeah, I didn't think so. If you change your mind, you know where to find me—or I'll find you."

I'm… He… He defended me? Even though he ran out on me?

Does he still like me? Am I still in the game?

Do I want to be?

Ali claps her hands, drawing everyone's attention. "All right, folks, playtime is over. Here's what we know."

She relays the story about Rebecca approaching Frosty. Everyone agrees we should give the antidote a shot—if we can get our hands on it—but no one trusts her to actually deliver it. Some are willing to trade Tiffany, others aren't.

Then Reeve tells us what she and Weber learned from the captured zombies. "If I were to cut off a chunk of my skin, new skin would grow. Right? Well, these new zombies operate just like that. When a spirit rises from a body, a shell, a new spirit grows."

It's a terrible cycle.

She continues. "These zombies have different levels of toxin, each creation weaker than the last. However, Rebecca told the truth about *thánatos*. When I introduced a sample of Milla's blood to the zombies, each one had the same reaction, becoming frantic to feed on each other. One bite caused their toxin levels to strengthen exponentially."

Great. If they bite me, they'll strengthen and only want more of me. Basically I'm a walking zombie juice box. "I didn't want to eat zombies," I say. "I wanted to eat…" Ugh. I can't say it.

"Like to like, remember?" Frosty says.

Our gazes meet…hold. I shiver.

"What do our witnesses say about all this?" Bronx asks.

"Ask them yourself," Ali says as both Kat and Emma appear. "They've ensured everyone will be able to see them."

The room grows quiet.

Beside me, River stiffens. "Her." He grits the word, leaving me confused. Her…who? Kat?

Frosty, I notice, turns his head, as if he can't bear to look at either girl.

"We've petitioned for answers," Emma says.

"Meanwhile, Camilla is the one who felt Tiffany's blade across her throat." Kat scans the room. "She's the one dealing with *thánatos* now. Let her decide what to do with the girl."

Every eye lands on me, but I focus on Frosty again and—

—in the blink of an eye, the walls of the room vanish. I'm suddenly surrounded by Anima agents. Each has a gun aimed at my chest. My attempt to break into the warehouse to save my brother has clearly failed. These guys were waiting for me all along. They knew I'd be coming, as if the bread crumbs I'd followed were purposely left. They probably were.

I've been beaten to hell and back, my jaw is on fire and the friends I convinced to join me are lying dead at my feet. All but one. Bettina. Like me, she's restrained by two agents.

We should be dead like the others, but for some reason, we were spared, punches pulled, no one shooting or stabbing us.

A pale-skinned brunette smiles and walks a circle around me. "Do you know who I am?"

Oh, yes. I've seen pictures. She's the epitome of evil, greed and everything wrong with the world. Her name is Rebecca Smith.

I spit at her feet.

She nods at the agents holding Bettina. Both men lift daggers and stab, stab, stab her in the chest and sides. She screams and screams.

I scream. "Stop! Please, stop." I struggle for freedom. My wrists are twisted behind my back, the backs of my knees kicked. My knees hit the floor.

And the guards…they just keep stabbing Bettina, blood spraying and pouring and dripping—blood and now other things. I want to look away, but I hold her gaze until the end—*I'm sorry, I'm so sorry.* She goes quiet, slumping in their arms. They let her go when her bowels empty. She drops with an unceremonious thump.

"Now you know I'm serious," Rebecca says. "Your brother, like your friend, is currently in my care. I would hate for something so tragic to happen to him."

I almost panic. I want to panic. This is my worst nightmare. I would rather die a thousand deaths than let my brother suffer a single moment of agony. He saved me, so many times he saved me. Now it's my turn to save him. I can't fail.

"You want something from me or I'd be dead too," I say. "What is it?"

"Ali Bell."

"I don't know an Ali Bell."

"You will. I'll make sure of it."

"But—"

"From now on, you will do what I say, when I say it. In return, your brother will walk away tonight. He won't know we met, and you won't tell him."

I nod. What else can I do?

"If you disobey me even once, I'll turn my sights to your brother once again, and we both know what will happen if I do." She motions to Bettina.

"Touch him and I'll—"

"What? You'll watch?" She smiles at me. "You're outmanned and outskilled, Miss Marks, and you know it. But if you need more incentive…" She holds out her hand. A guard gives her a small black remote. When she presses a button, a blind opens on the window behind her, revealing a small room.

Chains hang from the ceiling—River is attached to them, his arms trapped over his head. A blindfold covers his eyes, and a ball-gag fills his mouth. He's shirtless, and strips of flesh are already messing.

"You'll have to excuse his condition," Rebecca says. "He's one of the strongest slayers I've ever had in my lab, and I'd like to know just how much pain he can withstand before his mind breaks." She pushes another button, and River's body begins to shake and jerk, his limbs attempting to curl into his torso. "Right now, volts of electricity are shooting through him. It's excruciating, he could die any second—"

"Stop!" I shout. "Just stop! I'll do what you—"

—River is patting me on the back. "Milla! Can you hear me? Are you okay?"

I shake myself from the past. I'm trembling. I can't stop. And it's okay, I'll be okay, because Frosty strides across the room and throws his arms around me, offering comfort and support. I can feel his heart racing just as quickly as my own.

"What happened?" River demands.

"Nothing you need to concern yourself with." Frosty combs his fingers through my hair. "Whatever you decide, Milla, I'll back."

Black and white. Right and wrong.

My voice is soft, and it trembles like the rest of me as I announce, "We can't let Tiffany go. She tried to murder me, and she would have succeeded if you guys hadn't intervened. A girl like that can't be loosed on the general public."

Cole nods. "It's settled, then. We gear up and let Rebecca come to us."

One day passes. Two, then three, but nothing happens. Not from Rebecca's end.

I and the other blonde females in the house dye our hair brown. That way, Rebecca and her men might hesitate to take a shot, mistaking us for Tiffany.

The first time Frosty got a glimpse of my new hairstyle… well. I still haven't come down from the high.

"What the hell did you do to yourself?" he barked. "Change it back. Now."

He should be happy. Now I look more like the girls he picked up at the club. "No," I finally said.

"No? That's it? Just no?"

"Oh, good. Your ears are working."

"You were perfect the way you were, Mills."

Perfect? Me?

So why has he stopped sleeping in our room?

And if he doesn't want me, why does he watch me? In fact, his gaze is never far from me. He tracks me like he's a starving and I'm on the menu. But if I glance in his direction, he hastily looks away.

I have hope again.

Only one other time has he spoken to me, though, and only to ask about the visions. He wanted to know why the last one revealed my encounter with Rebecca. With a little Q and A, we came to the conclusion our thoughts direct the visions. He'd wondered about my meeting with Rebecca right before it happened. Just like I'd wondered about his name before the previous one.

These visions…they may be the complete opposite of Ali's, but they're helping us get to know each other better than any conversation. Which is why I love them almost as much as I dread them.

"An-n-nd…yes! We're done!" Love's excited announcement draws me from my thoughts. She pushes out of her chair. "I'm gonna spend the morning with Ali and just, I don't know, be a girl for a bit."

"Sounds nice." We've been monitoring the security cameras in twelve-hour shifts and last night Love and I were paired.

"Want to come?" she asks me.

I'm floored by the invite. And warmed. "Yes, actually, I do. But I missed dinner, and I'm starved. Let me grab a sandwich first."

"Okay, see you in a bit."

I make my way to the kitchen, where I find Chance pouring orange juice.

I swipe the glass and drain half the contents. "Thanks."

He snorts. "Anytime, apparently. Where's Love?"

"Headed to Ali's room."

He confiscates the juice and drinks the rest. "Well then, to Ali's room I go."

"First, bad Chance. Bad. She wants a girls' night, and you most definitely aren't a girl. Second, you are sooo whipped." I make a tsking sound.

"You mean I'm so happy."

"Wow. Way to rub it in." I lightly punch him in the stom-

A MAD ZOMBIE PARTY

ach, just hard enough to make him lose his breath. "What about now? Still happy?"

He laughs, bends down and rams his shoulders into my midsection, then straightens with me draped over his shoulder. "Just for that, I'm taking you to Love. You damaged her property, and you'll have to pay her fine."

"Certainly...after I tell her about the time you tried to collar a zombie, but actually collared yourself."

He smacks my behind. "You know what happens to rats, don't you?"

"They bite anyone who holds them?"

He gives me another smack, and I playfully kick at him. "Put me down. I'm hungry."

"Put her down. Now." The new voice is as hard as steel.

Frosty! I still, even as my heartbeat speeds up.

"Why? I'm not hurting her." Chance sets me on my feet. "I don't hurt my friends."

Frosty approaches us, trapping me in the middle of a testosterone sandwich. "Where were you a few months ago, when River kicked her out? She was sure hurting then."

"I know where I wasn't," Chance snaps. "At the bottom of a bottle, or in some random chick's bed."

Frosty draws back a fist, ready to strike.

"No!" I shout. "No. This isn't happening. We aren't fighting amongst ourselves. And over what? A little teasing?" I give Chance a push toward the exit. "Go tell Love goodnight, then go to your own room like a good little boy." I stare him down until he shuffles off—then I turn to Frosty. "What the hell was that?"

He leans down until we're nose-to-nose. "He's with some-one else. I won't let him lead you on."

"You mean the way you led me on?" My cheeks flash with heat. "Are you concerned for my feelings...or jealous?" I say the words to taunt him, but they echo in my mind and I gasp. *Is* he jealous?

"I'm not jealous." He steps away from me and rubs the back of his neck. "I'm your friend."

"Uh, you aren't my friend. Friends talk to each other. Es-pecially after they've kissed."

"Well. This is kinda awkward." Ali stands in the door-way, rocking back on her heels. "I came to get some cookies for girls' night, and if my craving wasn't so savage, I'd come back at another time."

Frosty opens his mouth, but the shatter of glass registers, then a loud thump. It comes from above us, and the three of us take off in unison, running for the stairs, palming weap-ons. Other slayers come out of their rooms, hastily dressing.

"Did you hear that?" Justin asks.

"Where'd it come from?" Jaclyn demands.

Pop, pop, pop.

Gunfire! "There!" I rush toward the door to Ali and Cole's bedroom.

Frosty grabs my arm to yank me behind him, making him the first to enter. Another round of gunfire rings out—courtesy of Frosty. I move beside him, determined to defend and protect, and see a black-clad figure propel out the shat-tered opening in the window, as if pulled by a rope.

I race over as violent gusts of wind lift strands of my hair. The sky is black, but it doesn't fully camouflage the helicopter hovering just above our roof. Once the black-clad guy is secured inside, the copter flies away.

Chance shoves me aside, looking as though he plans to jump. Blood trickles from a gash in his forehead and gushes from a wound in his chest. He's been shot.

"They took her," he croaks. "Took Love. There were three of them. They shot me as I entered the room."

"We have to do something." Ali's chin trembles. "Fast."

"First, let's get you patched up, Chance." I reach for him.

He steps out of reach. "Bullet only grazed me. I'm fine. I don't care what the rest of you do, but I'm gearing up and going after my girl."

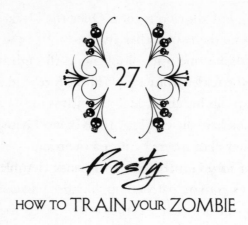

27

Frosty

HOW TO TRAIN YOUR ZOMBIE

Justin heads to the roof to watch for any other copters, or any agents who might be sneaking around the perimeter. The rest of us gather in the weapons room to arm up.

Rebecca wanted a war. She's got a war.

I've never seen the stoic Chance so panicked and inconsolable, and I sympathize. I'm not sure how I would react if Milla had been the one taken. At least his wound is a simple graze, as he claimed.

"How are we going to track her?" he demands. "Her phone is here."

"I think I know a way." Judging by the stubborn glint in Milla's pretty golden eyes, her way is going to put her in danger. My hands clench as she looks to River rather than me. "Do you still have the hazmat suits we stole from Anima?"

"Of course."

"Go get them, one for every slayer here. And hurry."

"Hurry?" He spreads his arms, all *shall I pull a rabbit out of my ass, too?* "The suits are at our house, an hour and a half away—and that's one way."

Your house isn't her house, prick. Not anymore.

"Then you better get going." She gives him a push.

"Tell me what you're planning." Chance grips her by the shoulders and shakes her. "I need to know."

A bolt of fury launches me to his side. I yank him away from her with enough force to damage. "You don't touch her. Ever."

Milla gives me a strange look before motoring on. "The plan is simple. Rebecca and Tiffany tried to destroy me with *thánatos.* Tonight I will use those flames against them."

"How?" Ali asks. "And how can you use them without destroying yourself in the process?"

Those words—*destroying yourself in the process*—are a punch in the gut.

Milla's nightmare is more reliable than a postman. Wind, sleet, rain or shine, it comes. Red flames hurt her, kill her. Now she plans to unleash them? Hell, no.

Forget losing another girl. I can't lose *her.*

"In the cemetery, zombies bit me and red flames appeared of their own accord. While it made the zombies crave me exclusively, it made *me* hunger for *you.*" Milla scans the room, but avoids my gaze. "The mix of *thánatos* and toxin, I mean. I sensed you. Blindfolded, I could have picked you guys from a crowd of thousands."

Reeve nods. "Like to like."

Realization clicks, horror on its coattails, and I curse. "You intend to let a zombie bite you." I get all up in Milla's personal space. "You want us in those suits so you won't sense us when you become a slayer GPS. But at what cost?"

"No cost on your part. Only mine. A few minutes of pain and suffering." She pushes me away. "My pain, my choice. Deal with it."

"No cost on my part?" What about the agonizing fear that is currently plaguing me? "You only have a ten-minute window before the toxin becomes too strong to neutralize."

"Probably closer to fifteen or twenty minutes," Reeve says. "Most of these zombies are clones, remember, and their toxin is weakened."

"That doesn't change my answer." I never look away from Milla.

"The vision," Ali says, as if I need the reminder. "We know she'll survive this—"

I point a finger at her, silencing her. "Don't you dare mention the vision to me."

She flinches. "Yeah. Okay. My bad."

"We'll find Love another way," I tell Milla.

She latches onto my shirt, giving me a shake. "There *is* no other way."

Desperation radiates from Chance. "The longer we wait, trying to think of something else, the more damage Anima can—and will—do to Love."

"But trading one life for another isn't our way. Is it?" I snap at Ali.

Ali withers. Milla only raises her chin.

I cup her cheeks. "I'm not willing to risk you." Not today, not tomorrow. Not ever. "We've got time. Love will be kept alive. She's a bargaining chip now."

"Frosty—"

"No." Since our kiss, my obsession with her has become as much a part of me as my arms and legs. I never should have walked away from her. I should have stayed with her, continued to lose myself in her. Should have told her how I felt—feel. I'm as desperate as Chance. As possessive as Cole. As determined as Bronx. But I didn't, and this is the price I must pay.

"Come with me." She takes my hand and draws me into the hallway. After shutting the door behind us, she anchors her hands on her hips and glares up at me—

—I'm in bed, curled in a ball and sobbing. I'm drowning in despair, dejection and a sense of rejection I can't shake. *I want him, I want him so bad I can barely breathe, but I'll never be more than a passing fancy to him and*—

—Milla gasps, and the vision fades.

I just saw the night we kissed. Through her eyes. *I'm* responsible for those tears. Me alone.

I'm gutted.

I'm ashamed.

"I'm sorry," I croak. "I'm so sorry. I never meant to hurt you."

Spots of heat ignite in her cheeks. Glaring, she waves my words away. "I don't want to discuss that. The only subject on the table right now is your attitude."

She wants to stick with business, fine. We'll stick with business. "What you suggested in there? The toxin? It's too dangerous."

"Don't pretend to care about my well-being, Frosty."

I care. I care too damn much. "I'm not pretending. You matter to me."

"Oh, really. I matter so much you left me seconds after your ex caught us together. I matter so much, you've kept your distance ever since. Sorry, but I can do without your particular brand of caring."

I guess business is over.

She reaches for the door. "I'm going forward with my plan, with or without your approval."

I cup her by the nape, holding her in place. I mean to tell her the terrible consequences she'll face if she saves my sorry hide. I mean to tell her the reason I've stayed away from her, the reason she has to stay here and stay safe. I can't handle even the thought of losing her. But the moment we're skin-to-skin, heat-to-heat, nothing matters but tasting her.

I rasp, "I owed Kat a goodbye," and smash my lips into hers. She doesn't open for me. Not at first. Then she moans, and our tongues find each other. I back her into the wall. Her hands tangle in my hair as I run my own down her sides, palm the back of her thighs and lift her off the floor. She wraps her legs around me and tilts her head, letting me take her mouth deeper, harder. I kiss her as if it's the last time I'll see her. As if it's my last night on earth. As if she's the only girl in existence—because she is. To me, she is.

The boy I was craved Kat. The man I am craves Milla.

The taste of her drugs me. She's headier than a bottle of Jack, and if I'm not careful, I'm going to lose track of my surroundings, forget the war and carry her to bed, where I'll keep her for at least a week.

I'm panting as I pull back and set her gently on her feet.

She peers up at me with passion-glazed eyes. "Are you going to run away now?"

"I'm done running. I'm right where I want to be." I flatten my hands beside her temples, my body caging hers, I breathe her in, enjoying the heat she radiates, and lean in to nuzzle her cheek. "I'll let you go after Love on one condition."

From languid to stiff in a blink. "You'll *let* me?"

"We need to reduce the risk to your life by pinpointing the path the helicopter took. Someone somewhere had to see something, maybe even posted about it online. Maybe satellites picked up images."

"Chance is an expert hacker. If he can focus, he can search for both."

"I'll make sure he focuses." I kiss the tip of her nose before returning to the weapons room. Chance is pacing back and forth, and I step into his path. He pauses. I punch him in the jaw, sending him reeling to the side.

When he straightens, blood trickles from his mouth. "What the hell, man?"

"Are you focused? Good." I tell him what I told Milla. "Maybe even search for nearby buildings with helicopter pads on the roof. There can't be very many."

"Brilliant," Ali says. "We should have all the equipment you'll need, Chance."

We make our way into the security room, where keyboards and monitors abound. As Chance works, Ali calls for Kat and Emma.

Emma arrives in a flash of light.

"Any details you can share?" Ali asks.

"Well, I've got bad news, good news and more bad news." The little girl plays with the hem of her tutu. "Here's the bad. Rebecca remains hidden from us. Here's the good. We sued her witnesses and won, and they're supposed to tell us Love's location. Kat is with them now, waiting for an answer. Here's the other bit of bad. The witnesses claim they don't know."

Ali scowls. "Are they lying?"

"If they are, they'll be punished. If they're telling the truth, they have to do everything in their power to find her." One of Emma's ears twitches, and she inclines her head. "I've got to go. I'll return when I learn more." A second later, she's gone.

That's something, at least. And by the time River returns, Chance has deduced the bird landed somewhere downtown. Everyone but Milla dons a suit, forgoing the face mask for now.

Rather than loading one of the collared zombies into a van we've doused with Blood Lines, Reeve hands Milla a syringe. "This is a weakened version of the toxin. Inject yourself right before you begin the search."

The group heads to the garage. Cole takes the wheel, and Ali takes the front passenger seat. The rest of us pile into the back. The entire drive, I hold Milla on my lap, protecting her while I can.

Cole parks in a darkened alley, and Milla turns to me, gifting me with a soft smile.

"I'm going to survive this, whatever it takes."

"Good. Because I want another kiss."

"More than one, I hope."

"Greedy girl." I lightly smack her ass. "All right. You talked me into it."

She flips me off before pushing her spirit from her body and stepping out of the van. It takes everything I've got to stay put when every protective instinct screams to go after her.

"Masks," Cole says, and we anchor our face masks into place.

I move to the front of the van, crouching between the seats, watching as Milla takes her place in the headlights.

She sits against a wall. Trembling, she lifts the syringe to her arm. Deep breath in...out... She injects the toxin. Her eyes go wide, in seconds turning neon red. Pain contorts her features, but she manages to stand.

I glance at the stopwatch hanging from my neck and press Start. In ten minutes, I will inject her with the antidote whether she's found Love or not. Nothing and no one will stop me.

She stumbles forward. One minute bleeds into two...three. Cole ensures the van remains directly behind her. The sun is in the process of rising, but it's so early in the morning that very few people are on the streets; those who are pay no attention to Milla, and she pays no attention to them. Civilian is not what's for dinner.

Four. Five. Six minutes.

Tension knots my stomach, ice chips crystallizing in my blood.

Seven. Eight. Nine.

I'm busting out of the van in thirty seconds flat.

"What's she doing?" Cole pulls over and throws the van into Park.

I focus on Milla, who is clawing at the glass doors of an office building.

Ali rips off her mask. "Love has to be in there."

Thank God. I fly out of the van and shove the needle deep into Milla's neck. She collapses in my arms, trembles as I carry her to the vehicle. As gently as possible I place her on the floorboards while the rest of the slayers strip out of their suits and pour into the streets, armed up and ready to go.

Milla struggles to sit up. "Did I find her?"

"We'll know in a few minutes." I slap a .44 in her hand. "Stay here. Make sure the van is ready to go when we come out."

"I will."

No argument?

I don't want to leave her behind, not weakened like this, but this is Milla—strong and stubborn Milla—and there's no way she'll let anyone get the drop on her.

I shed my suit.

"Frosty?"

"Yes."

"Stay safe."

"You owe me kisses, remember? There's no way I'm not coming back." I rush toward the building and take stock. The lights are snuffed out, and there are no shifting shadows to indicate movement. My friends are nowhere in sight, either, but a hole has been cut in the glass and the alarm system has already been disabled. I duck through the hole.

The rustle of clothing, the shuffle of shoes.

I follow the sounds and find Chance, who is standing behind a kneeling man, his gun aimed and ready. The other slayers are busy at the dock of monitors, rewinding and watching footage.

"One and only chance." Chance cocks the gun. "Tell me where she is."

The man actually pees himself. "Th-the injured girl? They

took her to the third floor. But I didn't hurt her, I swear. I was told to watch the monitors and report any suspicious activity. I—I didn't notify anyone about the brunette at the door. I wanted to help her, and I knew they'd tell me no."

"Thank you." Chance slams the handle of the gun into the guy's temple; he slumps forward, landing with a thud.

Had to be done. If we'd left him conscious, he could have pulled the alarm the moment we walked away.

"He was telling the truth." Bronx points to one of the monitors. "They're on the third floor."

Chance sprints to the elevator.

"Frosty, River, Gavin, Jaclyn, you guys take the stairs," Cole calls as he, Ali and Justin pile into the cart with Chance.

I get it. Just in case one entrance is guarded and the other isn't, we won't all be gunned down at once.

On high alert, we race up the steps. At the third floor entrance, River slides a tiny mirror under the bottom crack. When he ascertains no one is lurking nearby, I take the lead.

The lights are on. As quietly as possible we inch around the corner and—

Meet up with the others. So far so good.

Together, we stealth our way through a lobby, past a built-in reception desk and through a set of locked doors. I'm *very* good at B and E.

"—nice to me," a muted male voice says, "and I'll be nice to you. All right, pretty girl?"

The skid of chair legs, a thump…masculine laughter.

"Leave her alone," another man says. "We're supposed to watch her. Nothing else."

An animal growl erupts from Chance as he shoulders his

way into the room. Two muffled shots ring out—*pop, pop*—
the silencer on his semiautomatic doing its job. I'm right behind him, the others pouring in behind me. I take in the
scene. Love is bound to a chair and gagged; she cries with
relief when she spots us. There's a cut on her forehead and
dried blood on different parts of her body.

Five agents. Well, four now. One is writhing on the floor,
a bullet in each hand. The others are still on their feet, two
gaping at us, the other two reaching for weapons.

"I wouldn't, if I were you," I say, take aim. "All I need is
an excuse."

They still.

Yeah. That's what I thought.

"Get Love to the van," Cole commands, but he needn't
have bothered. Chance is already cutting her ties. "As for the
others…"

I smile. "Let's use them to send a message to Rebecca."

Milla

MY BRAINS AREN'T
WHAT THEY USED TO BE

I'm fading in and out as the van soars down the street. The moment everyone exited the building, I nearly collapsed with relief. Cole slid into the driver's side, nudging me away from the wheel. I would have landed on my butt if Frosty hadn't come up behind me and caught me.

I must have fallen asleep in his arms. Now voices jolt me awake.

"—should have seen it, Nana." Ali must be on the phone with her grandmother. "Five bodies, one of them bleeding profusely, each pinned to the wall in the shape of a letter. And do you know what four of those letters spelled? Yeah, you can guess. It starts with an *F* and ends with a *K*...are you kidding me? Nana, why would we spell *fork*?...seriously? What the heck is a *fink*? No, no, we made the last guy contort into the letter *U*, does that help...yeah, I know. I laughed so hard I almost pulled a muscle!"

Darkness tugs me back under...

"Dude!" Gavin's voice booms at high volume. "Milla brought the heat tonight. A real *fork you* to the enemy. You owe her your life, Love. And if I know Milla, and I do, all she'll want in return is for you to strip naked and dance for us."

"Do you *want* to die?" Chance asks.

"Barbie," Ali says, and I know she's speaking to Gavin. "Because you made such a ludicrous suggestion, *you* have to strip and dance for us. All of us."

Snicker, snicker.

"I thought you'd never ask." I can hear the smile in his voice.

"Oh, hell. He was serious. Put it back on!" Cole is laughing too hard; I can't make out his next words.

A chorus of "yes" rings out, but darkness returns, the world quiet once again.

The next thing I know, I'm rolling over in bed. Bed? Gasping, I jolt upright, waning sunlight greeting me. Wow. I must have slept the day away, drained by *thánatos* and toxin, a horrid cocktail. I shudder as I recall the pain, the unending, all-consuming hunger.

I'm alone, no sign of Frosty...who owes me a kiss.

As I shower, anticipation energizes me but also scares the crap out of me. Has he changed his mind? I tremble as I don a pink top with lace and a short white skirt. As good as it's gonna get right now.

When I emerge from the bathroom, Ali and Kat are sitting on the bed.

"Hey." I expected Kat to confront me sooner or later, but I should have known she'd bring backup.

"Let's just get it over with," Kat says. "But first, let's procrastinate. You look pretty, Milla. Tough and pretty. And it's totally not fair. I kinda wish you were a toad."

How am I supposed to respond to that? "Thanks?"

"We're not here to complain," Ali says.

"Right. We're here to, ugh, I can't believe I'm doing this, but...ugh." Kat meets my gaze, sighs. "Milla, I want to apologize."

Apologize? "For what?"

She gapes at Ali. "Fork! She still doesn't know?"

"Know what?" I demand.

"Good glory." Ali's shoulders slump in. "I expected Frosty to tell you."

"He's not here. You are. Explain."

Kat toys with the ends of her hair. "We told you that you'll save Frosty's life, and you will, but...you die doing it."

"Die." The word echoes in my mind, cutting like a dagger. I'm bleeding shock and betrayal, though I have no right to the latter emotion.

Sow and reap. I'm reaping.

But what of these two girls? They castigated me for something they themselves were doing. It's hypocrisy, plain and simple.

I want to lash out. *How dare they!* But feelings are fleeting, I remind myself, and right now, an outburst will be counterproductive.

"I'm sorry," Ali says. "I didn't know you when we first approached you, and granted, at the time I was angry with you, even hated you. You helped Anima hurt me. But I never should have—"

"Stop." I hold up my palm. "What's done is done. Now we move on and figure out what to do."

But…but…can we do anything? No one has ever changed one of Ali's visions.

I need to face facts. I'm going to die. Because, at the end of the day, I'm going to save Frosty. That's not even a question.

"I'd feel better if you yelled at me," she grumbles.

"I'm sorry, too," Kat say. "We had no right. We aren't your judge, jury or executioner."

The ragged edge of my anger dulls. "Here are the facts. If I knew in the beginning that I'd die, I might not have agreed to guard Frosty." I wouldn't have had a chance to get to know him. Or come to admire and respect him…to crave him more than I crave air to breathe.

As if on cue, the door opens, and he enters the room. He's wearing a black T-shirt and a pair of ripped jeans that hang low on his waist. His feet are bare, and he looks good enough to eat. Figuratively, I mean.

He notices the girls and pauses, then nods to Ali, to Kat, before staring hard at me. "I heard voices."

"We were just leaving." Ali stands, gives me a hug—a hug I return—and slinks from the room.

"Again, I'm sorry," Kat whispers. "I wish… Well, it doesn't matter, does it. Wishes mean nothing. Actions mean everything." Then she, too, is gone.

Frosty scowls. "They told you about the vision." A statement, not a question.

"Yes," I reply. "And I get why they kept quiet, I really do."

"You're taking it better than I did." He shuts the door with a firm click, then turns the lock, sealing us both inside.

"You wouldn't think so if you'd peeked into my mind a few minutes ago." I scrub a hand down my face. "I should have figured things out on my own. The guilt they so often projected, your treatment of me after Kat confessed all." As I speak, I'm hit by another realization; shock sends me into another tailspin. "You didn't want me near you, didn't want me acting as your shield because...you care about me. My life matters to you."

He raises his chin, unashamed of his feelings. "I told you that already."

Yes, but I never really believed it until now. "Frosty," I say, and take a step toward him, my heart singing. But another realization strikes and I still, the singing fading to quiet. Only one of us has a future. He's going to watch me die.

"I want you to leave town," he says. "You don't owe me. You don't have to atone for your past. Go to college. I'll pay—"

"Are you freaking serious? How about this? I'll leave if you leave."

He shakes his head, adamant. "I can't abandon my friends in the middle of a war."

"Neither can I, snowman." I *will* be here for him.

Navy blue eyes beseech me. "I need you alive, Milla."

And I need to touch him. I move forward; the moment I reach him, I sink my greedy hands under his shirt, directly on his chest—over his heart. His skin is white-hot, velvet over steel.

"No one is guaranteed a future," I remind him, and his

heart hammers so quickly I can't count the beats. "No one, not with a vision or without. All we have is today, this second." And I don't want to waste it. "You promised me a kiss."

He hooks a lock of hair behind my ear. "I promised you more than one. I'm addicted to the taste of you."

Hot shivers cascade through me. "Let's pretend, just for a minute, that you're a normal guy and I'm a normal girl, that we just got back from a date and we're standing at my door."

"Yes." His pupils flare, a full eclipse of desire. "I lean in to kiss you good-night…"

Breathing is impossible. "And I wait, excited and nervous."

"I hold out as long as I can, savoring every torturous second, but you smell so good, like roses and pecans, and I'm so worked up already, have wanted you all night…"

"I ache for you, and when I can stand it no longer, I wrap my arms around you. Like this…"

We're both panting. We're both trembling. Deep down I know he sees me, sees who I am, what I am, and he likes me anyway.

"I whisper your name…and then…finally I kiss you." His lips press gently against mine, his tongue seeking entry.

I open willingly, urging him inside, and he…utterly… *worships*…me.

This kiss is the total antithesis of the last one. There's no maddened rush to reach the finish line. No violence behind our actions, just languid relish. I've never been kissed like this. I'm not sure if it's a hello or a goodbye or both. But there's meaning to it. A promise.

When he lifts his head, his lips are red and slightly swollen. His eyes are wild, in direct opposition to his movements. I expect him to dive down and kiss me again, only harder and hotter, but he traces his thumbs over the rise of my cheekbones, his gaze never leaving mine, and I decide this is better.

"I haven't slept in days," he says. "Want to nap with me?" In his arms? "Yes." I don't care that I've only just woken up.

He sheds his weapons and gets comfortable on the bed. I crawl to him and rest my head on his shoulder, drape my arm over his stomach and bend one of my knees over his thighs.

"What if I have the nightmare?" I ask. "What if I catch fire?"

He plays with the ends of my hair. "I'll burn and I'll get over it. I've got you where I want you. I'm not letting go."

29

Frosty

THE EYE OF THE STORM POPS OUT

I hold Milla in my arms as she dozes. Sleeping is impossible for me, my mind a roller coaster of activity. I can't stop thinking about our kiss—can't stop craving another. I told myself I'd let her go afterward. I'd walk away and never look back.

But I kissed her and cuddled her closer, and now the thought of leaving her warmth and softness… Yeah, I'd rather eat nails.

I'm falling hard for this girl, and one way or another, I'm going to lose her the way I lost Kat. Even if we both manage to survive the vision, her brother still stands in our way, whether he supports us or not. I'll never be content playing second string to River—I was second string with my aunt and uncle, and it sucked—just like I know Milla will never be content playing second string to Kat.

The thing is, Kat is no longer my first priority. But River will always be Milla's.

Maybe she senses my tension. She mutters my name and stretches like a pinup, lifting her arms above her head, arching her back.

So beautiful.

The urge to touch her overwhelms me, and I shift her still-dark locks through my fingers, the strands like silk. The blood in my veins heats, boils…one touch isn't enough, will never be enough.

I should get up. Leave.

Too late. She blinks open her eyes and gasps. "You're still here."

"Where did you expect me to be?"

"Honestly? Anywhere else." A slow smile blooms. "But I'm glad you stayed."

There's a clench of desire low in my gut.

A hard knock sounds at the door. "Zombies are headed toward the house," Cole announces. "Gear up."

Zombies? Headed this way?

Mills and I scramble out of bed. The last time zombies approached a home I lived in, they wore bomb collars and destroyed everything in their path, distracting us and allowing Anima's most lethal agents to close in.

"Don't try to ditch me out there," Milla tells me, a tremor in her voice. She straps on the holster for her short swords. "Stay by my side."

No way in hell. The less time I spend with her during battle, the less likely Ali's vision is to come true.

"Frosty," she says, exasperated.

I ignore her and rip open the door. Other slayers are rushing out of their rooms, their expressions a mix of fury and dread. We congregate in the weapons room, hurriedly gathering extra daggers, guns and ammo.

"There are probably two hundred zombies," Cole says. "Justin and Gavin were on patrol and spotted them. In our favor, they aren't wearing collars so there are no bombs. Also, when our boys tried to engage, they were ignored. The hordes are acting just like Milla when she searched for Love."

"But I scented slayers," she says. "Why would zombies ignore Justin and Gavin?"

"The serum draws like to like, remember." I hand her my favorite guns, the ones with retractable axes, and show her how to work them. "But why aren't zombies fighting other zombies right now?"

"They scent Milla." Kat appears a few feet in front of me, her features tight with worry. "They hunger for *thánatos*."

"But she's not lit up with red flames." Ali slams a clip in place. "How can they scent it?"

"As with any fire, heat and smoke waft. In this case, spiritual heat and smoke," Kat replies. "And it's only growing stronger."

Milla flattens her hands over her stomach, clearly horrified. "I don't feel hot. Don't see any smoke. Should I wear one of the suits?"

"No. Let the hordes come," I growl. "Let them ignore us while trying to get to you, unable to reach you. Because yes, you'll ride the pine."

She stiffens, but nods.

"And if they can't scent you," Cole says, "they might attack any humans nearby. That, we can't allow."

"Okay. No suit," Milla says.

A thought—what if something goes wrong?

Worry twists my insides. Did Kat feel this helpless every time I went off to battle? Countless times she tried to stop me. *Don't go. Stay with me.* I always resisted, helping and guarding my friends far more important than saving myself from a few injuries.

"Be on the lookout," Cole says. "Smith might try to use our distraction against us and snatch Tiffany."

Bronx smiles an evil smile. "I wish her good luck with that. I set some wicked-ass traps around Tiff's cage."

No wonder I admire the guy so much.

"I'm thinking we need to stay together, just in case zombies turn on us," Ali says. "If someone gets bit, we do whatever it takes to inject him—or her—with antidote. Speaking of, Reeve and Weber played with the formula so that it works on anyone who's built up an immunity." She opens a case filled with instruments that look like EpiPens. "Take as many as you can carry."

I stuff a handful in my pocket, and everyone else does the same.

"I'm sorry," Kat says, at my side now.

Milla's head is high as she walks away, offering privacy.

"I know," I say. Kat did what she thought was necessary to protect me. Just like I'll do what I think is necessary to protect Milla. She learned from it, and now we move on. "You're forgiven."

Her shoulders slump with relief. "Frosty the softy," she says with a half smile. "Thank you."

"Let's talk later, okay?"

Kat nods and disappears.

Ali leads us to the roof. I close in on Milla and walk at her side. If anything happens to her...

Nothing better happen to her.

Halogen lights are anchored to the iron fence surrounding the property, and for the first time since I moved in, those lights are glowing. I take stock, watching as the hordes breach the property line and step into the high beams. Zombies in front hiss as they fall back, and the next in line step over them...only to hiss and fall back. But the creatures are determined to reach Milla and won't be deterred. Soon, even as their spirits sizzle, they are push, push, pushing at the gate.

"Milla," Cole says, "you stay up here to act as our bait."

Her nod is clipped.

Bait usually gets eaten. Not this time. I'll die first.

His violet gaze scans the rest of us. "Fight to kill." He steps out of his body, the new version of him grabbing the handrail that hangs on a nearly transparent wire, already covered in Blood Lines. He slides down, down, flying over the gate, landing just behind the crowd of zombies.

Ali is next, then Chance, Love and Jaclyn.

River pounds Milla's fist. "If I kill more zombies than Frosty, you have to do my laundry for a month."

"No way. I would rather *eat* a zombie," she says.

"I'll take that as a hell, yes." River steps out of his body and flies into the action.

My gaze follows him, and I see—

No way. Just no way. His spirit ghosts through two of the zombies. Zombies are spirits, not bodies. The two should have collided. There's only one explanation. Those weren't zombies but humans dressed as zombies.

Rebecca's agents are hidden in the masses.

Shit, shit, shit. I search the sea of rot, but it's too hard to tell real from fake. Except—

There! A collar is hooked to the zombie's belt loop. Not zombie. Human. Has to be. The agents hope to collar us.

I tell Milla, and she pales.

"We're in trouble," she says as she, too, scans the sea.

If the volts in the collars are strong enough, slayers will die in minutes. Or, maybe the goal is to make us solid to the touch, allowing agents to carry us away without civilians able to watch or cameras able to record.

"I have to disable the agents," I say, remaining in my body as I grip the rail.

"Go. Warn the others." Milla gives me a push, and I drop, wind slapping against my face.

I let go just before I reach the end of a wire: a giant oak. Landing is jarring, considering I'm moving at what has to be a thousand miles per hour, but I recover swiftly and roll with my momentum. As I straighten, I palm two semiautomatics and spray bullets in every direction. I'm in the physical realm, so I don't have to worry about hurting my friends, who are in the spirit realm. Grunts ring out, groans of pain soon following.

When I run out of bullets, I drop the empty clips and

jam the end of the guns onto new ones, which are currently strapped to my thighs. Then it's once again party time.

I stop only when Milla's flying form comes into view. She kicks the agent sneaking up on me and sends him to his back, allowing me to shoot him. She lands and rolls, and every zombie in the immediate area stops to face her.

"Go back," I snarl. "Now!"

"Clearly you need someone on your six." She withdraws her own semiautomatics and shoots up the area behind me.

More grunts. More groans.

I whip around to watch three agents topple. Damn it! Like the other one, they'd almost had me.

Zombies head straight for Milla. I drop my guns and reach for my swords, then step out of my body to remove any arms and legs that reach her way. Different parts soon form a wall between us and the rest of the horde.

When I return to my body, I look for Milla. There! An agent stands behind her, one arm snaked around her neck, the other around her waist. She bucks against him, slamming the back of her head into his nose. Howling in pain, he loosens his hold and she's able to break free by jamming her elbows into his stomach, then latching onto his arm, at the same time ducking and yanking him over her head.

I palm a gun and, while the guy is down, shoot him in the chest.

As zombies scale the wall of parts, I move in and out of my body. Milla cries out. I whip around. Two agents punch at her, keeping her distracted while a third sneaks up behind her, a collar ready to be snapped around her neck.

No way in hell! I aim, squeeze the trigger. He flies backward.

A frantic thud of footsteps behind me. I spin, ready to shoot, and come face-to-face with the barrel of a .38.

"Drop your weapon," a hard male voice demands.

Like hell. I go low and kick out my leg. Contact! He drops. I'm there when he lands, slamming my fist into his nose; cartilage snaps. His eyes close, his body going lax. I straighten—only to fly backward as pain explodes in my shoulder.

I've been hit.

Milla unleashes a blood-curdling scream, and I fight my way to my feet. Blood gushes down my shirt. Stars wink over my vision as I try to breathe. I step…step, moving forward. My knees give out, but it doesn't stop me. I crawl. Have to get to Milla… Can't let her get hurt…or worse.

"No, no. Don't hurt him." Suddenly she's at my side, her soft hands pressing my wound to stop the flow of blood. "Stay still, Frosty. Okay? All right? Just stay still. I'll take care of you."

Fog rolls in, but I manage to stay awake. "You…okay?"

"I'm fine. But you… I didn't shield you." Tears spill down her cheeks. "Couldn't get to you in time. I'm sorry. I'm so sorry."

I try to reach up and wipe those tears away, but movement is impossible. My muscles have seized. "No…tears. Not for… me." I have trouble catching my breath. "You…all that… matters."

The tears only fall faster.

"You have a choice," an unfamiliar voice says.

"I know. I know. We die or we go with you calmly," she snaps. "You don't need the collars, and you don't need to hurt him. We'll cooperate."

The tallest one smiles without humor. "I know you'll go with us calmly because, if one of you acts up, the other dies."

30

Milla

BODY MODIFICATION 101

We're disarmed, dragged to a van and stuffed in the back, and our friends have no idea, can't see us through the sea of zombies.

A guard barks "Patch him up" before slamming the door. At least we aren't handcuffed or tied down. More than that, we're alone in back, a clear plate separating us from the driver and his passenger.

I rip the hem of Frosty's T-shirt and use the material to bind his shoulder.

"You should have…continued to fight." He's panting more heavily now.

"And let them take you away from me? No."

"Exactly why you…should have stayed…on roof."

"My main objective has always been your safety. That hasn't changed." His skin is pale, and he's lost a lot of blood. He needs *dýnamis*.

Look inside…look inside…

I've looked countless times and failed to find it.

So what? Try again. Use faith.

Faith. Yes. When faith is low, build it up with words and thoughts. "I can do this." I can.

I sit back on my haunches, scoot away from Frosty—just in case *thánatos* escapes—and close my eyes. The mind is a beautiful, complex thing. It observes, stores. It's how my spirit communicates with my body. I go deep, deeper, enduring horrendous, blistering heat, at last spotting the smoke Reeve mentioned. I do my best to look past it, but it's just too thick.

Still I go deeper. Pain consumes me, burning, burning, *boiling*. Sweat breaks out on my skin. My lungs constrict, making it difficult to breathe. A high-pitched scream assaults my ears, and I want it to stop, need it to stop.

"Stop, Milla. Stop now."

My eyelids pop open, and I slump over, the hideous burn fading, the scream subsiding. "I'm sorry," I cry. "I'm so sorry."

He reaches out with his good hand to caress my cheek. "It's not your fault, sweet pea."

But it is. I had one job, just one. Save him. "We'll be okay. Maybe…maybe we can ambush them when they let us out." I search the back of the vehicle, but it's been emptied of anything we can use as a weapon. Helplessness bombards me.

"Whatever proves necessary," he says. "Survive."

"Ditto."

When the van suddenly jolts to a stop, I move in front of him, determined to protect him. He yanks me to his side. His body is weak, but his determination is strong.

The back door opens, revealing three agents with rifles already trained on us.

Guess we won't be doing any kind of ambush, after all.

"Out," the one in the middle commands.

Frosty gives me a comforting squeeze before he releases me. I slowly climb outside, where I'm swung against the side of the van, my hands tied behind my back. Frosty follows me under his own steam, only to be given the same treatment, despite being wounded.

I look around. We're in some kind of underground parking garage, but there are no other cars, no one to ask for help. We're herded to a bank of elevators and whisked to the eleventh floor, where I'm introduced to a nightmare worse than burning alive. The re-creation of Anima.

A handful of men and women in lab coats are bustling around counters scattered with vials, beakers and equipment I don't recognize. I've heard of labs like this. Ali and Jaclyn were tortured in one. River was kept in one for weeks before being moved to the warehouse he "escaped." He was injected with mysterious serums. His spirit was somehow yanked out of his body by force. His mind was shocked. His skin was torched.

Frosty and I are pulled apart. To be taken to separate rooms? But he erupts into action, throwing off his captors and tackling mine. I hit the ground, released as the guards do their best to defend themselves. Not that they do a very good job. Frosty is like a boy possessed. He head butts, throws shoulders and elbows and kicks. He bites off a piece of a guard's ear, then spits the bloody cartilage on the floor.

A chorus of pain, a macabre soundtrack as one of the guards

lunges at Frosty. I extend my legs, tripping him, and he lands hard, faceup. Frosty slams his booted foot into his neck, crushing his windpipe. The guy doesn't get back up.

Even without the use of his hands, Frosty is a master fighter, and he's determined to protect me whatever the cost. I can do no less.

"Put them in a room together." A dark-haired woman with hair as black as night and skin as white as snow steps into my line of vision. She's impeccably dressed in a black cashmere sweater and a pair of gray slacks that mold to her legs.

Rebecca Smith in the flesh. The devil pretending to be a business sophisticate. How adorable.

"If either one gives you any more trouble," she continues, "shoot the boy. He's damaged goods, anyway."

Panic claws at me, ripping at my insides. "We'll behave," I insist, my gaze beseeching Frosty.

Only two of the guards are able to crawl to their feet. They roughly haul Frosty to his. I stand on my own, only to be grabbed. I offer no protest. We're shoved into a ten-by-ten room with two-way mirrored walls and a padded floor. Anyone outside the room will be able to see us, making it harder to escape.

But that's the point, isn't it.

One of the guards pulls his gun and before I can kick it out of his hand, he smiles and shoots Frosty in his already injured shoulder.

Knocked backward, Frosty slams into the wall and drops, leaving a smear of blood in his wake. I scream and rush to his side.

"He gave me trouble," the guard says before slamming the door.

I rip off my shirt. I don't care that everyone can see my bra. Let them look. Fighting a fresh wave of panic, I bind Frosty's newest wound as best I can. "You'll be okay. You have to be okay."

Would he?

I have to reach *dýnamis*. I just have to. It's the only way he'll strengthen supernaturally fast. Maybe the only way he'll survive. But I try again and again and again—and I fail. No. No! I do not accept failure. I will never accept failure.

"I want you to know," he pants, "that I'm glad I met you, glad you were a part of my life. I had fallen down a very dark pit, but you pulled me out."

Damn him! He's talking like he's going to die.

Time for me to try something else. "Miss Smith," I shout. I stand and peer into the mirrored wall, my reflection wild. Hair still dyed brown is tangled with twigs and dirt. Frosty's blood stains my hands, smears my chest. There's a tear in my bra. Cuts in my arms, and rips in my pants. "Help him. Please."

A voice spills over the speaker. "I'll be happy to help him, Miss Marks. For a price. You remember how things work around here, do you not?"

"I do." I remember far too well.

"What will you give me in return?"

Nothing...while seeming to give everything. I told myself I'd never again betray my crew, and I won't. Not even for Frosty.

He's even paler than before, with a bluish hue becoming

more and more noticeable on his lips. His wounds are clean, at least, both bullets having gone out the other side, but infection is likely. The makeshift bandages won't last forever. Already the one on the left is soaked through.

How much time does he have? How much more blood can he stand to lose?

His eyes are on me, but they're closing. Still he's shaking his head no. "Don't do it."

I ignore him. I have to ignore him. I have a part to play. "What do you want, Rebecca? Name your price."

"I want Tiffany...and Ali Bell."

Of course she does.

"No." Frosty shakes his head more violently. "No."

Again, I ignore him. "Thanks to you, Ali lost all her abilities. She's useless to your cause."

"I took her abilities, and I can give them back. Will you do what I tell you or not?"

"Yes," I spit through clenched teeth. "If you help Frosty *now*."

"I'm not a cruel woman. You have my word he'll be on the mend by the time you return."

Her word means nothing to me.

"If you fail me, Frosty will die—and your brother will be my next target."

"Milla," Frosty croaks. "Don't. Please."

I close my eyes, tears leaking through my lashes. I don't have to fake it. So much rides on my ability to trick Rebecca and convince the other slayers I'm on the up-and-up. Two mountains I might not be able to climb.

But I have to try.

"Take me into the hall and tell me what you want me to do."

★ ★ ★

Rebecca's agents drop me three miles away from the mansion, not wanting to be noticed and followed by slayers. I have to run those miles. Every second counts. By the time I reach the mansion, the sun is at its pinnacle, its heat draining what little strength I have left.

The shirt I was given is drenched with sweat and plastered to my chest; I'm operating on nothing but fumes, desperation and determination.

One of the slayers must spot me on the monitors, because the wrought-iron gate whines open upon my approach.

There's no trace of the battle along the long, winding driveway, no bodies or body parts littering the yard. As I step inside the foyer, my friends—are they my friends?—run from different areas of the house to greet me. They're still armed, ready for combat, and I doubt they've had any sleep.

River yanks me into his arms, hugging me tight. "Are you okay?"

"I'm fine, but Frosty isn't." I fight past a fresh wave of tears. "We were captured by agents. He's badly injured, and he needs help." I make sure to say only what Rebecca told me to say. If I deviate from her script, she'll know.

There's a tiny camera and mic attached to the small, heart-shaped locket she hung around my neck.

One misstep, and Frosty will suffer.

Cole eyes me suspiciously. "I made it through the undead masses as you were being hauled away. I gave chase and tracked the van several miles, but they managed to lose me. Where is he, and how did you get away?"

"Rebecca still has him, but I don't know where she's keeping him. I was blindfolded on the drive out." I rub the tattoo on my wrist—the word *Betrayal*—and pray someone notices. "Rebecca set me free so that I could deliver a message. Give her Tiffany, and the war ends. Don't, and she'll kill us all."

Curses ring out. Amid them, Cole barks, "Go to your rooms. All of you. Now."

Several kids gape at him, but everyone obeys.

"You, too, Milla." He stares at me hard. "I need some time to think."

"Don't take too long." *Please.*

I hurry to my bedroom. How am I going to tell him what Rebecca really plans?

If I can't...I'll have to risk Frosty's life by telling everyone the truth outright. A whimper escapes me.

Kat appears in front of me and crosses her arms over her chest. As a spirit, the camera can't detect her and the mic can't pick up her voice.

Thank God! Cole understood.

"Is Rebecca watching you?" she asks.

I give the barest nod.

"Is she planning an ambush?"

Another nod, and Kat disappears.

She reappears a few minutes later. An eternity. "Okay. Everyone's gathered in the gym. Let's see if we can figure this out."

Yes. Let's. I walk into the bathroom, grab a bottle of Advil and fish out two little pills. I toss them in my mouth, drink straight from the faucet.

"Headache?" Kat asks.

A shake of my head.

"Advil...medicine...drug! You're supposed to drug every-one?"

I move away from the mirror and nod.

"To kill?"

A shake.

"To make everyone sick?"

A shake.

"Sleep?"

A nod.

I pace back and forth in front of my desk, ghosting my finger over my new cell phone.

"Is the phone significant?" she asks.

A nod.

"You're supposed to call Rebecca?"

A nod.

"When? Why?"

I lie on the bed and close my eyes.

"When everyone is asleep?"

A nod. How do I tell her agents will be waiting nearby? I'm supposed to let them in so they can grab Ali and Tiffany, and most likely kill everyone else.

"I'll be back." Kat vanishes.

These slayers have no reason to trust me, but I really, really hope that they do. It's the only way we'll make it through this alive. The only way Frosty will make it.

Kat appears. "We're trying to figure out a way to give Rebecca what she wants without actually giving her what she wants."

I roll my eyes—yeah, I'd already figured that part out, thanks—and she sighs.

"Emma is searching for Frosty, but so far no luck." She closes the distance, sits on the edge of the bed. "You've been good for him, you know. And I think he's been good for you, too. Your eyes light up every time you look at him."

He *has* been good for me.

"Do you love him?" she asks.

Do I?

I definitely chemistry him. He's real, and he's smart. He's driven. He's always willing to admit when he's wrong, and he's not afraid to apologize. I crave his kiss and his touch…his body pressing and rubbing against mine. I adore his smile, and his sense of humor. I love when he protects me, even though I'm capable of taking care of myself. I love the way he looks at me, as if I'm something special. I love his intensity and even his anger. He's passionate about what he believes in.

I love that he's guarded, and so few ever get to see the real him—I love it because I'm one of the blessed few. Just like he's one of the blessed few to know the real me. I let him in, even though there were a thousand reasons not to.

So. Yes. I do, I realize. I love him with all my heart.

I want him to love me, too, even though he's going to lose me.

A tear leaks from the corner of my eye.

Kat smiles at me. "Good," she says, shocking me.

Good? She's actually happy about this?

"Love always finds a way." She stands. "We're going to figure this out, don't worry. We won't let Frosty die."

Thank you, I mouth.

She reaches out to pat my hand, but all I feel is a rush of warmth. "In about five minutes, Ali's going to come in and ask if you're up to cooking dinner for everyone. You'll say yes, and you'll let Rebecca watch you pour the sedative, or whatever it is, into a pitcher of sweet tea. Ali will carry the pitcher out of the kitchen to fill the cups at the dining table, but as soon as she's out of range, she'll exchange it for an untainted one. While you eat, everyone will discuss what to do about the situation. Nothing they say will be true. As soon as we've got a real plan worked out, I'll let you know."

Great. All I have to do now…is wait.

31

Frosty

BREAKING BAD BONES

I'm given a couple bags of blood, my wounds stitched and bandaged *without* anesthesia—no need to waste it on me, I'm told. I hold my curses inside. These people are nothing more than walking lab coats, and they might actually enjoy my pain.

Screw 'em.

I'm cuffed to a gurney, the position pulling at the stitches. Screw the pain. I'm given my greatest wish: I'm left alone in the mirrored room.

Fighting a smile now, I give the cuffs a good tug. My shoulders scream in protest, but now I know what I wanted to know. The bedrail is solid.

I lift my knees and the sheet that drapes my lower body falls over my wrists. My next actions will be hidden from prying eyes. Perfect. With a few well-placed jabs, I can break my thumbs, contort my hands and slide free.

Easy.

In my dreams.

Before I can make the first jab, the door opens. A gleeful Ms. Smith strides inside. I scowl. She's changed into a tailored dress suit—window dressing to hide the monster living inside—and while she looks like money, she smells like death. The scent of rot clings to her. Been hanging out with zombies a little too long, have we.

A man comes in behind her. The man who shot me. He's sets a leather chair beside the bed. When Smith is comfortably settled, he meets my gaze and runs his tongue over his teeth.

Bastard wants another piece of me.

Suck my balls.

I blow him a kiss. He hisses, and Smith stiffens.

"Out." Without turning to face him, she waves a hand in dismissal.

His hands fist. I'm sure he's willing to strangle her to get to me. But she's his paycheck. He pivots on his heel and marches from the room.

She smiles at me. "Do you wish you'd taken me up on my first offer?"

Hell, no. "You never would have kept your end of the bargain."

"Oh, I would have. I tried to walk the straight and narrow to achieve my goals. Now it's too late. I got nowhere fast, and I'm tired of your constant interference."

Kat and Emma mentioned Smith's witnesses, those hoping to save her. Obviously they failed.

She continues. "You and yours screwed up from the very beginning, you know. You stopped my day-to-day activities, but didn't take away my funding. You hid my memories, but put me back on the streets. My people found me, helped me, and here we are, back where we started."

"Take away funding. Thanks for the tip."

She smooths an invisible piece of lint from her skirt. "We both know you'll never have another chance."

"Circumstances can change in an instant."

"True, and soon, yours will. Your friends will die tonight. Your precious Miss Marks and her brother will be blamed. I see the headlines now. Rival gang slaughters competition."

Yes, Milla is doing everything in her power to protect me. Yes, she took the threat to my life seriously. But she won't repeat the sins of the past. As she walked away from me, she looked back at me with tears and hope in her eyes. In that moment, I knew. Her feelings for me run deep. She won't hurt me by hurting my friends. Won't hurt *our* friends. This time, she's working *against* the enemy. I know it.

I unveil an ice-cold smile. "My friends won't be dying tonight. They'll be kicking your ass—again."

Unconcerned, she stands. "They'll need more power than they've got. Not that it will do them any good. I, Mr. Martin, am invincible." Her spirit steps out of her body, two versions of her peering at me. White flames leap to life at the end of her spirit hand—and yet, the flames are tipped with red and black. "Fire spreads so easily. With the right kindling, one spark can start an inferno."

The scent of rot intensifies, stinging the inside of my nose, and I grimace. "You're tainted with zombie toxin. Not what you gave Milla, but something else. Something stronger."

"I'm not tainted. I'm finally free! This particular strain of toxin is immune to any antidote." She giggles like a deranged schoolgirl, and her expression makes her look like one, too, shocking—and horrifying—me. "No one can cure me." She air quotes the word *cure.*

"You're *happy* about that?" Has the toxin already rotted her brain?

"Why would I be sad? I finally have what I've always wanted. I will never grow old, never weaken. Never die." She spreads her arms and twirls. "I'm immortal."

My stomach twists. "What do you plan to do with Ali?"

"Infect her, of course."

No. Hell, no. "She's your greatest enemy. Why not kill her?"

"Every hero needs a villain to fight. Forever and ever and ever." She giggles again—only to stop abruptly. She closes her hand, and the flames die. Her features smooth out. "Ali doesn't know it, but she possesses the ability to *create* slayers."

"You're lying." We would have known, suspected at the very least...right?

"All she has to do to light a fire in civilians is spark *their* faith—faith comes by hearing her story—then introduce her fire in small increments."

"Receptive civilian candidates," I echo.

"Like your girlfriend. What was her name? Kate...no, Kat. Kathryn Parker. If your little army had practiced on others, learned what to do—"

"You mean experimented. Learned what *not* to do."

"—she could have lived through the explosion, gunshots and zombie bites."

Rage blends with regret and vibrates in my bones. Maybe Smith is right. Maybe she's lying. But...what if?

Yeah. What if.

Dangerous words. They have the power to totally incapacitate me. I fight them. Now is not the time to cave to emotion.

Milla was right. Like circumstances, emotions can change in a blink. Why allow mine to pull my strings?

"It wasn't bombs, bullets or toxin that killed Kat," I say. "It was you. The orders you gave your men. But you'll come to regret it."

"You want me to regret. The thought of it makes you feel better." She returns to her body, and for a moment, her human eyes flash red.

Hell. She's not immortal. She's a living zombie.

"You will," I say. "Before, Kat could do nothing to fight you. Now she's a witness, and she has abilities she never had before. We need power, you said. Well, we've got it."

Paling, she walks around the gurney, her finger tracing over the rail. "I can't be killed."

"Rot is death sneaking up on you. And you, Smith, are rotting."

"I know what you're doing. Trying to undermine my confidence. Make me doubt myself—lose my faith. Too bad. I'm a god among men." She rips the bandage from my shoulder and presses her thumb against the stitches. "Now, let's get to the reason for my visit, shall we?"

Pain is a bitch, and I hiss in a breath.

"How did you retrieve Mackenzie Love?"

Sweat beads on my upper lip. "We followed the yellow brick road."

"How?"

"A little birdie told us."

She applies more pressure. *Breathe. Just breathe.*

Her phone rings, and glee returns to her features. "Goodie! News!" She releases me to place the device at her ear. "Is it done?" A pause, a toothy smile. "Wonderful. Bring them."

With a laugh, she focuses on me. "Miss Marks is such a darling girl. She came through for me. But then, I knew she would."

I brace myself. "What are you saying?"

"Was I not clear? Well, let's remedy that. Your friends are dead. Killed. Murdered. My men have Miss Marks, Miss Bell and Tiffany in custody, and they're en route now. Soon your only worth will be ensuring that Miss Marks cooperates as *she* answers my questions."

Outrage seeps from every cell in my body. Smith is wrong; I know she's wrong. I know Milla found a way to save our friends. I know...but I'm scared out of my ever-loving mind. Milla could have tried to warn Cole, and he could have ignored her, refusing to trust her.

What if they *are* dead?

I erupt, spitting and cursing. Laughing, Rebecca skips from the room.

With a roar, I slam my thumbs into the mattress. The bones shatter instantly. I lose the ability to breathe. Dizziness swims laps in my head while nausea stomps around in my stomach. But I don't care. I slide my hands through the cuffs at last and collapse against my pillows.

I'm not sure how much times passes before the door opens. Even though I want to leap up, I remain on the bed. Timing is everything.

My heart lurches as two guards escort Milla inside. Her

gaze is glued to the floor. She's pale and trembling, and there's a streak of blood on her cheek.

She's shoved into Rebecca's chair, her hands cuffed behind her.

The guards leave in a hurry. A commotion somewhere else?

"What happened?" I demand in a whisper. *Tell me everyone survived. Please.*

"Two minutes, thirty-two seconds," she whispers back.

Two minutes, thirty-two seconds...until the cavalry arrives? Hope is like an injection of pure adrenaline. "Where's Ali?"

Though her lips move, Milla remains quiet and I comprehend she's counting backward. Two minutes, twenty-six seconds. Two minutes, twenty-five seconds.

I let her do her thing. She's at one minute, two seconds when Ms. Smith strides into the room, her knuckles freshly cracked and bruised, as if she's been hitting a brick wall—or someone's face.

"What an extraordinary turn of events." The deranged schoolgirl is back. "Ali Bell once tried to ruin me. Now she's strapped to a bed and at my mercy."

My stomach drops into my feet. "Have you tainted her?"

"Soon, soon, so very soon." There's a creepy, sing-song quality to her voice. "I had to return her abilities first. That's what is happening right now. They're coming back and when they do, I'm going to steal them. My life will finally be perfect."

Fifty-three seconds.

"I'm sorry to say I've decided to kill you and your new girlfriend, Mr. Martin." She raises a .44—points it at Milla's head. "You've both proven to be more trouble than you're worth."

"Wait!" I leap off the bed, uncaring that my own advantage is gone. I put myself between Milla and the gun, my knees almost too weak to hold my weight. "Spare her, and I'll tell you anything you want to know. You'll have no more trouble from me."

Thirty-eight seconds.

Rebecca frowns. "She betrayed you and everyone you love, and yet still you want to protect her? Why?"

If I can just keep her talking... "Whatever she did, she did to save me."

"The end justifies the means? Is that what you're telling me?" She laughs again, but I hear bitterness rather than glee. "Hypocrite! The end justifies the means when it suits *you*, but not when it suits me."

"What did you have her do? What were her means?"

"She drugged your friends, let my men in your home. Those men shot each and every slayer in the head."

I flinch. No. No! "You asked how we tracked Mackenzie Love. I'm ready to tell you."

Milla quietly announces, "Ten," and a *clank* rings out, the cuffs hitting the floor. "Nine."

I leap at Smith, intending to break her wrist and take the gun, but she pulls the trigger before I reach her. *Boom! Boom! Boom!*

I expect another dose of pain, but it never comes. Milla, I realize, leaped a split second before me, putting herself in front of me. The bullets slam into her, throwing her backward.

"No!"

She hits the floor, and deep down I know this is it. The vision unfolding. *My* nightmare.

If she's shot, she'll die.

Rebecca has backtracked to the door; her gaze is on me as she blindly reaches for the ID scanner. Hoping to escape my wrath?

With a roar, I grab her by the shoulders and throw her against the mirrored wall. Glass shatters. She plunges to the floor, leaving a smear of blood in her wake. But she's back on her feet as I pick up the gun.

"Let me go, Mr. Martin." She holds up shaky hands, palms out. "I'm the only one who can help you—"

I empty the bullets into her chest.

She flies back, slams into the wall a second time and this time, when she slumps to the floor, she stays there. Immortal? Not even close.

"Frosty."

A soft voice. Milla's voice.

I race to her side. She's lying on her back, her skin pale, her lips blue. Lips that lift in a sad smile as blood gurgles from the corners. "Had to...be this...way. Made decision...only decision...saved..."

"Shut up. Just shut the hell up." I press my hands against two of the wounds, desperate to stop the bleeding. My efforts only create more problems, the third wound gushing.

"Two," she says. Still counting? While horror absolutely *ravages* me.

"How could you do this? How could you do this *to me*?"

"One," she whispers—and stops breathing.

No. Hell, no. I won't let her... She can't be...

I perform CPR, check for a pulse. Nothing. No, no. This isn't the end. I won't let it be the end. I continue CPR until I feel her sternum crack underneath my palms. Tears burn my eyes, blur my vision.

"Damn you," I croak. "Come back to me. Please. Please."

But she doesn't. Of course she doesn't. Because, no matter how much I want to deny it, the truth is the truth. She's dead. Like Kat, she's dead.

This time, I won't recover.

I roar up at the ceiling, just as an alarm blasts to life.

32

Milla

CAN'T HAVE MY HEART AND EAT IT TOO

Kat is waiting for me under the arch of a massive gate that looks to be made from a single, flawless pearl.

I would gawk at the beauty, the absolute majesty, but I'm once again connected to that stream of consciousness where faith saturates every thought.

"The journal!" Emma is running toward us. There's no sun here, not one that I can see, and yet light is everywhere. The most glorious light I've ever beheld, sparkling with diamond dust around the girl. "Remember the journal!"

"I won my case, Milla Marks. You're going back." Kat shoves me.

I fall down...down...and scream. Or try to scream. I only gasp. The pain! My body is too weak to fight it, blood pouring out of me at an alarming rate. My mind is hazy as another gasp escapes.

"Milla!"

Frosty's voice rises above the screech of an alarm, thick with relief. He's here…where is here? I crack open my eyes. The cell. Right. I've been shot, but the answer is in the journal… the journal…the journal.

Covered, covered, covered.

If something's been covered, you uncover it.

I know that. Have tried, have failed.

Try again. The only sure way to fail forever is to give up. *Darkness can always be chased by light.*

Hands press against my wounds. "Hang on, sweet pea. Just hang on."

My eyes close. Light erupts from behind my lids.

Light…

"Ali!" Frosty proclaims. "Help her! You have to help her."

Ali must have entered the cell. I don't have the strength to open my eyes a second time. A moment later, a white-hot fist punches through my chest and into my spirit. The pain intensifies exponentially, and I scream. This time, sound escapes. My back bows. *Thánatos* spills out of me of its own accord, trying to protect itself and drive Ali away. Ali…whose scream of pain rivals my own.

I do my best to extinguish the red flames…*have to protect…*

"Let them out," she commands. She's panting. "Don't fight the flames."

But…but…

"Uncover, Milla. Uncover."

Uncover…how? I'm too dazed to figure it out, but the first order I understand. *Don't fight the flames.*

So I don't. I…just…stop, allowing the floodgates to open and *thánatos* to pour out of me right alongside my lifeblood.

Soon I'm engulfed, and because I'm in the physical realm, my clothes are burned away. But...but...my wounds only grow worse. That can't be good for me.

I suspect Ali is experiencing the same reaction. When I scream, she screams. We scream together, again and again and again. The agony! It's too much, too much—it's my nightmare.

I'm burning to death. Soon I'll be nothing but ash.

Trickster. Darkness tricks. Darkness lies.

The nightmares...a trick to ensure I hold on to *thánatos*?

I want to hold on. I want to so bad. The pain will end, and I so desperately want it to end. I *need* it to end. But still I lie passive, accepting, the flames burning hotter and hotter, tremors wracking me. Of their own volition, my arms and legs curl inward, and even that is a new kind of agony.

Then, the strangest thing happens. The haze clears from my mind, and pain ebbs. Both Ali and I stop screaming. And for the first time in weeks, I can feel the comforting power of *dýnamis* healing me. Bone, muscle and skin begin to weave back together. Strength fills my spirit...my body.

Except, it doesn't last for long. *Thánatos* springs forth with new life, pouring out of me, flames blistering me, melting me, but it's worse now, it's so much worse...until it's not. Until I start to heal again.

"Three layers," Ali pants. "One more."

Before the last word leaves her, the pain kicks up yet again, and it's worse than the first two combined, but it doesn't last nearly as long, and when it's gone, it's gone. I'm free! I'm healing!

Thánatos might have covered my inner light, but it could not destroy it.

Not too strong, never too strong.

"Tell me," Frosty demands.

"She's going to survive," Ali replies.

Callused hands I know belong to Frosty skim over my torso, checking for wounds while also imparting strength. "She's really healed."

His shock matches my own. We did it. We did it!

"Thank God," Ali rasps.

Light and dark cannot coexist.

If we'd given up after the first layer…if we'd given up after the second…nothing good would have come of it. We had to fight till the very end, till we had the results we wanted.

Finally I have the strength to open my eyes and keep them open. "Frosty," I say on a raspy catch of breath.

"I'm here." He's shirtless, sweat dripping from his face, tension pulling at features I love and adore. Features I'm overjoyed to see again. "I'm here."

As I take his hand and twine our fingers, a single golden flame sparks between us. In seconds, it travels up his arm, his neck…soon, golden flames are dancing in his irises, and it's a radiant sight, absolutely mesmerizing. His wounds begin to heal.

"Rebecca snuffed out our lights. It's why we couldn't use our abilities." Ali stumbles to the bed—she's as naked as I am—and tosses a sheet at me before draping the mattress pad around her shoulders. "If a pilot light is out, you can't start a fire. She relit mine with a special antidote, and Milla, you just relit Frosty's with *dýnamis*."

I sit up and kiss him, because I can't not kiss him. Once, twice…three times.

He kisses me back, then helps me rip holes in the sheet to create a dress. I fit the material over my head saying, "If everything went according to plan, the others are here, and they need our help." I look around. The exit is closed. The only other door is a fiery hole in the wall that leads to the room I assume Ali just vacated. "Dude. Did you punch your way through?"

"A girl does what she's got to do."

"No worries. I've got this." Frosty stands, revealing charred patches in his jeans. He carries the dead-as-a-doornail Rebecca to the entrance and places her palm on the scan. The door opens with a soft snicker.

"Your heart is too soft," I say. "You should have cut off her hand."

"Next time, sweet pea."

He unceremoniously drops Rebecca, and with Ali watching our six, we exit the room together. There's no crack of gunfire to be heard, but the smell of gunpowder is thick in the air, the hallway littered with motionless bodies. No one I know, thank God.

Rebecca's men paid the ultimate price for aligning with Team Evil. And yeah, even Tiffany paid it. I find her slumped over in a corner, a wicked gash on her forehead, blood splattered on her face, her dull, cloudy eyes staring off in the distance.

The macabre trail leads us to the end of the hall...where Cole removes the head of the last agent standing.

I study my friends. Some are standing, some sitting. Justin, Bronx and Gavin have bullet wounds in their chests. Cole has a few cuts, nothing more. Chance, Love and Jaclyn are beat to hell, and River is without a single cut, bruise or wound. After years of our father's abuse, he learned to duck and dodge before anyone can land a blow.

"Ali!" Cole rushes to his girl and sweeps her into his arms for a bear hug.

"Milla." River does the same to me.

After a few seconds, I pull back. "I need to light your fire."

He releases me in a hurry. "I suddenly want to vomit."

"You know what I meant." I step out of my body, and I'm not sure whether I'm remembering things from the seconds I spent with Kat and Emma, connected to that stream of consciousness, but my next actions are automatic.

I reach past Frosty's skin and take his hand to free his spirit. I do the same to River. "Everyone separate and form a circle with us."

Ali takes River's hand, and offers the other to Cole. Jaclyn moves to Frosty's other side. Gavin latches on to her and Bronx to him. Justin joins us, then Love and finally Chance, who takes hold of Love and Cole, closing the circle.

"Summon *dýnamis*," I say to Frosty and Ali.

A second later, white flames burst from each of us. Those flames jump from person to person, until everyone is ablaze. There's a chorus of hisses and groans as bone, muscle and flesh weave back together, but my friends smile through it all, happy to be relit.

You can knock us down, but you can't keep us there.

Suddenly we're lifted off our feet by a blast of energy that comes from...us? We dangle in the air, the ends of our hair pointing toward the ceiling as if we stuck our fingers into a power outlet. And the peace! The most magnificent peace. I lose myself in a place where time no longer exists and nothing is impossible. I can do anything I can imagine. I can fight any fight and win any war. Nothing frightens me, because I know that I'm here for a reason; and I'm not alone. I have friends in high places. Friends here. Friends up there.

Victory is mine.

Faith, I realize. I might not be up there with Kat, but right now, I'm connected. I'm being filled with new faith. And for me, for all slayers, there's no greater power source.

As quickly as the energy appeared, it leaves. We lose our grip on each other and topple to the floor. Breath rushes from my lungs. When I recover, I sit up, and the others do the same.

Someone laughs. A second later we're all laughing.

"How did *that* happen?" Ali asks.

"No idea," Gavin says. "But let's do it again."

"Better than an entire bottle of vodka," River says, and the laughter starts up again.

Frosty moves in front of me to cup my cheeks, his features serious. "Are you okay?"

"Hundred percent. You?"

"Better than." He hugs me, and I cling to him. He's safe. I'm safe. The vision came true, but we both survived. The war is over. Finally. Blessedly.

Now...now we live.

"I'm sorry I made you think I was going to betray the group," I say. "Even for a little while."

"I never thought you would." He stands and offers me a hand.

I take it and he pulls me to my feet. "You trusted me."

"I did."

No wonder I love him. From the beginning, I'd chemistried him. The more time I spent with him, the more I got to know him, and the more I liked him. Sometime during our acquaintance, love clicked into place, a decision made by the very heart of me.

"I did. I do. Milla, I—"

Pop! Pop!

Two shots slam into my back, burning and stinging, throwing me against him.

He catches me before I fall and swings me around to shield me from any further shots.

"What the hell?" River shouts.

"Milla!" Ali calls.

"Rebecca," Gavin growls.

Rebecca is alive?

My view is blocked as every slayer rallies around us.

I catch my breath quickly and say, "I'm fine. I'm fine. Flames might not crackle over me, but my body is already healing."

The horror fades from Frosty's features. He presses a fingertip into the hole in the sheet one of the bullets caused. His eyes go wide.

"She's a zombie," Jaclyn says on a gasp.

Rebecca? Together Frosty and I step to the front of the crowd.

Rebecca *is* alive. Her hair is tangled around her blood-smeared face, her skin a hideous shade of gray...her eyes glowing neon red.

She's in bodily form, but she *is* a zombie.

Confused, she looks at me, then her gun, then me. With a screech, she shoots me three more times. When the same thing happens—Frosty catches me, I heal—she stumbles back, radiating fear.

"How do you want to handle this?" Cole asks me.

"I know!" Kat appears at my side, proclaiming, "We won our case. Join hands and light up. Hurry."

"Do it," I say.

Everyone leaps into action...and just like before, a great wave of energy bursts from us. Maybe it happens because the witnesses won their case. Maybe we've always possessed the ability and just didn't know it. Or maybe the faith still humming inside us is responsible. Whatever the reason, I sure do like the results.

Like us, Rebecca is cast into the air, where she hovers just below the ceiling, flailing for an anchor but finding none.

"Stop. Stop!" The gun falls from her grip, *clinks* on the ground. "Let me down! Let me—" Her back bows. She screams as her body goes up in flames—without being touched by any of us. She shakes and shakes and shakes... finally, she explodes.

The energy leaves us and we drop, our circle broken. Frosty wraps his arms around me as ash the color of ink rains upon us.

Dark can always be chased away by light.

"It's over now," he says and kisses my temple. "She can't come back from that."

"Now, all we have to do is…live."

33

Frosty

BEAUTY FROM ASHES

The drive home is a celebratory affair. The war is finally over—ding dong the witch is dead—and all of my friends are alive.

"Let Rebecca be a cautionary tale for all of us," Milla says. "Act like a hooker, get screwed."

I chuckle softly, but sober quickly. "River. Chance." The two sit across from me in the van. "You guys need to hack into Rebecca's accounts and drain her money. She's dead, yeah, but we can't allow anyone else to use her resources and keep the company afloat."

"I'll do it," River replies. "Then, I recover from battle, Marks-style."

Cole parks in our underground garage. Couples begin to dart upstairs, one after the other. I understand their urgency. I want Milla in my arms. I *need* her in my arms. I'm going to show her how much I love her.

She's my world.

The moment she put herself in front of me, taking the bullets meant for me, I knew. I could deny the truth no longer. I love her, and I'm never letting her go.

Before we make to the first step, River moves to block our path. "Is now a bad time to mention you guys have to do my laundry for a month?"

Milla flips him off.

He slaps her finger aside. "Is that any way to treat your favorite person on earth?"

"Currently you hold the exalted position of *least* favorite."

"Even though I promise not to stand in your way if you decide to live here?"

My smile is nothing more than a challenge. "Try and take her away. I dare you."

He studies me, silent, and nods. Then he turns away, calling, "Justin. We're the only smart—I mean, single—guys left. After I pad our bank accounts with Rebecca's money, we're going to Hearts, and I'm going to teach you how to score any chick you want—except the ones I want."

The two head for the door. Milla looks up at me and pouts. "You don't want to do long-distance with me?"

Hell, no. But would I be willing? Yes. If necessary. Thing is, I want her with me. Now and always. I want her in my bed every night, and in my arms every morning.

"Do you want to return with him?" Hell, if I must, I'll join River's crew.

"Well," she says, twirling a strand of hair around her finger. The finger I myself am wrapped around. "I haven't been offered an official position here."

Is that the problem? "Let's settle that once and for all." I heft her over my shoulder, sending her into peals of laughter. I carry her to our bedroom, then shut and lock the door. When I set her on her feet, she doesn't move away from me, but stands in front of me, nibbling on her bottom lip. Nervous now?

"I love you, Milla Marks." My gaze locks with hers. "I love you more than pizza and victory, which I used to think were my two favorite things. But it's you. *You* are my favorite hello. If you die, I die. We're bonded in a way I never expected and never before experienced. You are a treasured part of me, and I don't care if you put me first or last, just as long as you put up with me."

Tremors in her chin. "I don't… I can't… Aston. I love you so freaking much."

Waves of relief…waves of joy.

"I almost can't believe this is happening," she says. "Earlier I lived my worst nightmare. Now I'm living my greatest dream. But I still haven't heard an invitation."

Contentment settles deep in my heart. "Sweet pea, you are my favorite hello and my hardest goodbye, and I don't want to go a day without you. Consider that your official invitation."

A slow, sweet smile lifts the corner of her lips. "Consider this my official acceptance."

Darling girl. "Let's kiss on it."

"Let's do more than that." Smiling, she pushes me toward the bed.

My knees hit the edge of the mattress, and I fall. She jumps on top of me to straddle my waist. I grip her waist, holding her in place. And damn, I love the view. The sheet she's wearing is ripped in several places and gaping open.

"You think you can rough me up, sweet pea?"

"Oh, I know I can. You might be bigger than me—"

"A lot bigger." I arch my hips to show her just how much.

She moans, then manages to finish her sentence. "—but I'm spunky."

"And you sometimes like to perform that testicle removal," I add helpfully.

"Yes, I do. Which makes it strange that you keep calling me *sweet pea*."

"Why? You're delicious and nutritious, and I can't have just one taste."

Laughing, she braces her hands at my temples. "So...does this mean you're my boyfriend? Now...and in the morning?"

I move fast, so fast she's unable to counter, swinging her to her back. "I'm your boyfriend, and you are my girlfriend— now and *always*. I'll hear no arguments on the subject."

"What about complaints?" She rakes her nails down my chest. "You talk too much."

"Then let's put my mouth to better use."

I press my lips against hers, and she doesn't just return the kiss, she pours herself into it, giving me every part of her, nothing held back. She tastes so good, and she's so warm, so wonderfully warm, my need for her becomes frenzied. I run my hands over her, desperate to touch her, all of her.

But. Yeah. There's a but.

With a growl, I lurch back. "You're in charge of this. Whatever you want, I'll do." She's used to hit and runs, guys who care only about their own needs. I'm going to give her more, so much more.

I'm giving her everything.

"Aston..." As she studies me and the tattoos inked on my chest, her expression is luminous. "You said you didn't care if I put you first or last, but I want you to know that you're first with me. You'll always be first. And now I want you to kiss me again. Kiss me and never stop."

"That I can do." I swoop in for another kiss, and what begins as a sweet communion soon turns into a feral feeding. I can't get enough of her mouth, her tongue or her teeth.

Can't get enough of *her.*

I whisk the makeshift dress off her and look her over—and thank God for second chances. "You are perfect," I rasp, because it's the truth. "There's nothing about you I would change."

"Aston." A curse. A plea. "Less talking. More doing."

"Good. I like the way you communicate." I straighten to kick off my boots and strip. When I crawl back over her, she accepts my weight with a sexy moan. We rub against each other, creating the most beautiful friction.

"Please, Aston," she gasps. "More."

I grind against her with more force. "I love when you say my name."

"I love saying it." She glides her tongue over my lips then adds huskily, "I love the taste of it." The look she gives me is a little wicked and wanton—and a lot dirty.

"Taste...yes..." I kiss her from mouth to ankle and everywhere in between, until I'm drunk on all things Milla. The sweetness of her, the silk of her skin, the little sounds she makes when I do something she really enjoys. Sometimes I pause just to peer into her eyes, to convince myself she's real, and this is happening. It isn't long before she's writhing, begging me incoherently, a fine sheen of perspiration on her brow. But only when she's quivering and begging for release do I brace an arm at her temple and trail the other down—

"Oh!" she gasps. "That's…that's…incredible."

"I'm just getting started." I play with her some more, taking my time preparing her for what's to come. Not just physically, but emotionally. As I touch her, I tell her how much she means to me. I tell her how beautiful she is, and how lost I'd be without her. Soon, she's once again plagued by need and begging…and I'm on the verge of losing control. "Condom," I tell her, leaning over to grab one from the nightstand. I'm shaking.

As I roll on the latex, she nips at my mouth. She sucks on my neck and claws at my back.

"The way you make me feel…"

"If it's anything like the way you make me feel, we're going to have the *best* life together."

Of that I had no doubt. "Look at me."

Her gaze meets mine without hesitation. I hold her stare. I want her to know I'm here with her. I'm not thinking of anyone else. It's just the two of us in this bed.

"Aston," she whispers. "Now."

Yes.

Now.

I have never been so sated. Milla…she rocked my whole freaking world.

We doze for a bit, wake, make love again, then doze again.

The second time we awaken, I wonder how she tricked the agents who were supposed to kill the others. Our eyes meet—

—and I'm walking toward the front door of the house. The lights are out, and all is quiet. But I know trouble waits outside. When I turn the lock, the door bursts open and four men rush inside the foyer. They're dressed in black, and the one in front points his gun directly at my chest. I knew this was coming, prepared for it, but I hate that it's happening. Takes all of my willpower to remain calm. I have to remain calm. The life and death of my friends depends on me.

"The slayers are drugged and asleep," I say.

He motions toward the staircase with the barrel of the gun. "Take us to the bedrooms."

He keeps the weapon pressed between my shoulder blades as I lead the way. All he has to do is twitch his finger and boom, I'm dead. My knees threaten to buckle as I climb the stairs. If one thing goes wrong, just one...

"Here." I stop on the third floor. "Only two bedrooms are unoccupied."

"Ali Bell?" he demands.

"In the room at the far right."

The men branch off, each entering a different room. In the silence, I pick up the slight *pop pop* of silencers being put to good use, and hot tears streak down my cheeks. I know no one is actually in bed. I know test dummies from the work-out rooms are now dressed in wigs and clothes and they're the ones taking the bullets. I know lightbulbs have been re-moved from every lamp, just in case a bad guy decides to double-check his kill. I know my friends are hiding in clos-ets and bathrooms, just in case we have to fight our way out of this horrible plan.

But the stress just might kill me.

Two of the men return. The tallest one blows me a kiss.

"Shame to kill all the pretties without giving them a proper send-off." He looks me up and down and leers. I'll call him Target One. "Maybe you can make it up to me later."

I shudder with revulsion.

"Shut up," the other snaps. "Those girls are hard-core. They would've cut out your heart before you ever got your pants down."

Target One says, wiggling his brows at me. "Not if they were tied properly."

The remaining agents come out of Cole and Ali's room, dragging a sleep-rumpled and handcuffed Ali between them.

"Did you do this?" She tries to lunge at me.

Gold-star acting, right there.

"I'm sorry," I say, playing my part, as well. Not that I have to do much acting. I'm miserable.

"Let's go." My arm is gripped. I'm yanked forward and—

—the bedroom comes back into focus.

I'm yanked from Milla's memories, and I want to rage about the danger she faced. I want to rejoice at the results. "I'm surprised Cole allowed Ali to be taken."

"He didn't want to," she says, "but that girl can be persuasive."

"You mean bossy, stubborn and vengeful." She nods, and I add, "You suffer from the same afflictions."

She slaps my shoulder. "Why are girls bitches and boys authoritative?"

"Because we rule, and you drool."

"You did not just say that." She rolls her eyes.

"Had I been here," I say, wrapping my arms around her,

holding her the way I plan to hold her for the rest of our lives, "things would have gone down differently."

"Oh, yeah?" Her voice is low and husky.

"Oh, yeah. You are the most important part of my life, and I protect what's mine."

Her body softens, her legs parting to make a cradle for me. "So you're keeping me? Forever?"

"Forever...to start." I nip at her lips. "Mills, maybe I failed to make it clear. I'm never letting you go."

Milla and I leave the bedroom only once, and we do it only because we're dying of hunger. Once she's fed, she tells me she can finally think straight and she's no longer certain she should live in the mansion.

She's teasing, I know, but I protest. A lot. We spend a hot, sweaty hour negotiating. In the end, we are both exhausted, and we agree she'll live here, and I'll do whatever she wants, whenever she wants, and I'll like it.

You know, I kinda feel like I got the better end of the deal.

But now we're hungry again. I leave her lounging in bed, excited about the future, my head buzzing with plans. I head to the kitchen to fix up her favorite bowl of SpaghettiOs and bake—or try to bake—red velvet brownies. The rest of the house is still in bed, and I'm going to romance the hell out of my girl, take her on her very first date.

"Hello, Frosty."

I almost drop the bags of sugar and flour, but manage to set them on the counter before I face Kat. "Hey."

She smiles at me. "I came to say congratulations on your victory."

"We couldn't have done it without you."

"I know."

I laugh. Such a Kat response.

"I just came to tell you that I'm glad you ended up with Milla," she says. "You two fit in a way we never did. One day you would have resented me for my fears, for trying to keep you out of danger, and I knew it."

"Kat—"

"No, don't try to deny it." She hurries on before I can respond. "I'm glad you're at peace, Frosty. You deserve a happily-ever-after."

"So do you."

"Don't worry. It's not too late." She blows me a kiss. "Well, I better go. Petitions to file, people to help." She turns, and I realize Milla is standing in the doorway. "If you ever need advice about the best ways to torture him, all you have to do is call for me. Kat to the rescue!" She's gone a second later.

34

Milla

TEAM LOVE TAKES THE CAKE

"Hi," I say with a little wave. "I woke up, you weren't there..."

Frosty smiles at me, and it's the warmest, sweetest smile I've ever seen. It lights me up inside. "Come here."

I close the distance, and he folds me in his arms. "I know I can't replace Kat," I say.

He kisses the tip of my nose. "You don't need to replace her, sweet pea. There's room in my heart for both of you."

Those words... *Room in my heart.* They hit me and hit hard, because they are so beyond right. Not just for him, but for me. A heart can be filled with love or it can be filled with hate, but never both. The two emotions simply cannot coexist—like light and shadow, one always chases the other away. I can't love Frosty and hate myself for my past sins; I have to make a choice. Hold on to love or hold on to hate.

Like I really need to think about it. I'll always choose Frosty.

I have to forgive myself. Finally. I have to let go, just like River said.

I told my brother it would be impossible. I was so certain the past had its claws buried deep. But that's not true, is it? The past is nothing but a memory. *I* sank my claws in *it*.

Closing my eyes, I rest my forehead on Frosty's shoulder. I inhale…exhale. Letting go doesn't have to be some grand gesture, I admit now, just a flip of a switch inside my mind. A decision to do and follow through.

I flip the switch.

I don't actually feel any different, but that's okay. Feelings always follow action.

Frosty combs his hands through my hair. "You okay?"

"I am. I really am." I meet his gaze and smile.

He cups my cheeks, his thumbs stroking my flushing skin. "I'm a slave to that smile."

I melt against him. "You're also an amazing boyfriend."

"I know."

"And modest."

He winks at me. "I hope you're ready to have your mind blown, because I'm taking you on a date. I was going to call you down in an hour, when I had all your favorites on the table. Plus candles. And rose petals. And soft music playing in the background. After dinner, I thought I'd take you to a movie. You know, act normal for a change."

My mouth drops. A date. Our first. *My* first.

If I didn't already love this boy…

"Frosty," I say, breathless.

"I know. I'm amazing." He leads me to the table, helps me sit and kisses my forehead. I'm in awe as he chops and mixes and bakes, pours the juice I favor and massages my shoulders. We talk and laugh, and for the first time in my life, I *feel* normal.

"By the way," he says, moving beside me, "you're going to tattoo me."

What? "No way. I might mess up."

"You won't. I want your name on me."

Wait, wait, wait. He wants to wear my name? Forever? "Aston," I whisper, overwhelmed.

"I'm proud to be with you, and I want the world to know it."

How can I say no to that? "Yes. I'll do it."

"In black and white."

Could this boy be any sexier? "In black and white. But I'll wear your name in color." What I feel for him is beautiful and vibrant.

He leans over and kisses me. "You make me happy."

Cole and Ali snake around the corner. They are kissing and laughing—nope, kissing again. Immersed in each other, they fail to notice the oncoming wall and ricochet backward. They break apart, laughing again.

Both have sleep-rumpled hair. Ali is wearing a T-shirt that reads Gotta Get Some Killer Zs and a pair of boxers. Cole is shirtless, like Frosty, and wearing a pair of low-slung sweats.

"The men in this household are hot," I say and fan myself. I stand to take my plate to the sink.

"Hey." Frosty slaps my butt. "Eyes on me, sweet pea. I'm the only hot you need to concern yourself with. Besides, if you look at Cole, Ali will cut out your eyes."

"*Ali* will?" I ask with a smile.

"I most certainly will not," Ali says. "I know my guy is a prime piece of grade A man-steak. If I wanted to keep him from being eye-mauled on a daily basis, I'd have to blind every woman in the world."

I nod in agreement. "See?" I say to Frosty, then face Ali. "I know just what you mean. The difference is I *am* willing to blind every woman in the world."

Frosty laughs. "Suck it, Cole. My girl loves me more than yours loves you."

Ali chokes back her chuckles as she waves a fist at me. Cole just flips off Frosty.

"You made SpaghettiOs, Frost?" Ali asks. "I'll have a bowl. Thanks."

"Ditto," Cole says. They both sit at the table, waiting expectantly.

"You're both douche-purses," Frosty mutters. "You know that, right?"

I watch him as he prepares a bowl for each, and I smile. All my life, I never thought I'd have *this*. I'm loved by the sexiest guy in existence. I'm cherished. I have friends who trust me and count on me. I'm not looking over my shoulder every few seconds, knowing another blow is coming, it's just a matter of time. I'm not the girl who betrayed everyone. I'm the girl who helped save everyone.

Frosty carries the bowls to the table, but rather than taking his own chair, he picks me up, sits down and settles me in his lap.

"I remember when you liked having me on *your* lap," Ali says to Cole after swallowing a spoonful. "We must be getting stale."

Cole stands—and then sits in her lap. "How's this, honey?"

The four of us erupt into peals of laughter.

"You really *are* a douche-purse." Ali pushes Cole away and says, "So…tell them what we saw."

Cole steals Ali's bowl and finishes off the contents. "All our abilities—"

"All our abilities are back," she blurts, taking over the story. "This morning we sat out on a swing outside, holding hands like we once saw in a vision. I had the journal in my lap, and when the wind kicked up, it opened. Pages that were once blank are now filled with writing, and nothing is in code. Anyway, I digress. Cole and I looked at each other and we had a *new* vision. One of our entire group standing around the perimeter of Shady Elms. We weren't touching, but had our arms extended toward each other. A gust of power exploded from us and swept through the entire graveyard, cleansing every shell and spirit of zombie toxin. We didn't have to get bitten, and we didn't have to fight."

I don't doubt the vision will come true. "Can you imagine?" I ask Frosty, excited by the possibilities. "We're not slayers anymore. We're janitors. The clean-up crew."

His arms tighten around me. "We'll go to college. I'll get my degree in criminal justice and become the youngest, hottest detective on the force."

"Second-youngest and hottest," Cole interjects.

Please. "Sorry, Holland, but you might as well get used to being second best when you're around my guy."

Frosty smirks. "You hear that, Holland?"

"Meanwhile, I'll be the youngest, hottest surgeon in town."

I kiss Frosty on the forehead. "I'll make all your boo-boos better."

He barks out a laugh. "If you're going to be kissing my boo-boos, don't be surprised when I come home with suspicious wounds in suspicious places. Speaking of…" He jumps to his feet, keeping me in his arms. "If you guys will excuse us," he says to Ali and Cole, "we're in the middle of a date."

They boo and hiss, but Frosty keeps going, carrying me away.

"No movie?" I tease.

"Oh, you'll get your movie. I'll pop in a DVD."

"Desperate to be alone with me?"

"You have no idea."

Joy practically fizzes in my veins as we enter our bedroom. People usually say some variation of "this is life, get used to it" when bad things happen. But right now, everything is just right. Everything is perfect. And to me, *this* is life. I'll get used to it.

★ ★ ★ ★ ★

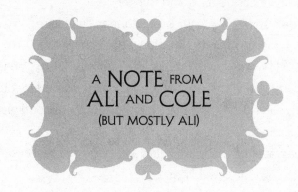

A NOTE FROM
ALI AND COLE
(BUT MOSTLY ALI)

Ten years have passed since I first fell down the zombie hole. I woke up and discovered zombies are real and only slayer light can destroy their darkness. I lost so much. My parents, my little sister. My grandfather. But I gained so much, too. Cole, friends who understood me in a way no one else ever did, and now...a family of my own.

Cole proposed to me my freshman year of college. I said no—but only to make him beg. Which he did. Fun! Then, of course, I said yes. He's my best friend, my heart and soul, my future. We married a year later, and I've been Ali Holland ever since, the happiest girl in the world (and probably ever, of all time)!

Cole did, in fact, become one of the youngest, hottest detectives on the force. I say "one of" because Frosty did, in fact, become one of the youngest, hottest detectives on the force. Women go crazy for the two of them, but Milla and I just laugh about it. Our boys are devoted. (AKA whipped.) The four of us,

we've been to hell and back, and the bonds between us are un-
breakable. That's never going to change.

Besides, why would our boys want anyone else? We're awesome! I'm a counselor for troubled teens, and get this...I'm a mom!
Cole and I have two rug rats. A boy, Phillip Tyler (Ty), named for
our dads, and a girl, Miranda Janelen (Rane), named for our moth-
ers. Both darlings see zombies, and their abilities...good glory, both
Ty and Rane far surpass Momma and Daddy.

I have a feeling our third munchkin—due any second—will surpass even his—her?—siblings.

Speaking of our third, we'll name the darling Emerson, whether
boy or girl. A tribute to my little sister.

If you couldn't tell, we've settled into our "normal" lives quite
nicely. Anima hasn't been resurrected, but zombies still rise. At
least we've learned the root cause of the infection. Our actions
here, in this physical world, dictate the condition of our spirits when
we die. Evil deeds cause rot, and rot spreads. So, as long as there's
evil in the world, there will be zombies. And as long as there are
zombies, there will be slayers. (Or janitors.) But now, thanks to a
little tip Rebecca gave Frosty, we can turn average citizens into
slayers. They just have to believe us when we tell them about the
spirit world in operation around them, and they have to want to
do what we do. That desire does something to their spirits, brings
dýnamis to life.

We cleanse the zombies we can, without fighting them, without being bitten by them. But we've discovered a resistant strain
of zombie toxin that doesn't respond to our waves of power—
zombies we have to take down the old-fashioned way. These un-
clean zombies are the ones that rain black ash when they die. The
others rain white-as-snow ash.

We do what we can.

You'll be happy to know the gang is still together. Bronx and Dr. Reeve are married. In fact, they were the first to tie the knot. They have a daughter, Allison (named after me!) but delivery almost killed Reeve, so they decided to adopt the rest of their kids. They run Sunlight, a foundation for the troubled teens I send their way. Teens who don't yet know—or aren't ready to accept—they are slayers. Or, if they aren't, that they can be.

Gavin and Jaclyn got married, divorced, then married again. They think it's fun and keeps their spark burning white-hot. Jaclyn is now pregnant with twins, so I'm pretty sure they'll stay together this time. Gavin is a fireman, and she's an instructor at Sunlight.

Chance and Love live together, and after babysitting Ty and Rane decided they never ever never wanted to have kids. Go figure. Chance runs some sort of software company (he starts talking shop, I tune out), and wears pin-striped suits on a daily basis. Even though I'm a married woman, I'm not blind, and the guy looks go-o-o-od in those suits. Love, on the other hand, ended up famous. Someone posted pictures of her all over the internet. She was dressed in slayer gear and strapped with weapons, and people couldn't get enough. Those pictures went viral, and a very well-known company hired her to model swimsuits (she was on the cover!). Now, she's in high demand.

Emma, Kat and Helen visit me when they can. Both Ty and Rane can see them, and boy, do the kids love their aunt Em and auntie Kat, and they think Grandma Helen is the prettiest grandmother in the entire world.

They love Nana, too. She lives with us, and helps us with the kids. Actually, she's more like a second mom to them. I don't know what I'd do without her.

As you can see, life is good. We weathered the storms and came out stronger on the other side.

—Because I'm an amazing leader.

Cole has entered the building, everyone.

—What? You know it's true.

I do. I also know behind every excellent decision you made, there I was, directing you.

—And behind every crappy decision?

You were on your own.

—So that's how this works?

I thought you knew. But, uh...honey? I think my water just broke.

(I wish you could see my husband right now. He's chalk white, and there's panic in his eyes. He can take down a horde of cleanse-resistant zombies with a crossbow, but he flips his lid every time I go into labor.)

I guess this is goodbye. Better now than when I start cursing—labor is the only time I suspend the Kat-rule about a lady never dirtying her mouth with foul words. Please know that we're happy, and we're excited to see what the future holds. (Also know that if you turn into a zombie, we're coming for you. Just saying.)

Let your light shine!

Ali and Cole

A NOTE FROM MILLA
(AND FROSTY)

Life didn't turn out the way I once envisioned it.

Milla Martin here. I never get tired of saying my name—my legal tie to Aston. Once, I saw myself as a dedicated surgeon, but the night we cleansed Shady Elms of evil, Frosty and I got a little too excited to be together and didn't use a condom. Nine months later, we welcomed Ryn into the world.

(We spent months agonizing over our son's name. In the end, we wanted our firstborn to honor Kat. Kathryn. Without her, we would have been two ships passing in the night, blowing our horns at each other and threatening to war.)

During my pregnancy—when Frosty wasn't pampering the crap out of me—I began to cook for the slayers.

—Yes. I rock.

He so does! But back to me! I cooked breakfast to start everyone's day right. Lunch to fuel them for the coming battle, if zombies were spotted. Dinner to recharge them when they returned from patrol. I rediscovered my love of the kitchen. And then, when Ryn arrived, I didn't want to leave his side.

Ryn has grown into an amazing boy. He's quiet, but he's smart. He studies a situation before he comments or acts. Like Ali's kids, he's a brand-new breed of slayer. He has abilities, and then some. The things he can do while he's in the spirit realm... I'm still shocked sometimes. On his first hunt, he somehow stopped time, cleansed all the zombies he could, then restarted time, leaving the rest of us floundering in the seemingly instant change of situation.

Uncle River says Ryn will be the next leader of his crew. My brother hasn't settled down, or found a nice girl to love (or even a mean one). In fact, he's wilder than ever. He's convinced another war is headed our way. Evil isn't dumb, he says; it waits for the perfect time to strike.

I worry for him sometimes, for all of us, but I know that no matter what happens, we're in this together, and together we will prevail.

—Also, we're kind of badass.

This is true.

—And now I would be forever grateful if you'd stop writing your— our—letter so I can start loving you properly. Ryn just left to spend the day with Uncle Riv...

Got to go!

Never look back,

Milla and Frosty

A NOTE FROM KAT

THE GREATEST PETITIONER
OF ALL TIME AND EVEN
BEFORE TIME EXISTED

I'm awesome. Just thought you needed the reminder.

My friends are so happy. Their kids are little terrors—but adorable! I love watching their lives unfold. Do I wish I walked among
them? Yes. I'd be crazy not to. But I also wouldn't give up my
amazing afterlife. Dude. I'm, like, forever HAWT. Not that I know
how hot I am. And the fact that I don't know just makes me hotter.

When kids die before their time, they enter the holding zone,
where they continue to age. Of course, everyone stops aging
somewhere around thirty-three. I'm twenty-eight now and I've
only gotten awesomer. My peers can't get enough.

That's right. This little Kitty Kat is playing the field and loving it.
Hear me purr! Except...none of the guys up here compare to one
I can't seem to stop watching down there...and no, it's not Frosty.
The horror! He's totally nuts for Milla, and that's the way it should
be. It's—ugh, I can't believe I'm admitting this, but...it's River.

There. Now you know. The boy is a ten on my bow-chica-wow-

wow scale. And you've heard the old saying, right? Two hawts can totally make a right.

Anyway. I'll get to spend real time with River soon enough. I'll get to spend time with all the slayers. You know they won't live forever, right? You heard what Frosty once said: death is hereditary. An-e-way. I know my friends will be surprised to find out what, exactly, happens up here. Like, we seriously have our own war going on. I've had to learn to fight, and yeah, you guessed it, I'm pretty amazing at it. Probably the best ever. If *probably* is the new word for *definitely*. When you got it, you got it. No use denying it.

An-n-nd speaking of the war, I'm being summoned for a court appearance. Time for another battle (for me to win)!

Live as if today is your last day...because it just might be.

Love,
Kat

*Ali's adventures in Zombieland may have ended—for now.
But Gena Showalter is ready to sweep you away with a
brand-new series.
Turn the page to read an excerpt from her next unforgettable novel
FIRSTLIFE
Book One of the EVERLIFE series.*

*Think you know the truth about life and death?
Think again.*

CHAPTER ONE

"All are welcome. None are turned away." —Myriad

I've been locked inside the Prynne Asylum—where happiness comes to die—for three hundred and seventy-eight days. I know the exact time frame, not because I've watched the sun rise and set, but because I mark my walls in blood every time the lights in the good-girls-gone-bad wing of the facility are turned on.

There are no windows in the building, and I've never been allowed outside. None of us have. To be honest, I don't even know what state—country?—I'm in. Like every other patient, I was drugged before being flown, driven or shipped here. But wherever I am, I know it's cold. Every day, every hour, every second, heat wafts from the vents.

I can't ask the doctors, nurses and guards for information. They aren't exactly the talkative types.

There's only one downside to my blood-calendar. Ugly scars now mar my hands. But I'm strangely okay with every jagged pink line. Gives me something else to count.

I have a thing for numbers and what they mean. Maybe because my name is Tenley—Ten to my friends.

Ten commandments. Ten fingers and ten toes. Ten years in a decade. Ten, the standard beginning for a countdown.

Maybe I'm obsessed with numbers because every breath we take is another tick on a clock, putting us one step closer to death. Or maybe because numbers always tell a story, and unlike people, they never lie.

Here's my story in a nutshell:

Seventeen—the number of years I've lived.

One—the number of boyfriends I've had.

Four—the number of friends I've made and lost since being committed.

Two—the number of lives I'm told I have. That we *all* have. Firstlife, and then Everlife.

Two—the number of choices I've been given for my eternal future. Do as my parents demand or suffer.

I've chosen to suffer.

"Seriously? You're using a finger-pen?" Bow, my brand-new roomie, rubs her eyes and eases into a sitting position on her twin-size bed, the springs creaking. "No wonder everyone calls you Nutter," she says, and I detect a slight English accent.

"Actually, everyone calls me Nutter because I tend to spread my haters over the floor—like butter."

I expect her to pale. She smiles. "Mmm. Nutter Butter. I'd do bad, bad things for a single bite."

I'm impressed. In this place, a lack of fear is rare and precious. Of course, if she threatens me, I won't hesitate to do to her what I had to do to my last roommate and a guard. Not just hurt—but kill. If there's one thing I've learned in my three hundred and seventy-eight days here, it's this: an enemy will always strike back. Why not end the war before it can begin?

"You should probably be called Madame Chats-a-lot," she says matter-of-factly. "You talk in your sleep nonstop."

"Impossible. I don't sleep." I catnap here and there, but fight rest—and vulnerability—as long as I can.

"You count from ten to one over and over again."

"I—" Might. When I do sleep, despite my best efforts to the contrary, I dream about numbers. About a song I sang as a child.

Ten tears fall, and I call…nine hundred trees, but only one is for me. Eight—

Stop. Can't afford to get lost in my head.

Finished with my latest marking, I stride into our "bathroom." There are no doors to offer even a modicum of privacy, just a small, open shower stall next to a toilet. For our safety, we've been told. For our humiliation and others' amusement, I suspect. Our room is monitored 24/7. At any given time during any given day, Dr. Vans, the nurses and even the guards are allowed and encouraged to watch live camera feed. And they do. A lot.

Dr. Vans taunts. *I see and know everything.*

The nurses belittle. *Put on a little weight, haven't we?*

The guards grin and leer. *Just begging for it, aren't you, and one day you'll get it.*

Just some of the many perks offered Chez Prynne.

As I strip, Bow makes a big production of throwing her legs over the side of her bed and showing me her back. Even though I've long since lost all sense of modesty, I wash as fast as I can. Inmates aren't given razors, so I keep my legs and underarms smooth with threads I've pulled from my uniform. Not that a well-groomed appearance matters. While we're allowed to socialize with the opposite sex at mealtime, I have no interest in dating. Too much energy is needed to sneak around. Besides, the people I care about are used against me sooner rather than later. But I already feel like an animal; there's no reason to look like one, too.

As I towel off, Bow cups her breasts and grins. "Boobs are bloody awesome, yeah? Literal fun bags. I don't know what you girls are always complaining about."

I got a crazy one this time. Noted.

"Don't you mean *us* girls?" I ask as I dress in the requisite uniform. A white jumpsuit that actually glows in the dark.

She pales, and her hands fall away from her *fun bags*. "Dude. There's nothing wrong with enjoying the equipment and getting a little some-some of my own goods and services. I mean, I'm so hot even *I* want a piece of me."

Not just crazy, but a frat boy trapped in a female body. Delightful.

"Forget anatomy." Bow runs a hand through her short, spiky hair. When she arrived at the asylum yesterday morning, she somehow managed to get hold of a kitchen knife and hacked off all her pretty pink curls before being tackled by the guards. "Let's talk Everlife. Got any plans for the Unending?"

Could no one have a conversation with me without mentioning the Unending? Where Myriad and Troika—the two realms in power in the afterlife...the *Everlife*—are supposedly located. Where "real" life is said to begin. "Not a single one," I say, choosing honesty over a lie. Do I believe there *is* an afterlife? I've rolled that question through my mind more times than I can count. And for me, that's saying something.

Here's what I do know: over the years, the world has been divided into three factions. Those who support Myriad, those who support Troika and those who don't believe either realm actually exists. The three are not segregated but coexist in imperfect harmony, with an underlying hum of tension between them. A hum it's "impolite" to acknowledge.

"Do *you*?" I ask.

"Of course."

Her confidence irritates me. I'm desperate for answers, for proof, and I've struggled to pick a side for so long. The very reason I'm here. "Since you're in a Myriad facility, I can only assume you're considering signing a contract with Troika."

"Not considering. I've already done it." I hear the note of pride in her voice, and it irritates me further. "They ensure I never go hungry, I have shelter and friends who will back me up no matter what trouble I'm in."

If that were true, why did her friends allow her to be locked up in the first place? Why hasn't she been rescued already?

See! This is why I remain unconvinced there's actually an Unending. Both sides make promises, but neither one seems to deliver.

"Are your parents hoping to change your mind?" I ask. It's not an impossibility. Until death, firstlifers are allowed to take their spiritual benefactor to a court and fight to rework or improve their contract. In extreme cases, void it.

Ask me if such cases actually mean anything.

Bow looks away from me, remaining silent.

"If you're with Troika, why aren't your hands branded?" Those who sign a contract with Troika always brand or tattoo themselves with three-point stars on the tops of their hands. Those who sign with Myriad brand or tattoo themselves with interlocking jagged lines on their wrists. An outward sign of an inward commitment.

Again I'm met with silence. I'm tempted to shake the answers out of her.

"I had friends who signed with Troika," I say, "and they immediately stopped answering calls. Some turned their backs when they saw me in the halls at school, and some gossiped about me nonstop." My parents are extreme Myriad loyalists, and up until my sixteenth birthday, they were allowed to make my decision for me, giving both my Firstlife and Everlife to Myriad.

A woman claiming to be a Myriad representative visited me once every month. Madame Bennett. A flawless beauty with pale hair and dark eyes. She would spend hours with me, prying into every area of my life, as if she had every right to know. Was I doing drugs? Dating…having sex? Who was I hanging out with? What did I talk about with my friends?

I later learned she would dictate which friends I was allowed to keep and which ones my parents were supposed to cull from my life.

Now, because I'm a free agent—I laugh bitterly at the thought that *this* is freedom—my parents have until my eighteenth birthday to convince me to select Myriad on my own. Little wonder my stay here is growing increasingly worse. Longer therapy sessions. Harsher punishments.

Only three hundred and fifty-two days to go.

$3 + 5 + 2 = 10$

The day after my eighteenth birthday, when my decision will no longer affect any Firstlife or Everlife but my own, I'll be released on my own recognizance. Maybe. Hopefully.

Everything depends on whether or not Myriad truly exists. If they do, and I continue to refuse to sign a contract with them, I'll have the distinct privilege of watching my parents lose everything they've been given. Everything they've loved more than they've ever loved me. Money, prestige. The homes. The cars. The boats. *Everything.*

Maybe it's wrong of me, but I smile. I've kept a mental ledger with all my parents' crimes, and yes, I blame them for everything that happens here. They have a lot to answer for.

"I have yet to meet a person from Troika I like," I add. "I *have* fallen in love with someone who signed Myriad." My ex-boyfriend, James. He worked here, and he lost everything trying to escape with me.

I wonder, every day, what happened to him. If he's out there, or if he's really gone.

He vowed to return, if he were to die first, and tell me the truth about the Unending. If at all possible. Nine months have passed since his death.

A baby spends nine months in a womb.

The ninth commandment says we aren't to lie.

Nine planets in the solar system. Pluto counts, I don't care what the haters say.

"What your friends did..." Bow shakes her head. "That's not our way. That was humans being humans."

"Shouldn't you be more careful about the humans you accept, then?"

"If we were, do you really think you'd be a contender?" She softens her tone, saying, "Everyone deserves a chance, Ten."

I'm actually impressed. Finally, an answer I respect. "Did Troika send a Laborer to talk with you? Surely they did." Or someone *pretending* to be a Laborer. How else would Bow have made a decision? "What was he—she?—like? How did you know they were what they claimed to be?"

At my high school, the daily operations of the Unending was required learning. According to my teacher, both Myriad and Troika have Headhunters who scour the land of the living for recruits. When a decision is made, a Laborer is sent to negotiate terms.

Bu-u-ut...once again I'm met with silence.

"Why won't you answer me?" I demand.

"I see the disbelief swimming in your eyes. Whatever I tell you, you'll doubt."

"True, but maybe later I'll convince myself you're right."

"I bet that's what you said every time you questioned someone about this very subject. How's that working out for you?"

I glare at her.

With an unfeminine grunt, she falls onto her pillow.

"By the way," I mutter, "you look like Hair Salon Disaster Barbie."

"What? I needed a trim." She fluffs the ragged ends of her new *style.*

Something else to admire about her: her positivity.

I study her. She's short and big-boned, with a plain face. A forgettable face. Only her eyes are memorable. They're odd yet captivating, the color of copper, and right now they are smoldering with an intensity that should've been too much for any one person to contain.

"Uh-oh. We've run out of time." Bow jumps to her feet. "Our cell will open in three...two...one."

Sure enough, the door slides open.

Yes, we're like dogs in a crate, taken out only at scheduled times.

We have thirty seconds to leave; if the door closes and we're still in our room, we'll miss breakfast. We dart into the hallway along with the girls from the other rooms. There are twelve girls in total. One of them—Jane—mutters to herself as she bangs her forehead against the wall, splitting skin and causing blood to trickle. Almost everyone else keeps their head down and their arms wrapped around their torsos, as if to protect their vitals—or stop an avalanche of pain and misery from spilling out. My guess is the former.

I walk beside Bow. She hasn't showered or brushed her teeth, and yet she smells like a mix of wildflowers and lemon drops.

How has she managed *that*?

A high-pitched whistle cuts through the air and makes me cringe. "Well, well," a voice says behind us. "I just lost a bet I'd assumed was a sure thing."

I don't have to glance over to know who's just spoken. Sloan.

"Tenley's new roommate survived the first night, y'all," she continues, her Southern twang ridiculously adorable even when she's sneering.

A few boos erupt. A couple of cheers.

"What'd you lose?" Bow asks her.

I almost sigh. I know what's coming next.

Sloan jumps into Bow's path, forcing her to halt.

That.

I stop just for the hell of it. Sloan and I have been here the longest, and I've seen this song and dance a thousand times before (thirty-eight, to be exact). Her philosophy differs from mine. While I wait until I'm provoked, she attacks the new-comers first, certain there will be fewer challengers later.

Life sucks. We've adapted.

"Bless your heart. You're either extremely brave or termi-nally stupid." Sloan plants her hands on her hips. Tall, blonde and model-pretty, she's the girl every other longs to be. Until she opens her mouth, when her outer beauty stops compen-sating for her inner bitch. "I don't remember speaking to you and until I do, you will keep your eyes down and your tongue quiet...or you'll lose them both."

Bow flicks me an amused glance. "Is she serious?"

"Hey!" Sloan reaches out to grab Bow by the collar of her uniform, but I catch her wrist just before contact.

"Hands off." I don't know Bow, and I certainly don't trust her—and to be honest, I will never let myself like her—but today I'll have her back.

"Or what?" Sloan snaps at me, yanking free of my hold.

Usually we steer clear of each other. We fought once be-fore, when I first arrived at the asylum, and we almost killed each other. "Do you really want to know?" I ask softly.

The next words she utters will decide both our fates.

I'm hit with surprise when my roommate says, "Tell me something. Is your ass jealous that your mouth is full of shit?" removing attention from me.

Sloan bares her teeth in a scowl as another round of boos and cheers erupt.

"Girls," a harsh voice booms from the other end of the hallway. "Go to the cafeteria or to your rooms. You know the rules. No loitering outside of either."

With a final glare at Bow, one promising brutal vengeance, Sloan turns on her heel and flounces toward the cafeteria.

I'm left reeling. A confrontation didn't lead to bloodshed. *What?*

"Come on," I mutter, dragging Bow with me. There are multiple doorways along the way, each painted puke-green. The walls are medicine-tray gray, and the floor some type of soil-your-pants brown. I know this for a fact. Last week, when an orderly threatened a new guy with castration, all hell broke loose...among other things.

Fun times.

"You protected me." The awe in Bow's tone is unmistakable. "I mean, I could have taken her down, no problem, but you still put yourself on the line for me."

"Don't get used to it. Just...keep your head on a swivel and the insults to a minimum and you might live till lunch."

We pass through the commons, a space that offers the illusion of comfort with plush leather couches and large-screen TVs mounted to the walls. But this is where group therapy takes place, and there's nothing comforting about that.

Around the corner and through a wide set of double doors is the cafeteria. A colorless utilitarian room with a sea of bolted-down tables and benches.

The boys are already seated, each with a tray of indistinguishable slop. As Bow and I take our place in line, I try to take in everything at once. The number of people in the room: thirteen female inmates versus seventeen male inmates. It's uneven. I don't like uneven. The scales should always be balanced. There are six guards: four are male, two are female. Multiple conversations are happening at once.

"—too bad. I call dibs."

"—where they are? Tell me!"

"—ten minutes. If you're late this time, I'll pick someone else."

My gaze lands on a boy I've never before seen. He's new, like Bow. He leans back and drapes his tattooed, muscular arms over the chairs of the inmates flanking him. He has dark hair shaved military short and I can't make out the color of his eyes, but as with Bow, I can feel the intensity of them—because they are locked on me.

"Son of a Myriad-whore," Bow snarls. "How dare he use a Shell! That's *my* play. I'm going to murder him. Murder him so hard."

Shell?

She takes a step forward, about to step out of line. *Her* gaze is locked on the new boy.

I shackle her wrist with my fingers and hold her in place. When she continues to struggle, I move in front of her, blocking her view of the newcomer. "Calm down. Now. Or you'll be dragged out of here kicking and screaming."

She huffs and puffs, but she eventually settles.

"You know him?" I ask.

"I know he's pure evil, and you have to stay away from him." She fists my shirt, clinging to me. Her dark eyes implore me to understand. "I mean it. He's bad news. Okay? All right?"

I twist, daring another glance at "pure evil." He's focused on Bow, looking her up and down—a predator at mealtime. He smiles slowly and runs his tongue over his teeth.

"Move," the inmate behind Bow commands, pushing us forward.

I toss the girl a scowl that rivals Sloan's, promising violence. Only when she is staring at her feet do I step forward and accept my tray from a creeper with greasy hair and an even greasier mustache. I think the asylum purposely hires the scourge of the earth to make us more willing to do what we're told, if only to get the hell out of here.

After accepting her own tray, Bow comes up beside me and shepherds me across the cafeteria, as far away from New Guy as possible. I let her get away with it for only one reason: curiosity. Along the way we pass Sloan, who just can't resist the opportunity to stick out her leg to trip Bow. Only, Bow jumps over the obstacle and kicks back, hooking Sloan's ankles between her feet, ripping the girl out of her chair.

Sloan lands with a hard thump and her tray dumps over. She shrieks as food pours over the top of her head, and the rest of the cafeteria grows quiet. A chuckle escapes someone, and it's like a starting bell. The rest of the room explodes into squawks of laughter. Grinning now, Bow starts to skip. I'm utterly impressed and suddenly I'm following without needing any kind of encouragement.

When we sit, Bow loses her amusement and focuses on me. "Listen. Some things are about to go down. Things you won't understand. But I need you to trust me and stay with me. No matter what. Okay? All right? I'll protect you."

"I don't need your protection." But...a sense of foreboding suddenly floods me, and not just because of her warning. I have a knack for knowing, bone-deep, when trouble is on its way, and she's right. Some things are about to go down. Bad things. I sense it with every cell in my body.

For some reason, my gaze is drawn to New Guy.

He's staring at me again and this time, he blows me a kiss.